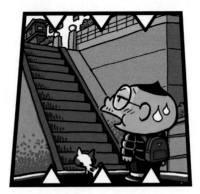

YASUNARI NAGATOSHI

I wish they'd put an escalator on the stairs in my neighborhood... Anyway, thank you for buying Volume 9! I hope you enjoy it!!

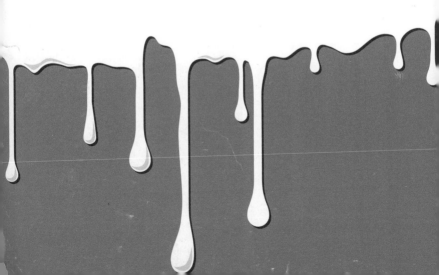

ZOMBIE BOY'S METAMORPHOSIS COLLECTION

BABY ZOMBIE BOY

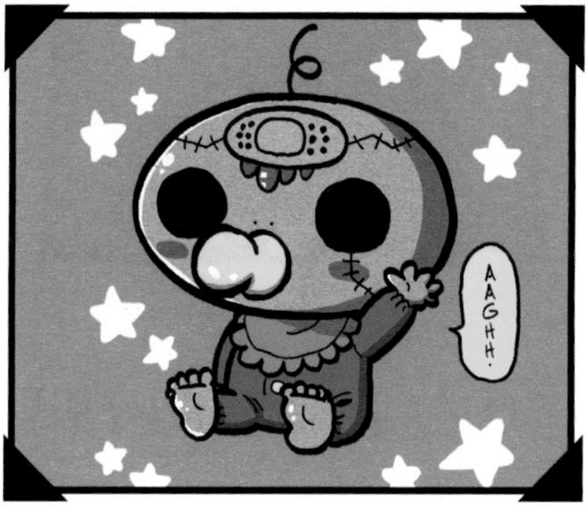
AAGHH.

He uses his cuteness as a weapon to get close to people and attack them. If his pacifier is taken away, he flies into a terrible rage powerful enough to destroy an entire town, so you need to be very careful.

ZO ZO ZOMBIE

VOL. 9

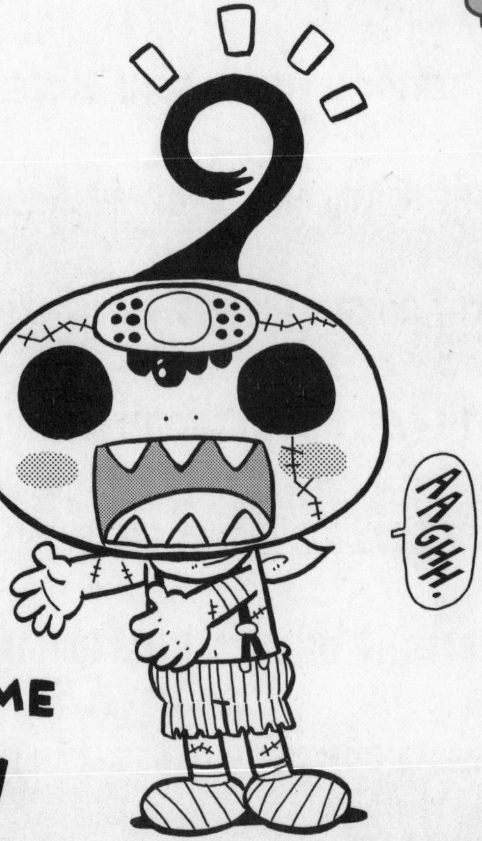
AAGHH.

WELCOME TO VOL. 9

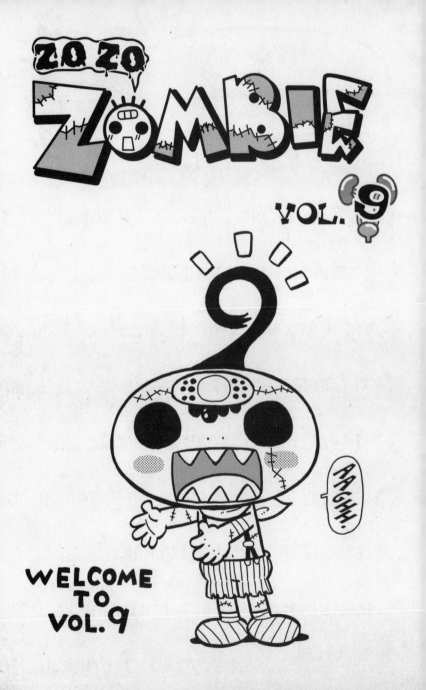

IT'Z THE INDEX!!

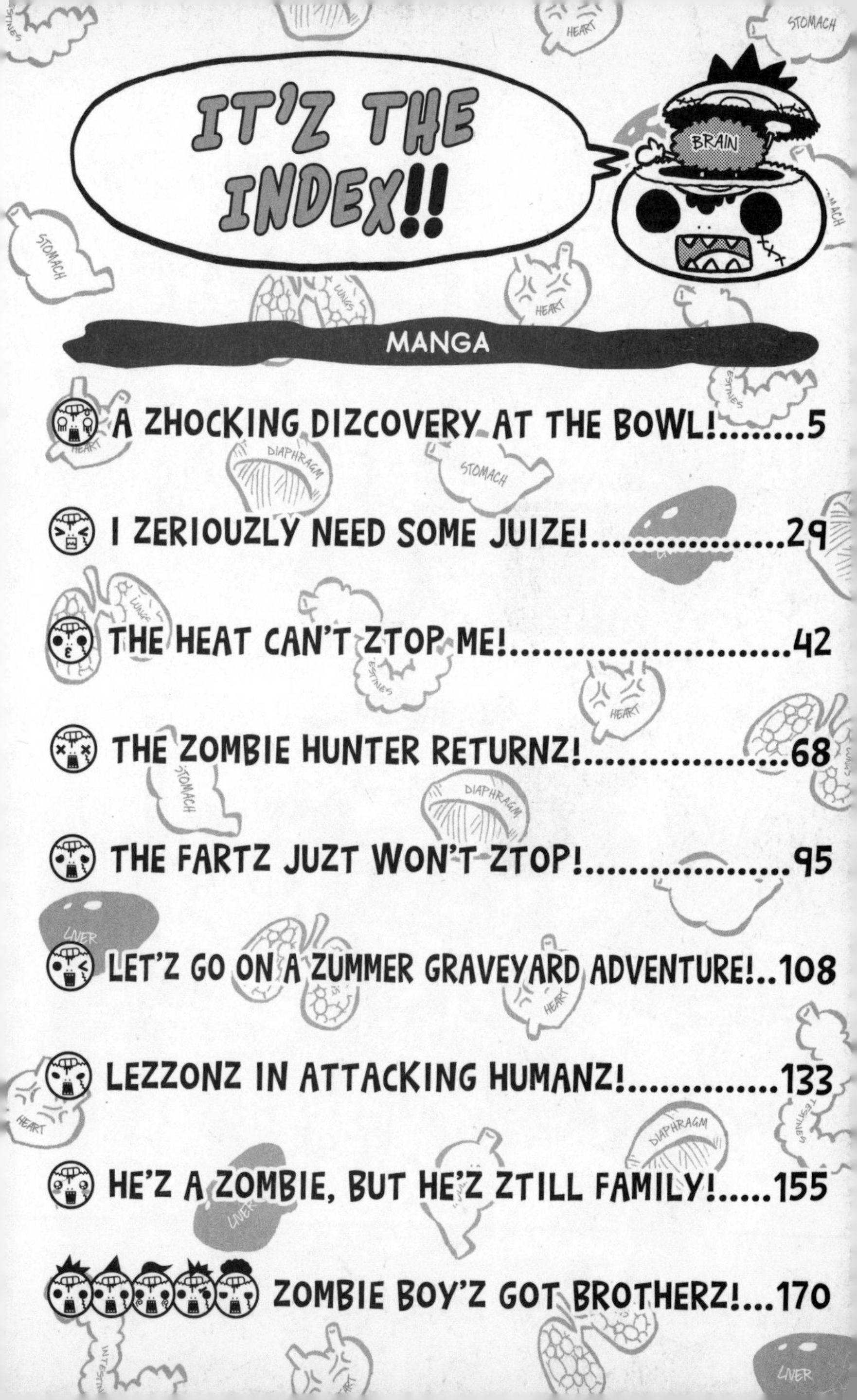
BRAIN

MANGA

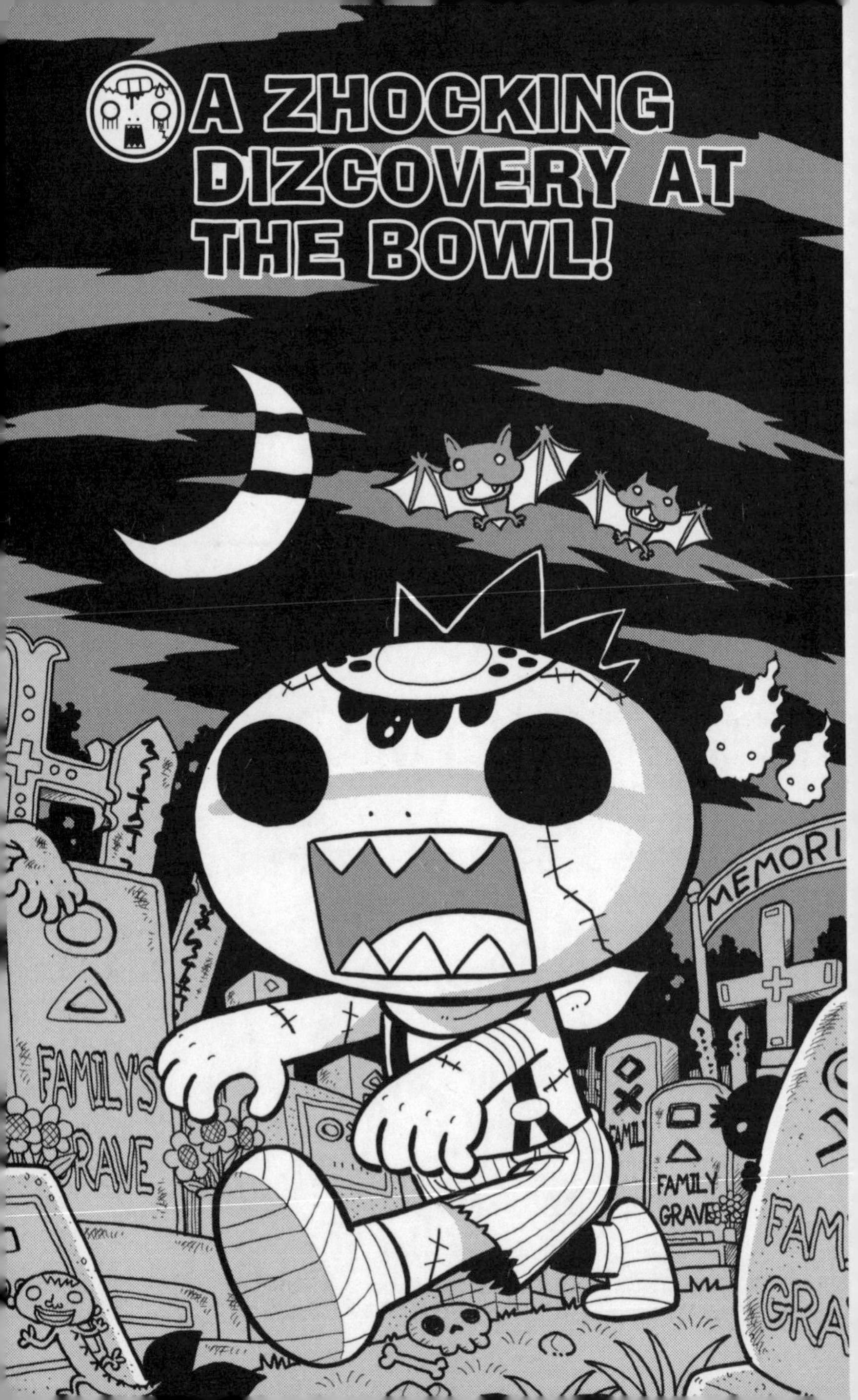
A ZHOCKING DIZCOVERY AT THE BOWL!
MEMORI
FAMILY'S GRAVE
FAMILY
FAMILY GRAVES
FAM GRA

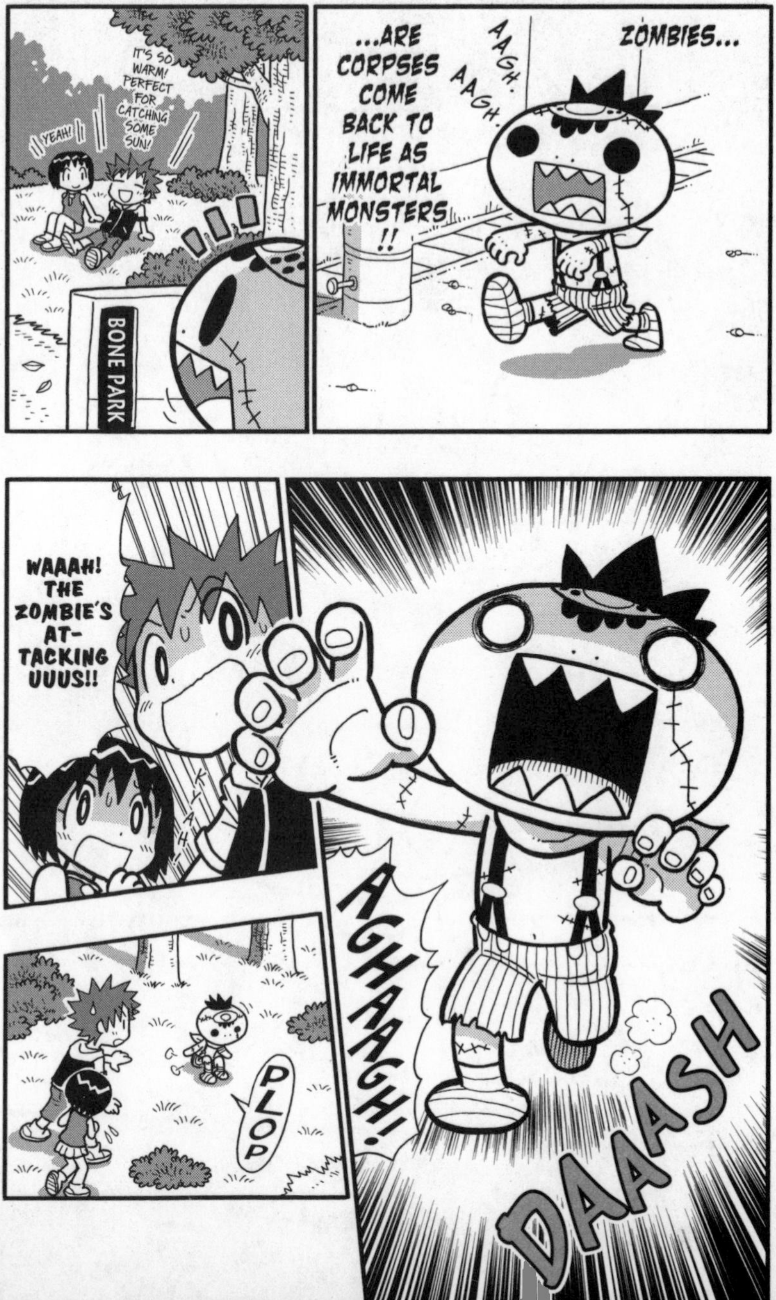
ZOMBIES...
...ARE CORPSES COME BACK TO LIFE AS IMMORTAL MONSTERS!!
AAGH. AAGH.
IT'S SO WARM! PERFECT FOR CATCHING SOME SUN!
YEAH!
BONE PARK
AGHAAAGH!
DAAASH
WAAAH! THE ZOMBIE'S AT-TACKING UUUS!!
KYAAH.
PLOP

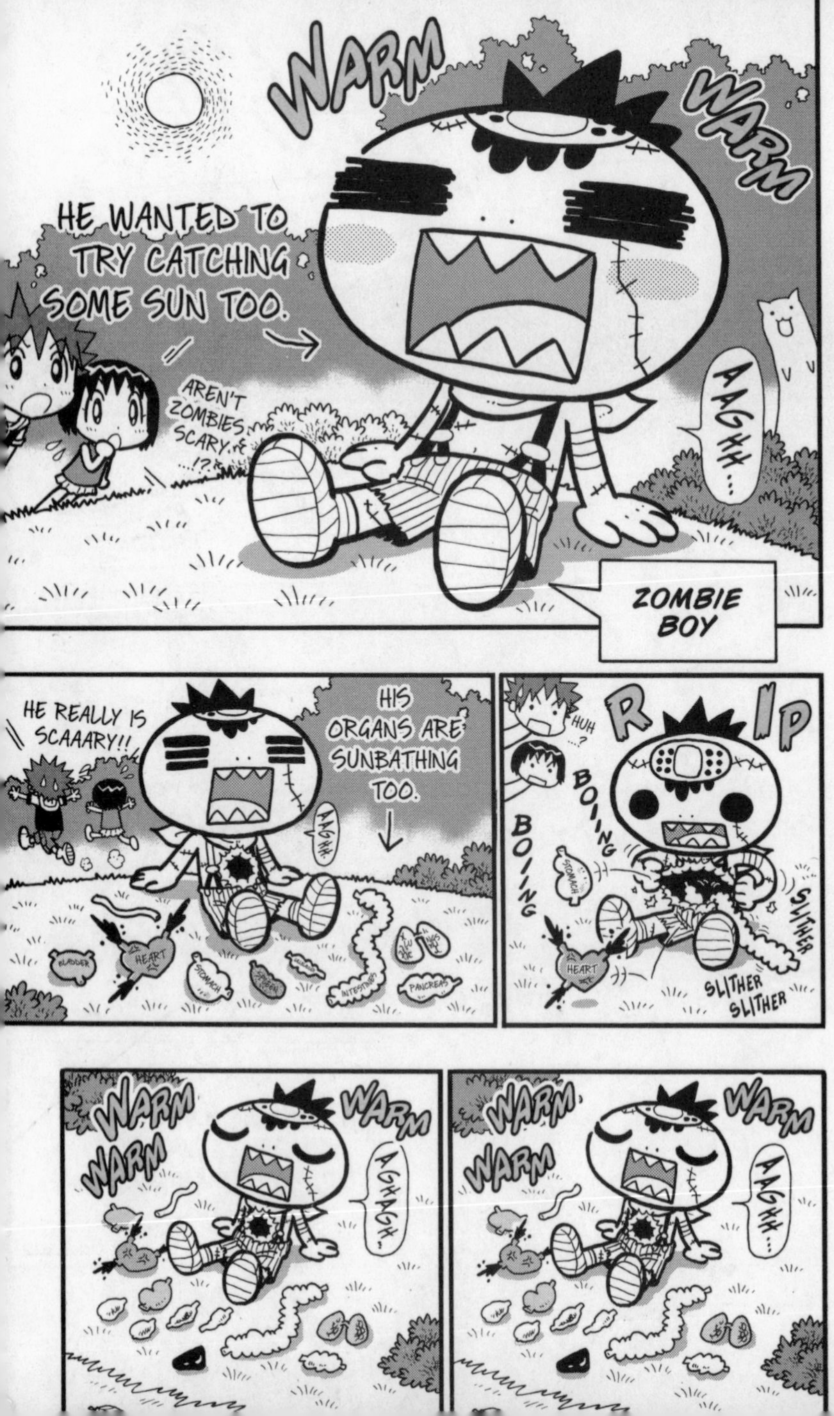
WARM WARM
WARM
AAGHH...
HE WANTED TO TRY CATCHING SOME SUN TOO.
AREN'T ZOMBIES SCARY...!?
ZOMBIE BOY
RIP
HUH...?
BOING
BOING
STOMACH
SLITHER
HEART
SLITHER SLITHER
HIS ORGANS ARE SUNBATHING TOO.
AAGHH...
HE REALLY IS SCAAARY!!
BLADDER
HEART
STOMACH
SPLEEN
INTESTINES
PANCREAS
WARM WARM
WARM
AAGHH...
WARM WARM
WARM
AGHAGH...

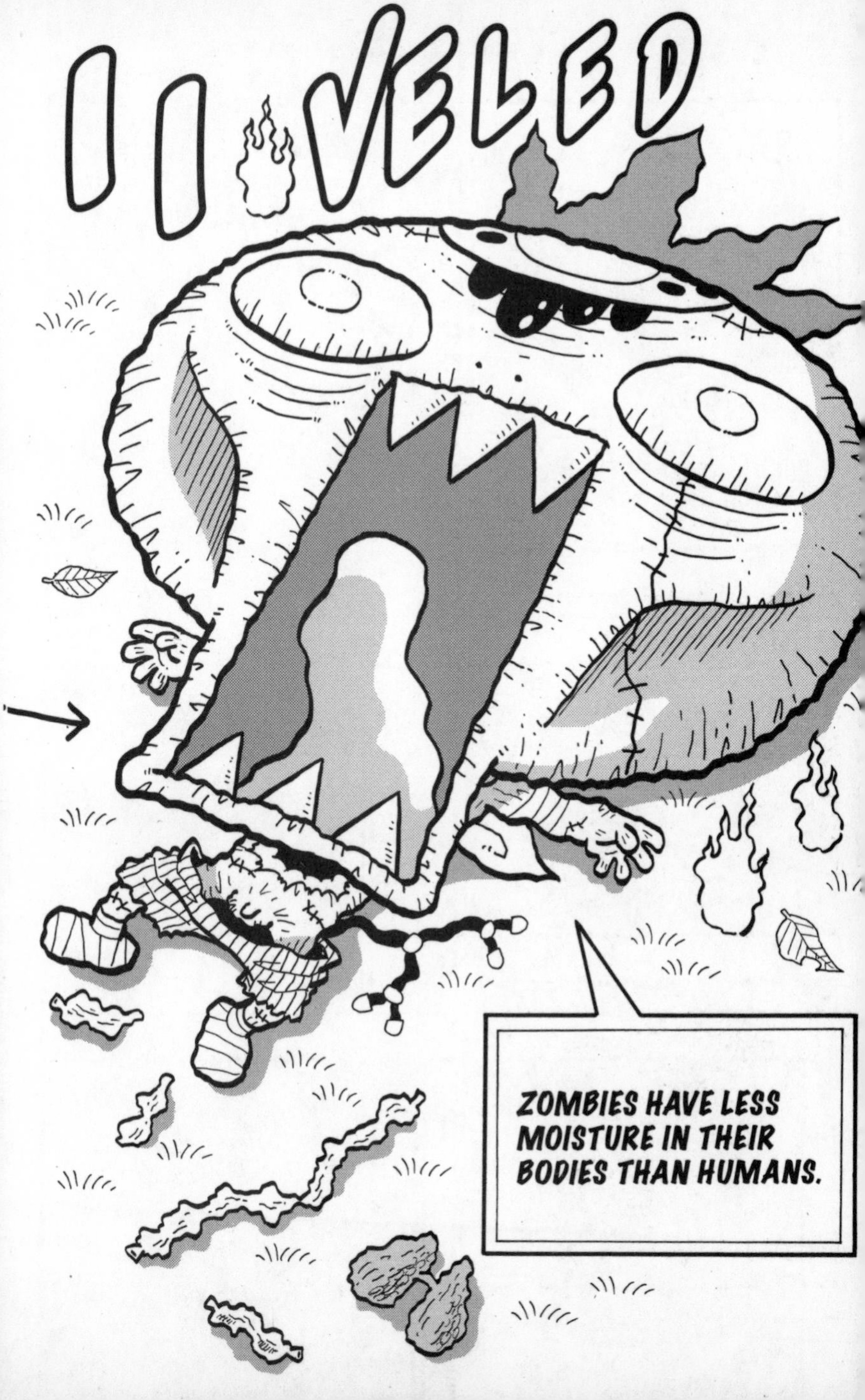
ZOMBIES HAVE LESS MOISTURE IN THEIR BODIES THAN HUMANS.

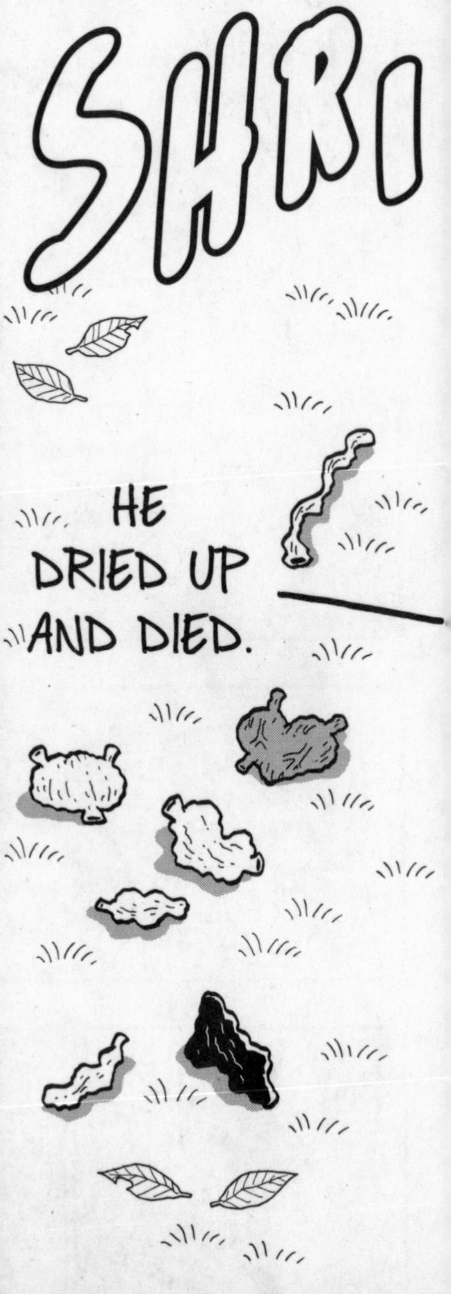
SHRI
HE DRIED UP AND DIED.

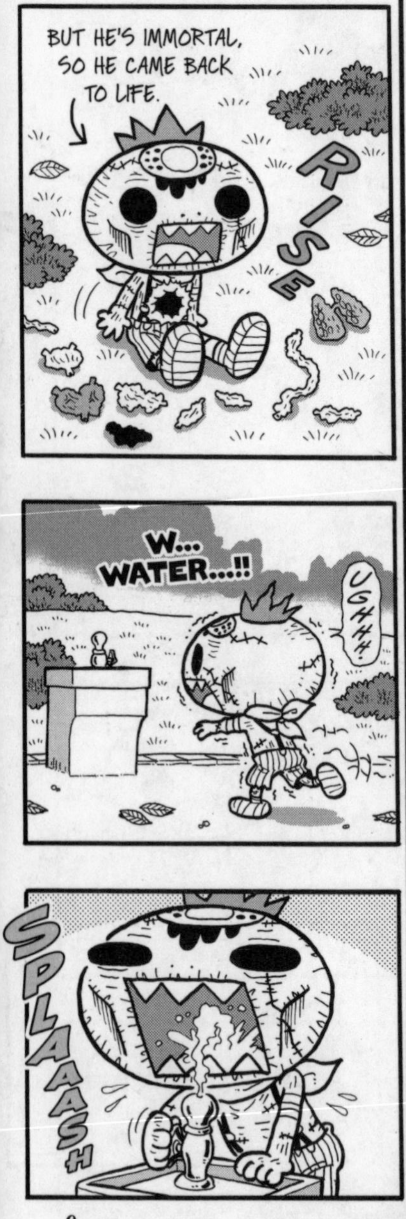
BUT HE'S IMMORTAL, SO HE CAME BACK TO LIFE.
RISE
UGHHH.
W... WATER...!!
SPLAAASH

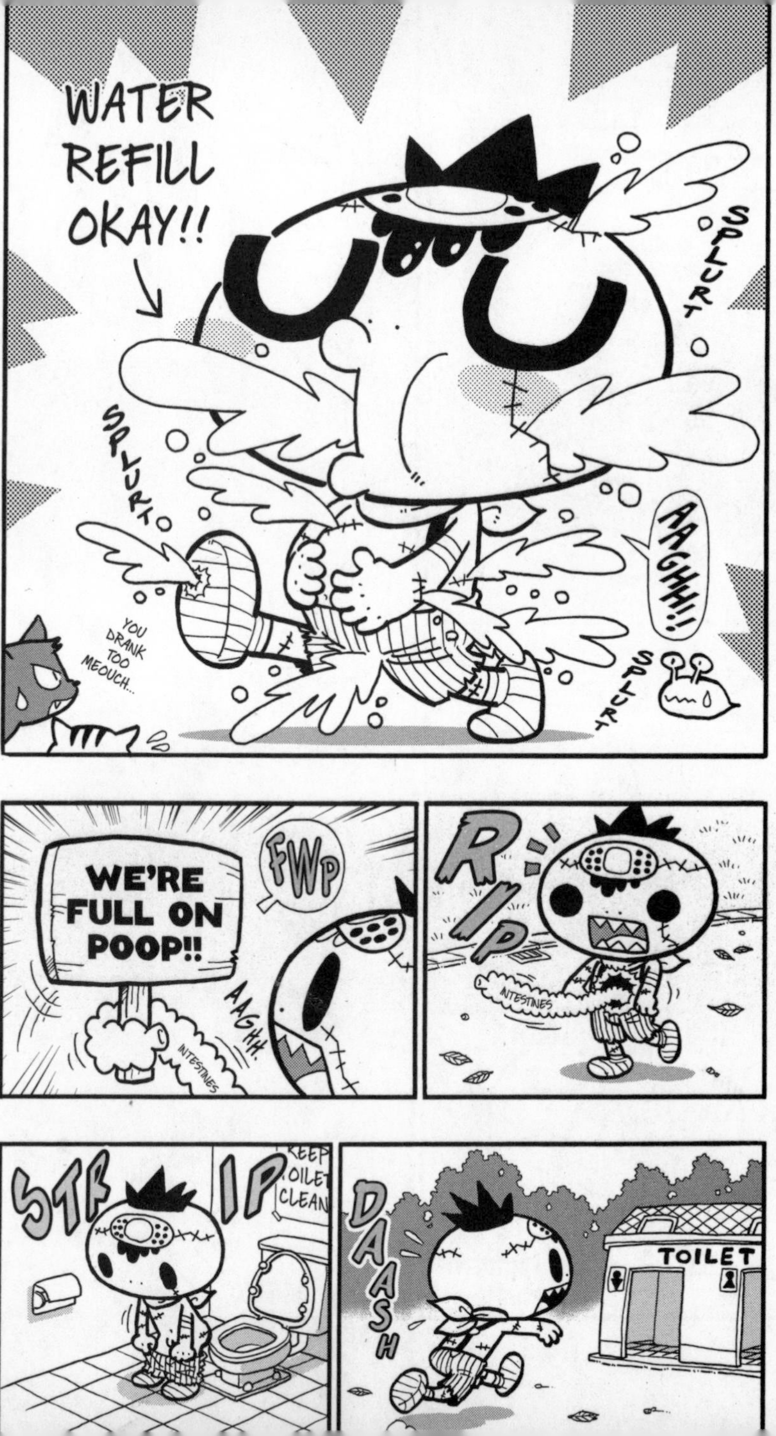
SPLURT
WATER REFILL OKAY!!
AAGHH!!
SPLURT
SPLURT
YOU DRANK TOO MEOUCH...
RIP
INTESTINES
FWP
WE'RE FULL ON POOP!!
AAGHH.
INTESTINES
DAASH
TOILET
STRIP
KEEP
OILET
CLEAN

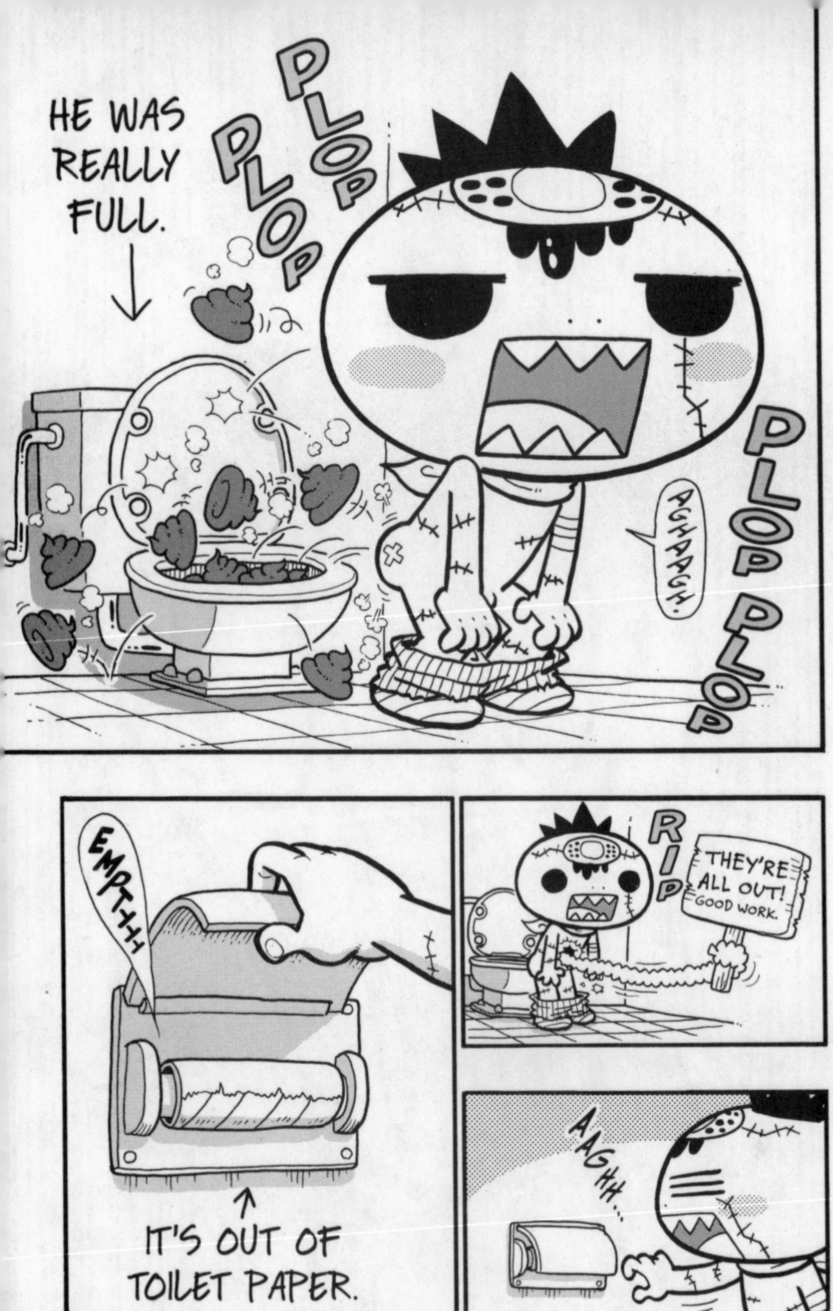
HE WAS REALLY FULL.
PLOP PLOP
AGHAAGH.
PLOP PLOP PLOP
RIP
THEY'RE ALL OUT! GOOD WORK.
AAGHH...
EMPTYYY
IT'S OUT OF TOILET PAPER.

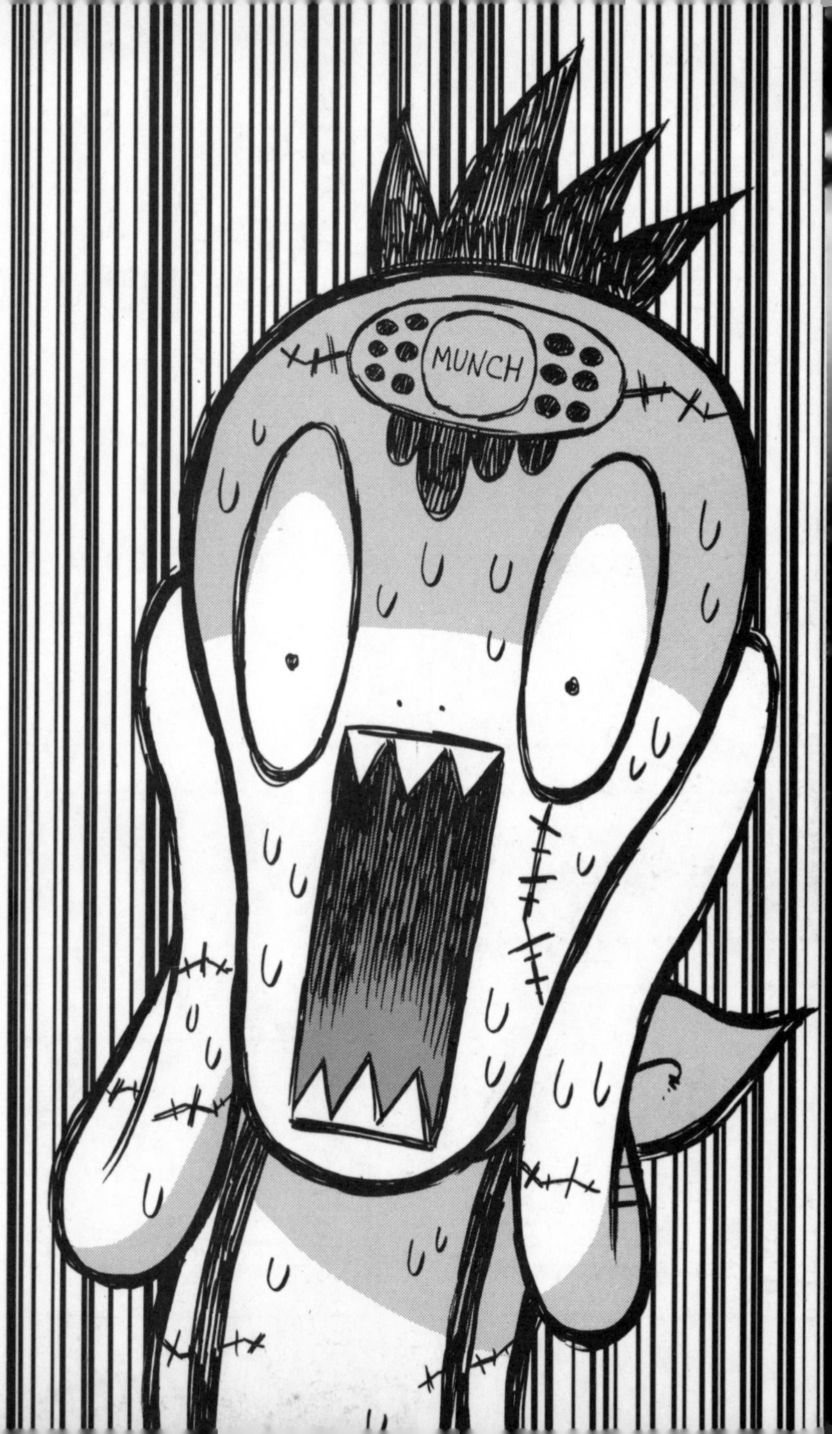
MUNCH

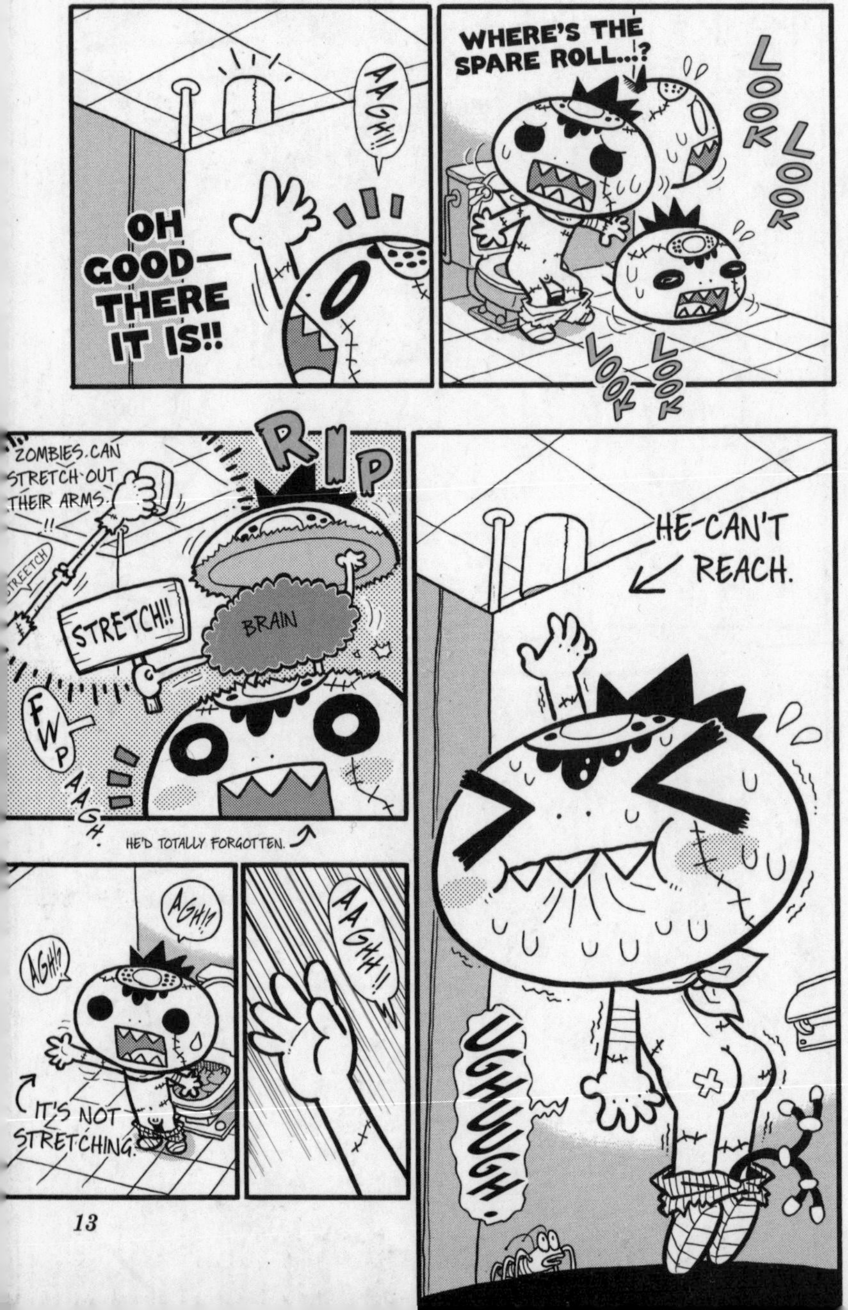

WHERE'S THE SPARE ROLL...!?
LOOK LOOK
LOOK LOOK
AAGH!!
OH GOOD—THERE IT IS!!
HE CAN'T REACH.
UGHUUGH.
RIP
ZOMBIES CAN STRETCH OUT THEIR ARMS.
!!
STREETCH
STRETCH!!
BRAIN
FWP
AAAGH.
HE'D TOTALLY FORGOTTEN.
AAGHH!!
AGH!?
AGH!?
IT'S NOT STRETCHING.

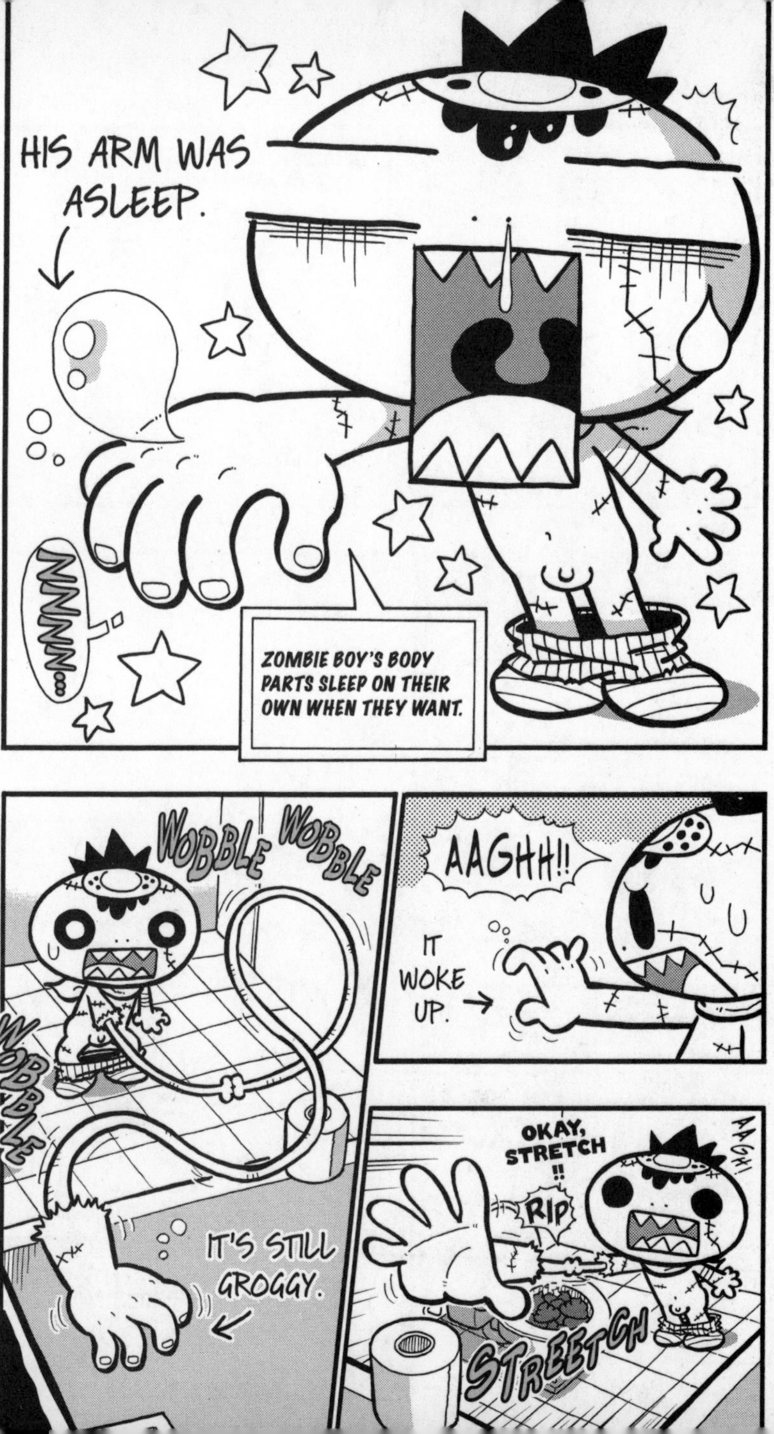
HIS ARM WAS ASLEEP.
ZOMBIE BOY'S BODY PARTS SLEEP ON THEIR OWN WHEN THEY WANT.
ZZZZZ...
AAGHH!!
IT WOKE UP.
OKAY, STRETCH!!
AAGH!
RIP
STREETCH
WOBBLE WOBBLE
WOBBLE
IT'S STILL GROGGY.

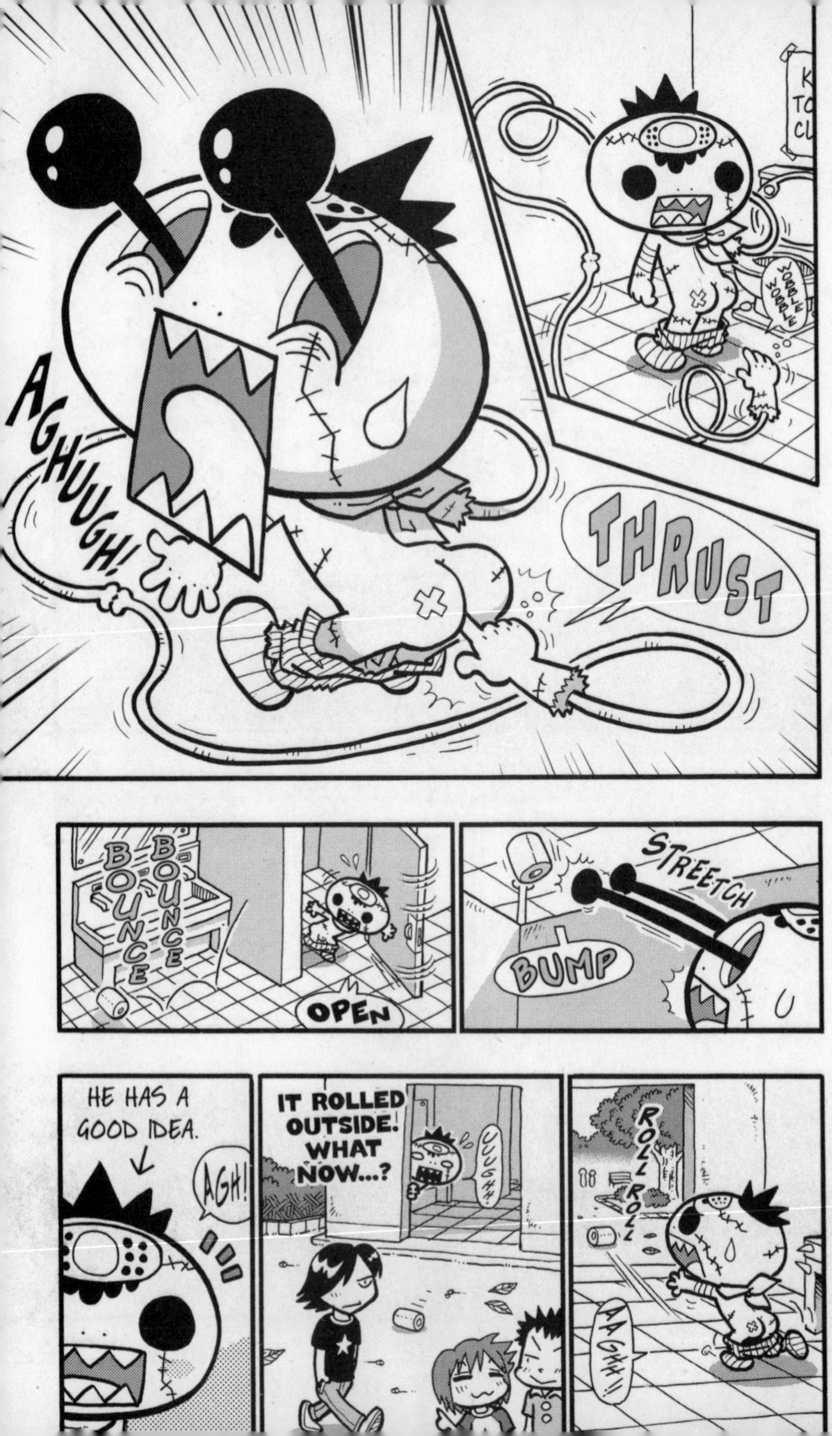
WOBBLE WOBBLE
THRUST
AGHUUGH!
STREETCH
BUMP
BOUNCE BOUNCE
OPEN
ROLL ROLL
AAGHH!!
IT ROLLED OUTSIDE. WHAT NOW...?
UUUGHH
HE HAS A GOOD IDEA.
AGH!

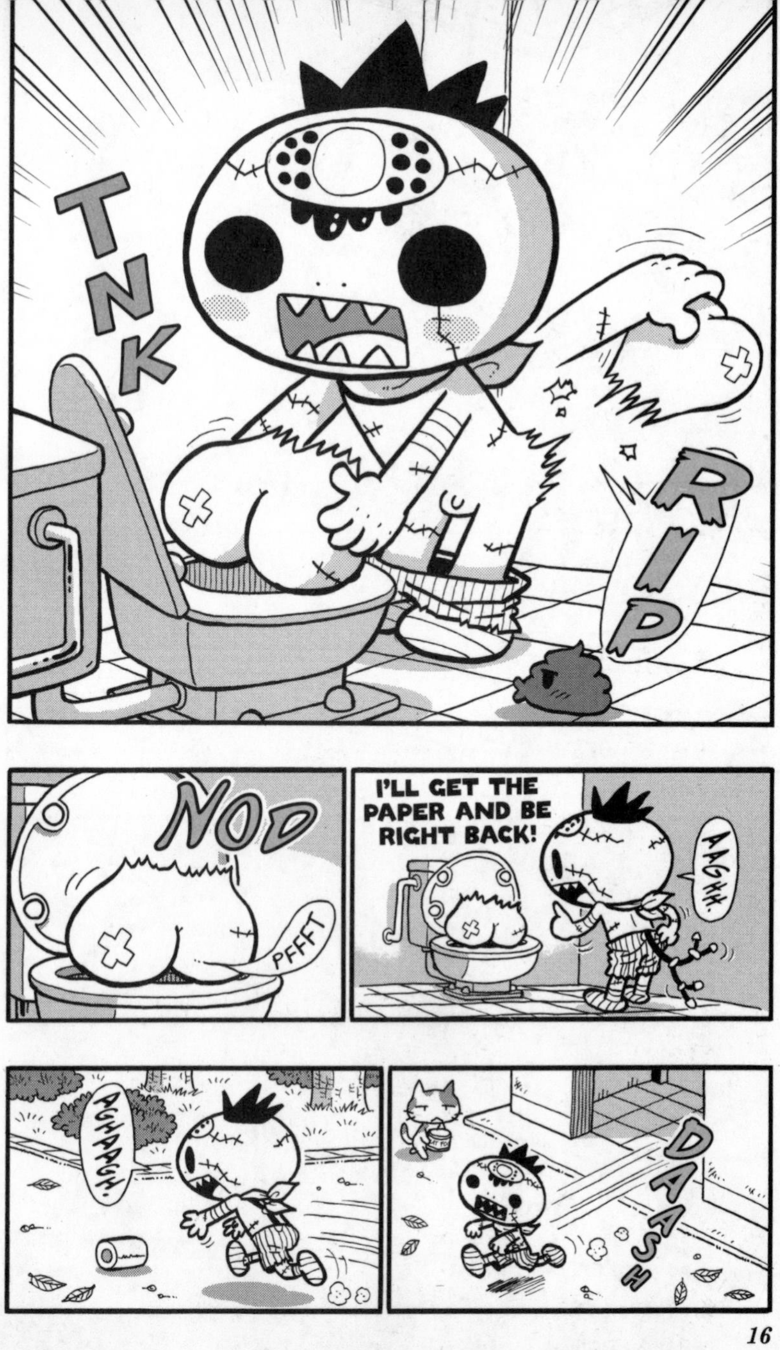
RIP
TNK
I'LL GET THE PAPER AND BE RIGHT BACK!
AAGHH.
NOD
PFFFT
DASH
AGHAAGH.

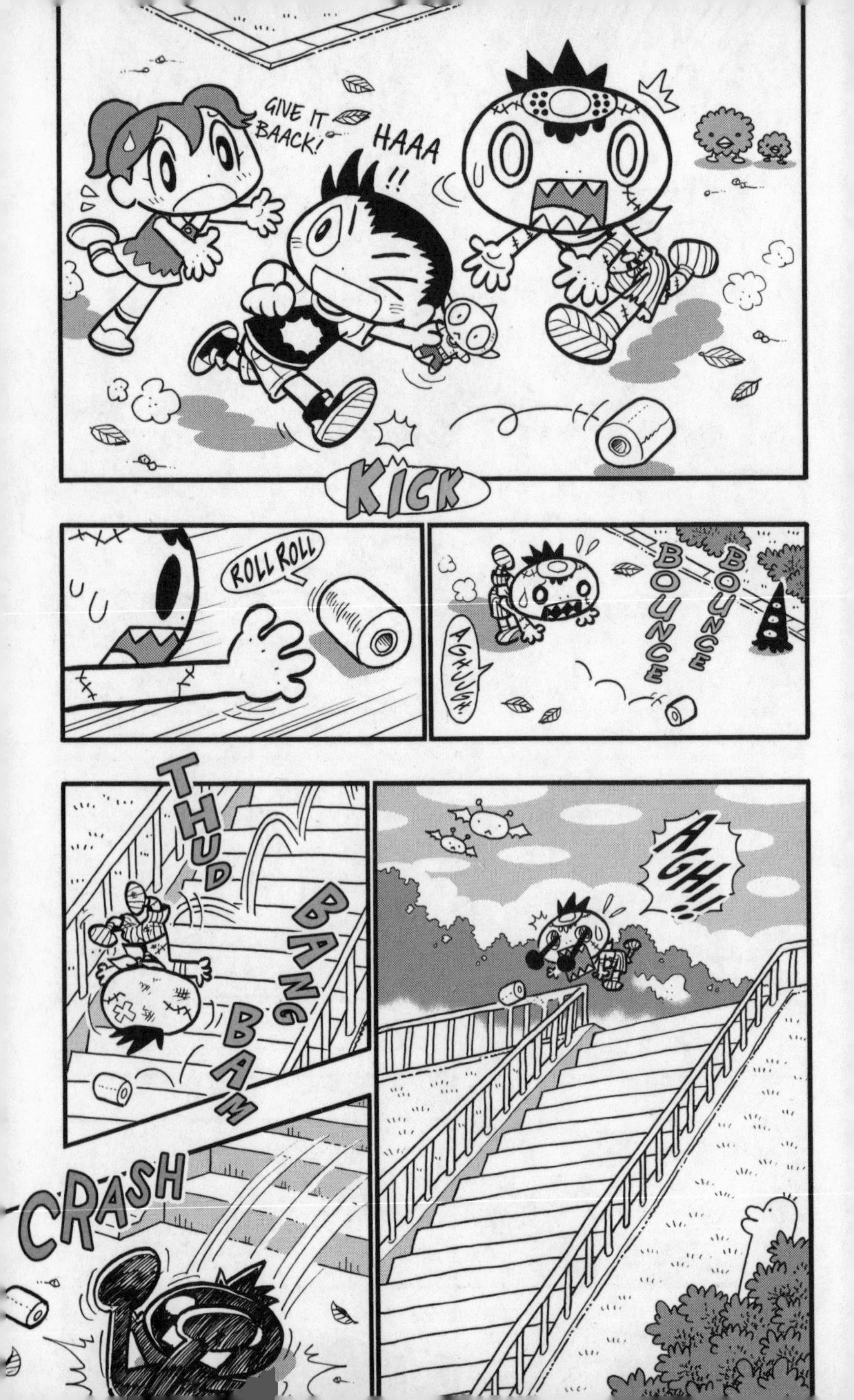
GIVE IT BAAACK!
HAAA!!
KICK
BOUNCE
BOUNCE
AGHUGH.
ROLL ROLL
AGH!!
THUD
BANG
BAM
CRASH

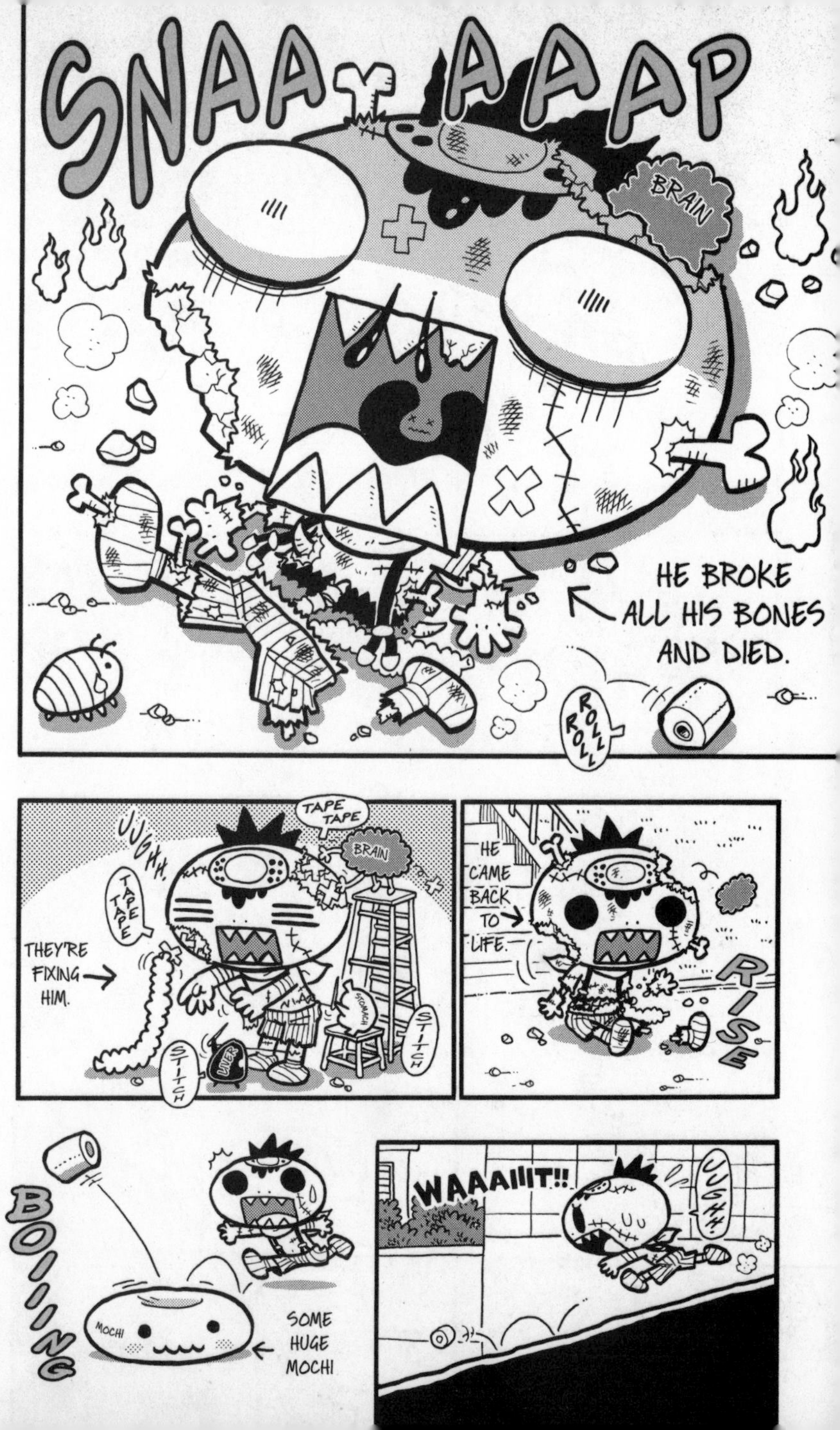
SNAAAAAAP
BRAIN
HE BROKE ALL HIS BONES AND DIED.
ROLL ROLL
HE CAME BACK TO LIFE.
RISE
TAPE TAPE
UGHH.
BRAIN
TAPE TAPE
THEY'RE FIXING HIM.
STOMACH
STITCH
LIVER
STITCH
UGHH.
WAAAIIIT!!
BOIIIING
MOCHI
SOME HUGE MOCHI

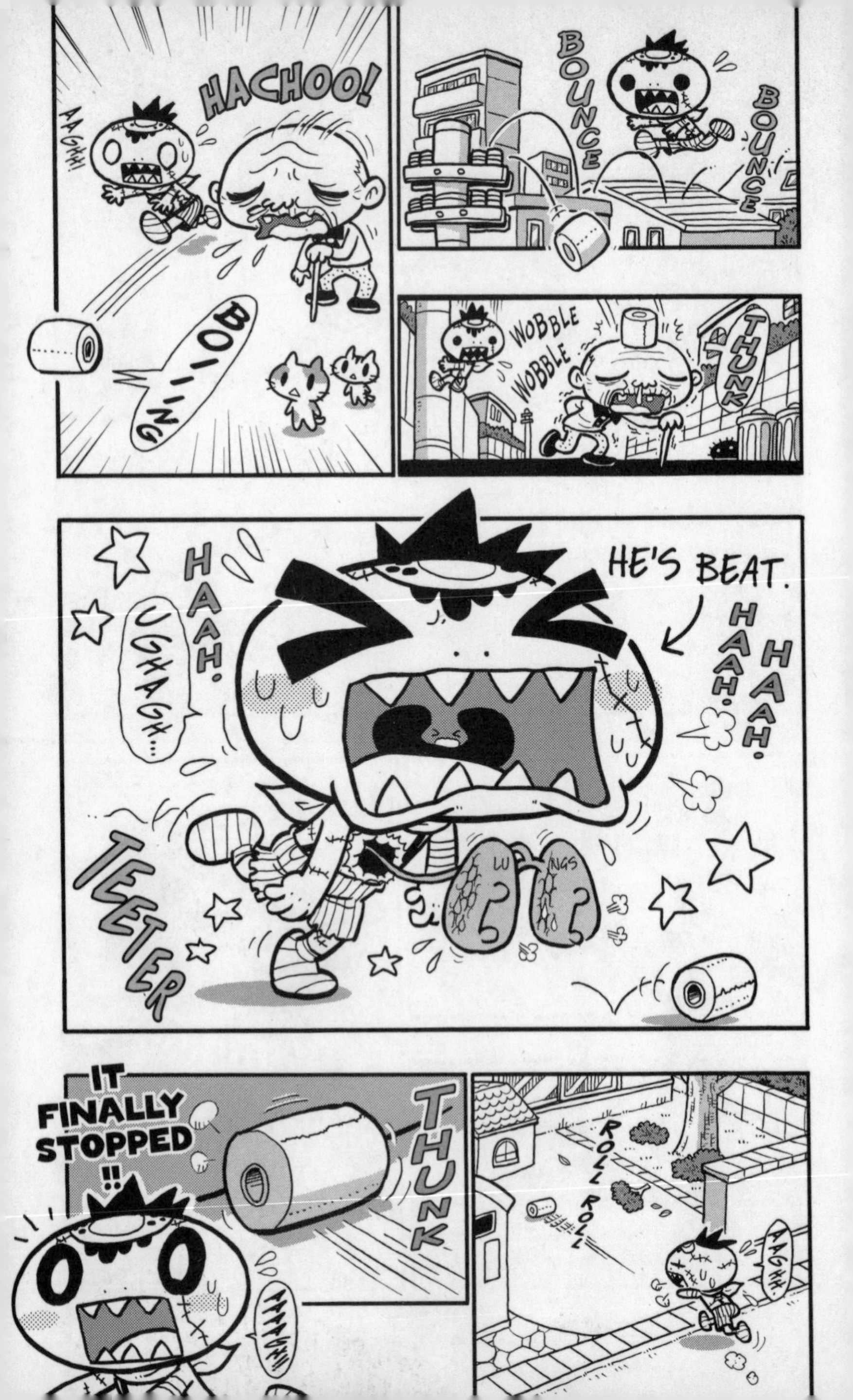
BOUNCE
BOUNCE
THUNK
WOBBLE
WOBBLE
HACHOO!
AAGHH!
BOI-I-NG
HE'S BEAT.
HAAAH. HAAAH.
HAAAH.
UGHAGH...
TEETER
LU
NGS
ROLL ROLL
AAGHH.
THUNK
IT FINALLY STOPPED!!
AAAAGH!!!

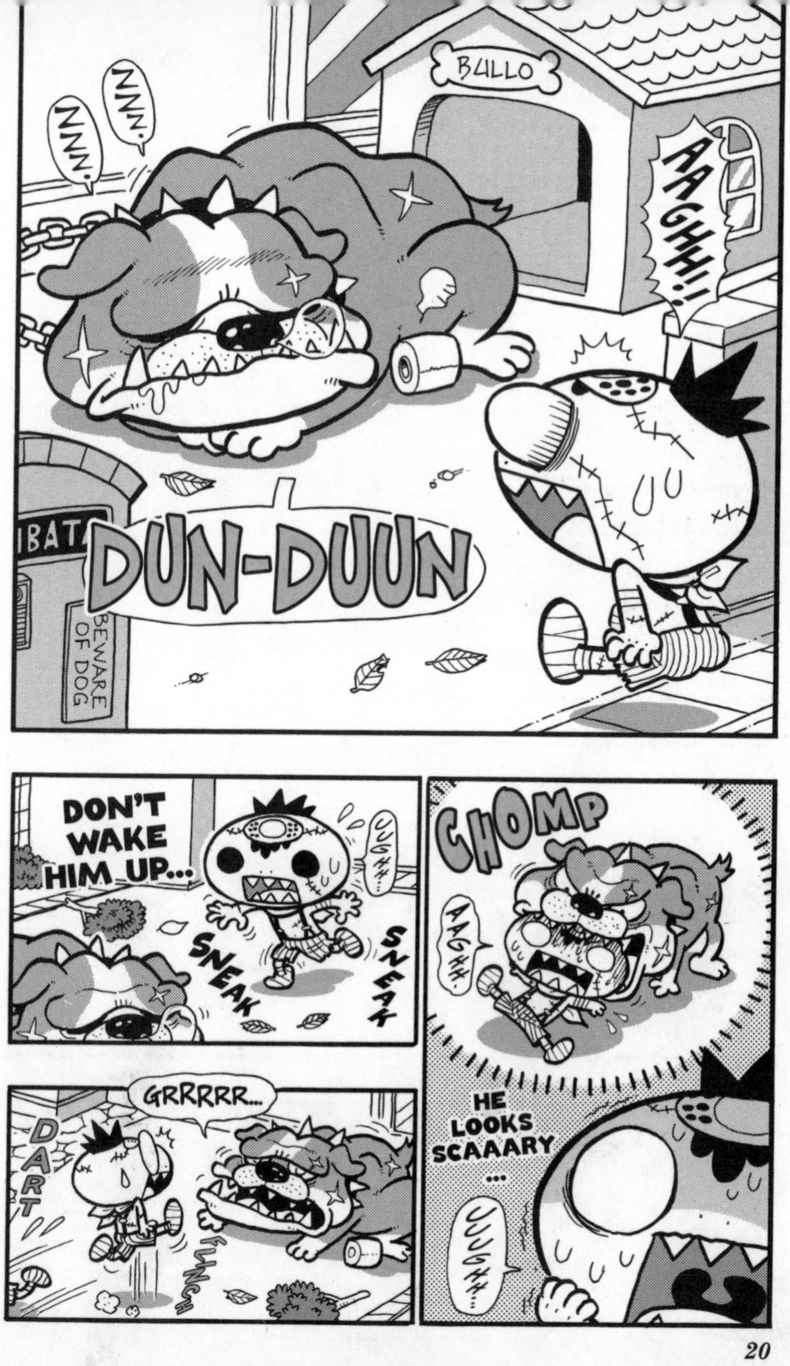
BULLO
AAGHHH!!!
NNN.
NNN.
DUN-DUUN
IBATA
BEWARE OF DOG
CHOMP
AAGHH.
HE LOOKS SCAAARY...
UUGHH...
UUGHH...
DON'T WAKE HIM UP...
SNEAK
SNEAK
GRRRRR...
DART
FLINCH

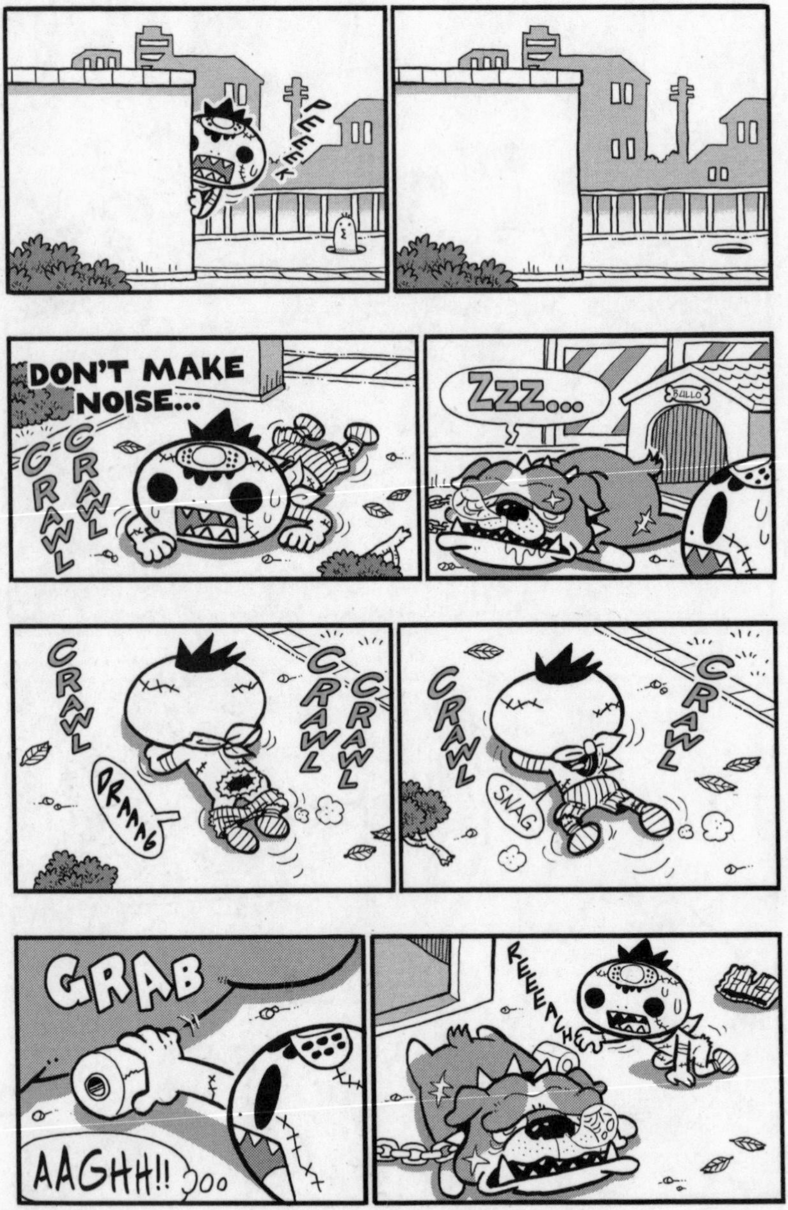
PEEEEK
Zzz...
DON'T MAKE NOISE...
CRAWL
CRAWL
CRAWL
SNAG
CRAWL
CRAWL
CRAWL
CRAWL
DRAAAAG
REEEACH
GRAB
AAGHH!!

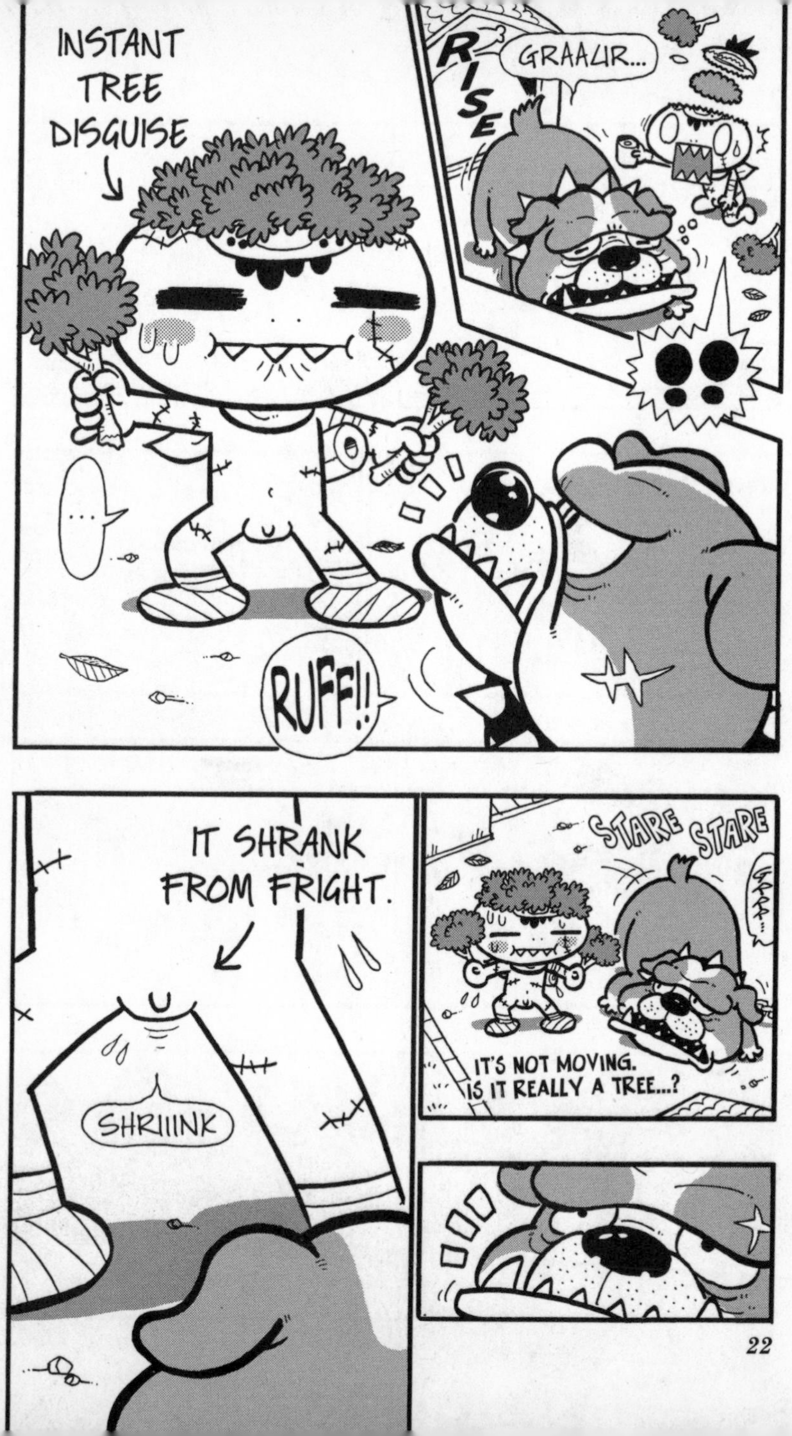
RISE
GRAAUR...
!!
INSTANT TREE DISGUISE
...
RUFF!!
STARE STARE
GRRR...
IT'S NOT MOVING. IS IT REALLY A TREE...?
IT SHRANK FROM FRIGHT.
SHRIIINK

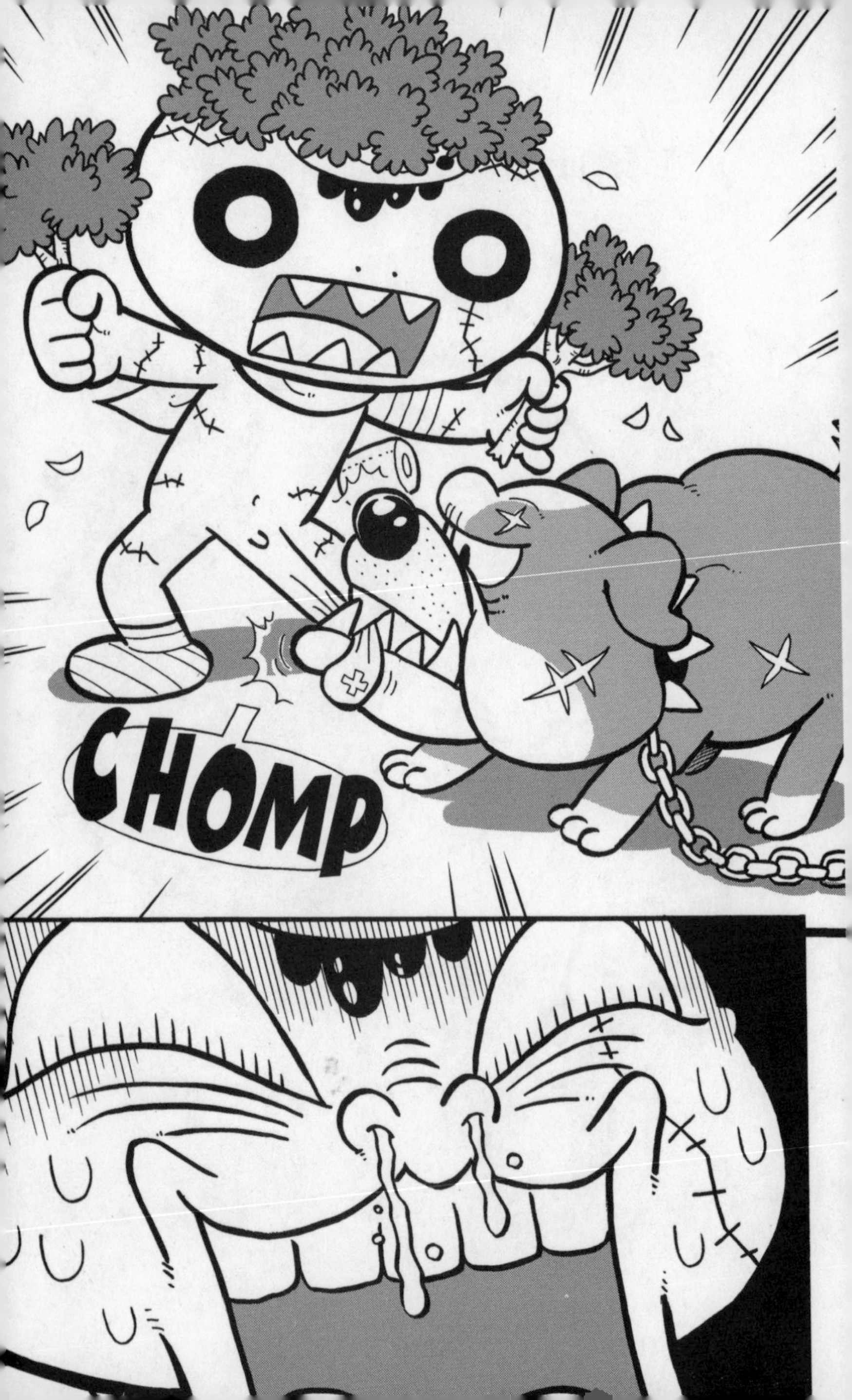
CHOMP

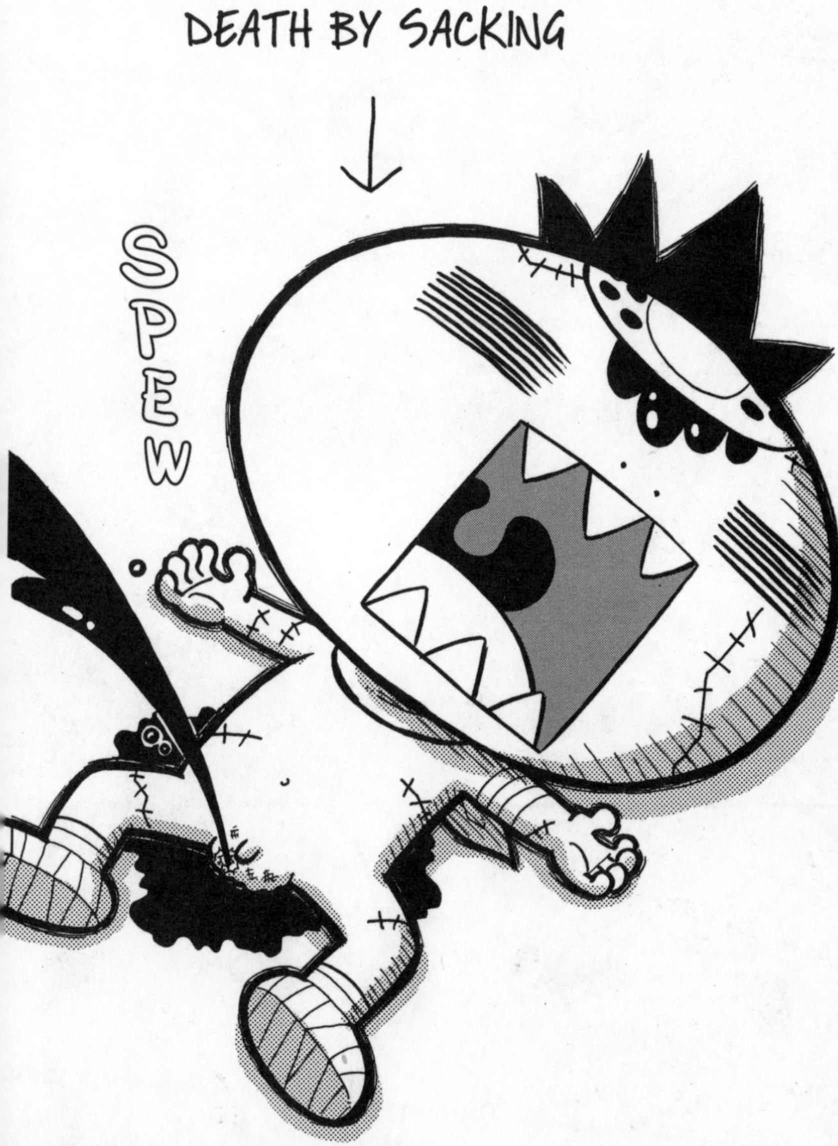
DEATH BY SACKING
SPEW

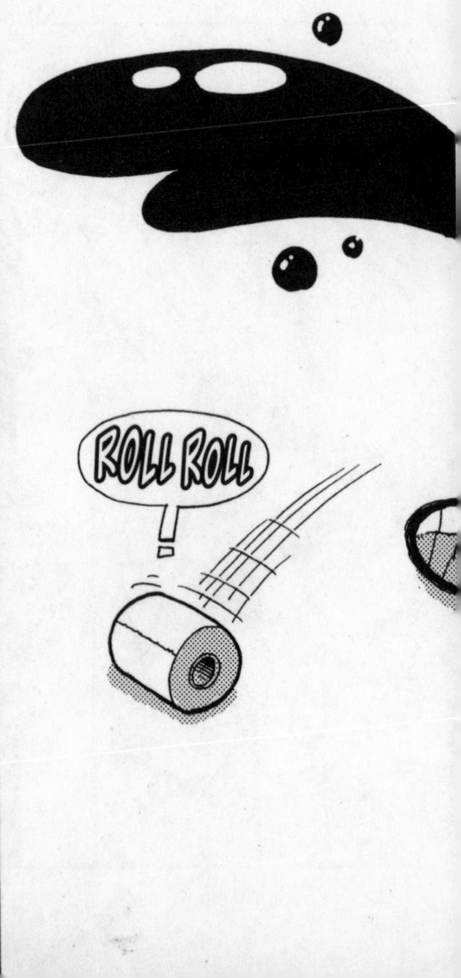
ROLL ROLL
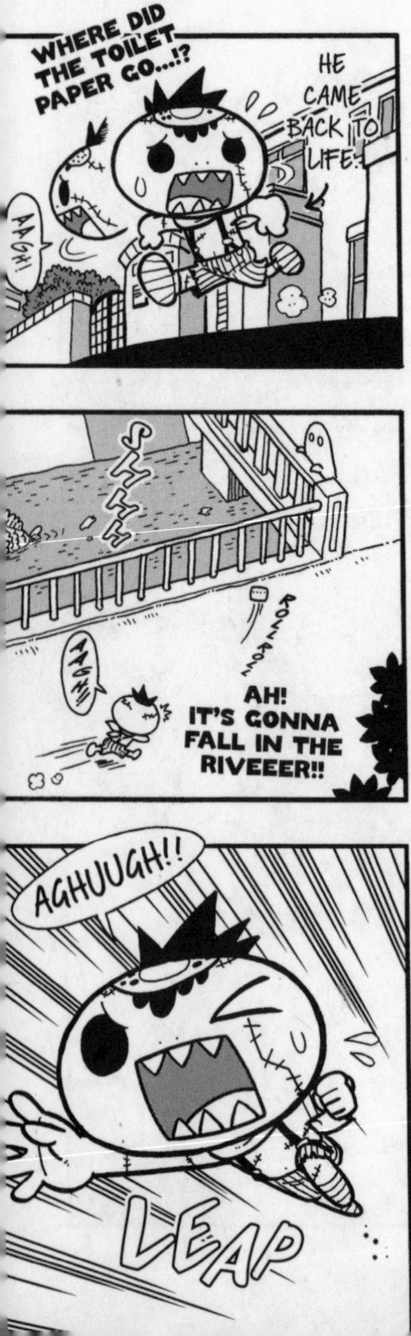
HE CAME BACK TO LIFE
WHERE DID THE TOILET PAPER GO...!?
AAGH!
ROLL ROLL
AH! IT'S GONNA FALL IN THE RIVEEER!!
AAGH!!!
AGHUUGH!!
LEAP

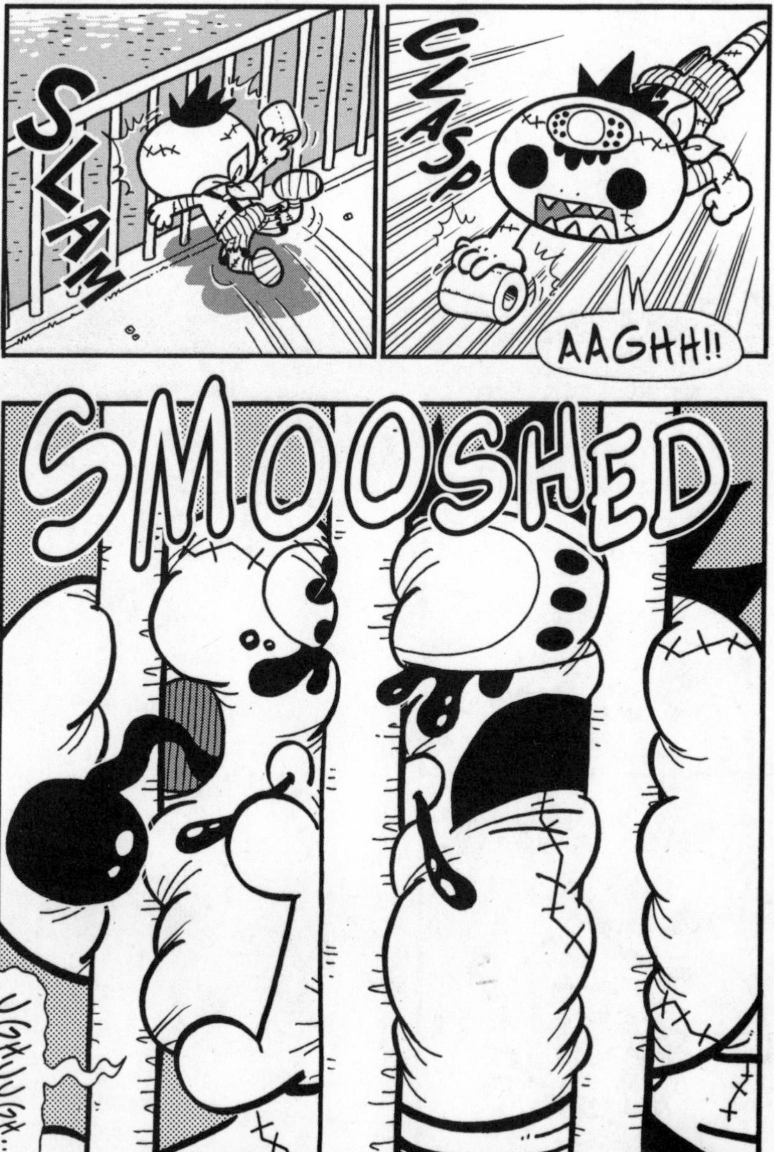
CLASP
AAGHH!!
SLAM
SMOOSHED
UGHUGH...

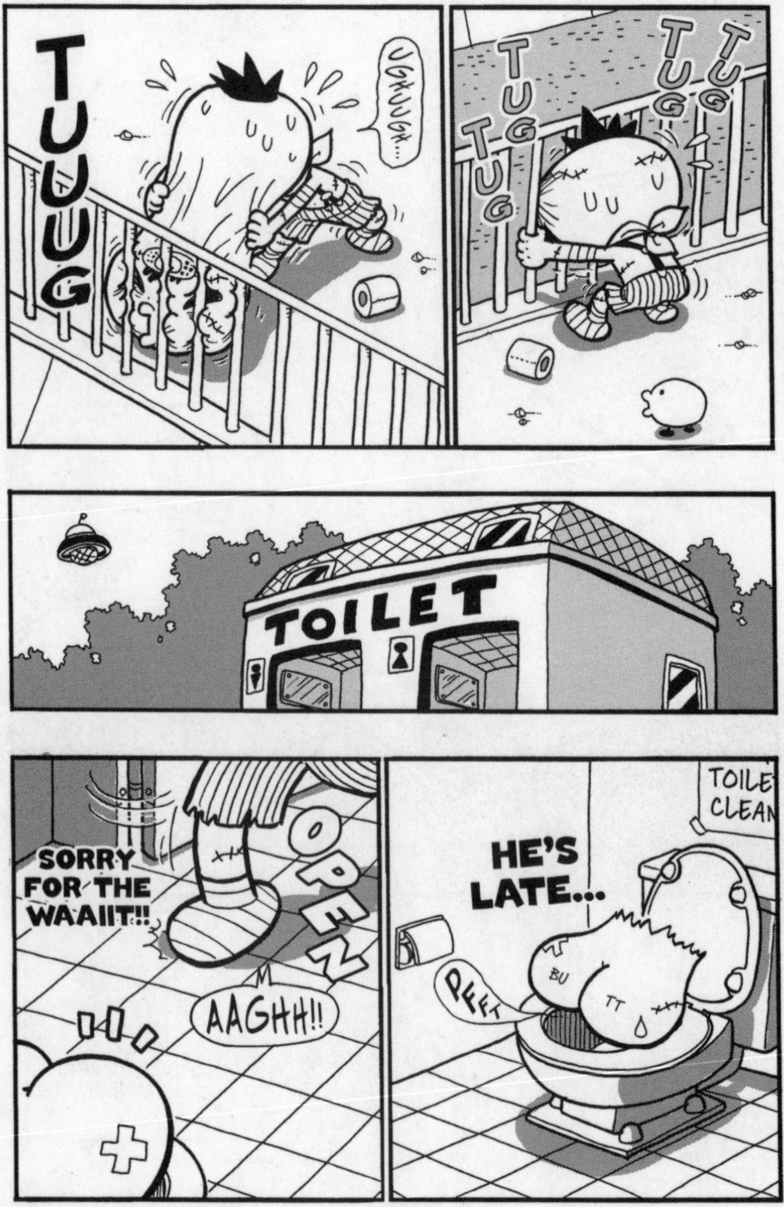
TUG
TUG
TUG
TUG
TUG
TUUUG
UGHUUGH...
TOILET
TOILE
CLEAN
HE'S LATE...
BU
TT
PFFFT
OPEN
SORRY FOR THE WAAIIT!!
AAGHH!!

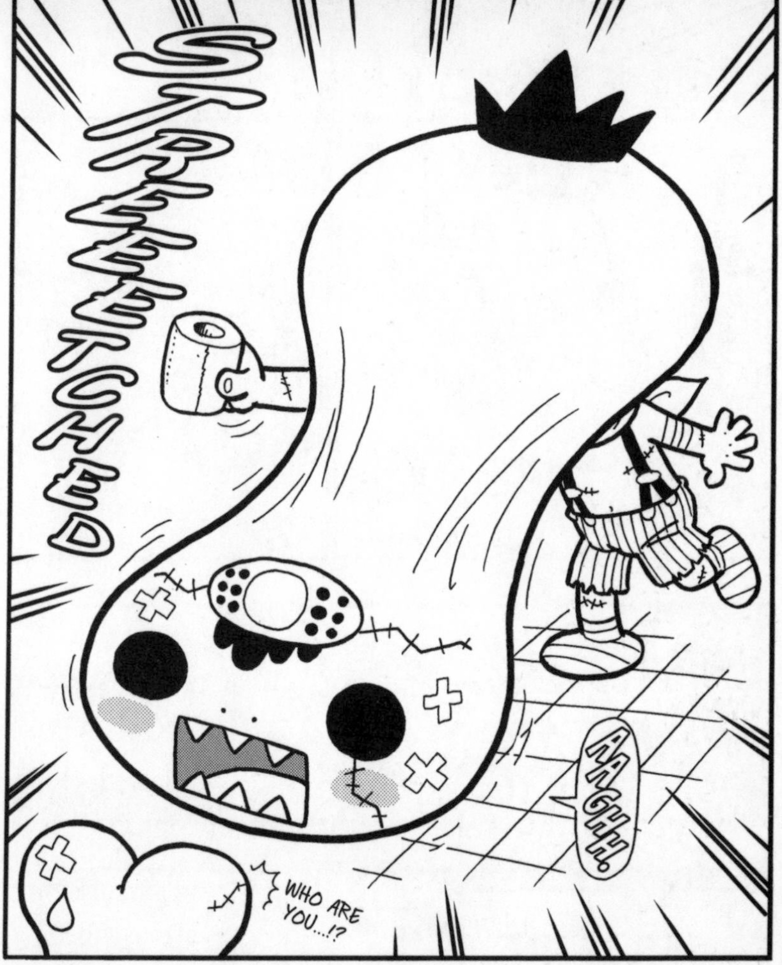
STRETCHED
AAGHH.
WHO ARE YOU...!?

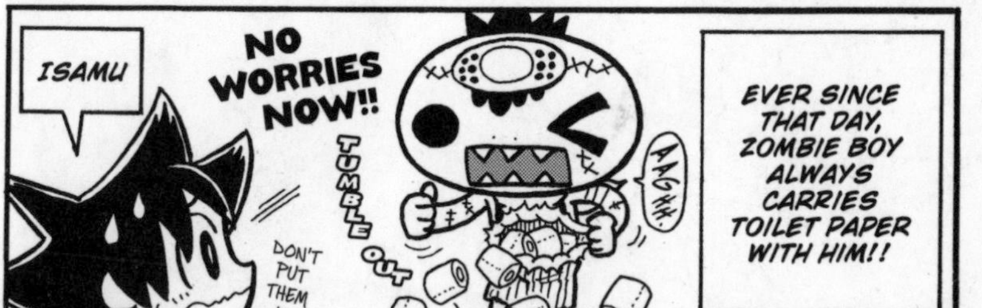
EVER SINCE THAT DAY, ZOMBIE BOY ALWAYS CARRIES TOILET PAPER WITH HIM!!
AAGHH.
NO WORRIES NOW!!
TUMBLE OUT
ISAMU
DON'T PUT THEM IN THERE!

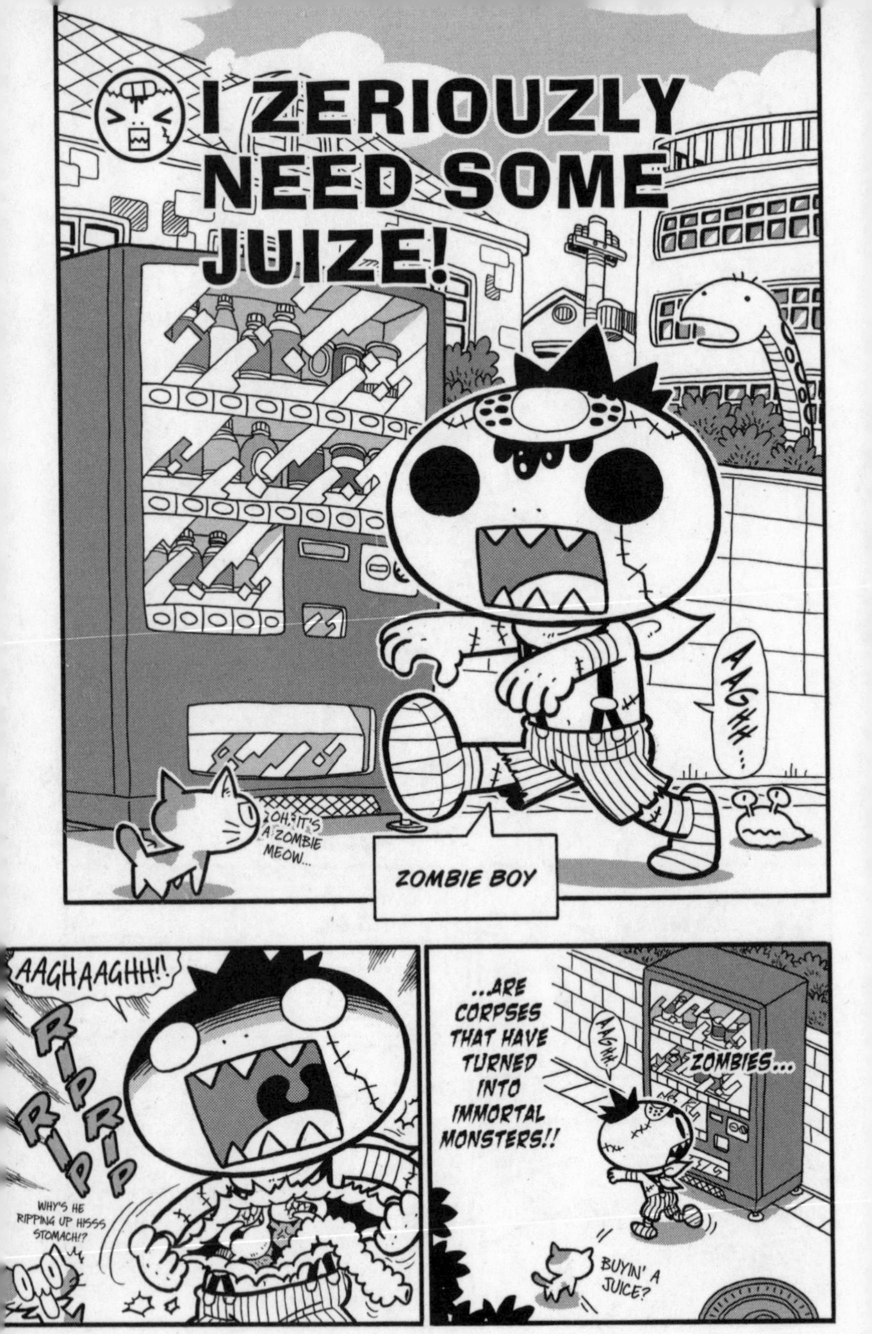
I ZERIOUZLY NEED SOME JUIZE!
AAGHH...
ZOMBIE BOY
OH, IT'S A ZOMBIE MEOW...
ZOMBIES...
AAGHH
...ARE CORPSES THAT HAVE TURNED INTO IMMORTAL MONSTERS!!
BUYIN' A JUICE?
AAGHAAGHH!!
RIP RIP RIP
WHY'S HE RIPPING UP HISSS STOMACH!?

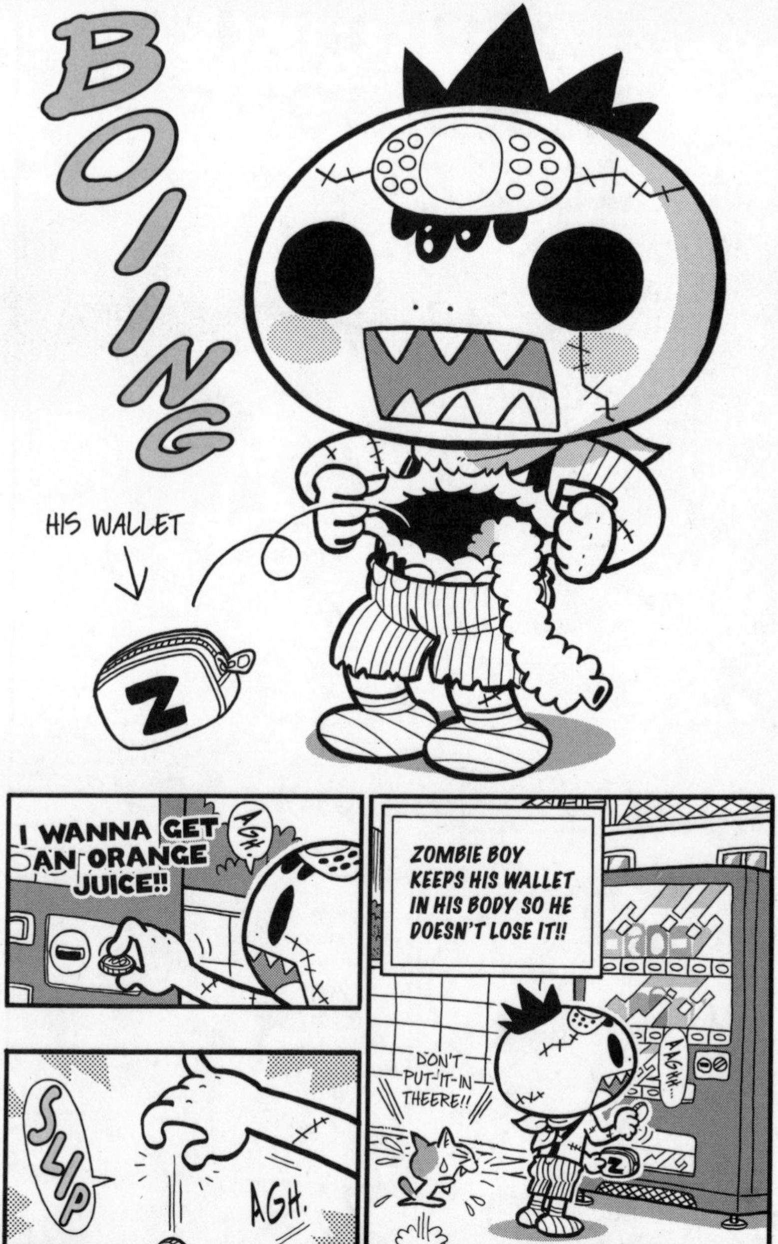
BOING
HIS WALLET
ZOMBIE BOY KEEPS HIS WALLET IN HIS BODY SO HE DOESN'T LOSE IT!!
AAGHH...
DON'T PUT-IT-IN THEERE!!
AGH.
I WANNA GET AN ORANGE JUICE!!
SLIP
AGH.

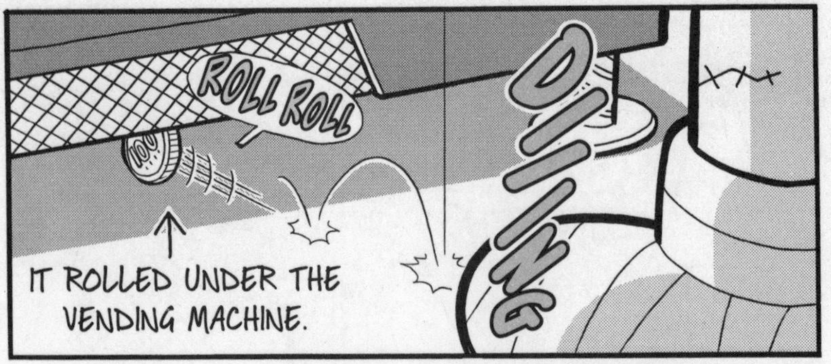
DIIING
ROLL ROLL
100
IT ROLLED UNDER THE VENDING MACHINE.
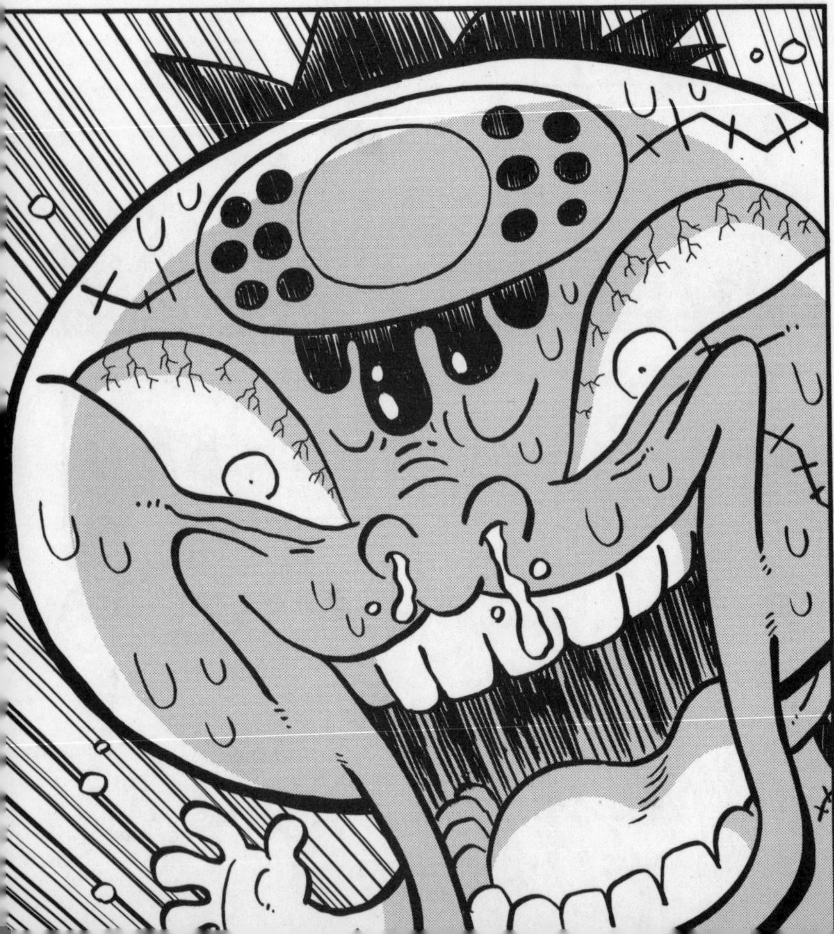

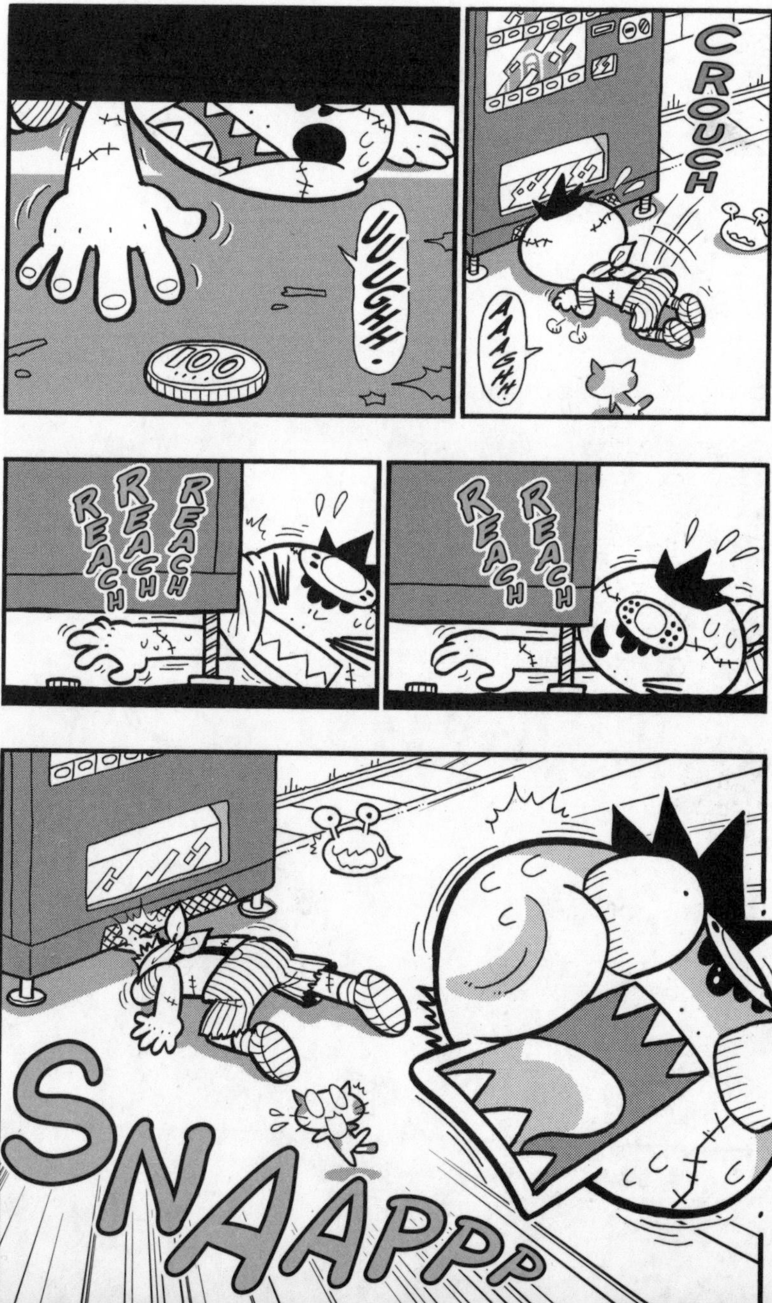
CROUCH
AAAGHH.
UUUGHH.
REACH REACH
REACH REACH REACH
SNAAPPP

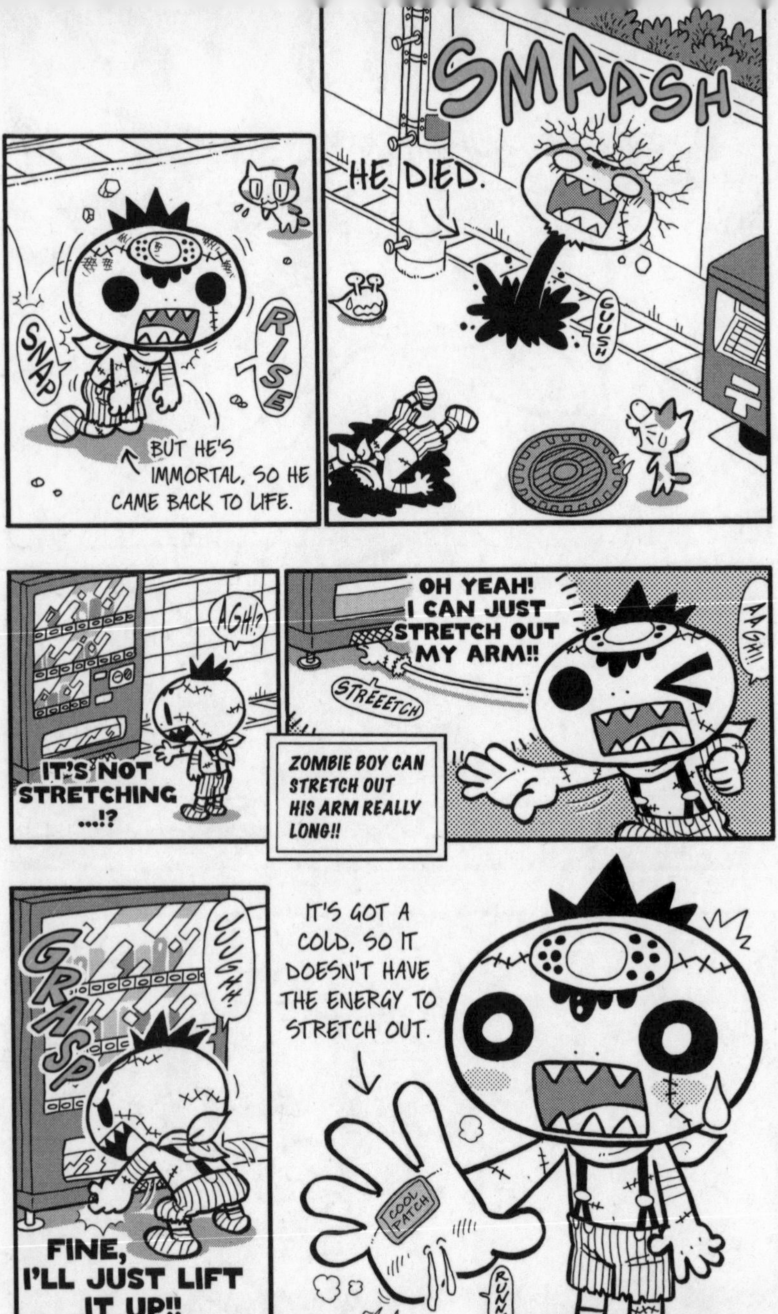
SMAASH
HE DIED.
GUUSH
SNAP
RISE
BUT HE'S IMMORTAL, SO HE CAME BACK TO LIFE.
OH YEAH! I CAN JUST STRETCH OUT MY ARM!!
AAGH!!
STREEETCH
ZOMBIE BOY CAN STRETCH OUT HIS ARM REALLY LONG!!
AGH!?
IT'S NOT STRETCHING ...!?
IT'S GOT A COLD, SO IT DOESN'T HAVE THE ENERGY TO STRETCH OUT.
COOL PATCH
RUNNY
KOFF KOFF!
UUGHH
GRASP
FINE, I'LL JUST LIFT IT UP!!

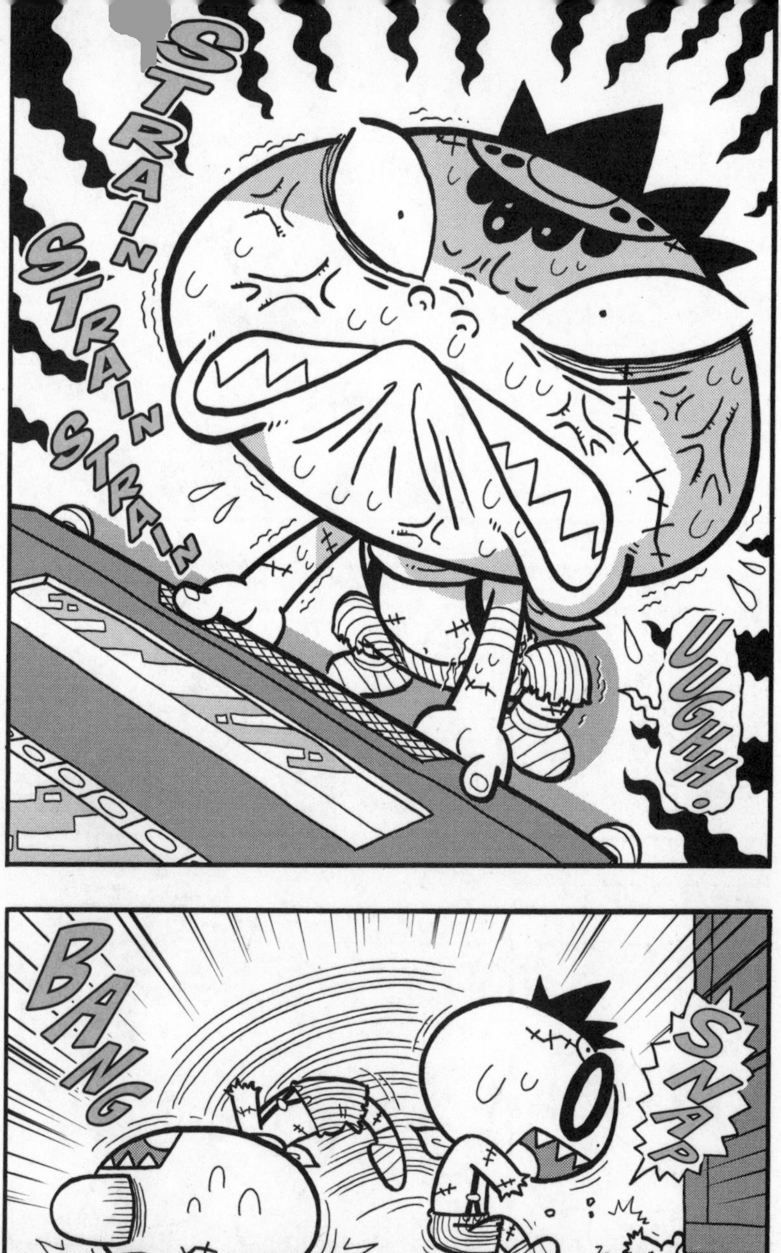
STRAIN
STRAIN
STRAIN
UUGHH.
SNAP
BANG

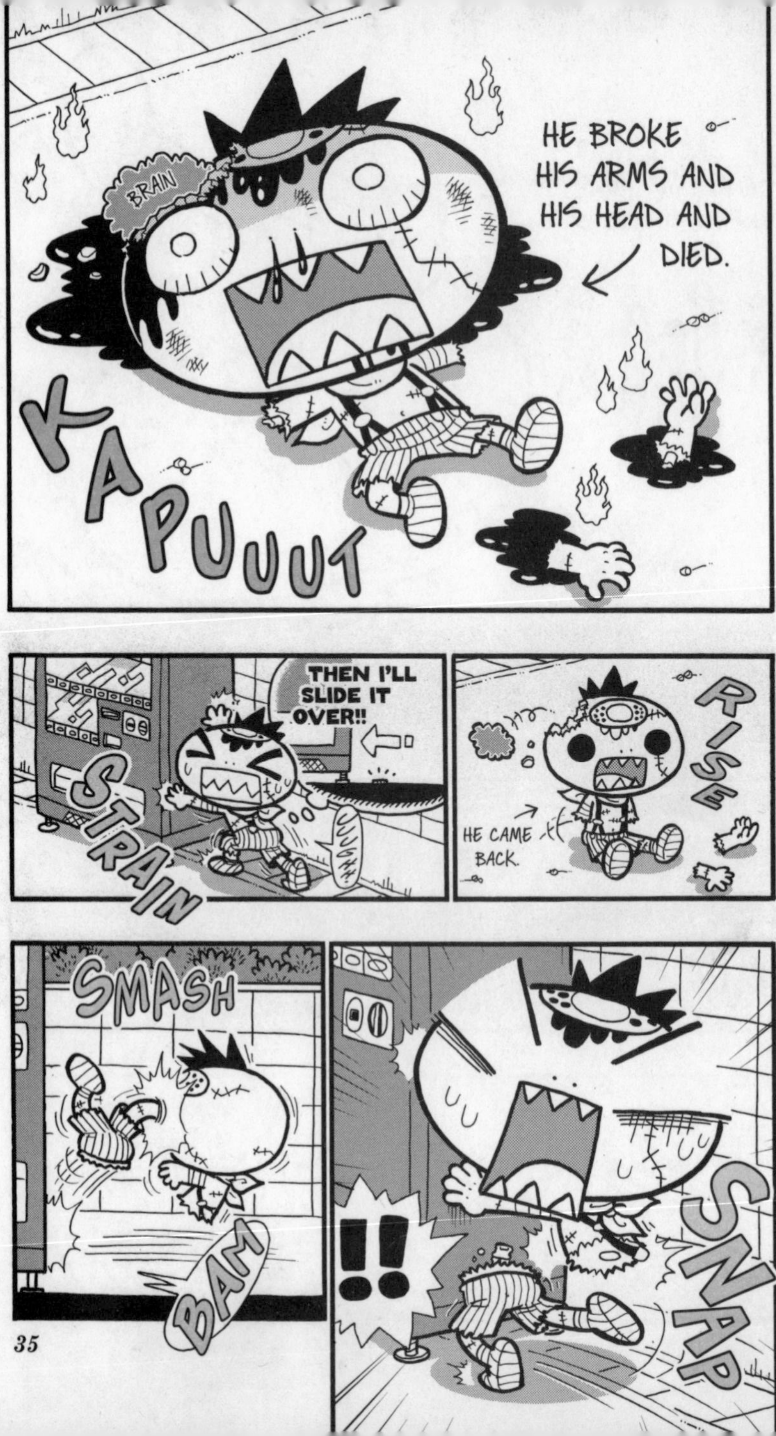
HE BROKE HIS ARMS AND HIS HEAD AND DIED.
BRAIN
KAPUUUT
RISE
HE CAME BACK.
THEN I'LL SLIDE IT OVER!!
STRAIN
SNAP
!!
SMASH
BAM

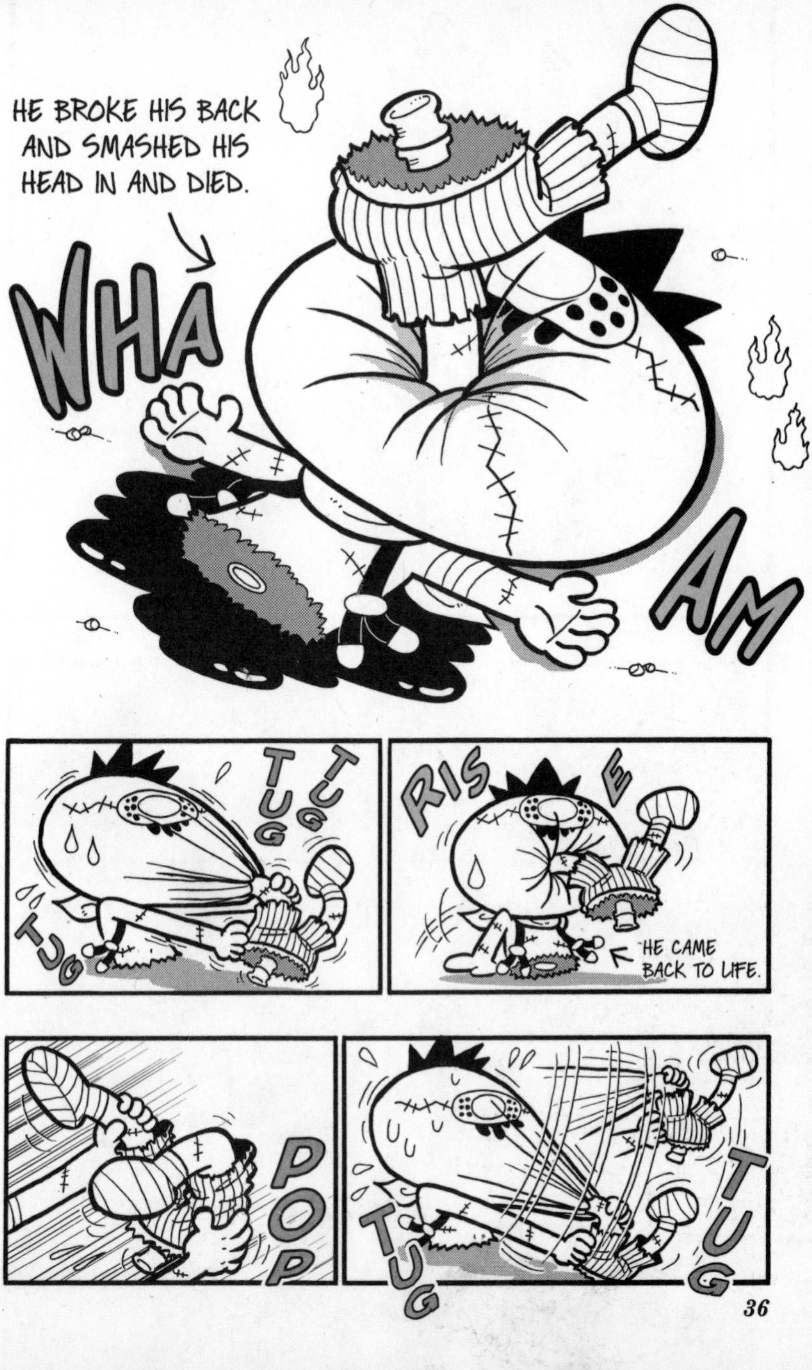
HE BROKE HIS BACK AND SMASHED HIS HEAD IN AND DIED.
WHA
AM
RIS
E
HE CAME BACK TO LIFE.
TUG
TUG
TUG
TUG
TUG
POP

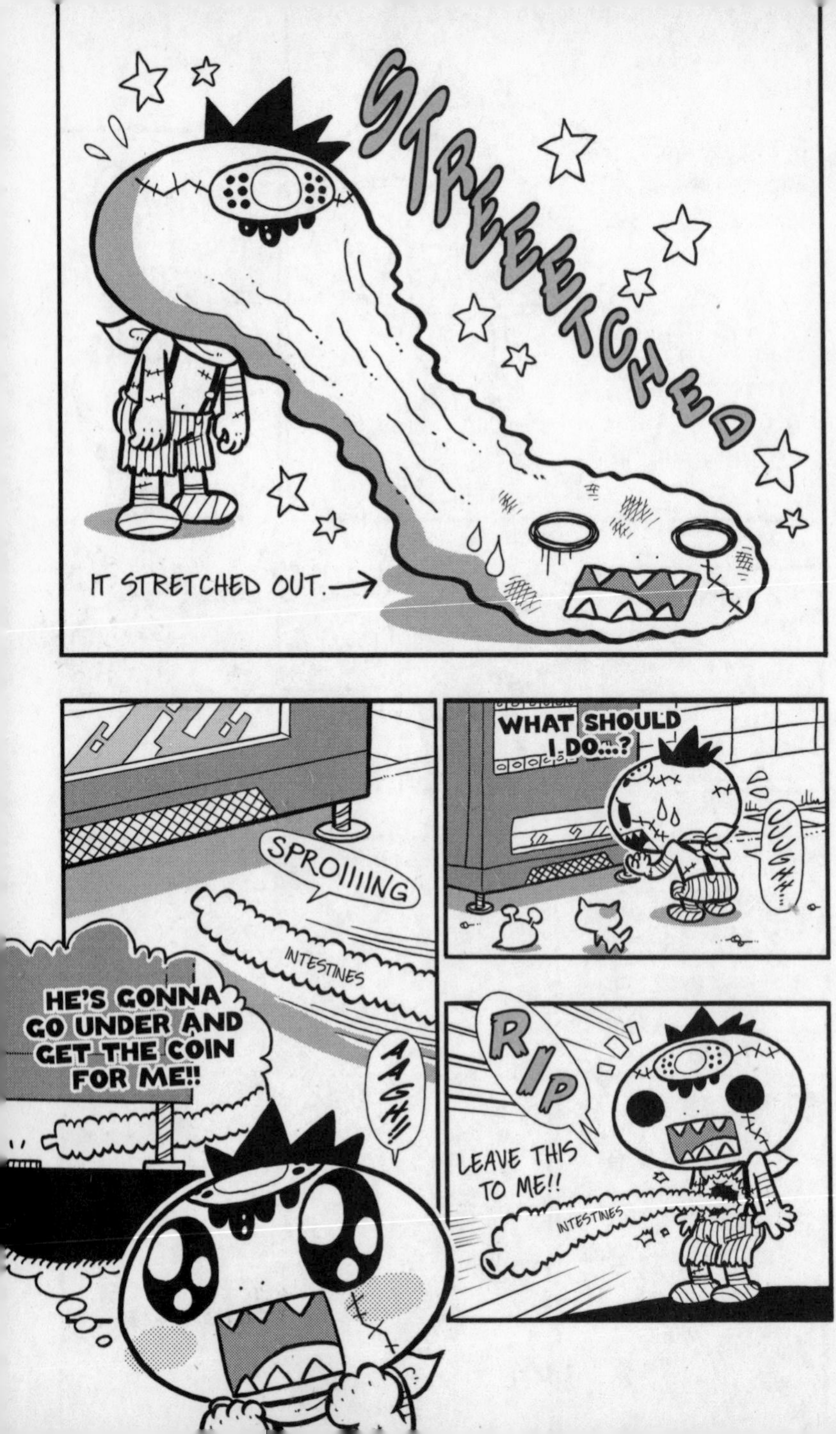
STREEETCHED
IT STRETCHED OUT.
WHAT SHOULD I DO...?
UUGHH...
RIP
LEAVE THIS TO ME!!
INTESTINES
SPROIIIING
INTESTINES
HE'S GONNA GO UNDER AND GET THE COIN FOR ME!!
AAGH!!

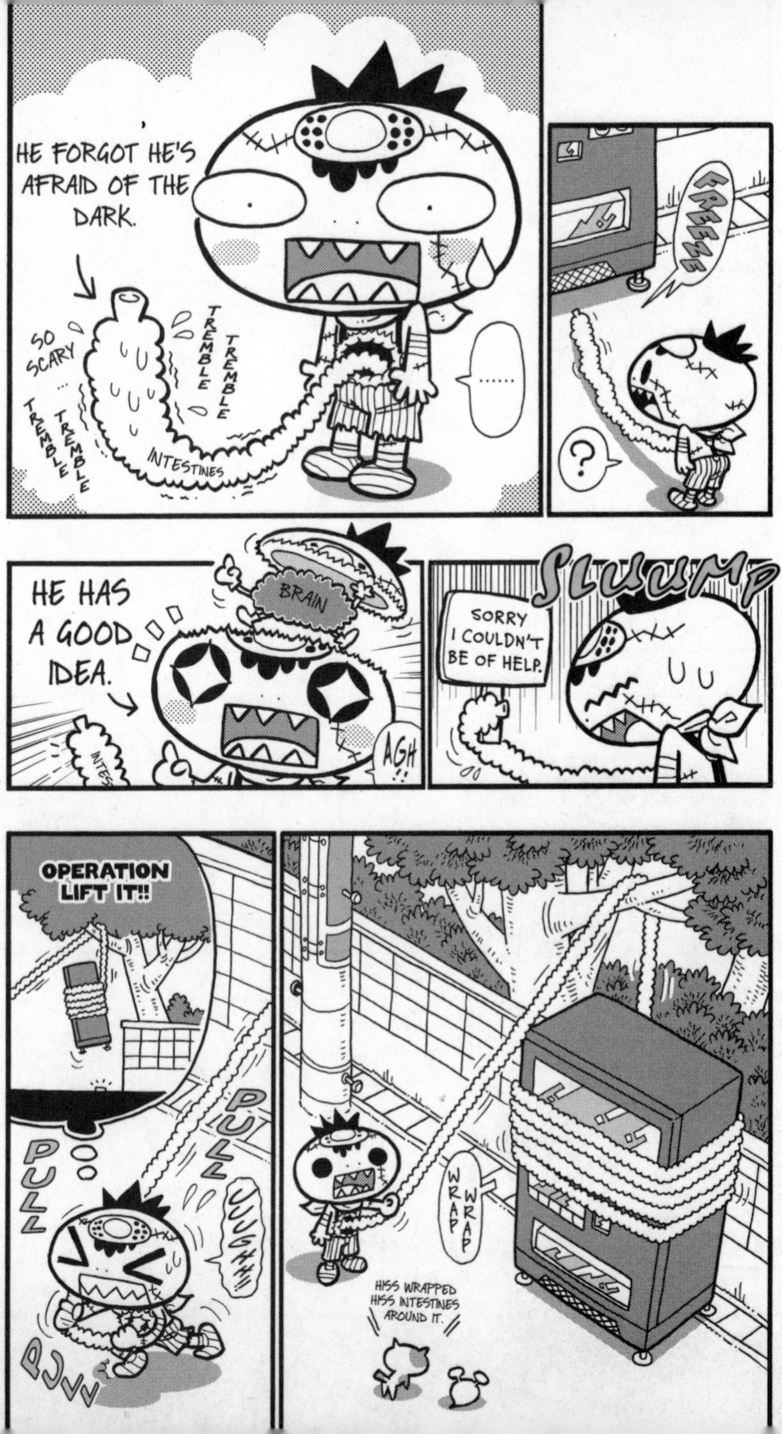
FREEZE
?
HE FORGOT HE'S AFRAID OF THE DARK.
SO SCARY...
TREMBLE TREMBLE
TREMBLE TREMBLE
INTESTINES
......
SLUUMP
SORRY I COULDN'T BE OF HELP.
HE HAS A GOOD IDEA.
BRAIN
AGH!!
INTES
WRAP WRAP
HISS WRAPPED HISS INTESTINES AROUND IT.
OPERATION LIFT IT!!
PULL
PULL
UUGH!!

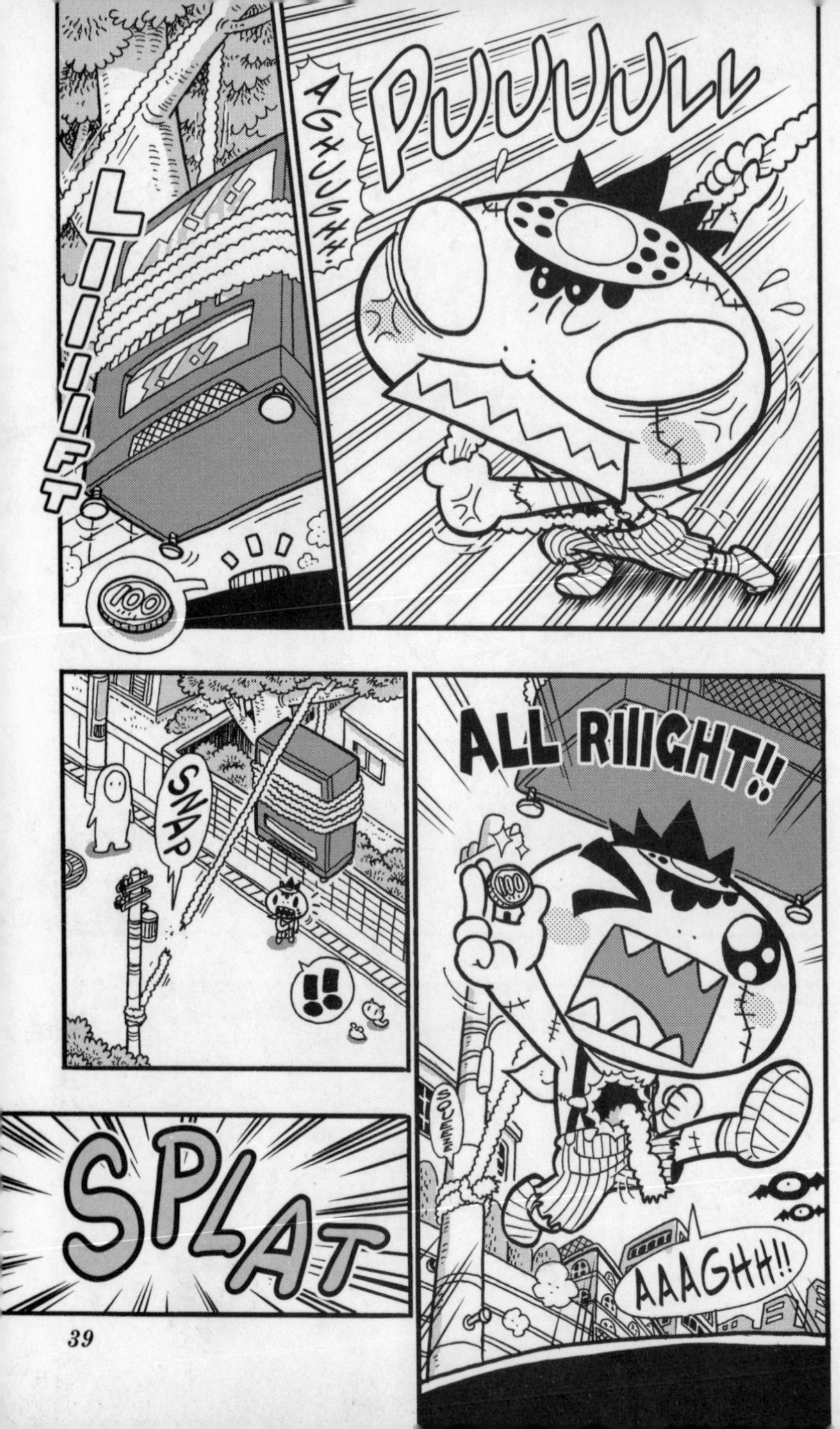
PUUUULL
AGHUUGHH.
LIIIIIIFT
ALL RIIIGHT!!
SQUEEZE
AAAGHH!!
SNAP
!!
SPLAT

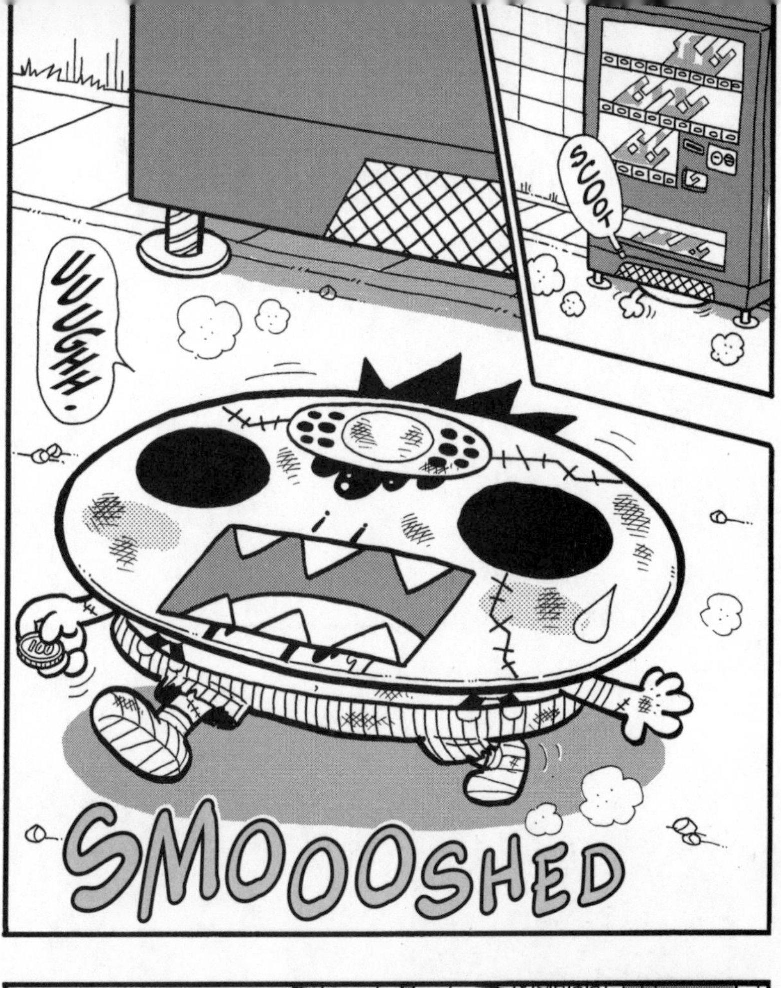
SCOOT
UUUGHH.
SMOOOSHED

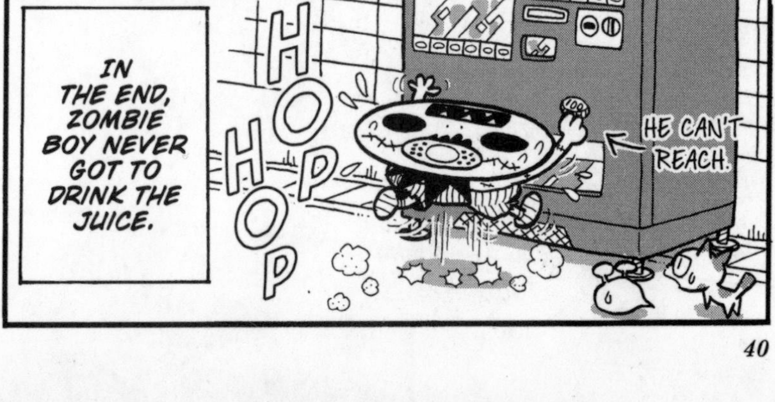
HE CAN'T REACH.
HOP HOP
IN THE END, ZOMBIE BOY NEVER GOT TO DRINK THE JUICE.

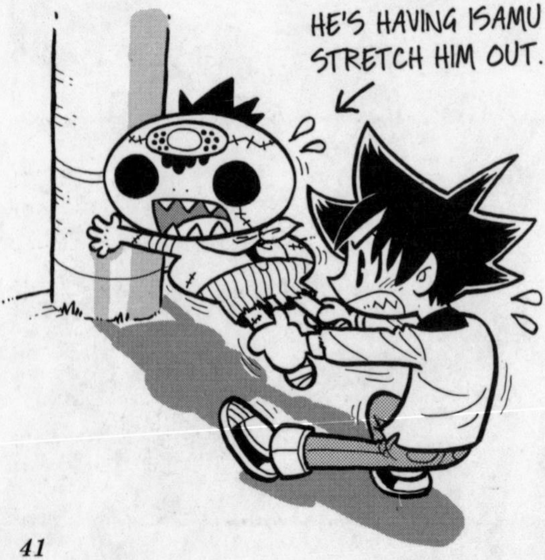
HE'S HAVING ISAMU STRETCH HIM OUT.

THE HEAT CAN'T ZTOP ME!

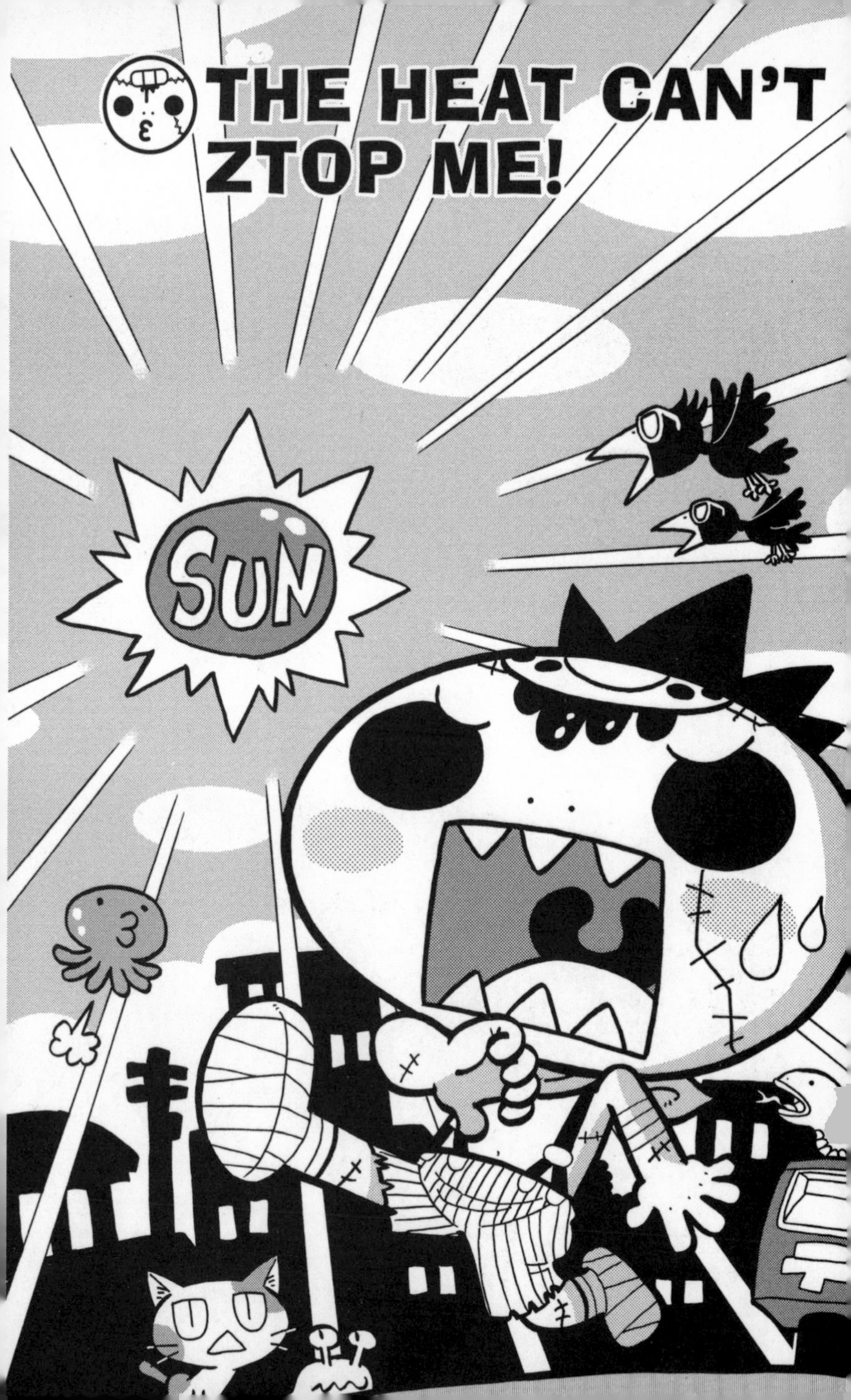
SUN

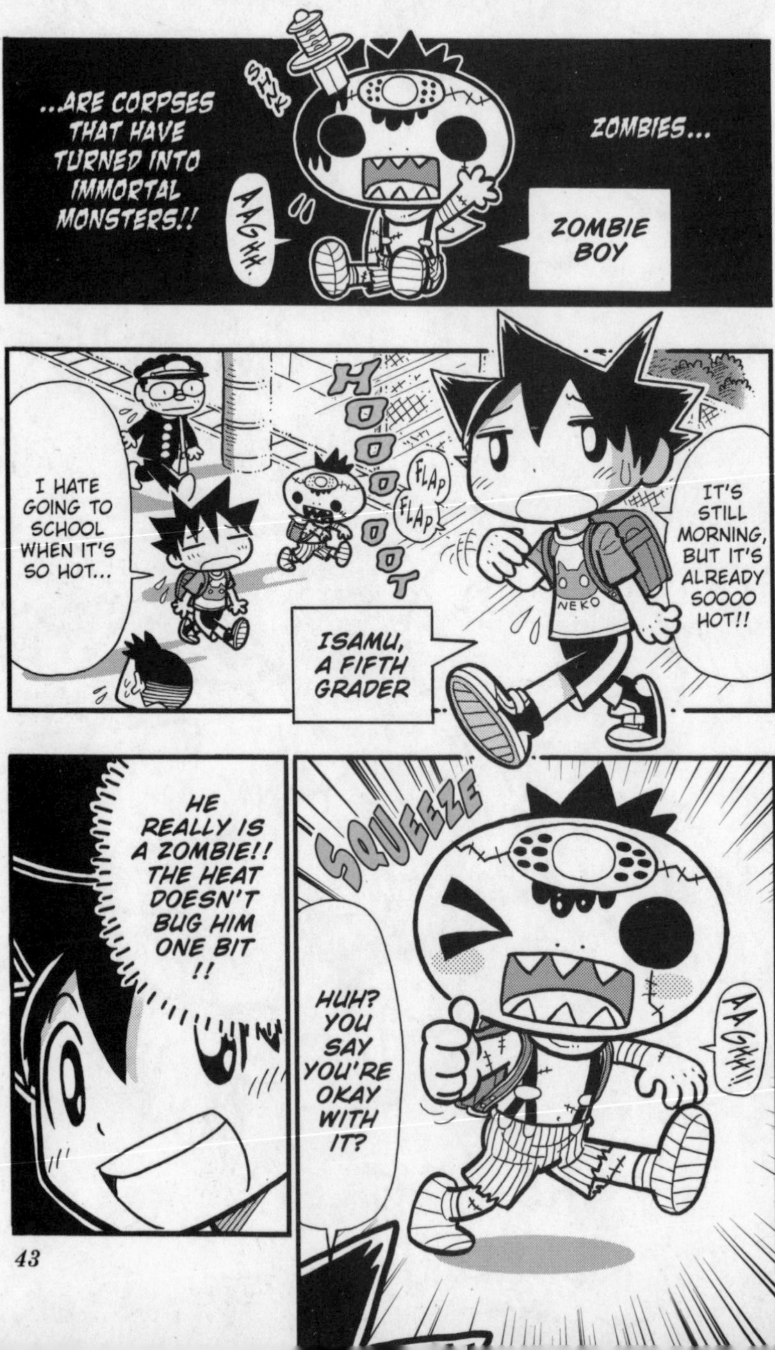
ZOMBIES...
ZOMBIE BOY
AAGHH.
...ARE CORPSES THAT HAVE TURNED INTO IMMORTAL MONSTERS!!
IT'S STILL MORNING, BUT IT'S ALREADY SOOOO HOT!!
ISAMU, A FIFTH GRADER
HOOOOOOT
FLAP
FLAP
I HATE GOING TO SCHOOL WHEN IT'S SO HOT...
AAGHH!!
SQUEEZE
HUH? YOU SAY YOU'RE OKAY WITH IT?
HE REALLY IS A ZOMBIE!! THE HEAT DOESN'T BUG HIM ONE BIT!!

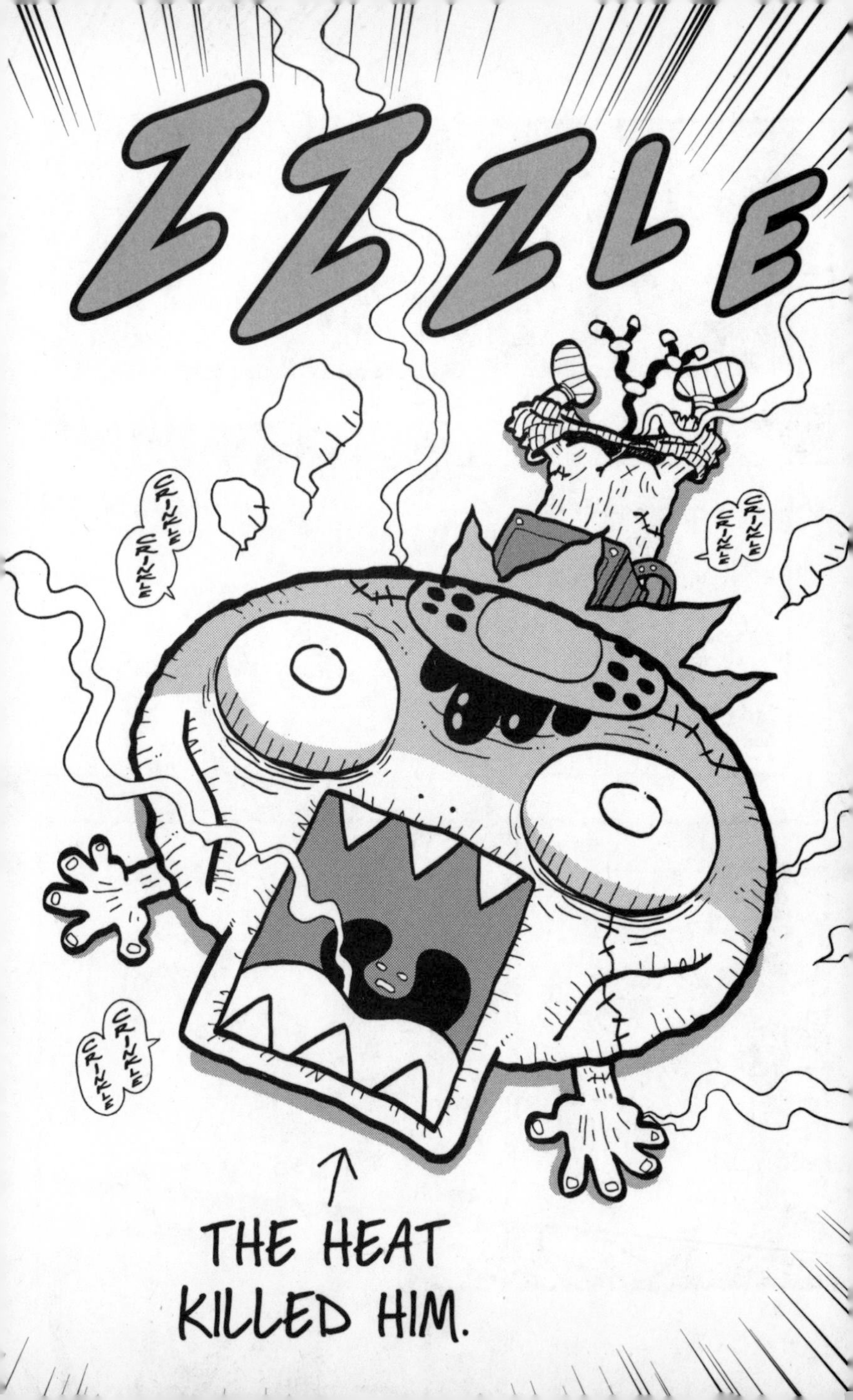
ZZZZLE
CRINKLE CRINKLE
CRINKLE CRINKLE
CRINKLE CRINKLE
THE HEAT KILLED HIM.

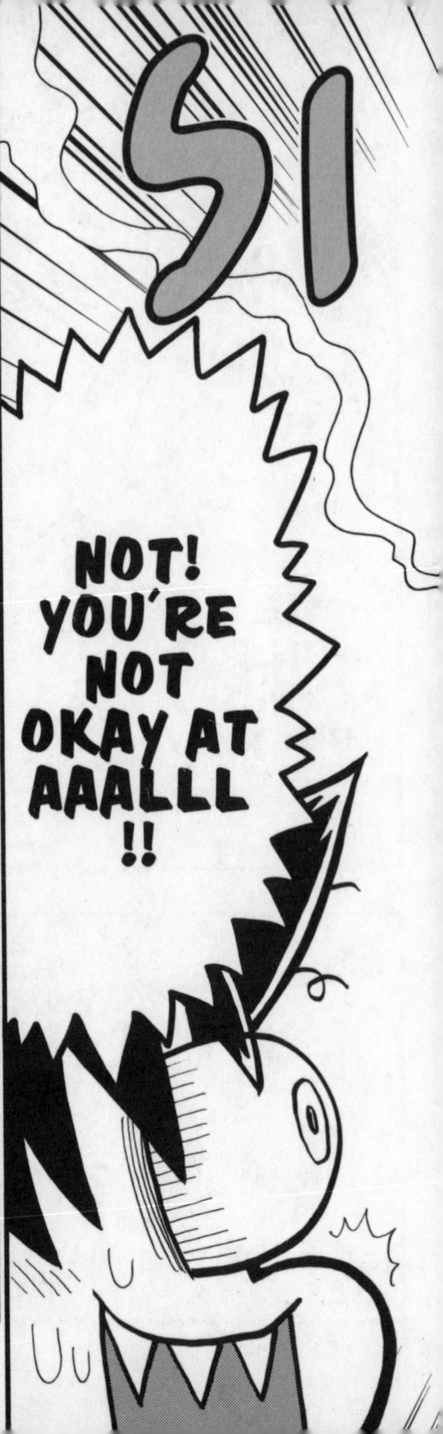
SI
NOT! YOU'RE NOT OKAY AT AAALLL !!

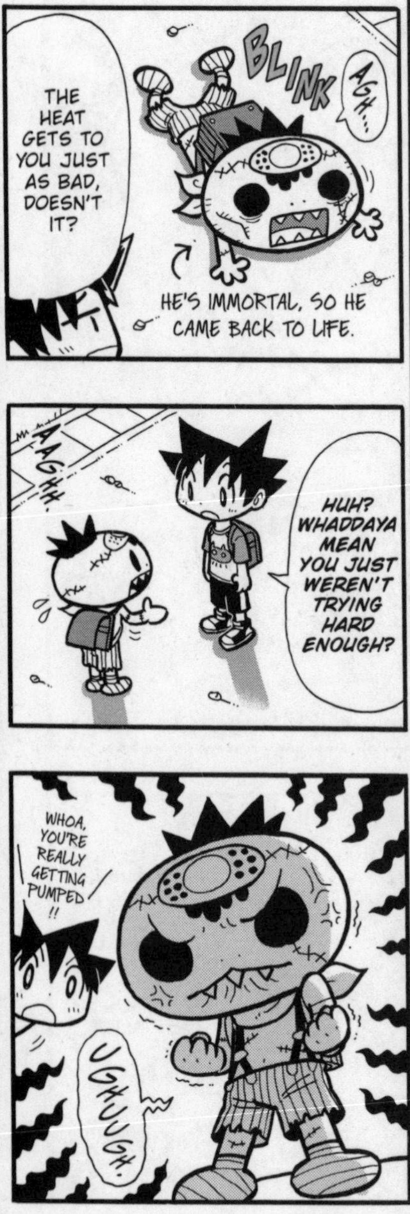
BLINK
AGH...
THE HEAT GETS TO YOU JUST AS BAD, DOESN'T IT?
HE'S IMMORTAL, SO HE CAME BACK TO LIFE.
HUH? WHADDAYA MEAN YOU JUST WEREN'T TRYING HARD ENOUGH?
AAGHH.
WHOA, YOU'RE REALLY GETTING PUMPED !!
UGHUUGH.

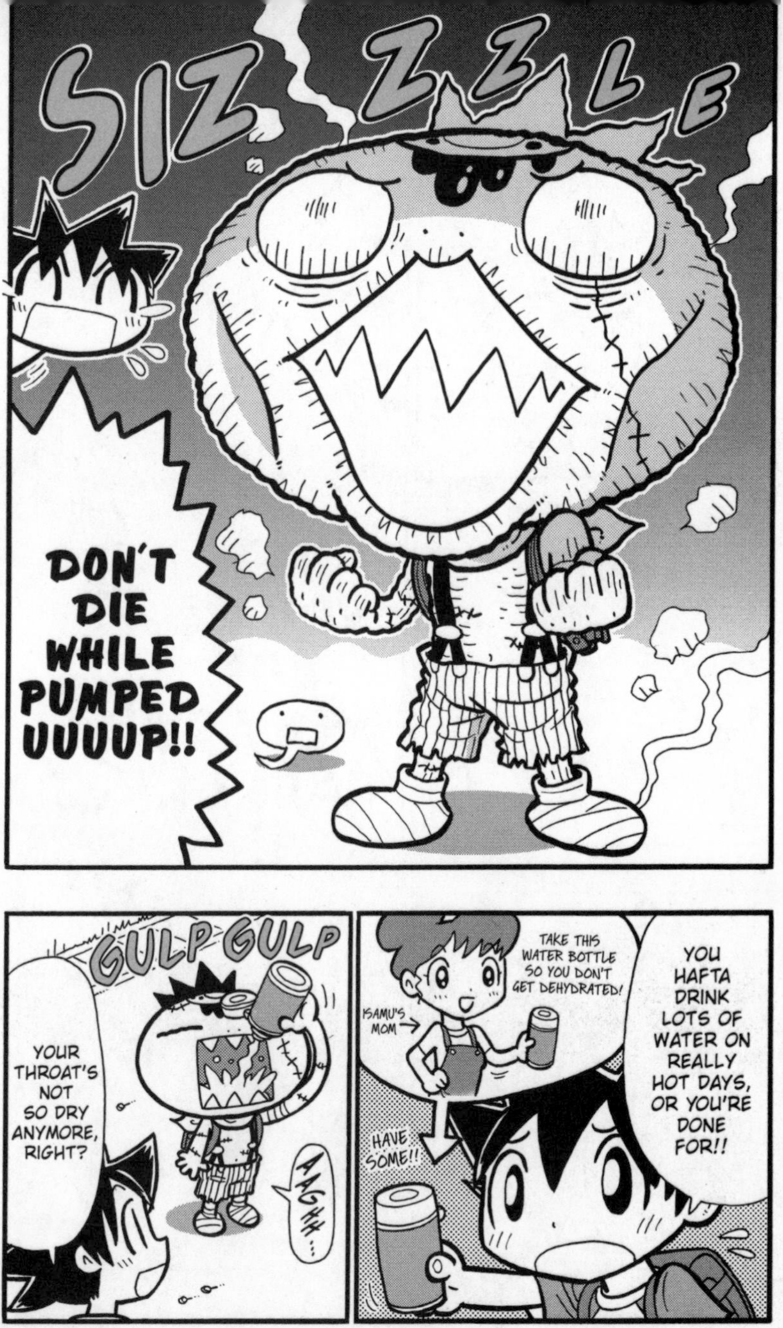
SIZZZLE
DON'T DIE WHILE PUMPED UUUUP!!
YOU HAFTA DRINK LOTS OF WATER ON REALLY HOT DAYS, OR YOU'RE DONE FOR!!
TAKE THIS WATER BOTTLE SO YOU DON'T GET DEHYDRATED!
ISAMU'S MOM
HAVE SOME!!
GULP GULP
YOUR THROAT'S NOT SO DRY ANYMORE, RIGHT?
AAGHH...

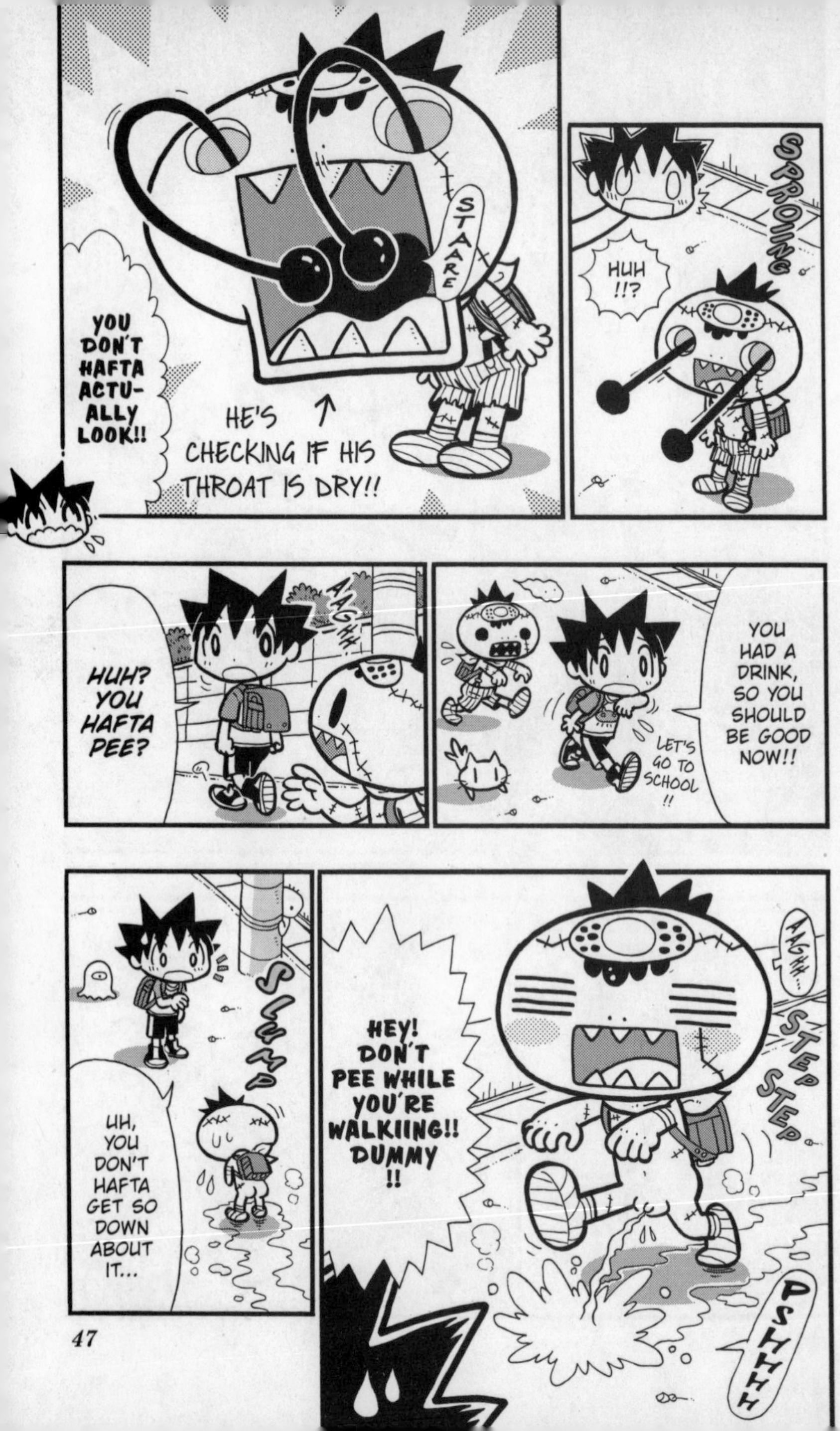
SPROING
HUH !!?
STAARE
HE'S CHECKING IF HIS THROAT IS DRY!!
YOU DON'T HAFTA ACTU-ALLY LOOK!!
YOU HAD A DRINK, SO YOU SHOULD BE GOOD NOW!!
LET'S GO TO SCHOOL !!
AAGHH
HUH? YOU HAFTA PEE?
AAGHH...
STEP STEP
HEY! DON'T PEE WHILE YOU'RE WALKIING!! DUMMY !!
PSHHHH
SLUMP
UH, YOU DON'T HAFTA GET SO DOWN ABOUT IT...

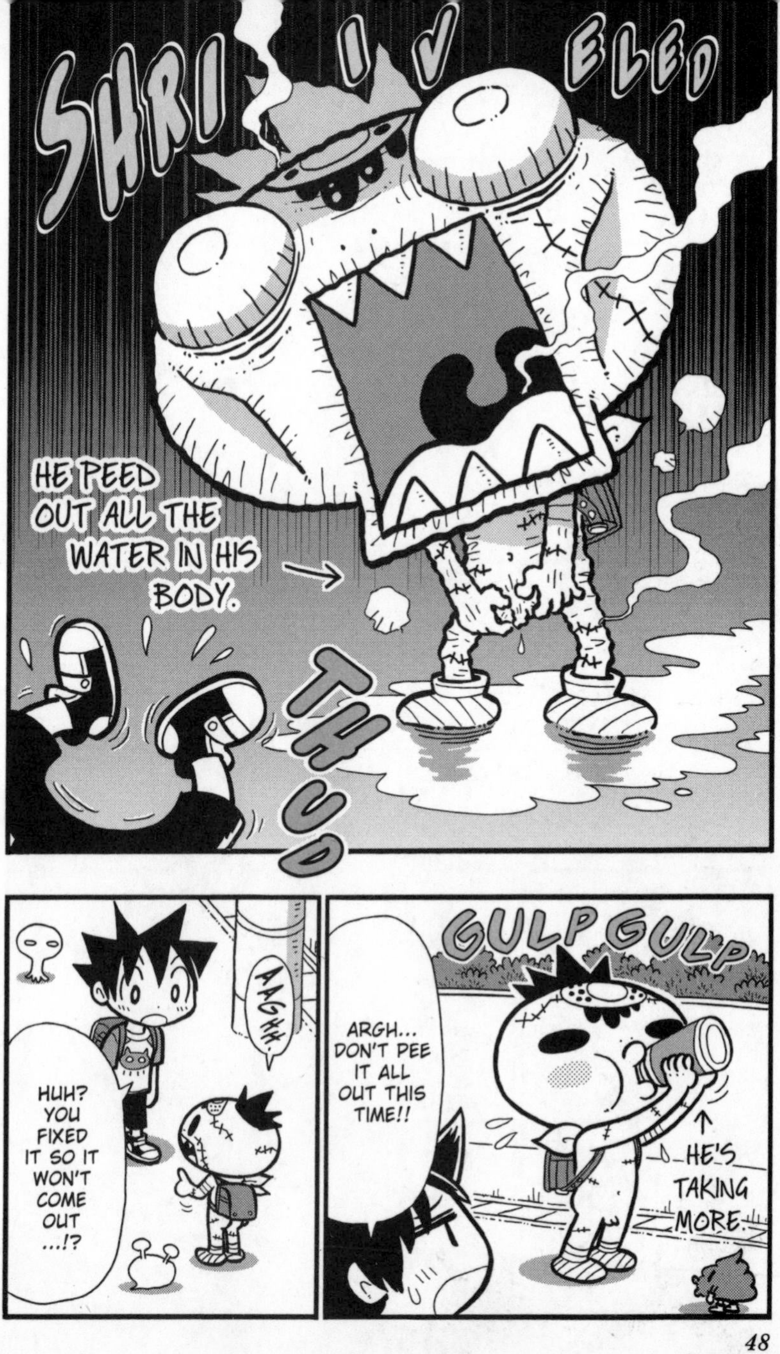
SHRIIVELED
HE PEED OUT ALL THE WATER IN HIS BODY.
THUD
GULP GULP
ARGH... DON'T PEE IT ALL OUT THIS TIME!!
HE'S TAKING MORE.
AAGHH.
HUH? YOU FIXED IT SO IT WON'T COME OUT ...!?

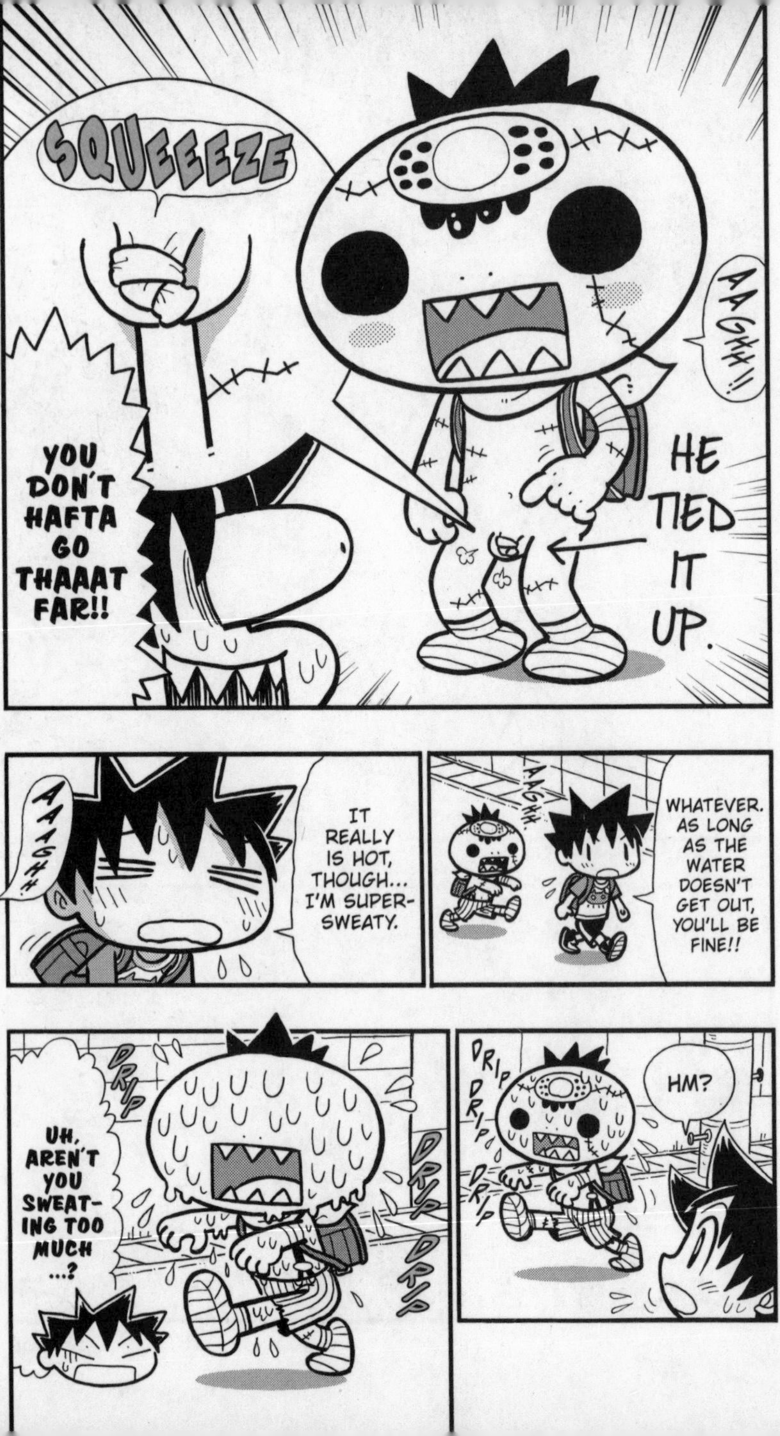

AAGHH!!
HE TIED IT UP.
SQUEEEZE
YOU DON'T HAFTA GO THAAAT FAR!!
AAGHH.
WHATEVER. AS LONG AS THE WATER DOESN'T GET OUT, YOU'LL BE FINE!!
IT REALLY IS HOT, THOUGH... I'M SUPER-SWEATY.
AAAGHH
HM?
DRIP
DRIP
DRIP
DRIP
DRIP DRIP
UH, AREN'T YOU SWEATING TOO MUCH...?

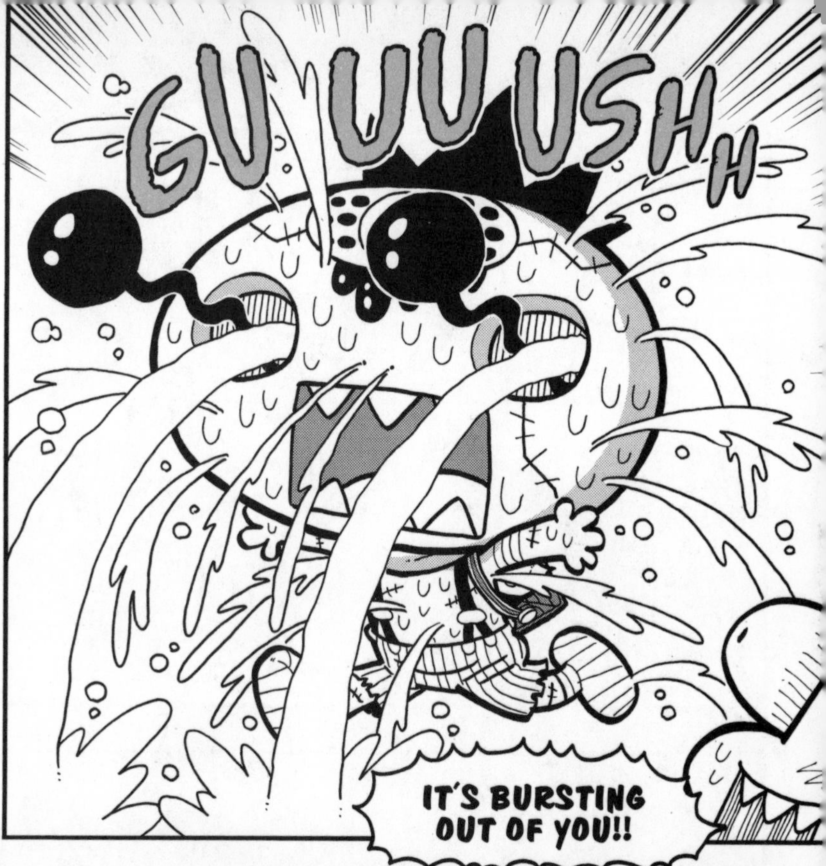
GUUUUSHH
IT'S BURSTING OUT OF YOU!!
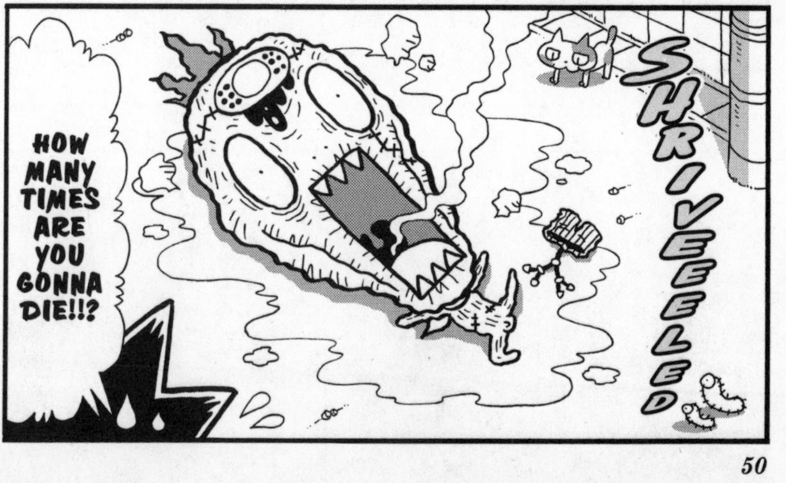
SHRIVEEELED
HOW MANY TIMES ARE YOU GONNA DIE!!?

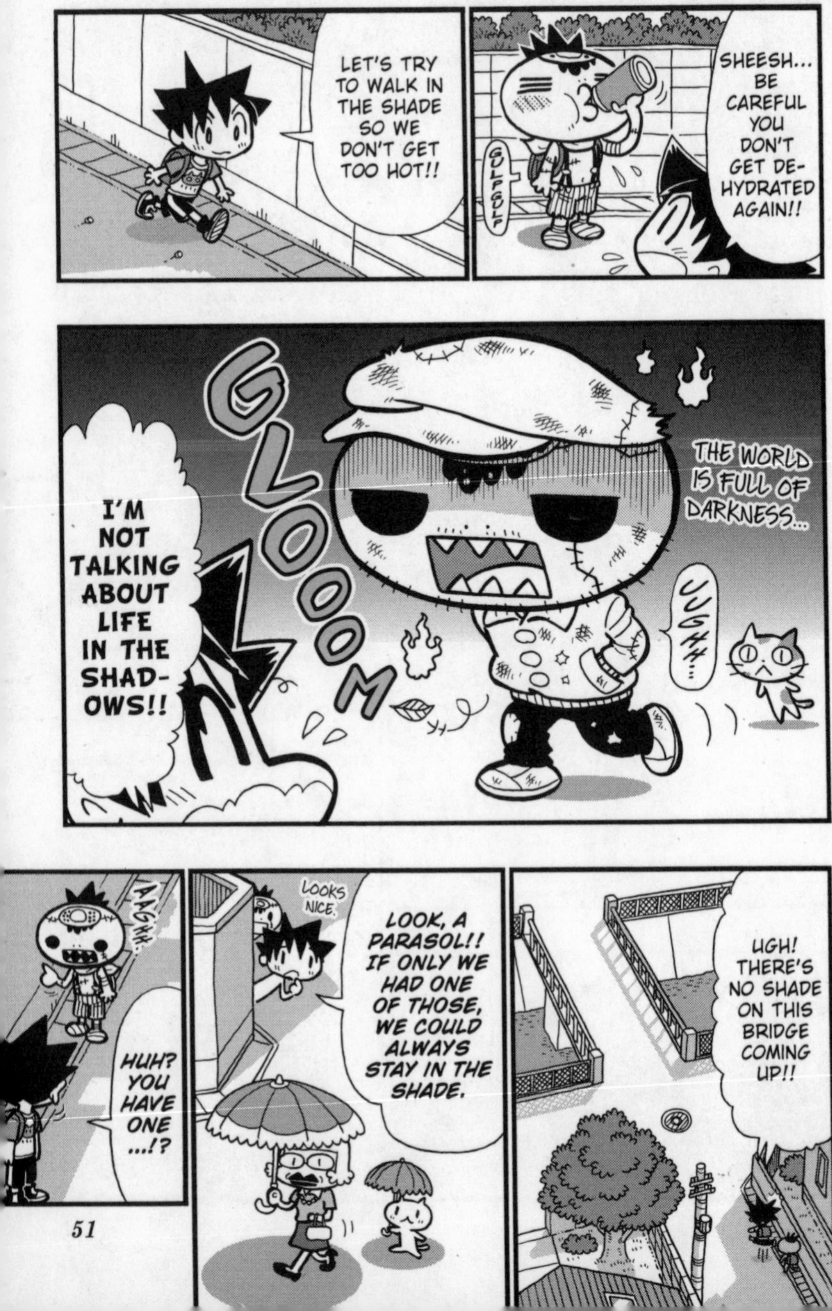
SHEESH... BE CAREFUL YOU DON'T GET DE-HYDRATED AGAIN!!
GULP GULP
LET'S TRY TO WALK IN THE SHADE SO WE DON'T GET TOO HOT!!
THE WORLD IS FULL OF DARKNESS...
UGHH...
GLOOOM
I'M NOT TALKING ABOUT LIFE IN THE SHAD-OWS!!
UGH! THERE'S NO SHADE ON THIS BRIDGE COMING UP!!
LOOKS NICE.
LOOK, A PARASOL!! IF ONLY WE HAD ONE OF THOSE, WE COULD ALWAYS STAY IN THE SHADE.
AAGHH.
HUH? YOU HAVE ONE ...!?

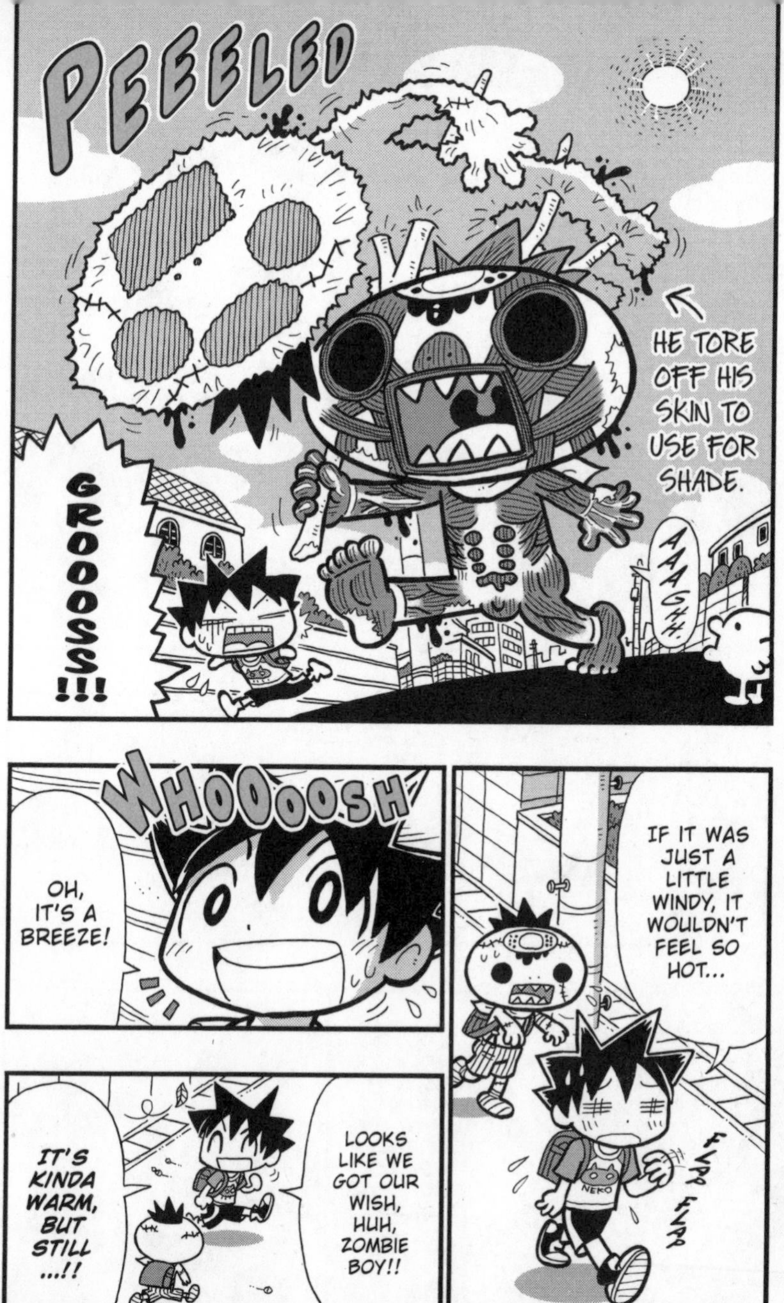
PEEELED
HE TORE OFF HIS SKIN TO USE FOR SHADE.
AAAGHH.
GROOOOSS!!!
IF IT WAS JUST A LITTLE WINDY, IT WOULDN'T FEEL SO HOT...
WHOOOOSH
OH, IT'S A BREEZE!
LOOKS LIKE WE GOT OUR WISH, HUH, ZOMBIE BOY!!
IT'S KINDA WARM, BUT STILL ...!!

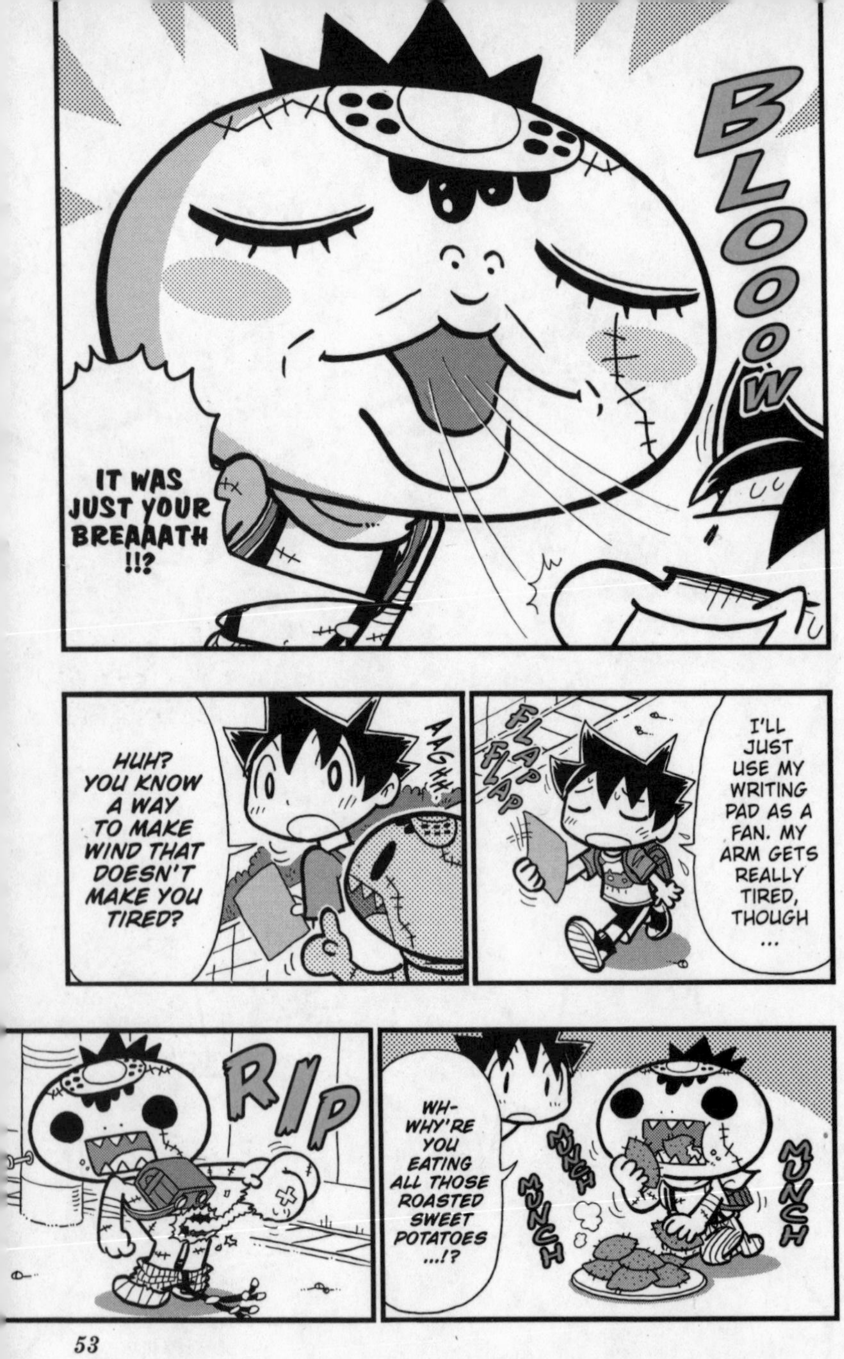
BLOOOOW
IT WAS JUST YOUR BREAAAATH !!?
I'LL JUST USE MY WRITING PAD AS A FAN. MY ARM GETS REALLY TIRED, THOUGH ...
FLAP FLAP FLAP
AAGHH
HUH? YOU KNOW A WAY TO MAKE WIND THAT DOESN'T MAKE YOU TIRED?
MUNCH
MUNCH
MUNCH
WH- WHY'RE YOU EATING ALL THOSE ROASTED SWEET POTATOES ...!?
RIP

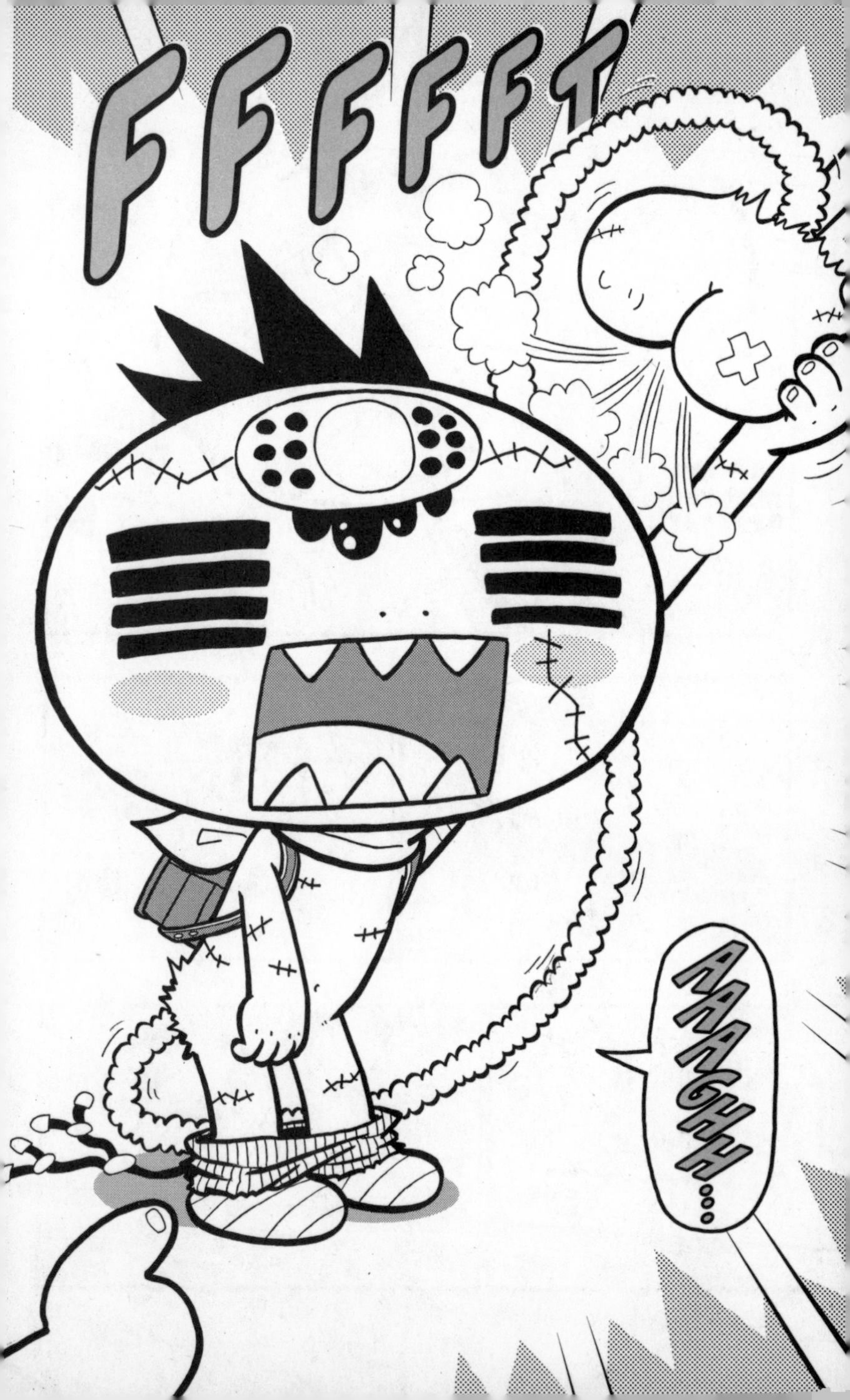
FFFFFT
AAAAGHHH...

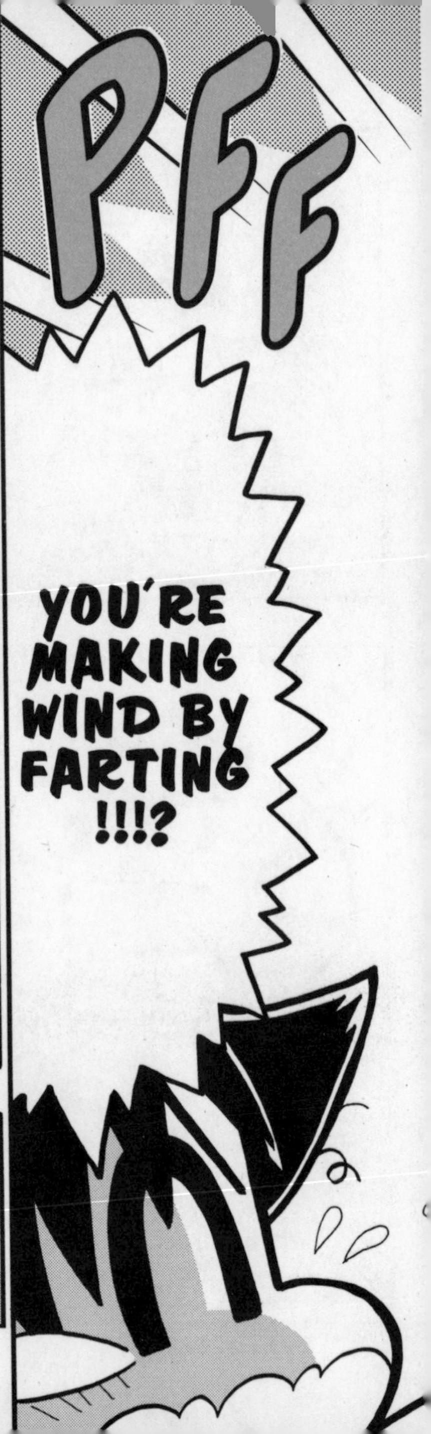
PFF
YOU'RE MAKING WIND BY FARTING!!!?

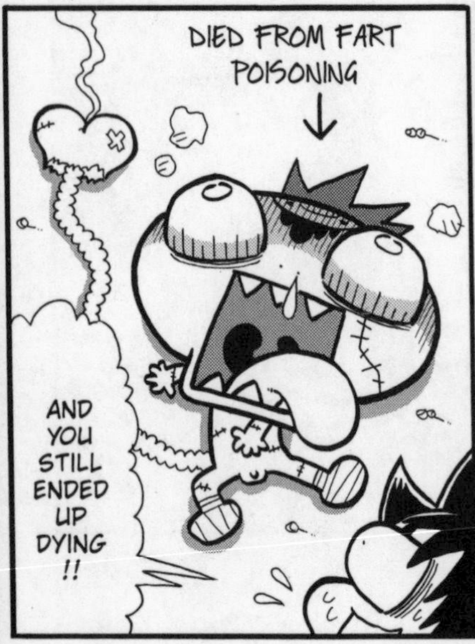
DIED FROM FART POISONING
AND YOU STILL ENDED UP DYING!!

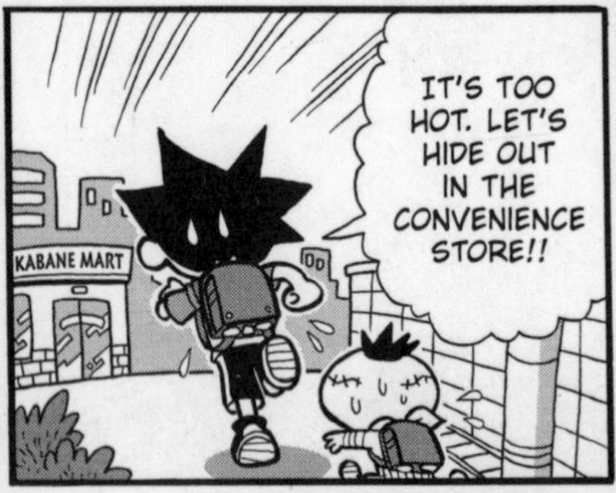
IT'S TOO HOT. LET'S HIDE OUT IN THE CONVENIENCE STORE!!
KABANE MART

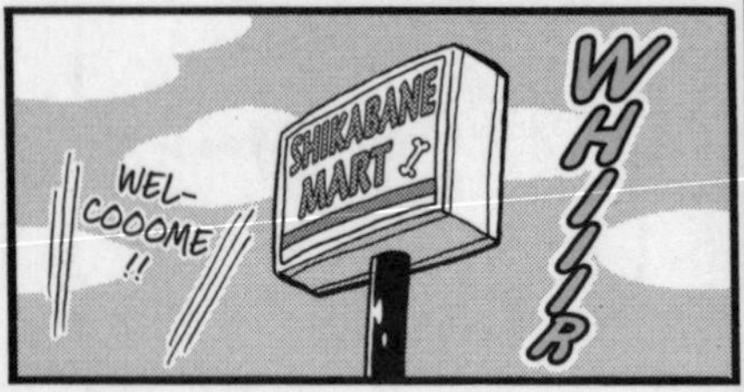
WHIIIR
SHIKABANE MART
WEL-COOOME!!

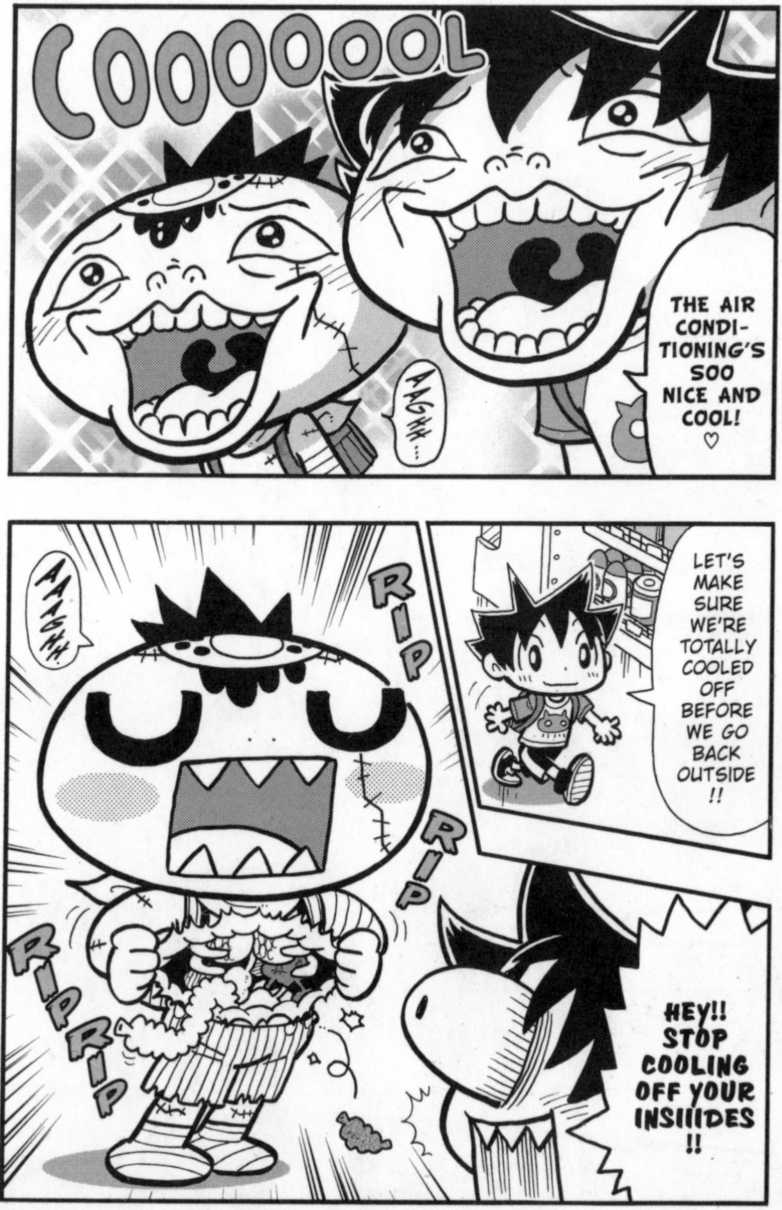
COOOOOOL
THE AIR CONDI-TIONING'S SOO NICE AND COOL! ♡
AAGHH...
LET'S MAKE SURE WE'RE TOTALLY COOLED OFF BEFORE WE GO BACK OUTSIDE !!
AAAGHH.
RIP
RIP
RIP RIP RIP
HEY!! STOP COOLING OFF YOUR INSIIIDES !!

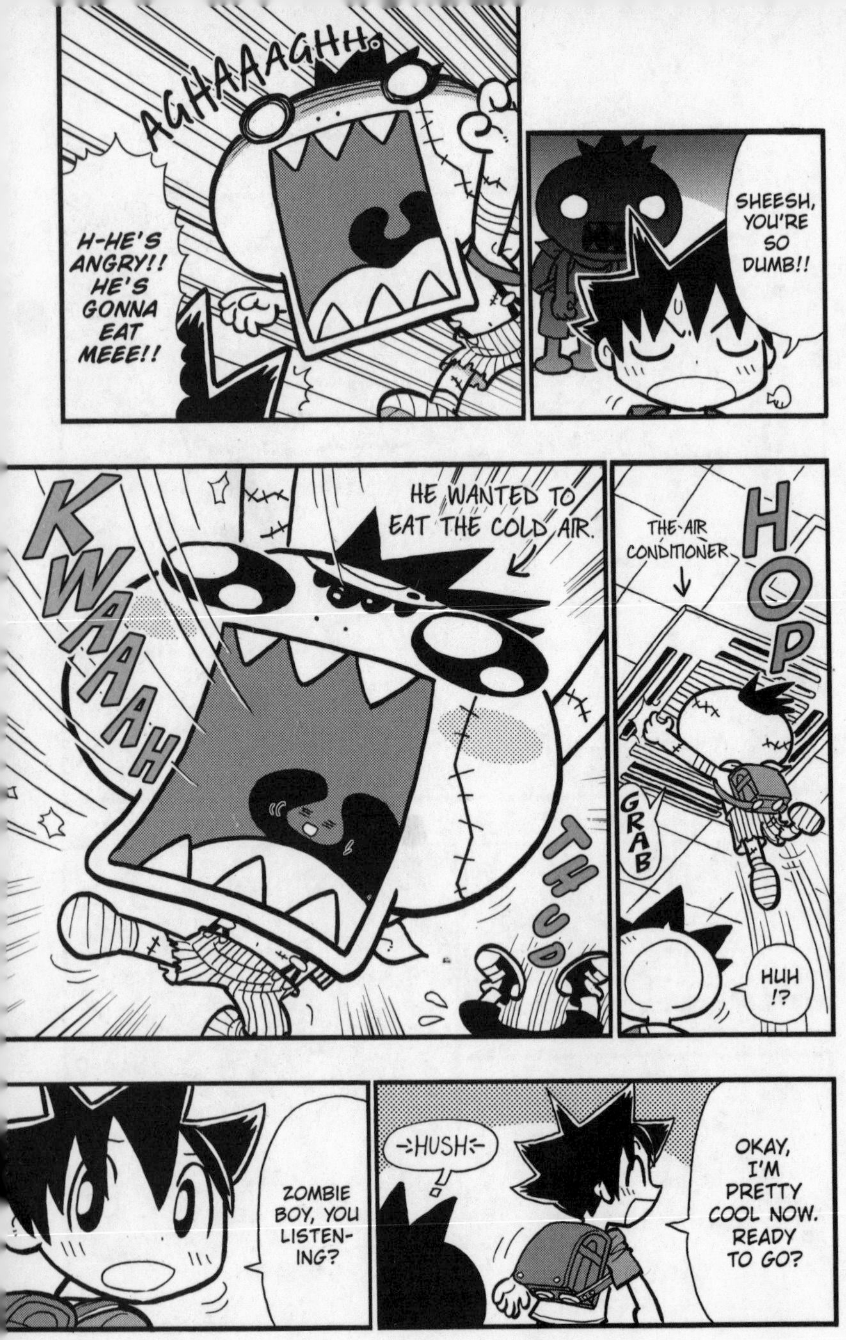
SHEESH, YOU'RE SO DUMB!!
AGHAAAAGHH.
H-HE'S ANGRY!! HE'S GONNA EAT MEEE!!
HOP
THE AIR CONDITIONER
GRAB
HUH!?
HE WANTED TO EAT THE COLD AIR.
KWAAAAH
THUD
OKAY, I'M PRETTY COOL NOW. READY TO GO?
HUSH
ZOMBIE BOY, YOU LISTENING?

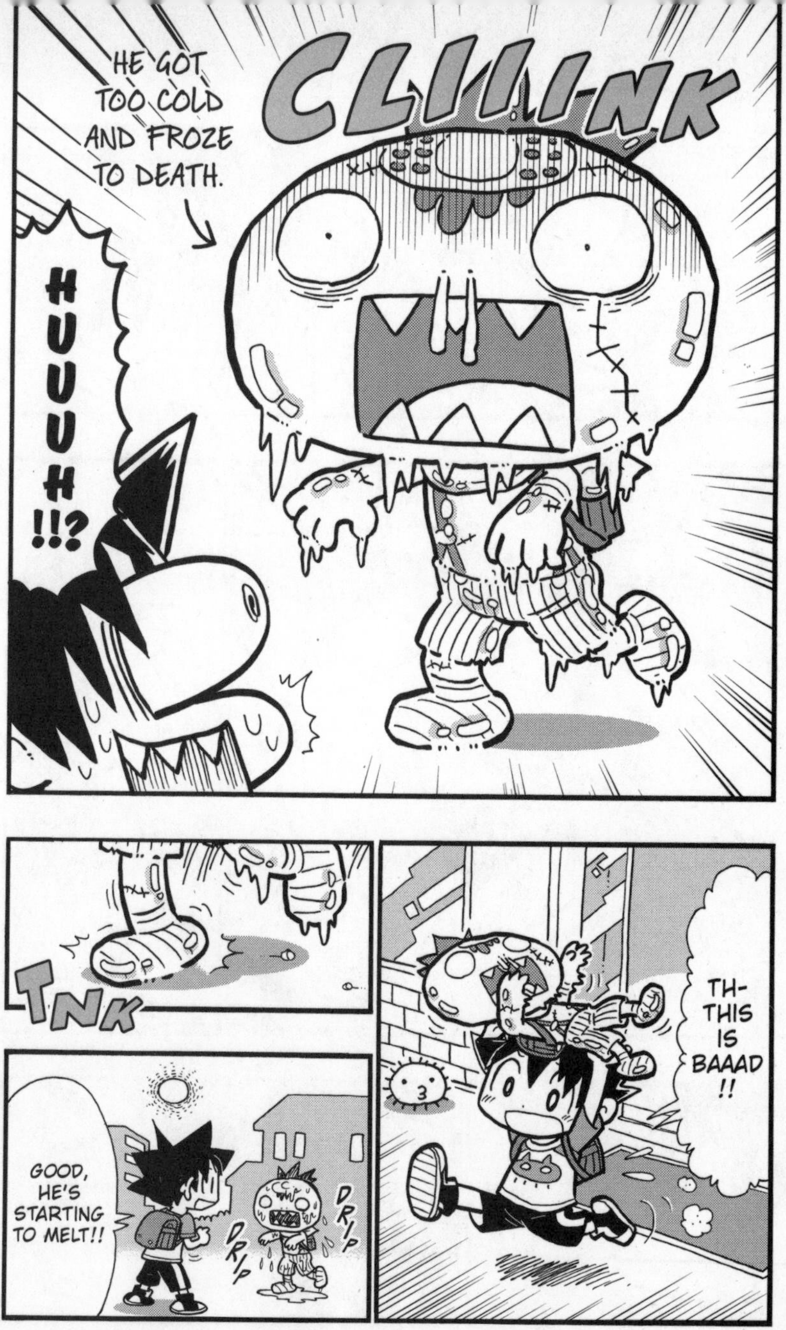
CLIIIINK
HE GOT TOO COLD AND FROZE TO DEATH.
HUUUUH!!?
TH-THIS IS BAAAD!!
TNK
GOOD, HE'S STARTING TO MELT!!
DRIP
DRIP

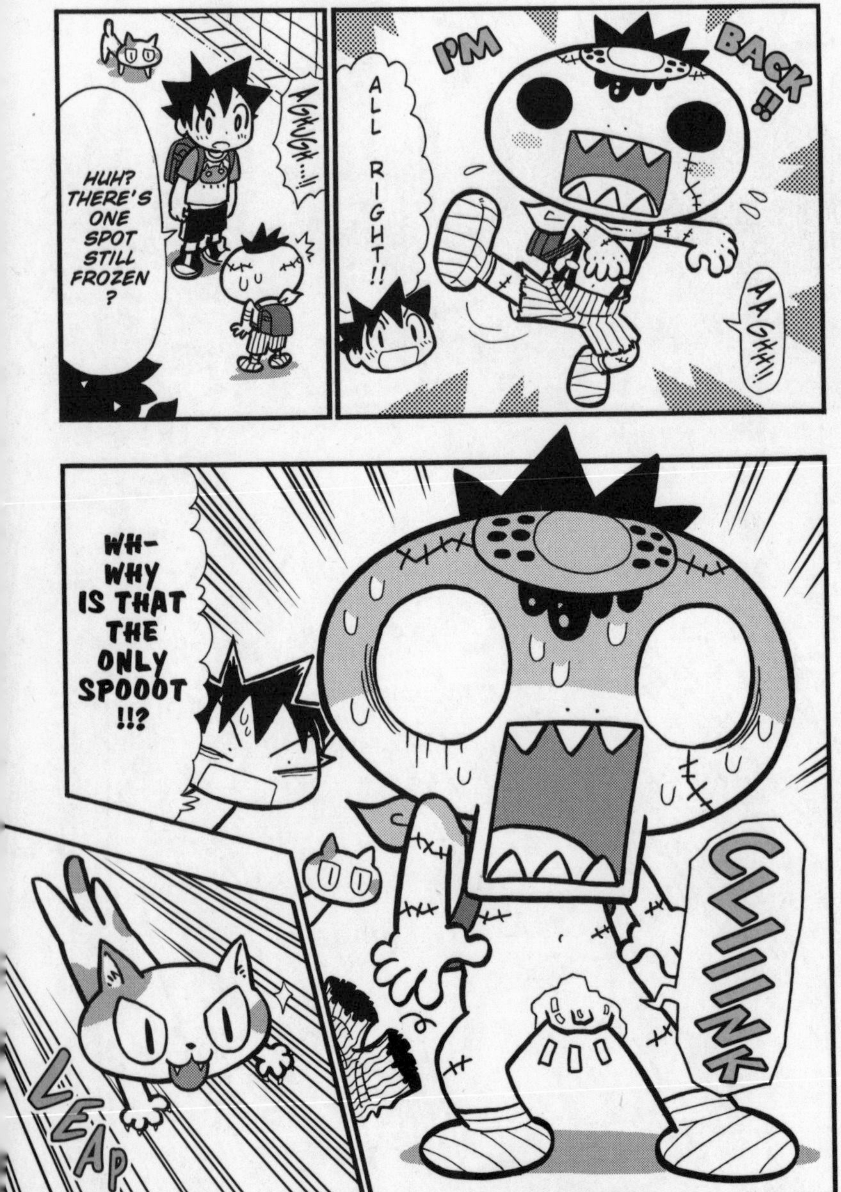
I'M BACK!!
ALL RIGHT!!
AAGHH!!
AGHUGH...!!
HUH? THERE'S ONE SPOT STILL FROZEN?
WH-WHY IS THAT THE ONLY SPOOOT!!?
CLIIIINK
LEAP

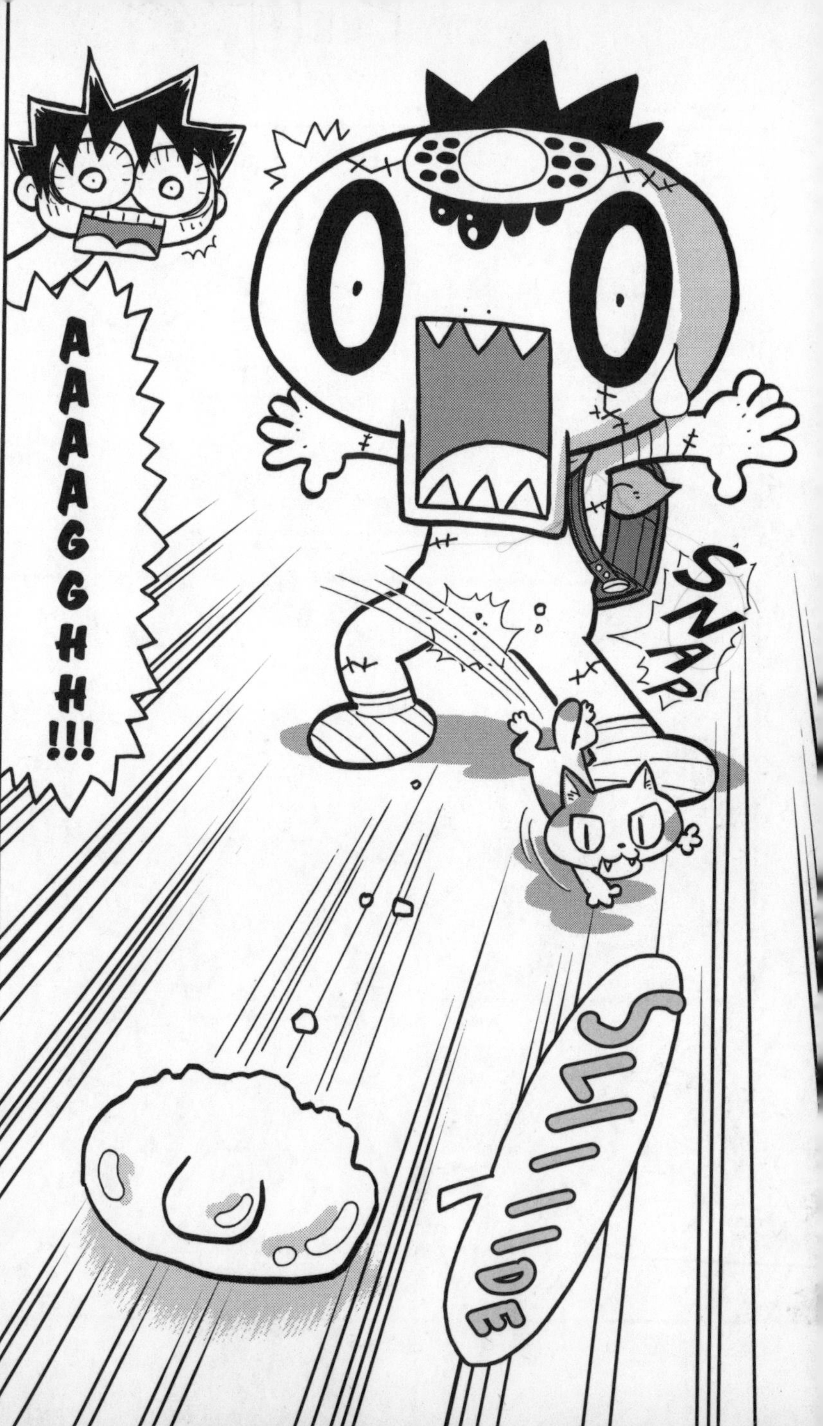

AAAAAGGHHH!!!
SNAP
SLIIIIDE

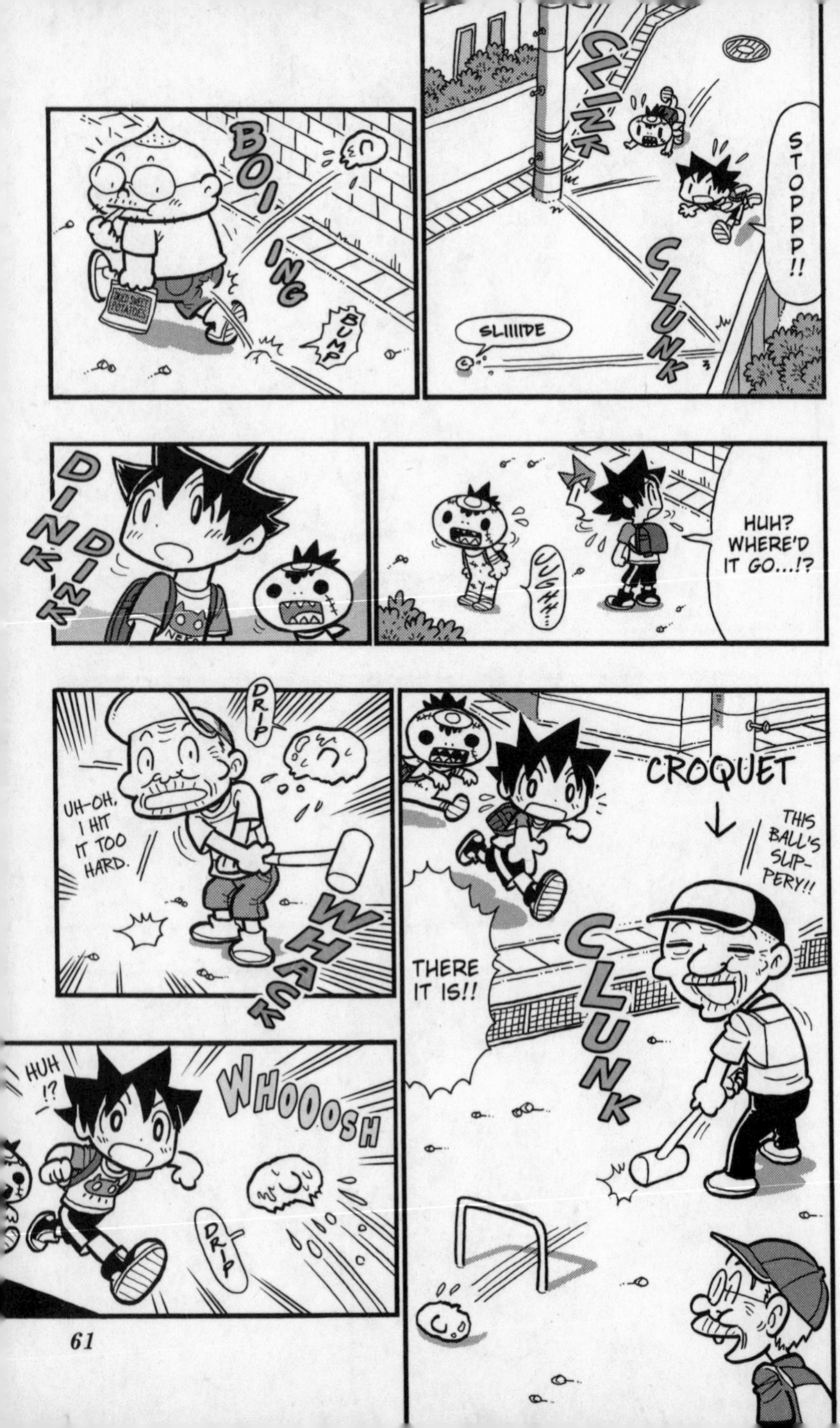
STOPPP!!
CLINK
CLUNK
SLIIIIDE
BOI
ING
BUMP
HUH? WHERE'D IT GO...!?
UGHH...
DINK
DINK
CROQUET
THIS BALL'S SLIP-PERY!!
CLUNK
THERE IT IS!!
UH-OH, I HIT IT TOO HARD.
DRIP
WHACK
HUH !?
WHOOOSH
DRIP

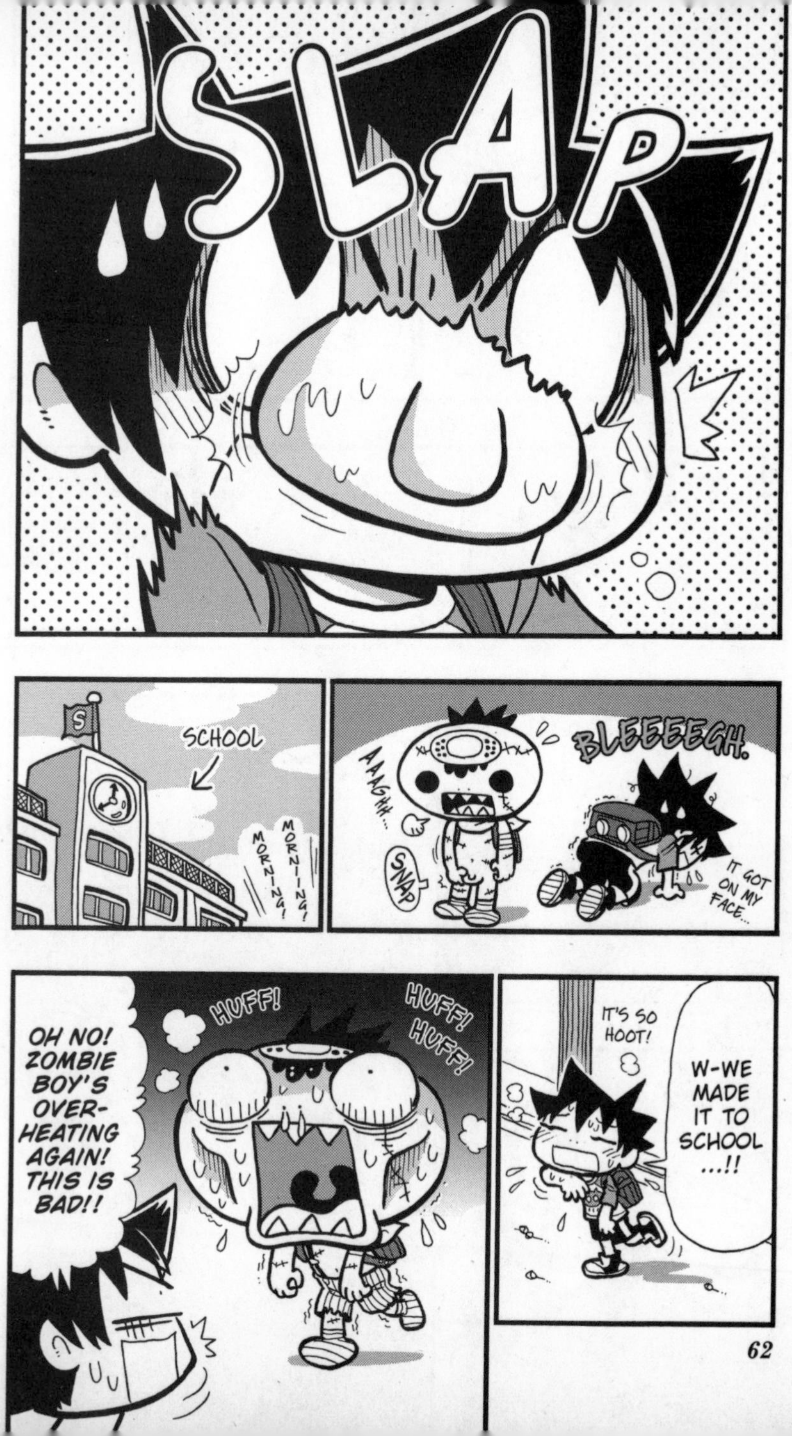
SLAP
BLEEEEGH.
AAAGHH...
SNAP
IT GOT ON MY FACE...
SCHOOL
MORNING!
MORNING!
W-WE MADE IT TO SCHOOL ...!!
IT'S SO HOOT!
HUFF! HUFF!
HUFF!
OH NO! ZOMBIE BOY'S OVER-HEATING AGAIN! THIS IS BAD!!

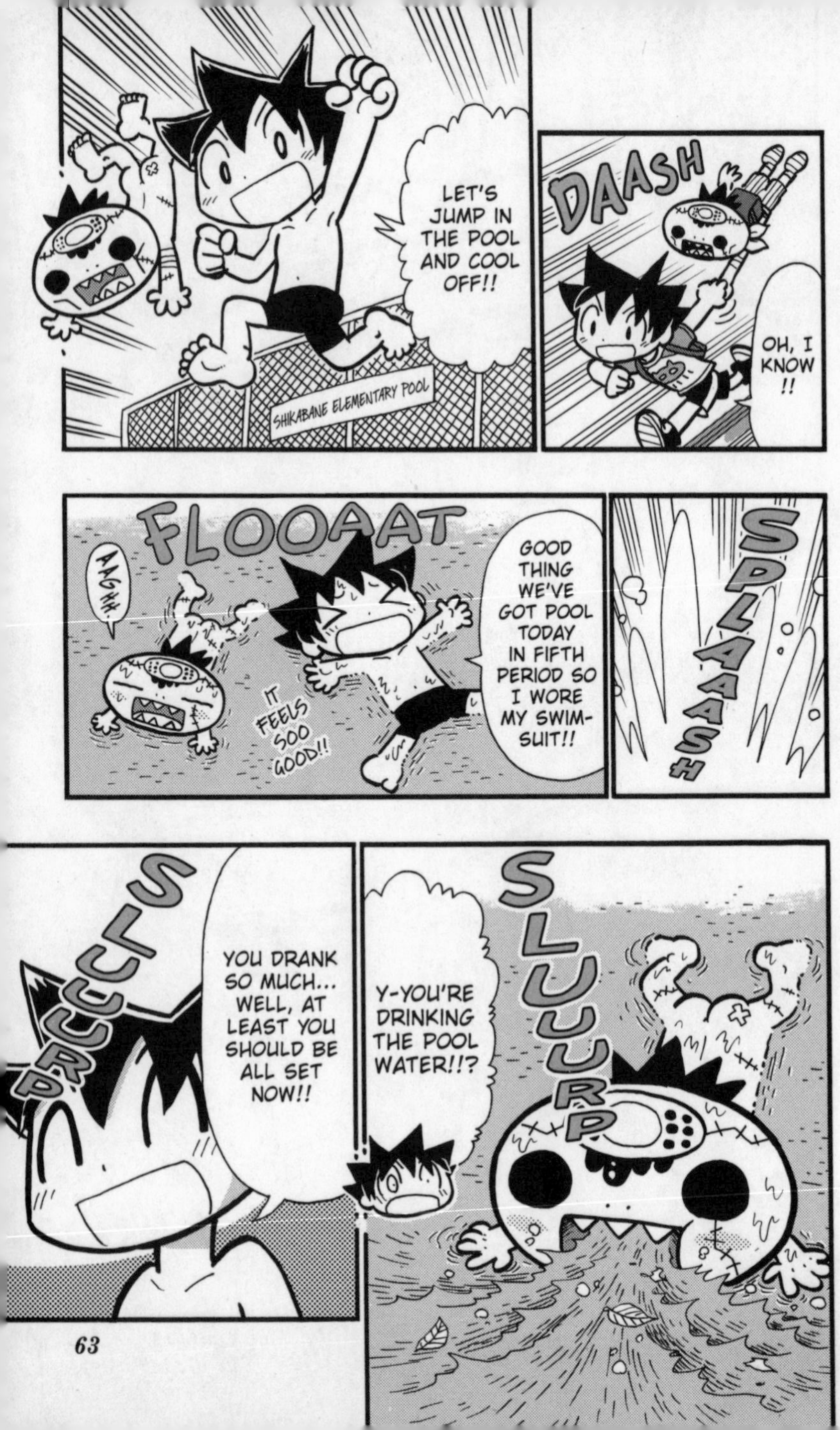
DAASH
OH, I KNOW!!
LET'S JUMP IN THE POOL AND COOL OFF!!
SHIKABANE ELEMENTARY POOL
SPLAAAASH
GOOD THING WE'VE GOT POOL TODAY IN FIFTH PERIOD SO I WORE MY SWIM-SUIT!!
FLOOAAT
AAGHH
IT FEELS SOO GOOD!!
SLUUURP
Y-YOU'RE DRINKING THE POOL WATER!!?
SLUUURP
YOU DRANK SO MUCH... WELL, AT LEAST YOU SHOULD BE ALL SET NOW!!

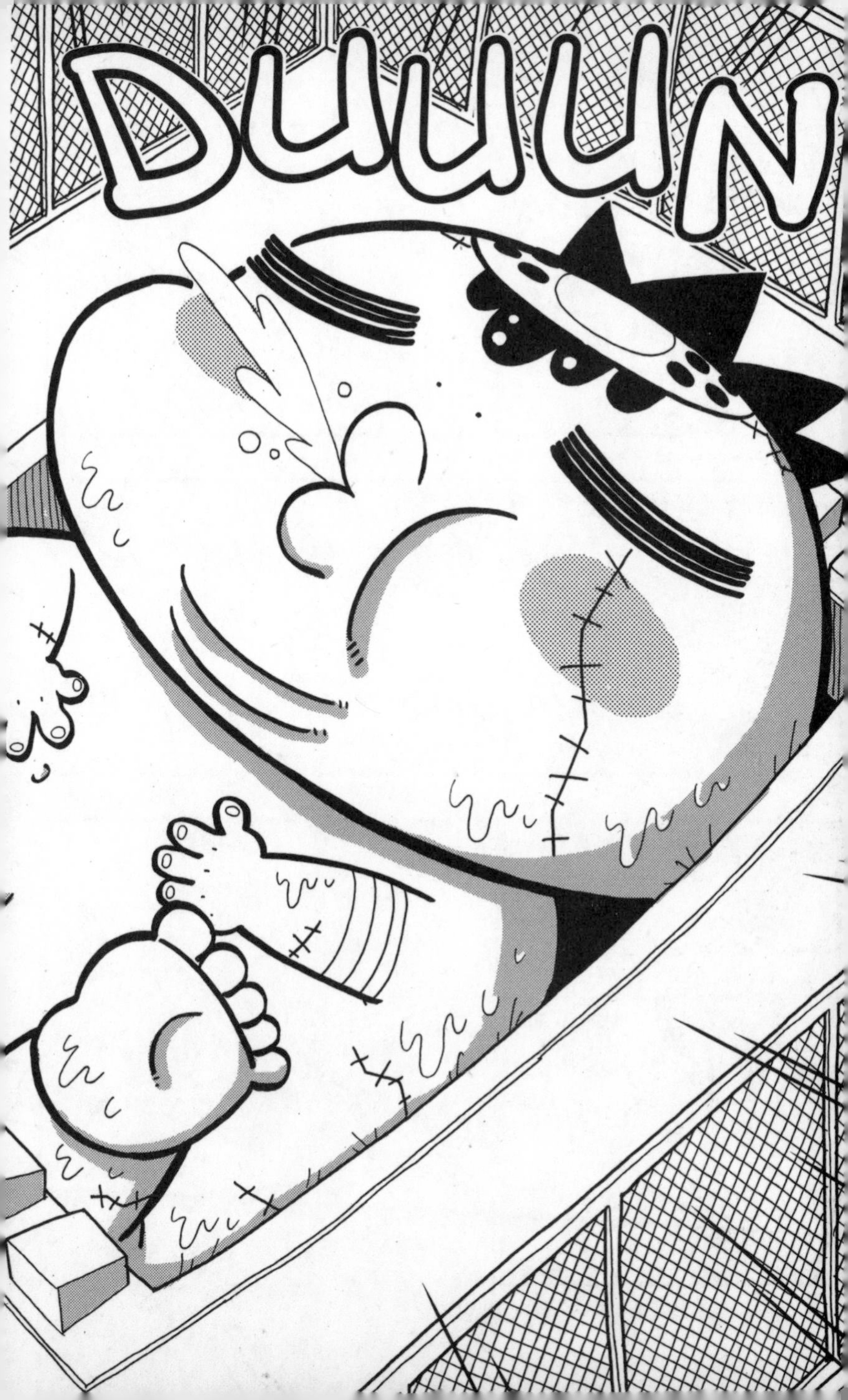
DUUUN

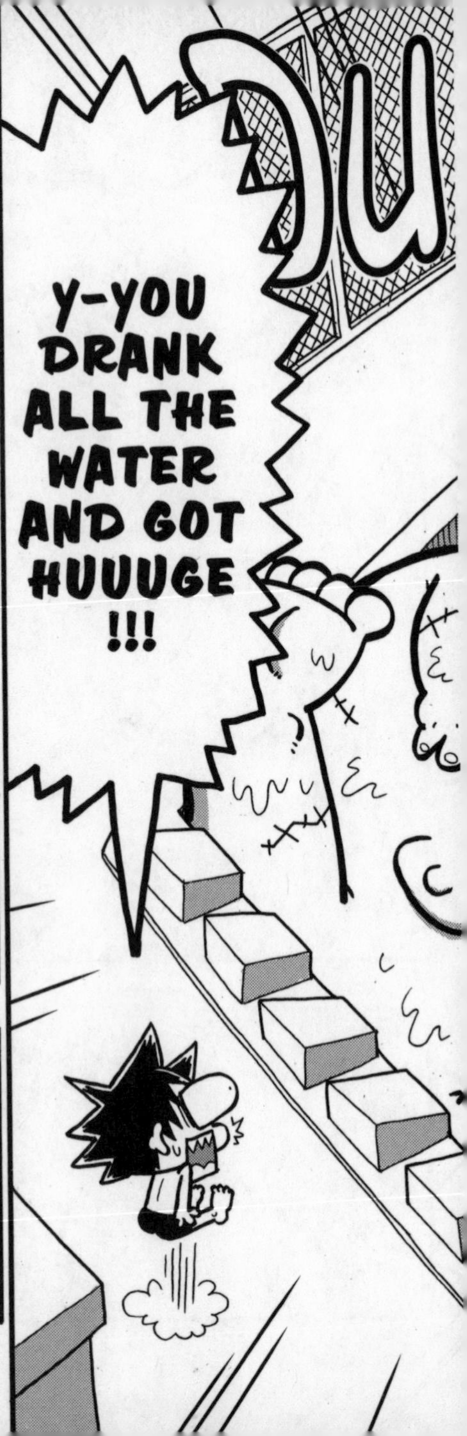
Y-YOU DRANK ALL THE WATER AND GOT HUUUGE !!!

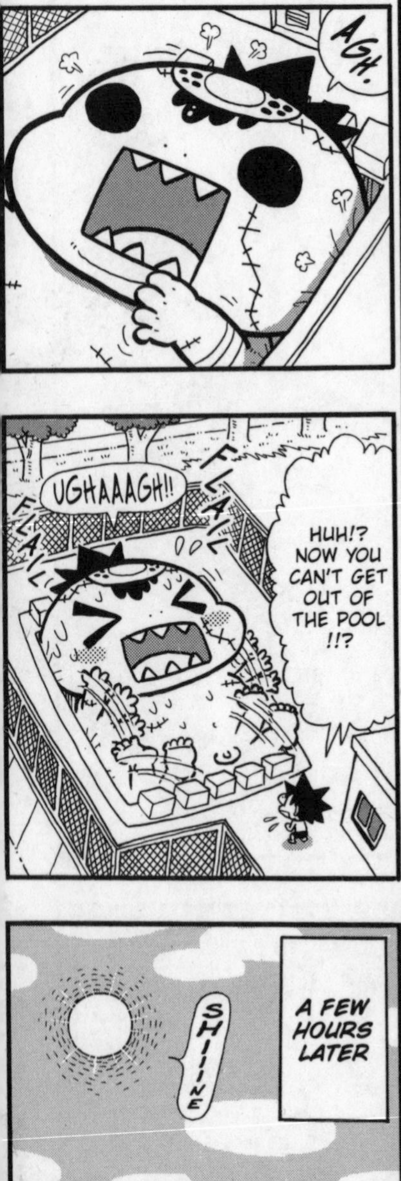
AGH.
HUH!? NOW YOU CAN'T GET OUT OF THE POOL !!?
FLAIL
FLAIL
UGHAAAGH!!
A FEW HOURS LATER
SHIIINE

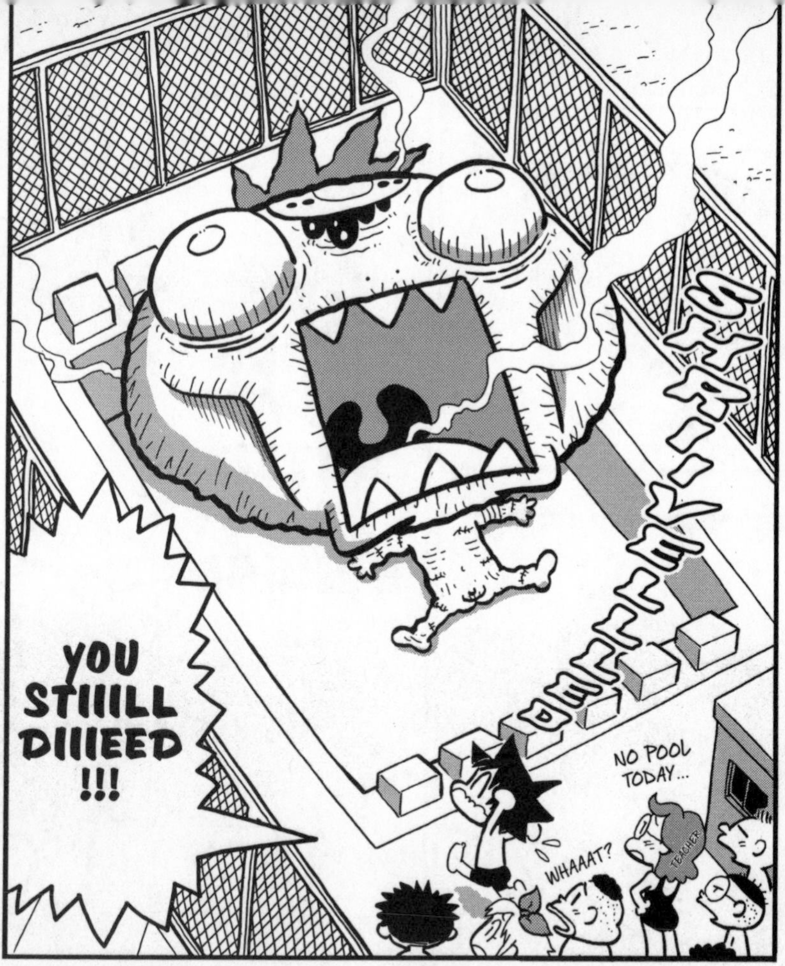
SHRIIVELLLED
NO POOL TODAY...
WHAAAT?
YOU STIIIILL DIIIEED !!!

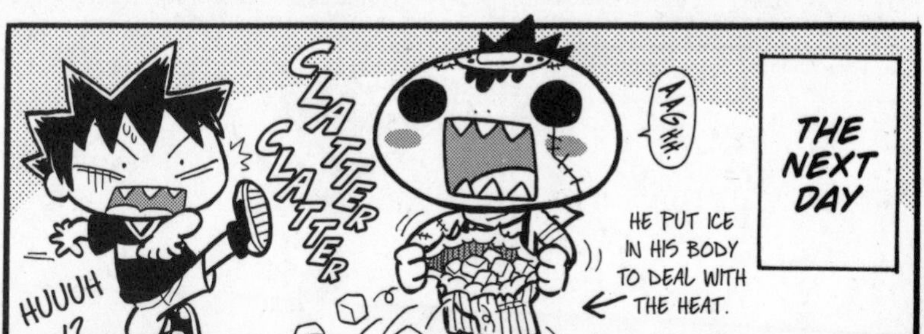
THE NEXT DAY
AAGHH.
HE PUT ICE IN HIS BODY TO DEAL WITH THE HEAT.
CLATTER CLATTER
HUUUH !?

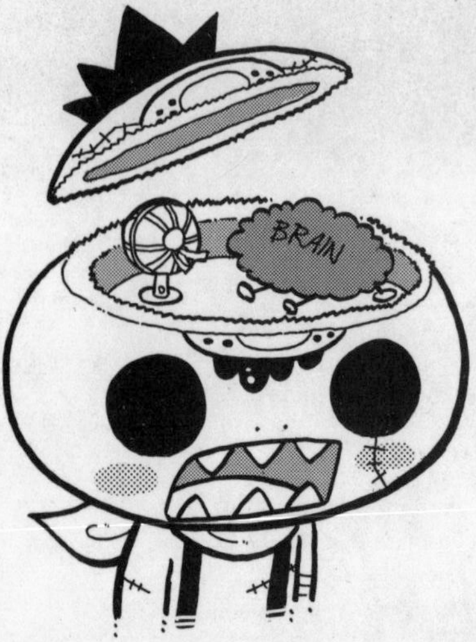
BRAIN

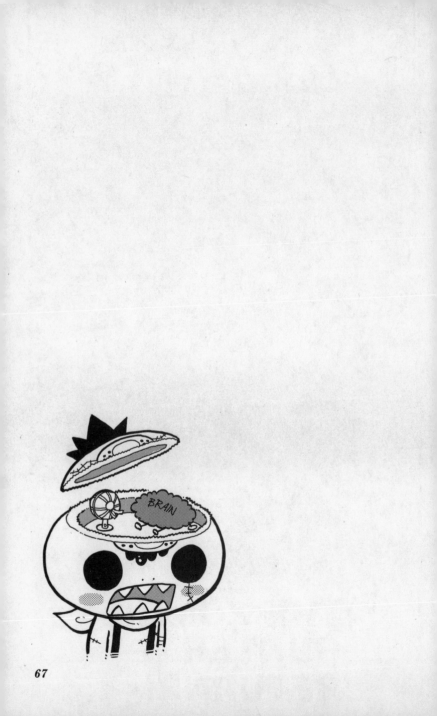

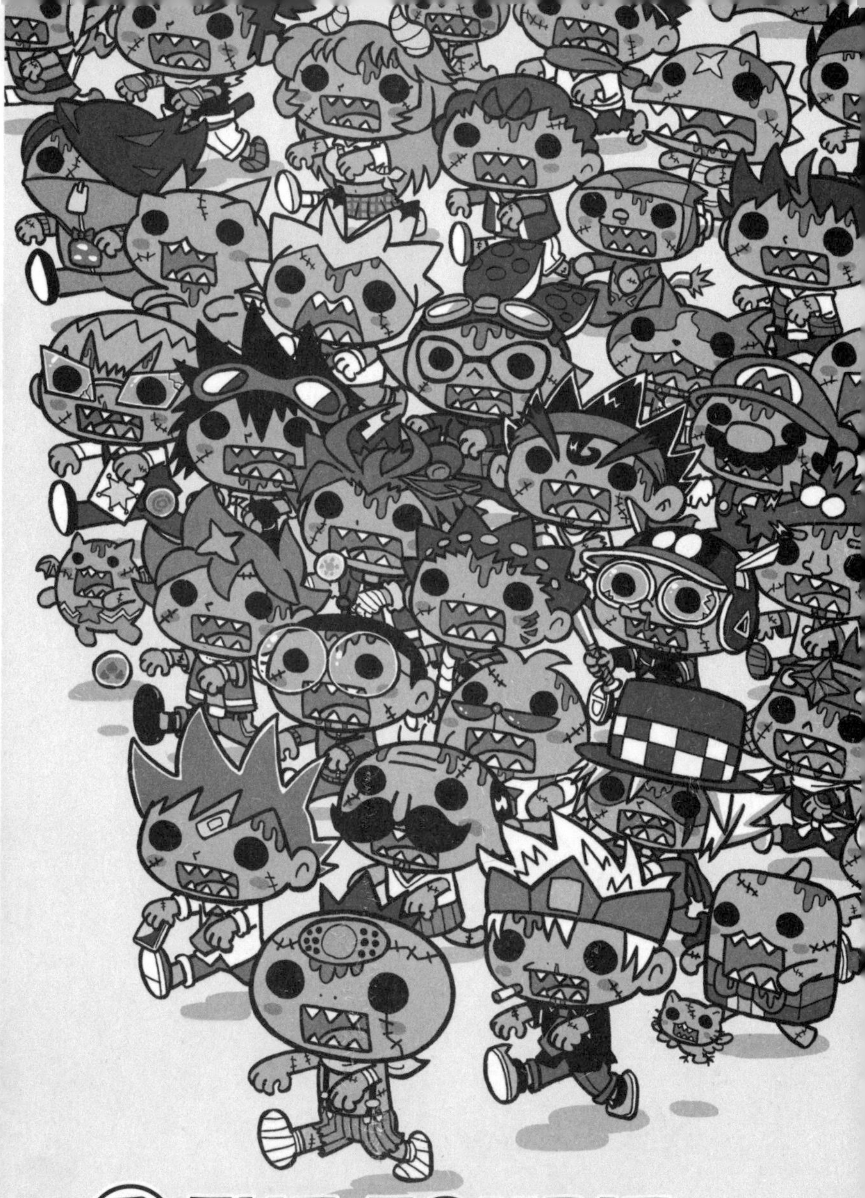

THE ZOMBIE HUNTER RETURNZ!

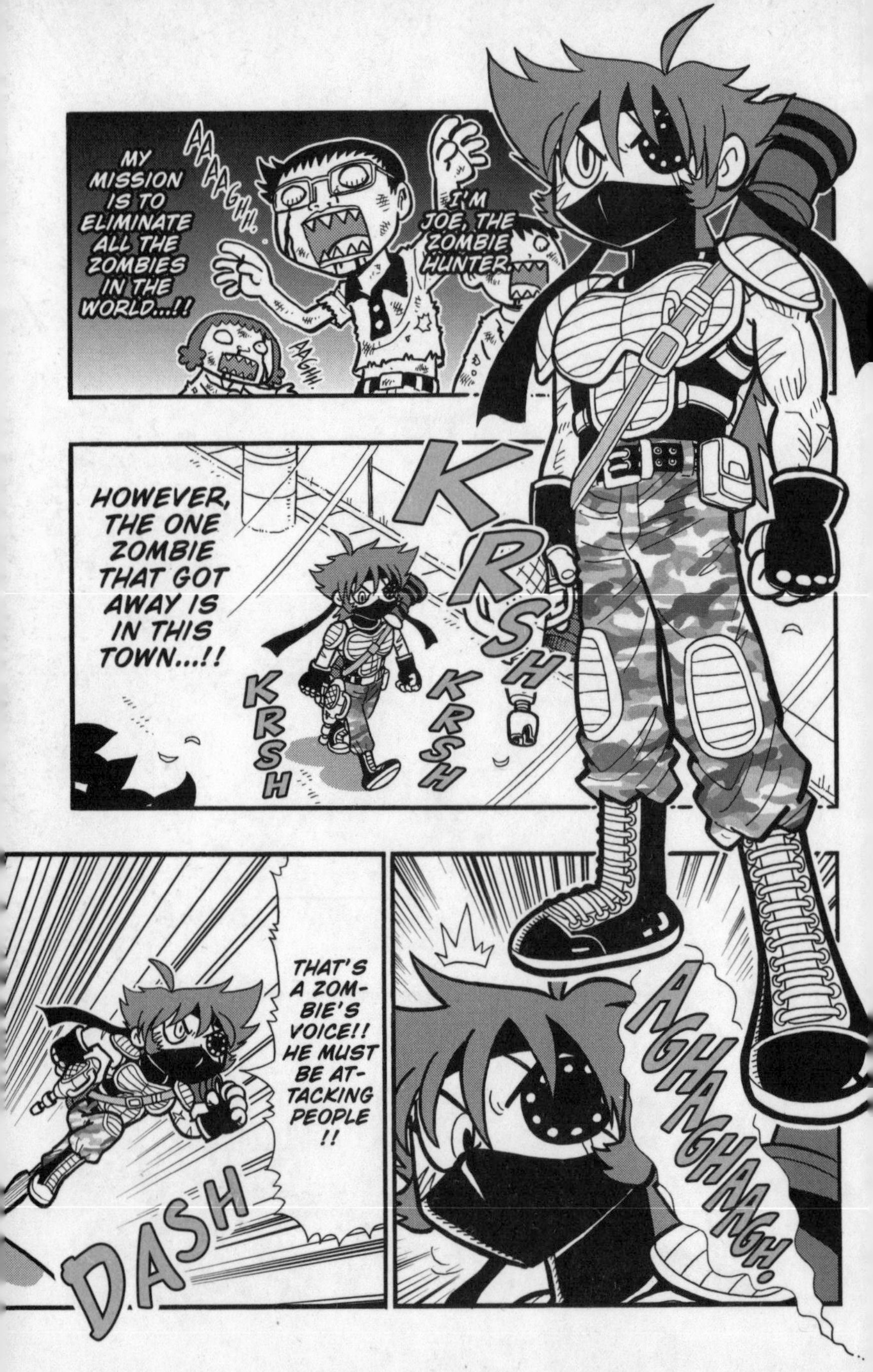
I'M JOE, THE ZOMBIE HUNTER.
AAAAAGHH.
MY MISSION IS TO ELIMINATE ALL THE ZOMBIES IN THE WORLD...!!
AAGHH.
KRSH
KRSH
HOWEVER, THE ONE ZOMBIE THAT GOT AWAY IS IN THIS TOWN...!!
KRSH
AGHAGHAAAGH!
THAT'S A ZOM-BIE'S VOICE!! HE MUST BE AT-TACKING PEOPLE!!
DASH

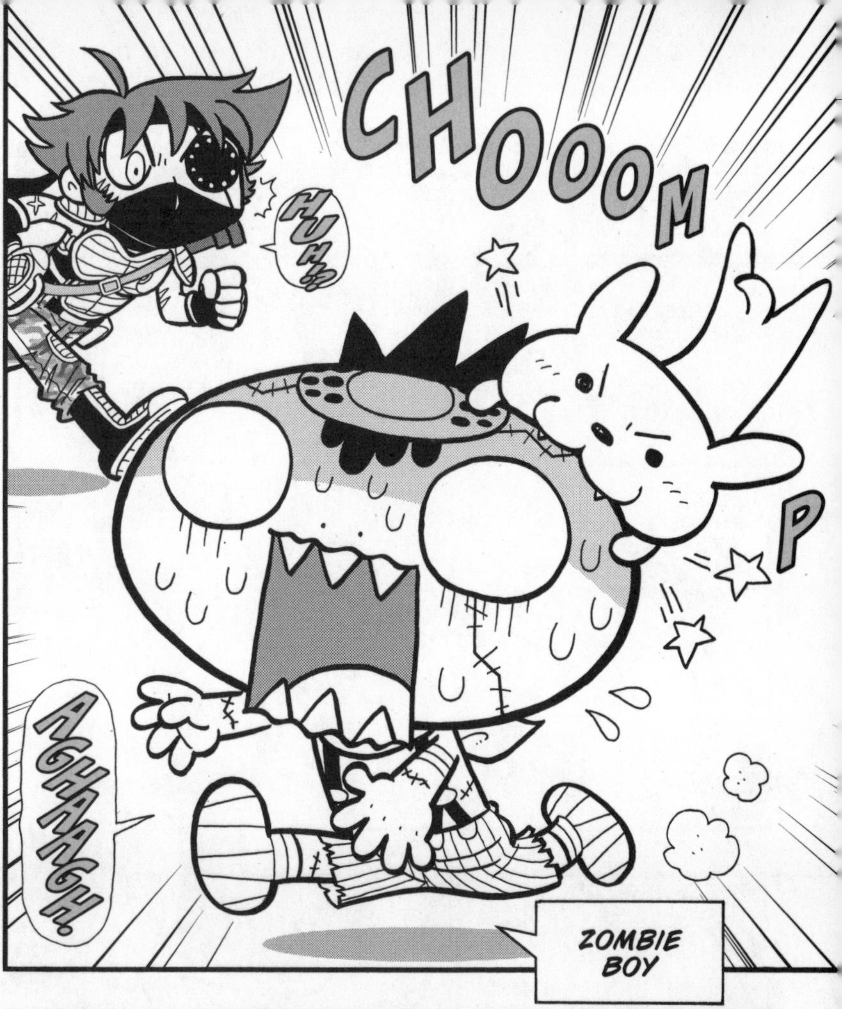
CHOOOMP
HUH!?
AGHAAAGH!
ZOMBIE BOY
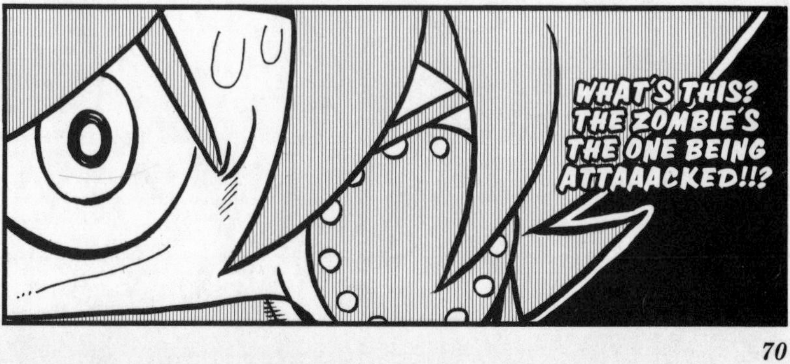
WHAT'S THIS? THE ZOMBIE'S THE ONE BEING ATTAAACKED!!?
...

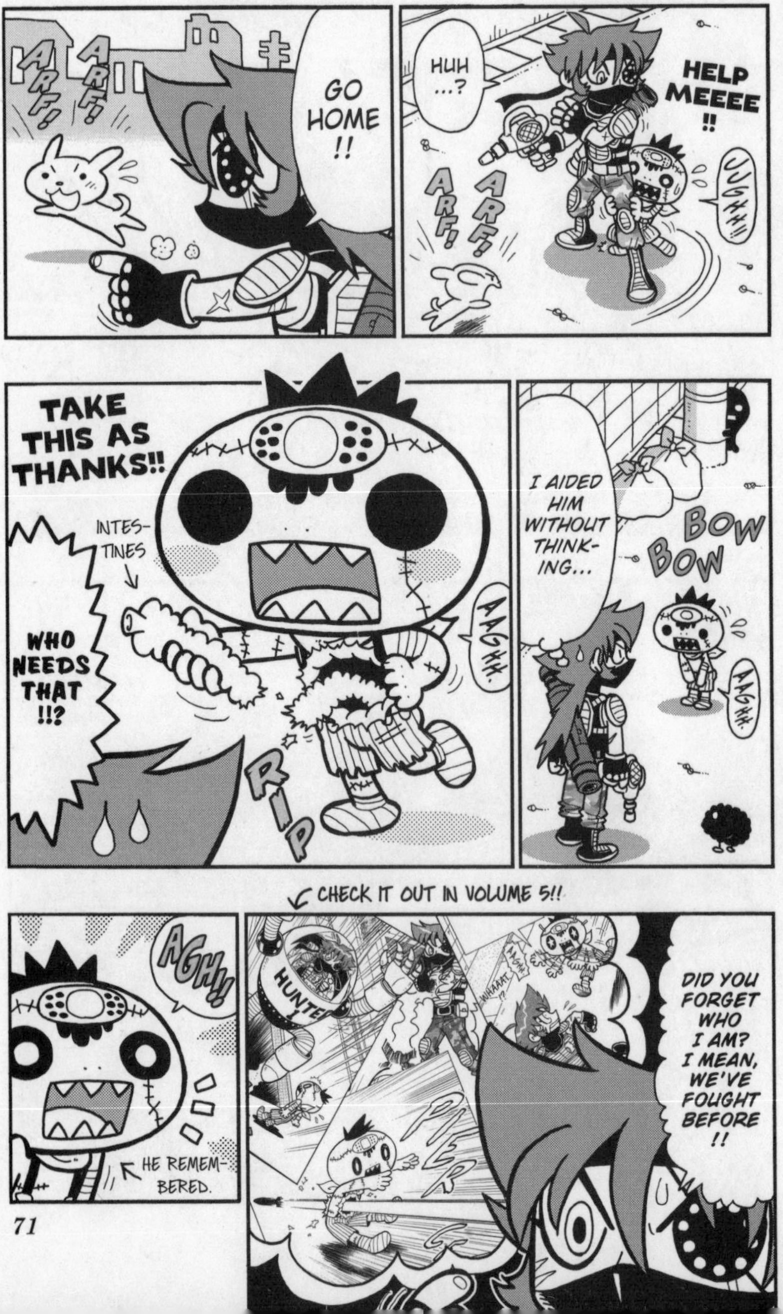
HUH ...?
HELP MEEEE!!
UGHHH!!
ARF! ARF!
GO HOME!!
ARF! ARF!
I AIDED HIM WITHOUT THINKING...
BOW BOW
AAGHH.
TAKE THIS AS THANKS!!
AAGHH.
INTES-TINES
WHO NEEDS THAT!!?
RIP
CHECK IT OUT IN VOLUME 5!!
DID YOU FORGET WHO I AM? I MEAN, WE'VE FOUGHT BEFORE!!
HUNTER 1
AGH!!
HE REMEM-BERED.

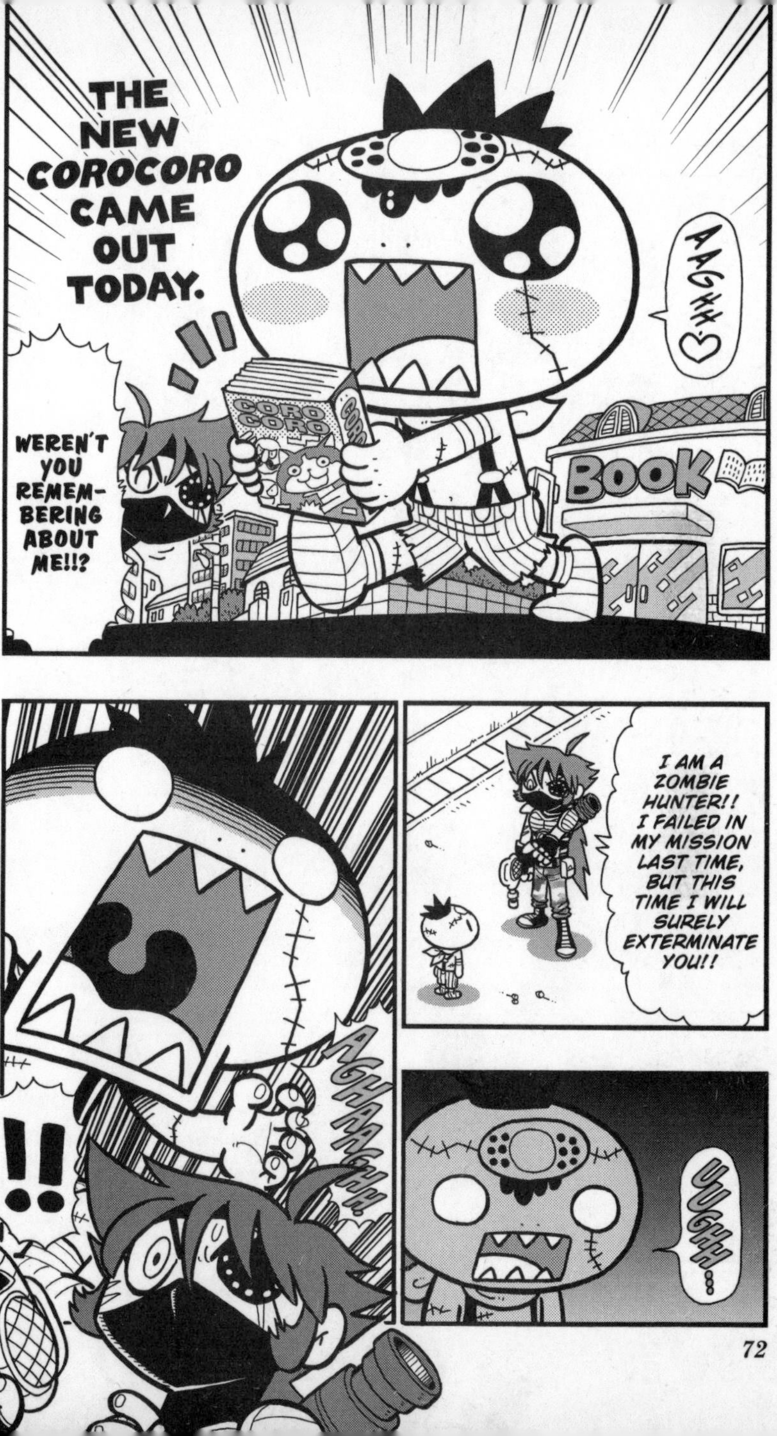
THE NEW COROCORO CAME OUT TODAY.
AAGHH♡
BOOK
COROCORO
!!
WEREN'T YOU REMEMBERING ABOUT ME!!?
I AM A ZOMBIE HUNTER!! I FAILED IN MY MISSION LAST TIME, BUT THIS TIME I WILL SURELY EXTERMINATE YOU!!
UUGHH...
AGHAAAGHH.
!!

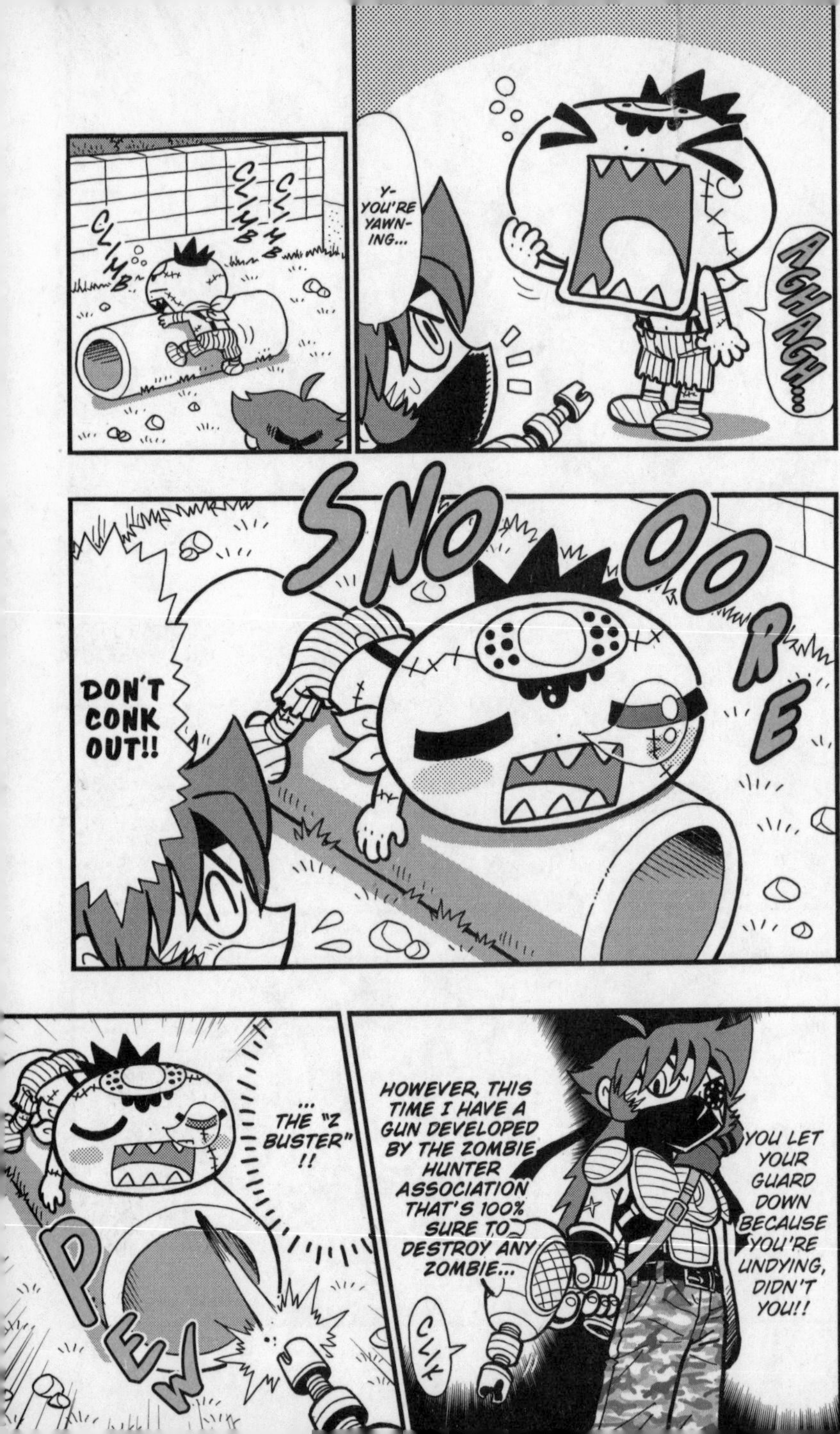
AGHAGH...
Y-YOU'RE YAWNING...
CLIMB
CLIMB
CLIMB
SNOOORE
DON'T CONK OUT!!
YOU LET YOUR GUARD DOWN BECAUSE YOU'RE UNDYING, DIDN'T YOU!!
HOWEVER, THIS TIME I HAVE A GUN DEVELOPED BY THE ZOMBIE HUNTER ASSOCIATION THAT'S 100% SURE TO DESTROY ANY ZOMBIE...
CLIK
... THE "Z BUSTER" !!
PEW

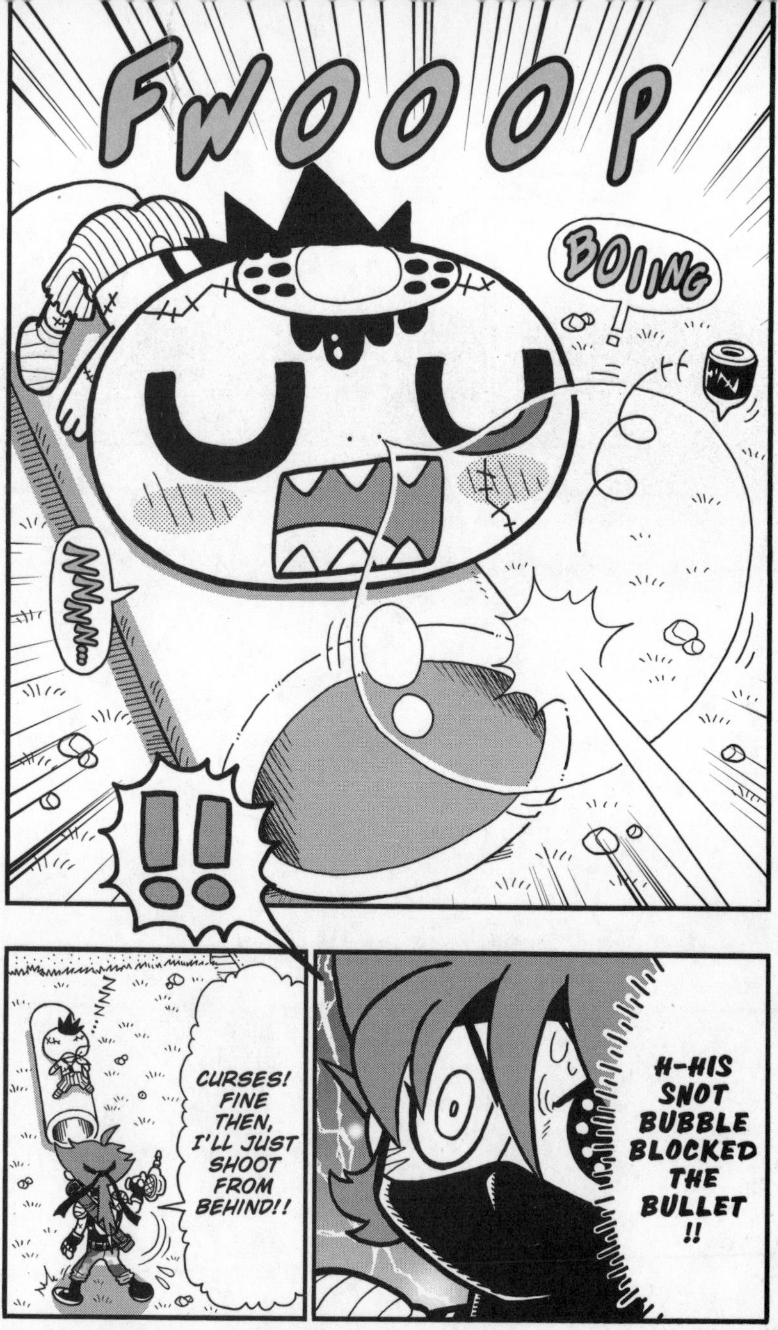
FWOOOP
BOING
NNNN...
!!
H-HIS SNOT BUBBLE BLOCKED THE BULLET!!
NNN...
CURSES! FINE THEN, I'LL JUST SHOOT FROM BEHIND!!

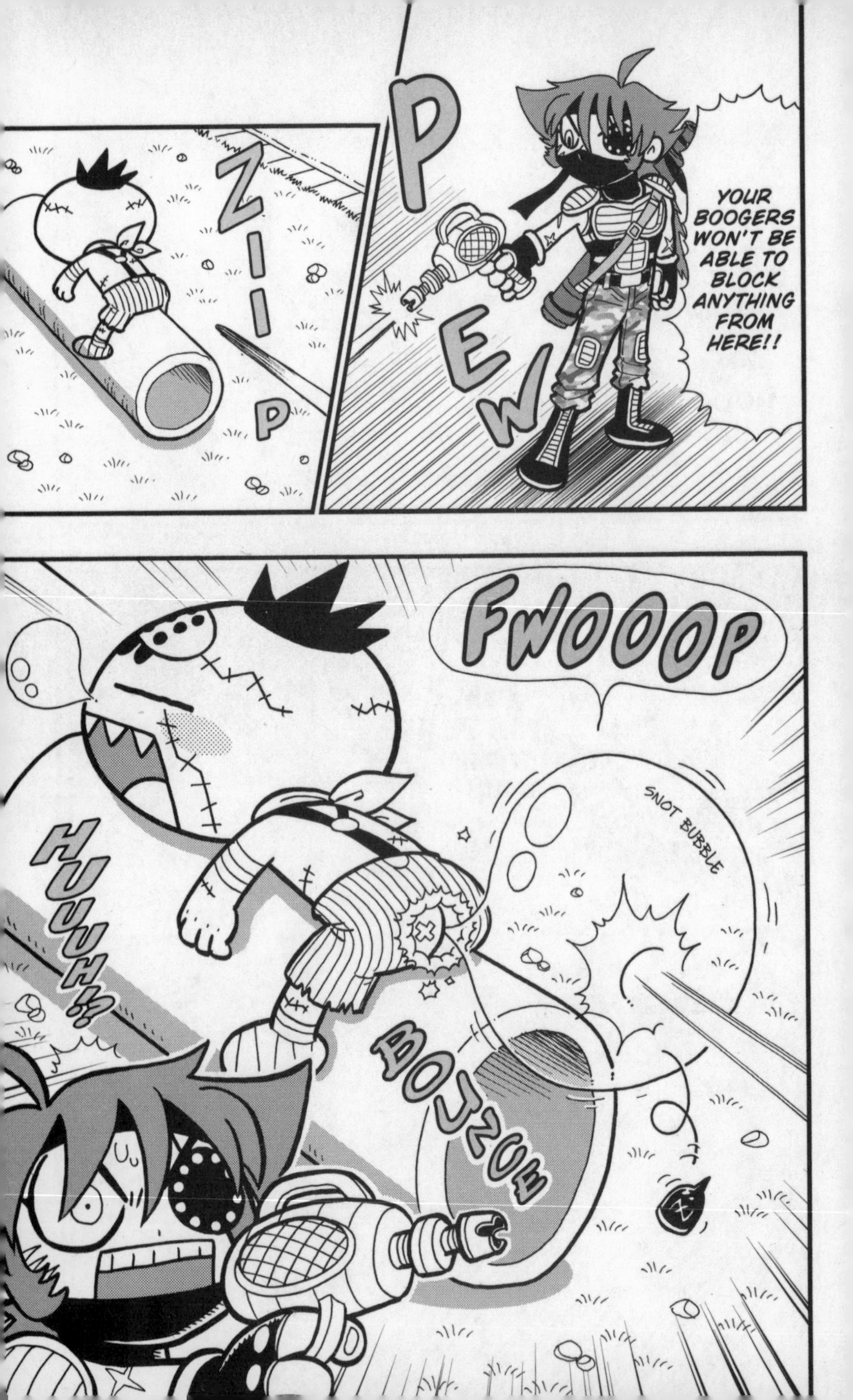
PEW
YOUR BOOGERS WON'T BE ABLE TO BLOCK ANYTHING FROM HERE!!
ZIIP
FWOOOP
SNOT BUBBLE
BOUZOE
HUUUH!?

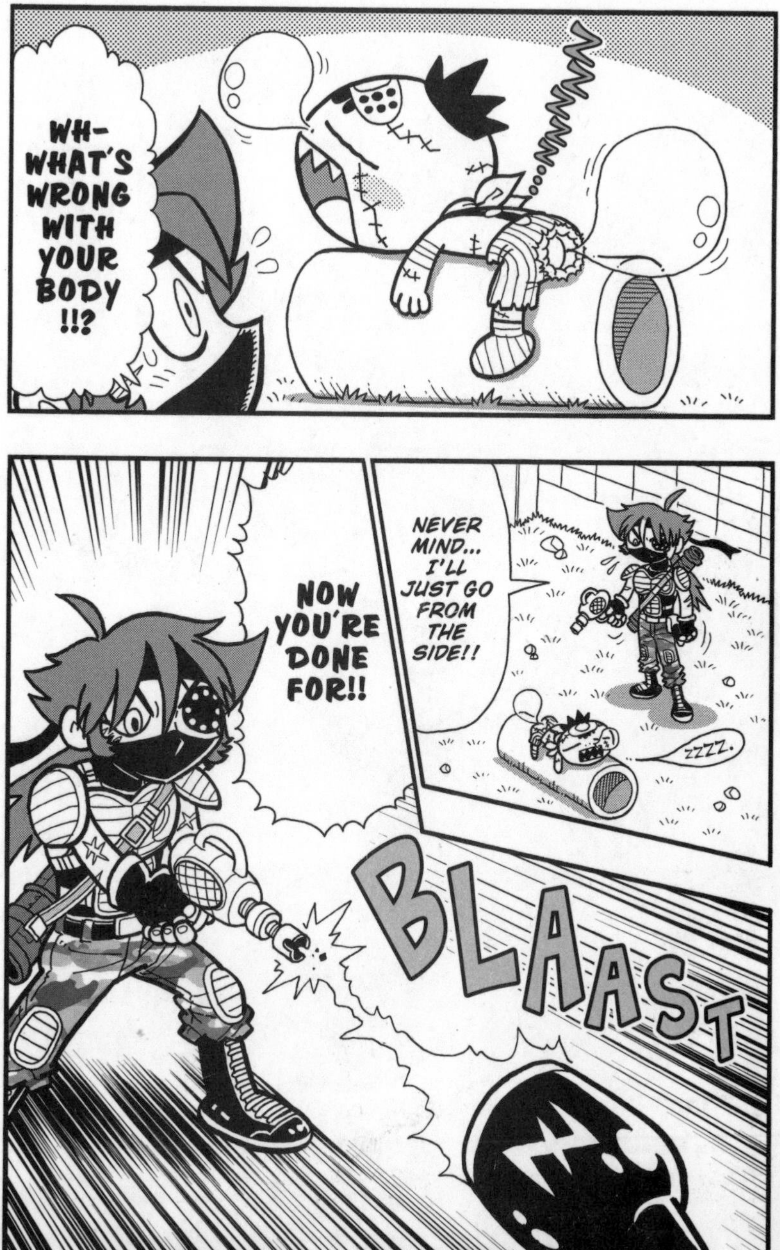
WH-WHAT'S WRONG WITH YOUR BODY!!?
NEVER MIND... I'LL JUST GO FROM THE SIDE!!
ZZZZ.
NOW YOU'RE DONE FOR!!
BLAAST

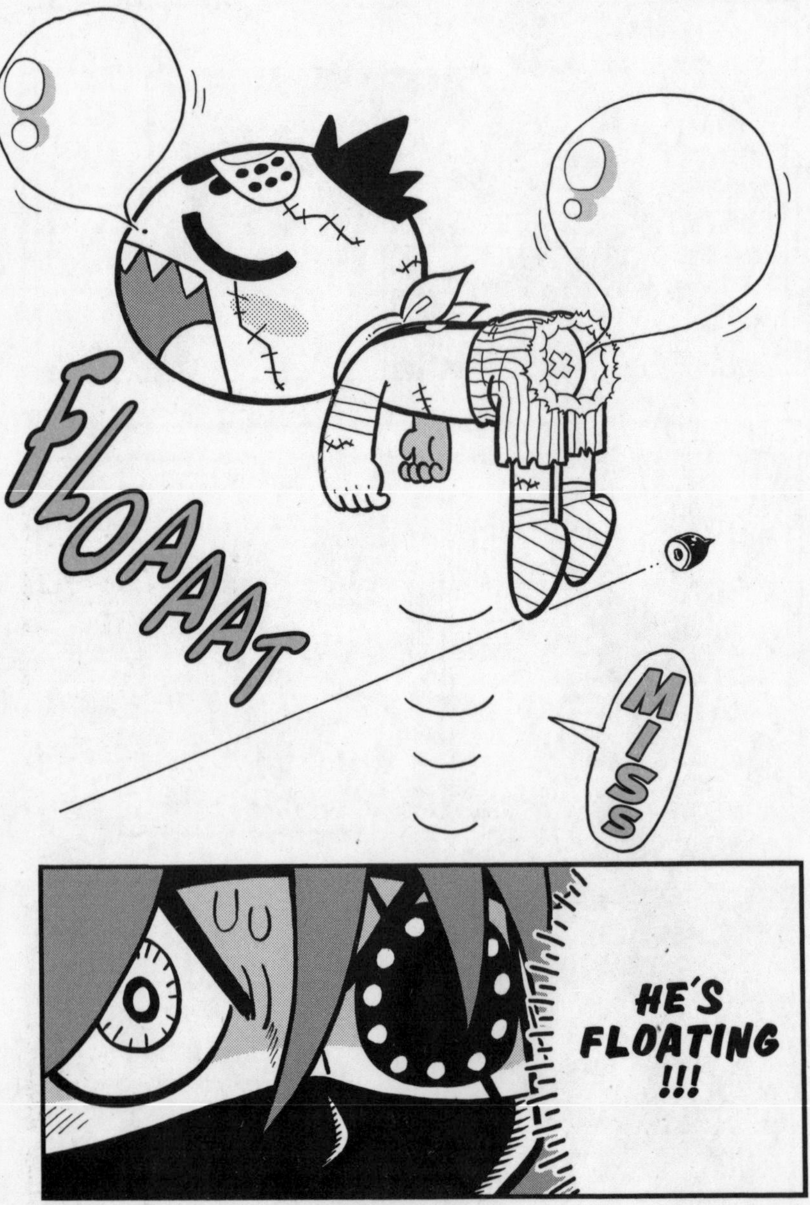
MISS
FLOAAAT
HE'S FLOATING !!!

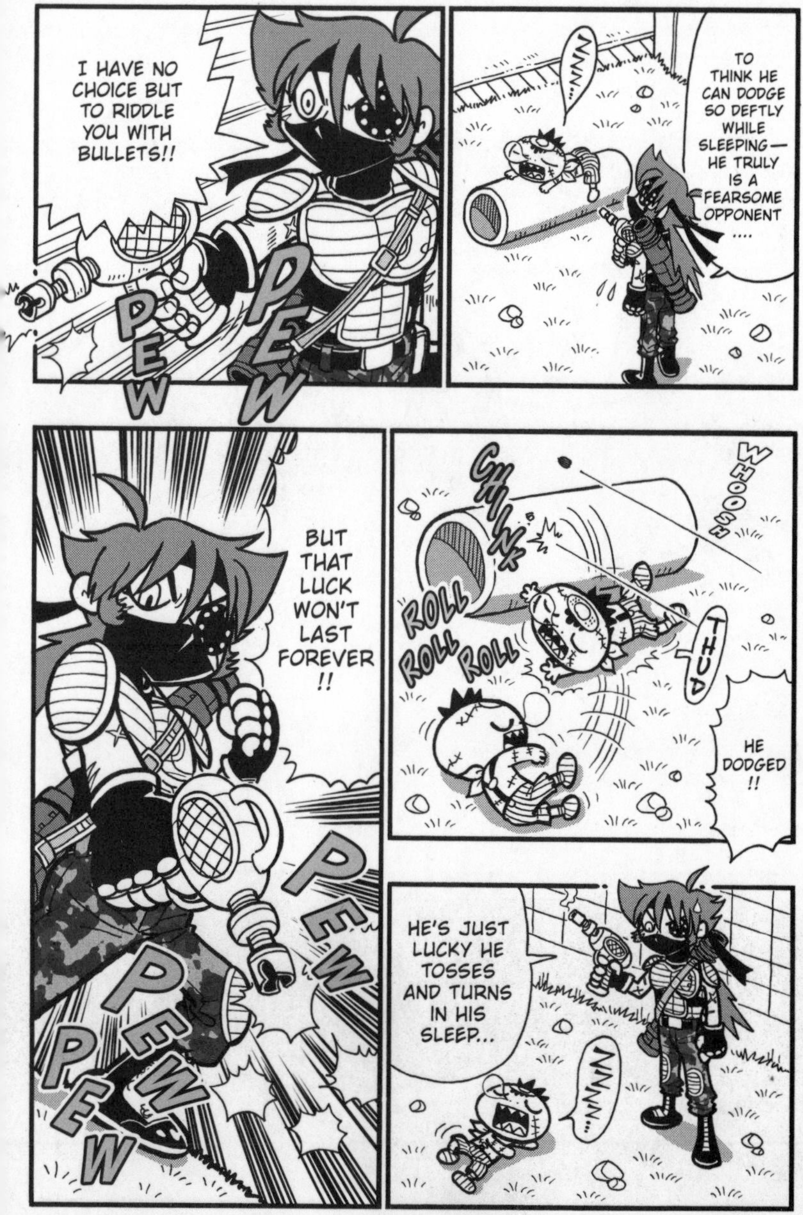

TO THINK HE CAN DODGE SO DEFTLY WHILE SLEEPING—HE TRULY IS A FEARSOME OPPONENT....
NNN...
I HAVE NO CHOICE BUT TO RIDDLE YOU WITH BULLETS!!
PEW
PEW
WHOOSH
CHINK
THUD
ROLL
ROLL
ROLL
HE DODGED!!
HE'S JUST LUCKY HE TOSSES AND TURNS IN HIS SLEEP...
NNNN...
BUT THAT LUCK WON'T LAST FOREVER!!
PEW
PEW
PEW

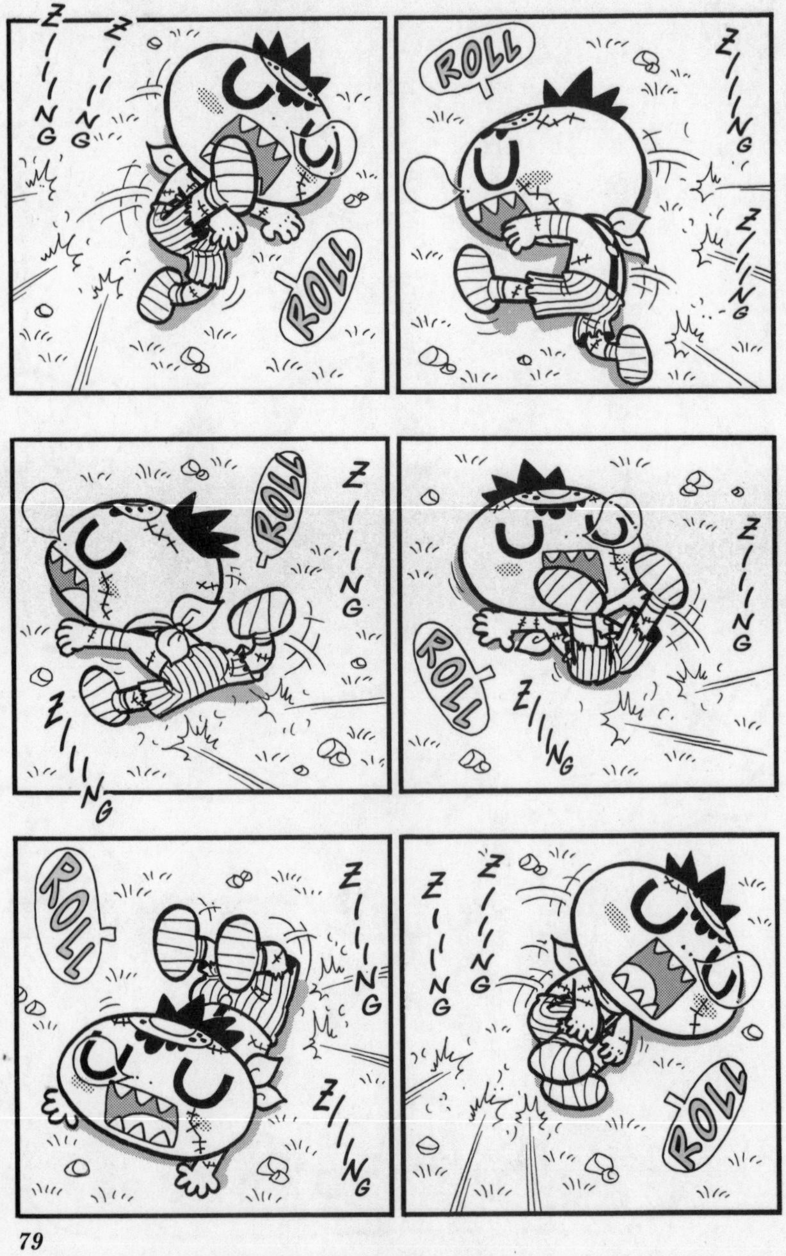
ROLL
ZIIING
ZIIING
ZIIING
ZIIING
ROLL
ZIIING
ROLL
ZIIING
ROLL
ZIIING
ZIIING
ZIIING
ZIIING
ROLL
ROLL
ZIIING
ZIIING

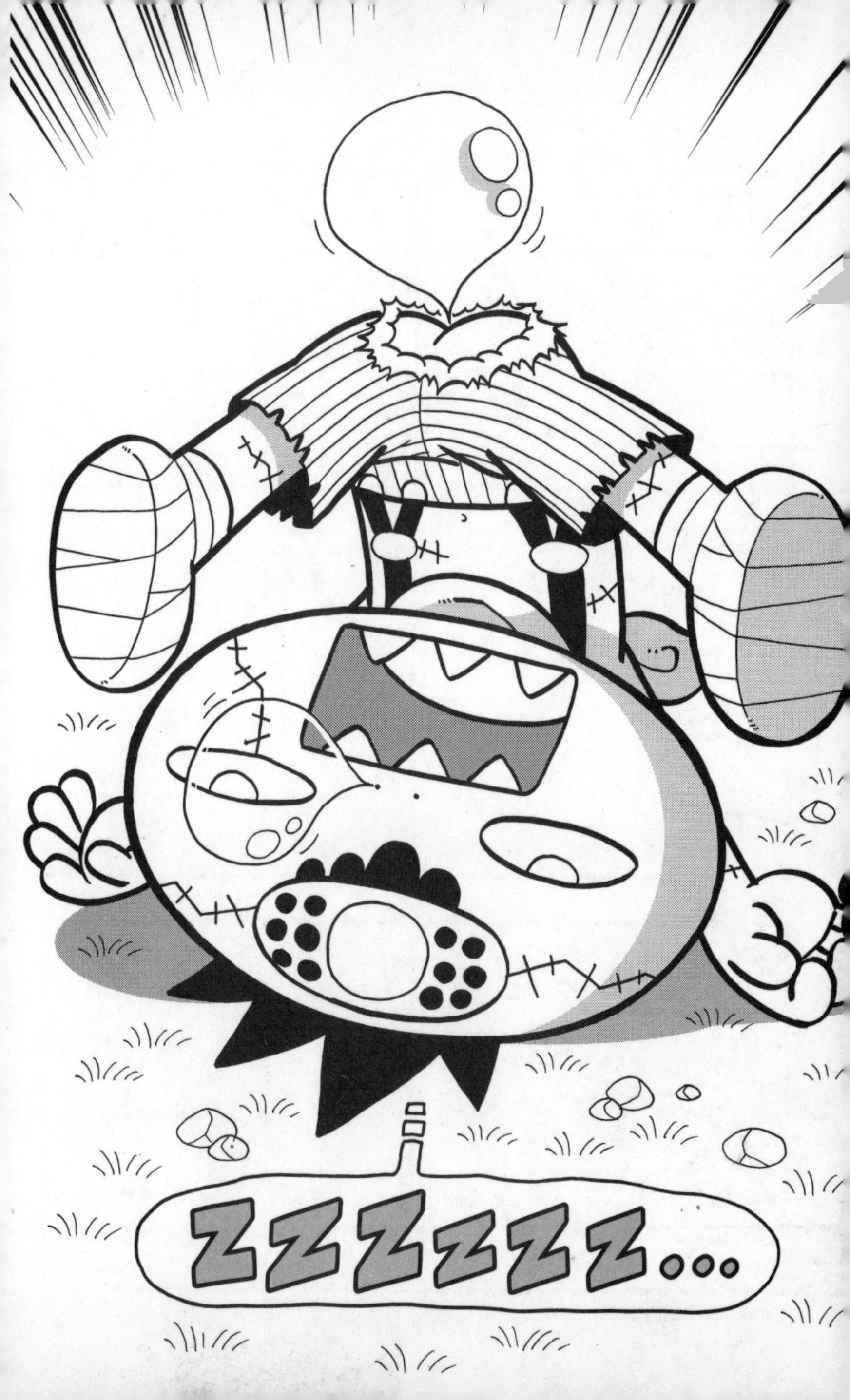
ZZZZZZZ...

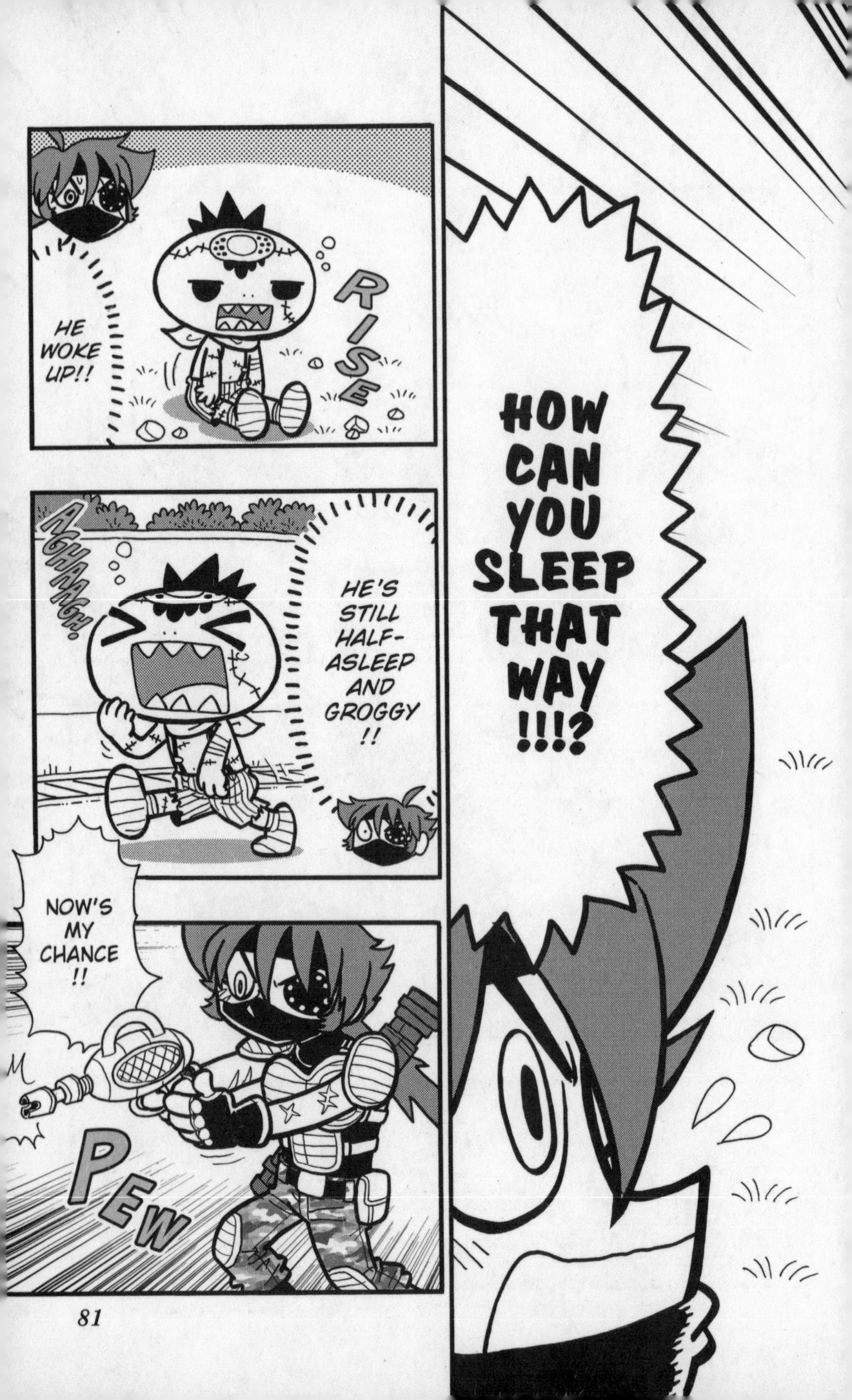

HOW CAN YOU SLEEP THAT WAY!!!?
HE WOKE UP!!
RISE
HE'S STILL HALF-ASLEEP AND GROGGY!!
AGHAAGH!
NOW'S MY CHANCE!!
PEW

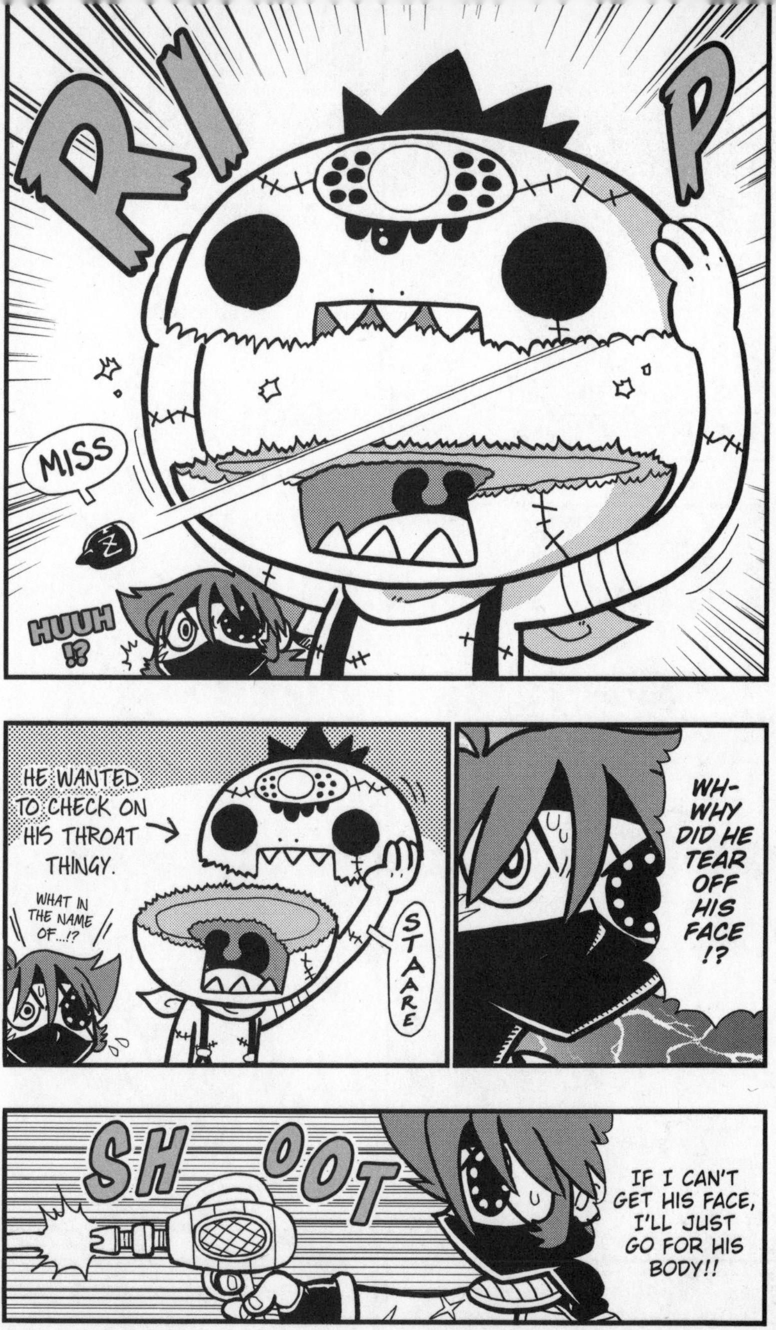
RIP
MISS
HUUH!?
WH-WHY DID HE TEAR OFF HIS FACE!?
HE WANTED TO CHECK ON HIS THROAT THINGY.
STAARE
WHAT IN THE NAME OF...!?
IF I CAN'T GET HIS FACE, I'LL JUST GO FOR HIS BODY!!
SHOOT

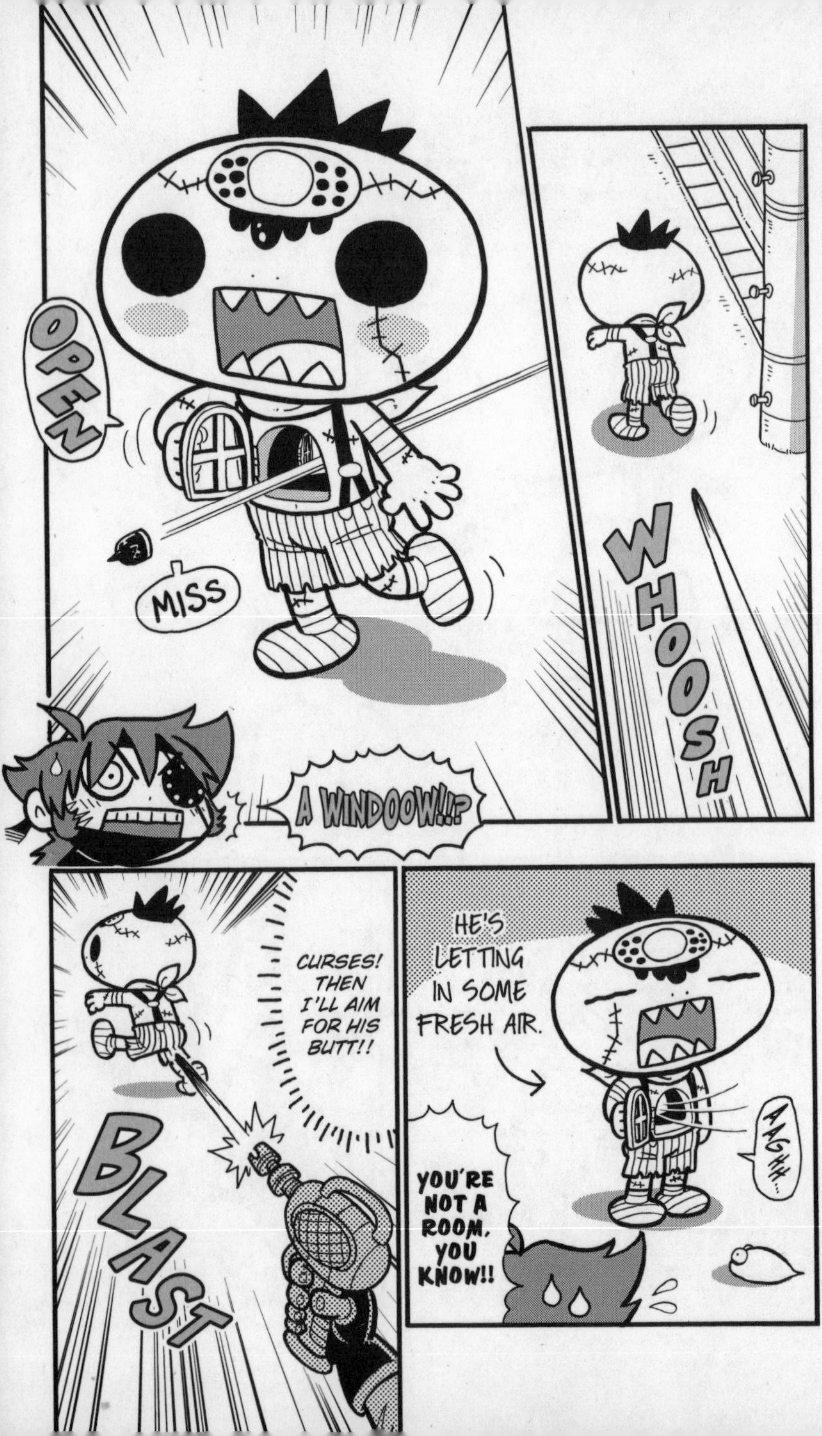
OPEN
MISS
WHOOSH
A WINDOOW!!?
CURSES! THEN I'LL AIM FOR HIS BUTT!!
BLAST
HE'S LETTING IN SOME FRESH AIR.
AAGHH...
YOU'RE NOT A ROOM, YOU KNOW!!

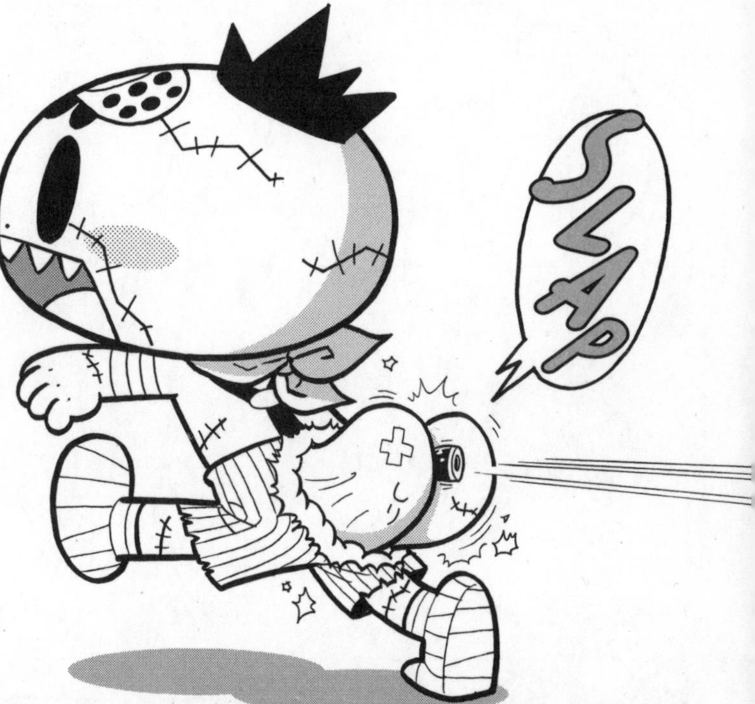
SLAP

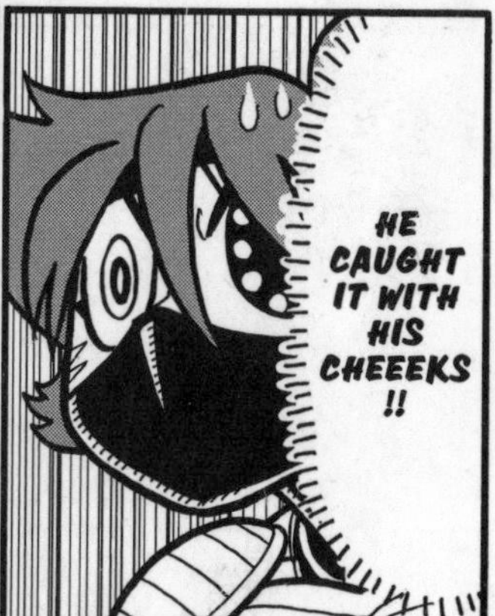
HE CAUGHT IT WITH HIS CHEEEKS !!

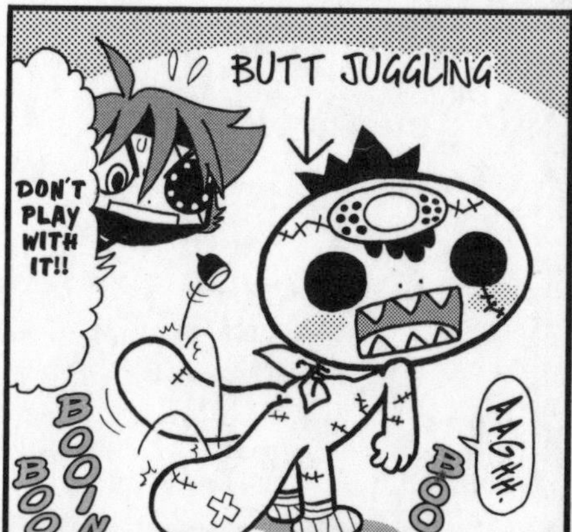
BUTT JUGGLING
DON'T PLAY WITH IT!!
AAGHH.
BOOING
BOOING BOOING

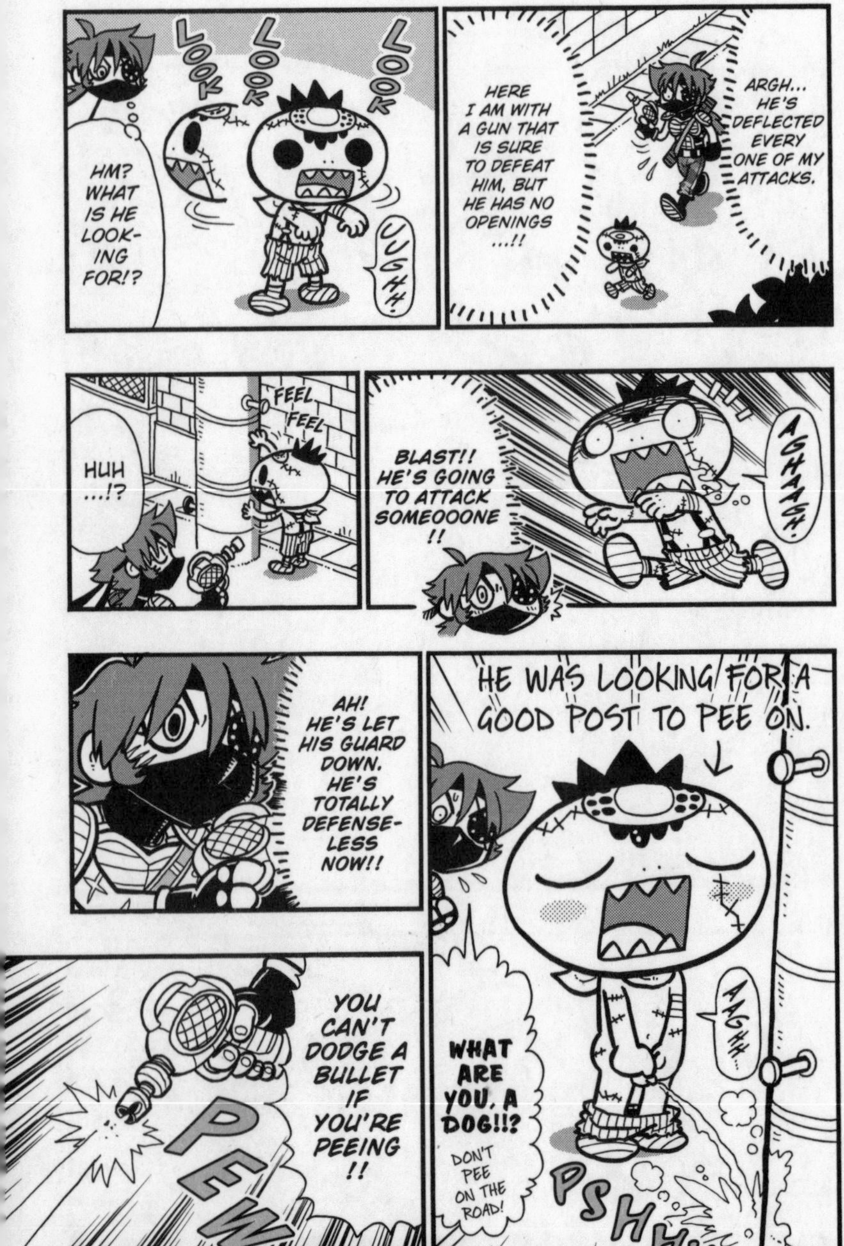
ARGH... HE'S DEFLECTED EVERY ONE OF MY ATTACKS.
HERE I AM WITH A GUN THAT IS SURE TO DEFEAT HIM, BUT HE HAS NO OPENINGS ...!!
LOOK
LOOK
LOOK
UGHH
HM? WHAT IS HE LOOKING FOR!?
AGHAAAGH
BLAST!! HE'S GOING TO ATTACK SOMEOOONE !!
FEEL
FEEL
HUH ...!?
HE WAS LOOKING FOR A GOOD POST TO PEE ON.
AGHH...
WHAT ARE YOU, A DOG!!?
DON'T PEE ON THE ROAD!
PSHHHH
AH! HE'S LET HIS GUARD DOWN. HE'S TOTALLY DEFENSELESS NOW!!
YOU CAN'T DODGE A BULLET IF YOU'RE PEEING !!
PEW

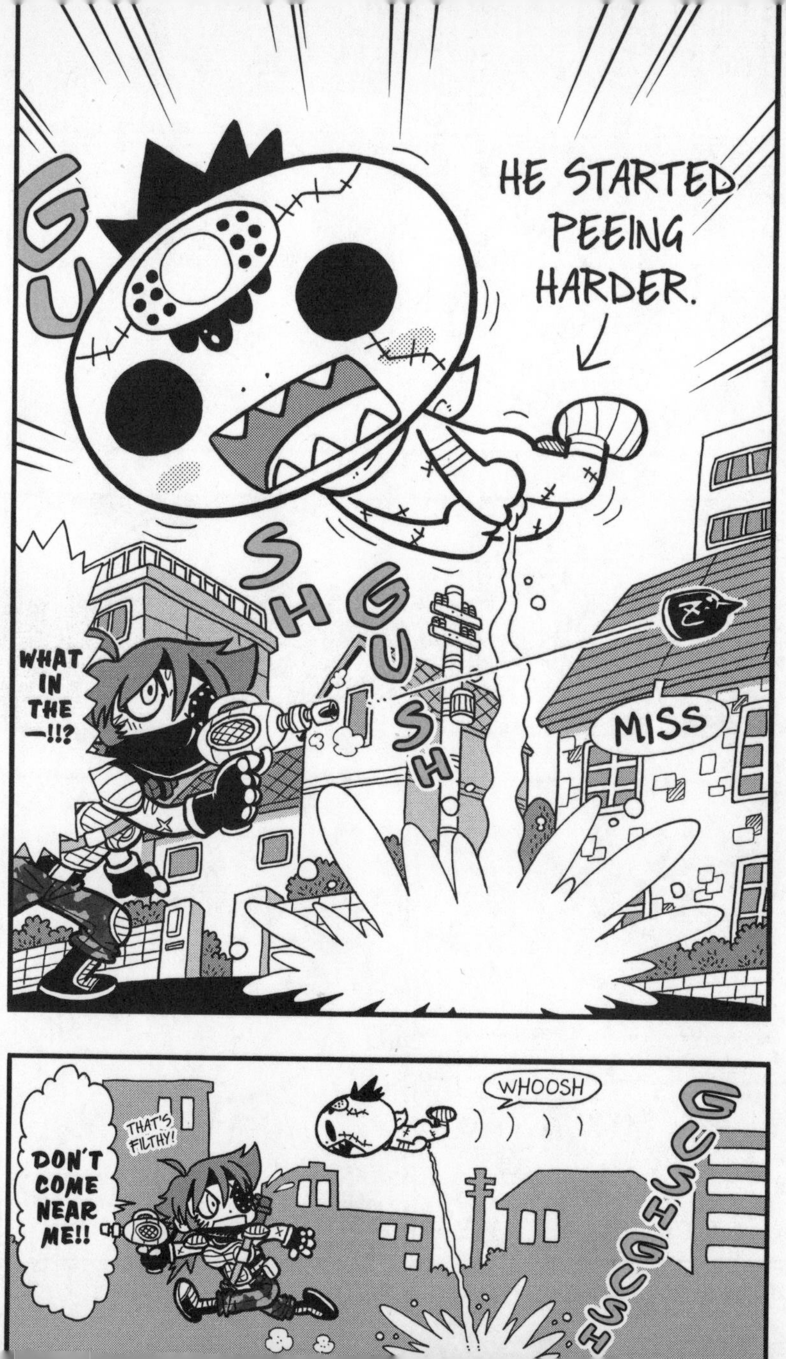
HE STARTED PEEING HARDER.
GU
MISS
SHGUSH
WHAT IN THE—!!?
GUSHGUSH
WHOOSH
THAT'S FILTHY!
DON'T COME NEAR ME!!

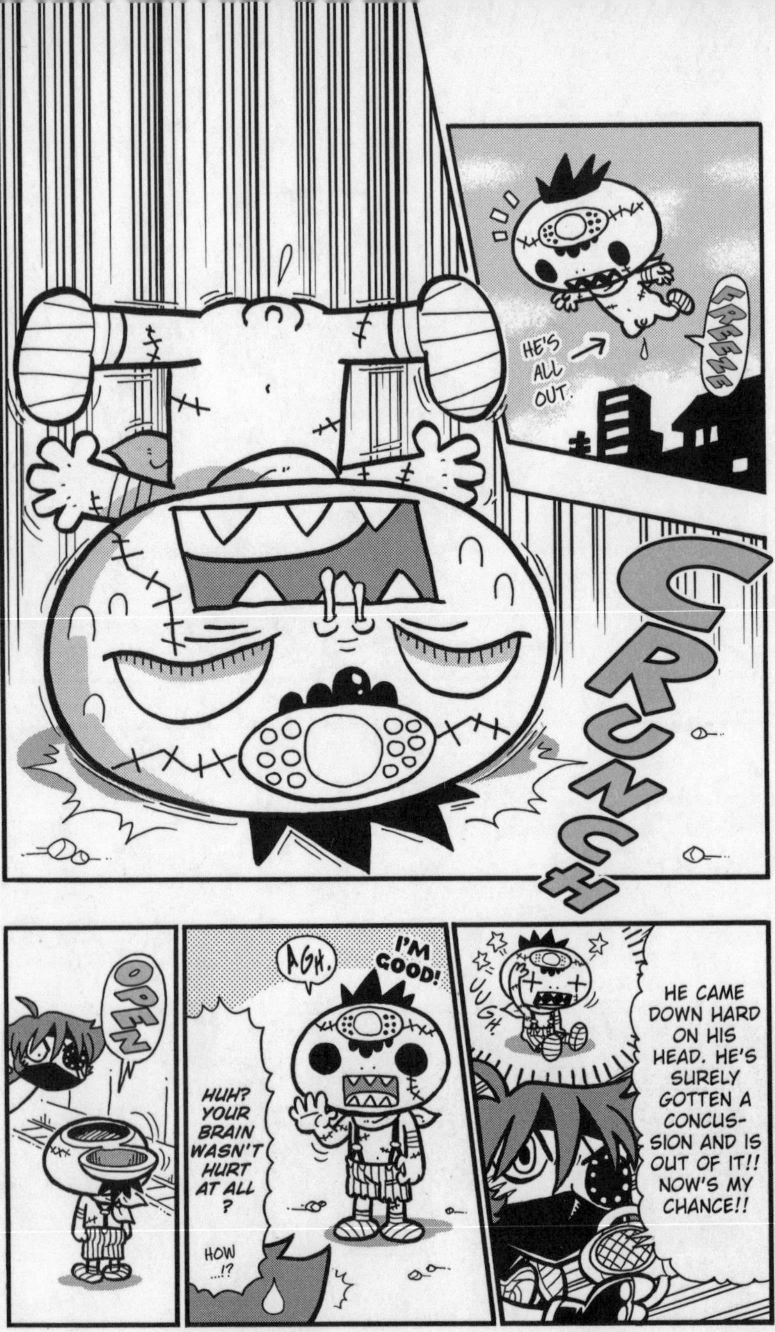
FREEZE
HE'S ALL OUT
CRUNCH
HE CAME DOWN HARD ON HIS HEAD. HE'S SURELY GOTTEN A CONCUSSION AND IS OUT OF IT!! NOW'S MY CHANCE!!
UUGH.
I'M GOOD!
AGH.
HUH? YOUR BRAIN WASN'T HURT AT ALL ?
HOW ...!?
OPEN

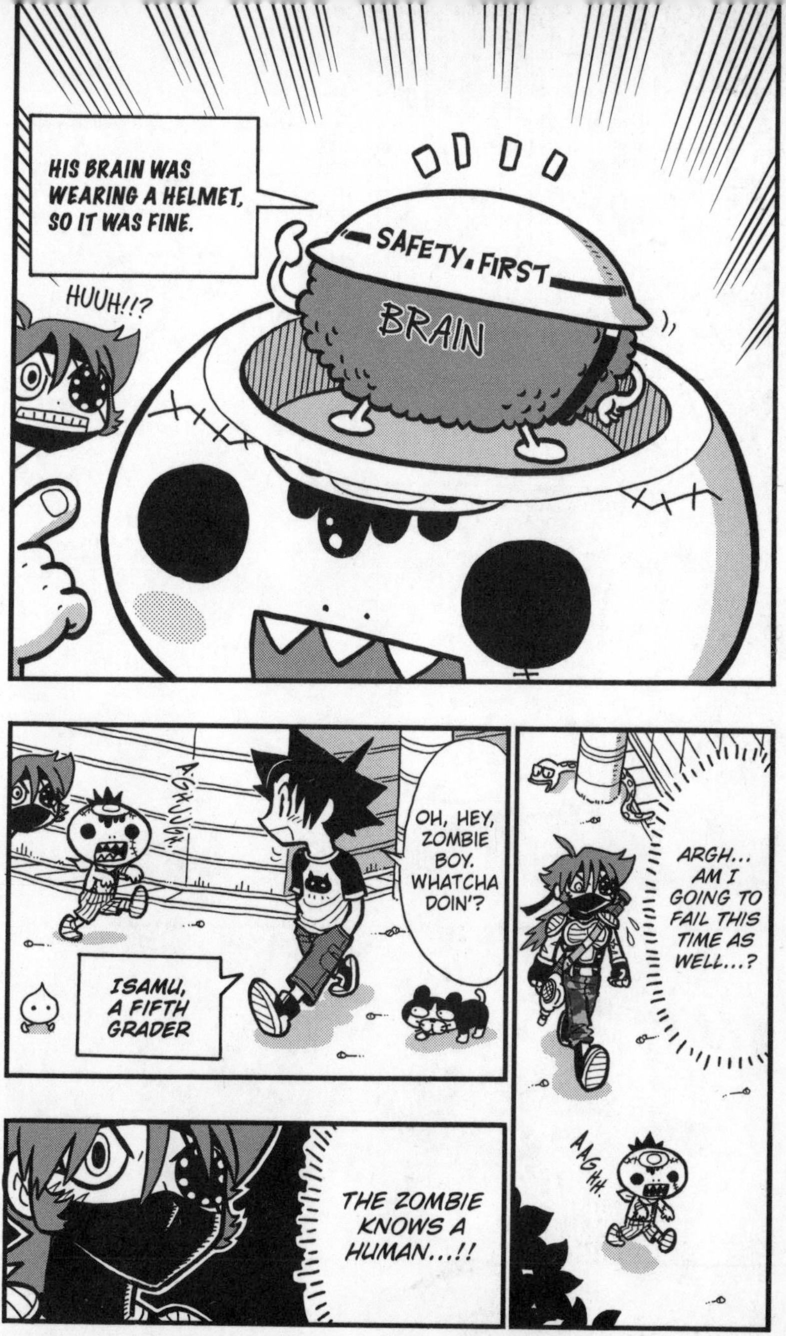
HIS BRAIN WAS WEARING A HELMET, SO IT WAS FINE.
SAFETY FIRST
BRAIN
HUUH!!?
ARGH... AM I GOING TO FAIL THIS TIME AS WELL...?
AAGHH.
OH, HEY, ZOMBIE BOY. WHATCHA DOIN'?
A·GHUUGH.
ISAMU, A FIFTH GRADER
THE ZOMBIE KNOWS A HUMAN...!!

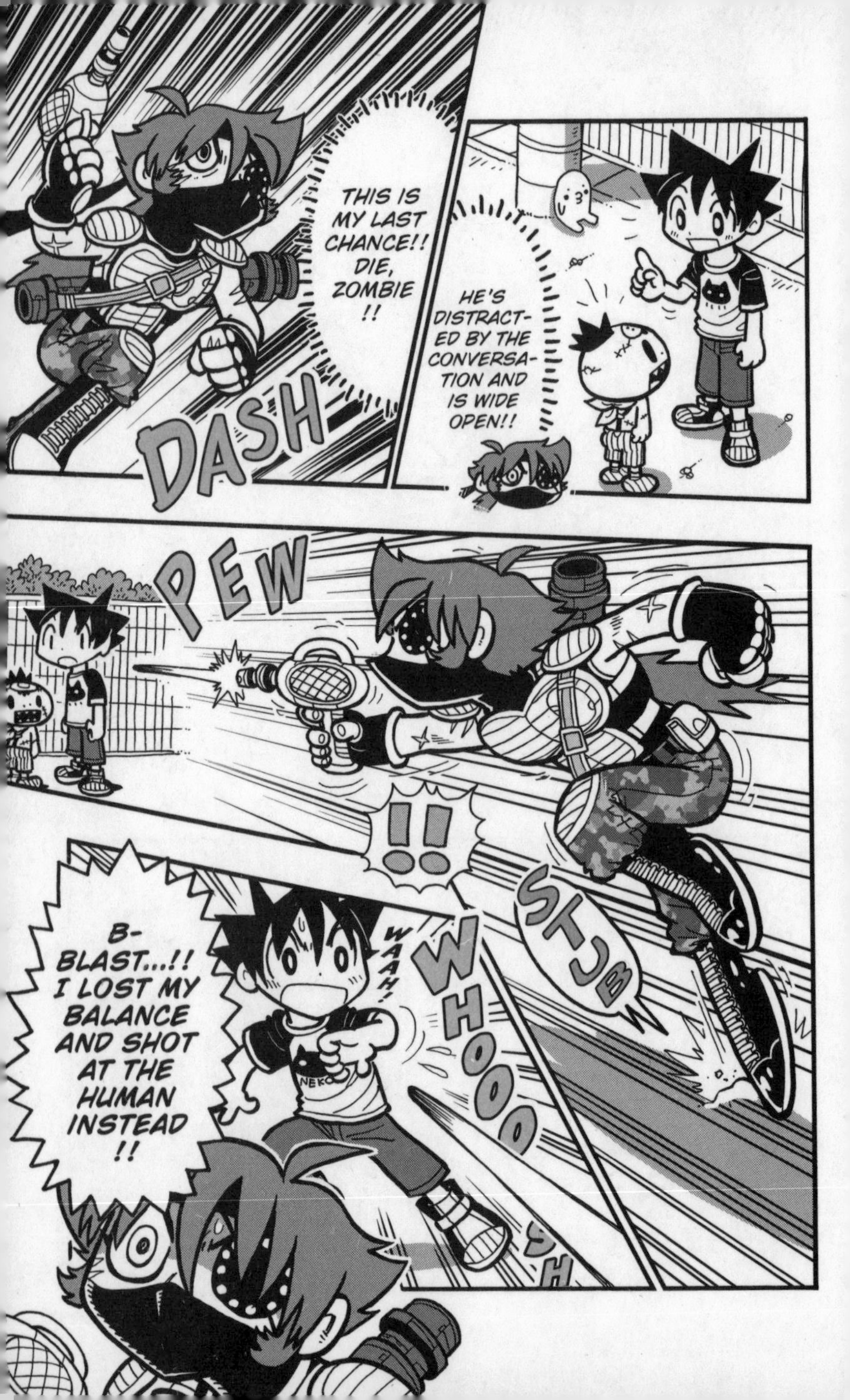

HE'S DISTRACTED BY THE CONVERSATION AND IS WIDE OPEN!!
THIS IS MY LAST CHANCE!! DIE, ZOMBIE!!
DASH
PEW
!!
WHOOOOSH
WAAAH!
B-BLAST...!! I LOST MY BALANCE AND SHOT AT THE HUMAN INSTEAD!!
NEKO

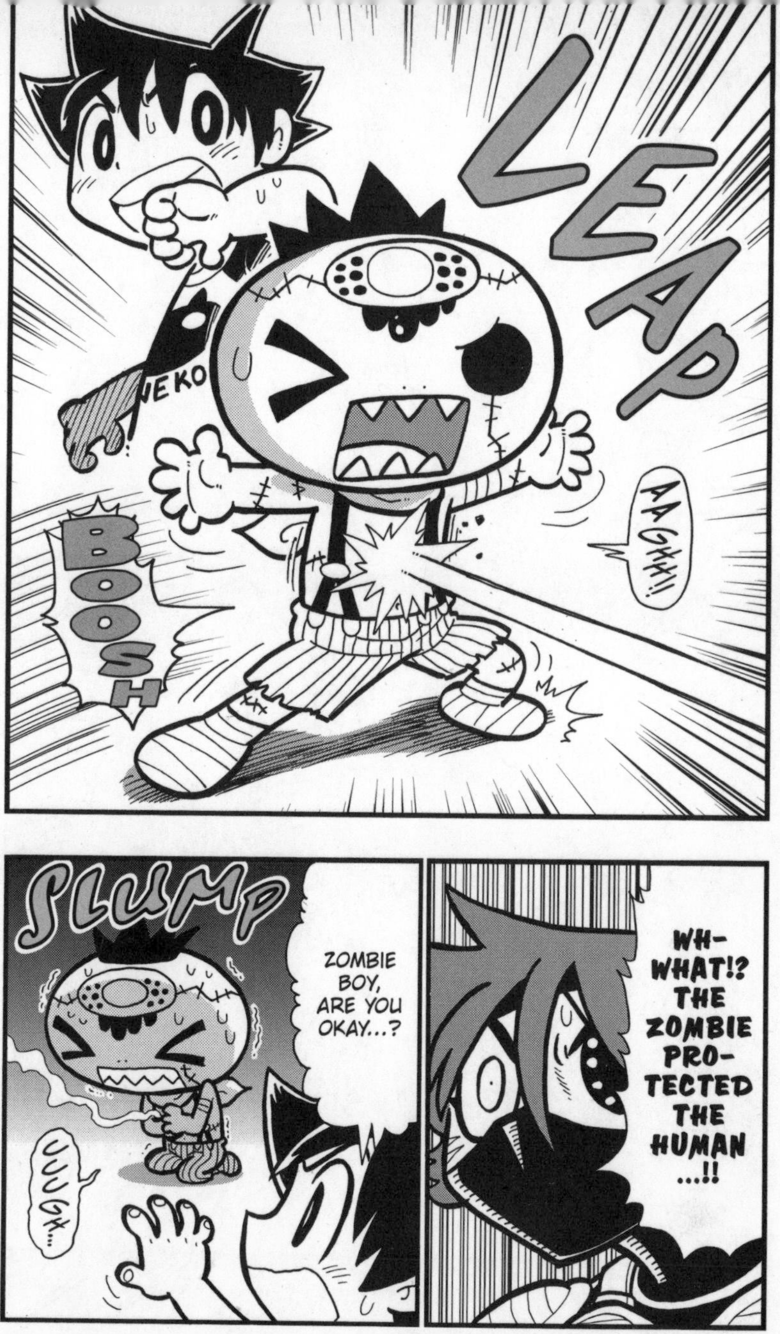
LEAP
AAGHH!!
BOOSH
NEKO
WH-WHAT!? THE ZOMBIE PROTECTED THE HUMAN...!!
SLUMP
ZOMBIE BOY, ARE YOU OKAY...?
UUUGH...

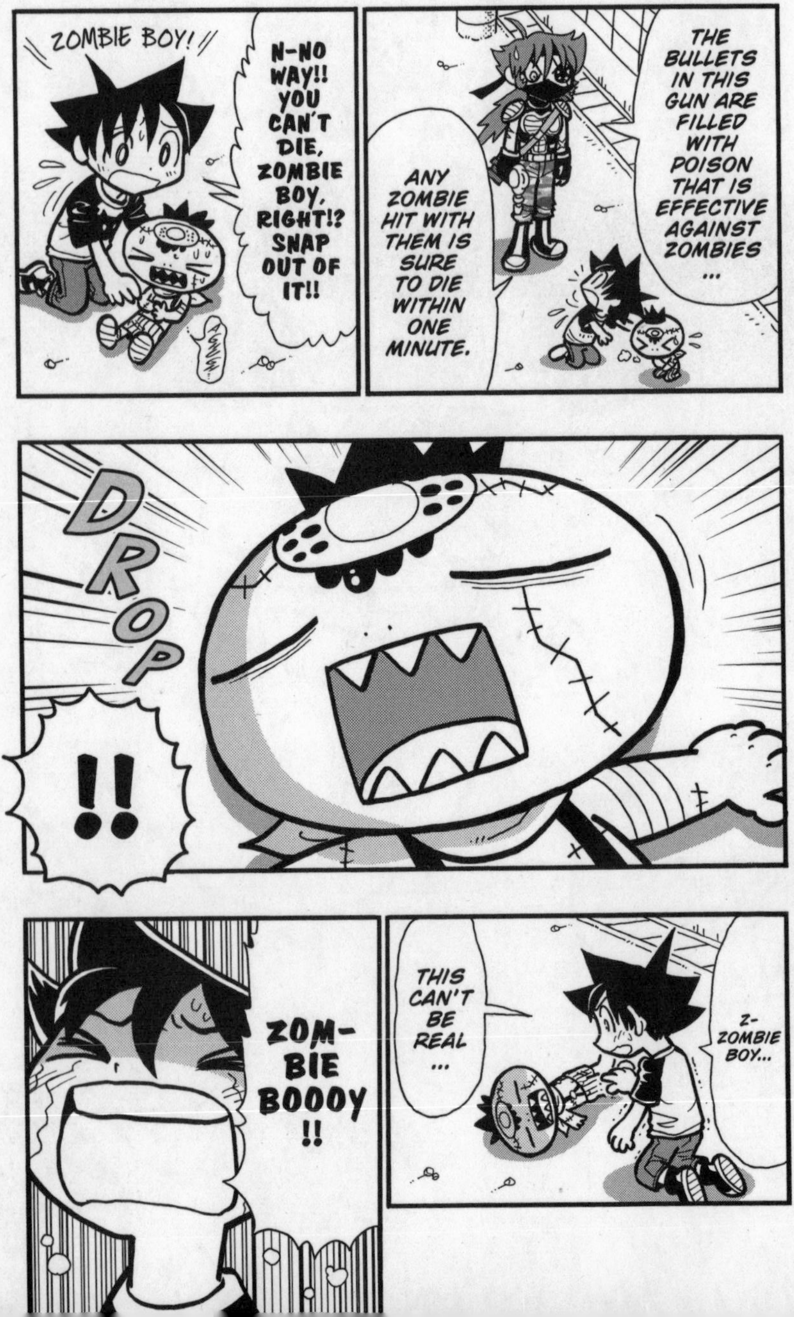
THE BULLETS IN THIS GUN ARE FILLED WITH POISON THAT IS EFFECTIVE AGAINST ZOMBIES ...
ANY ZOMBIE HIT WITH THEM IS SURE TO DIE WITHIN ONE MINUTE.
ZOMBIE BOY!
N-NO WAY!! YOU CAN'T DIE, ZOMBIE BOY, RIGHT!? SNAP OUT OF IT!!
DROP
!!
Z-ZOMBIE BOY...
THIS CAN'T BE REAL ...
ZOM-BIE BOOOY !!

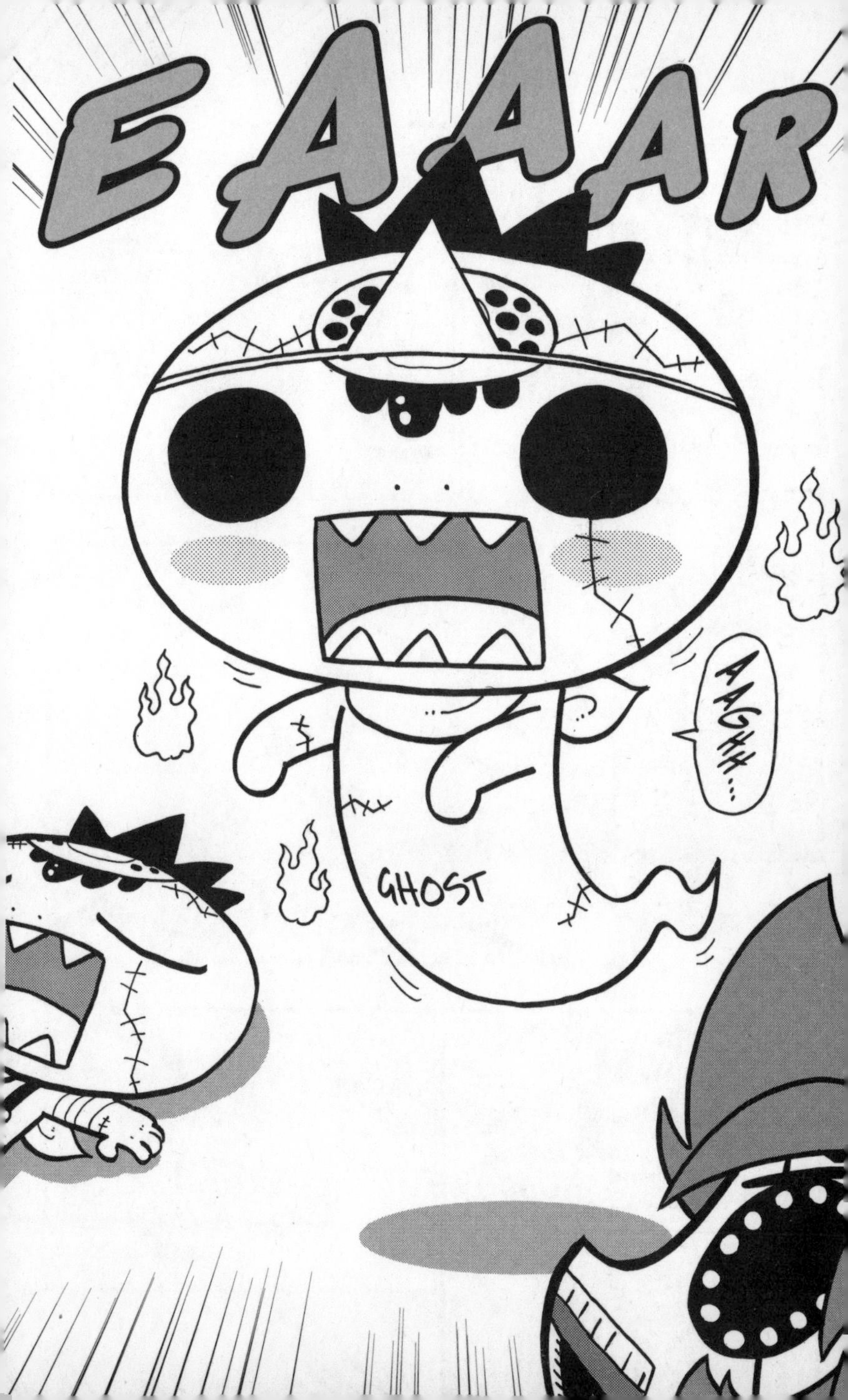
EAAAR
AAGHH...
GHOST

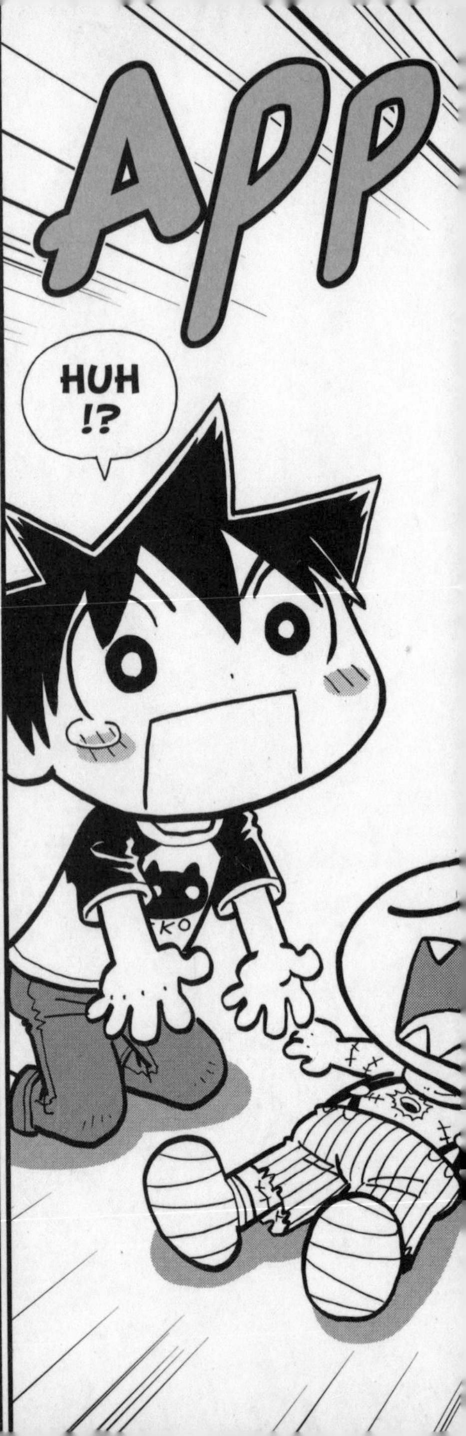
APP
HUH!?
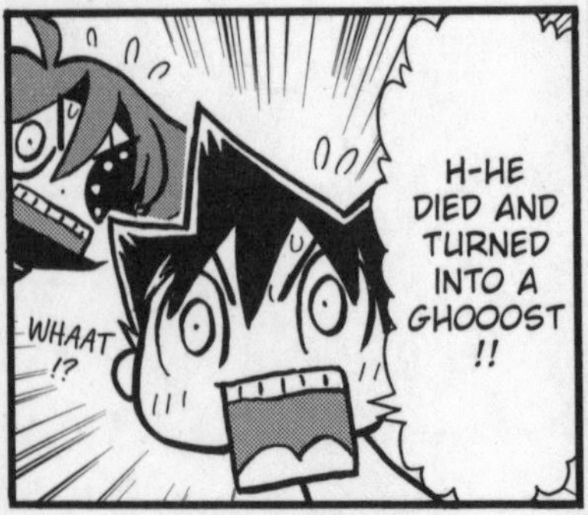
H-HE DIED AND TURNED INTO A GHOOOST!!
WHAAT!?
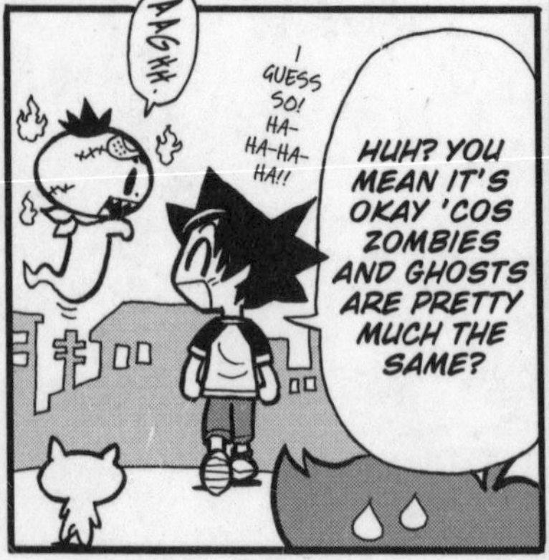
HUH? YOU MEAN IT'S OKAY 'COS ZOMBIES AND GHOSTS ARE PRETTY MUCH THE SAME?
I GUESS SO! HA-HA-HA-HA!!
AAGHH.
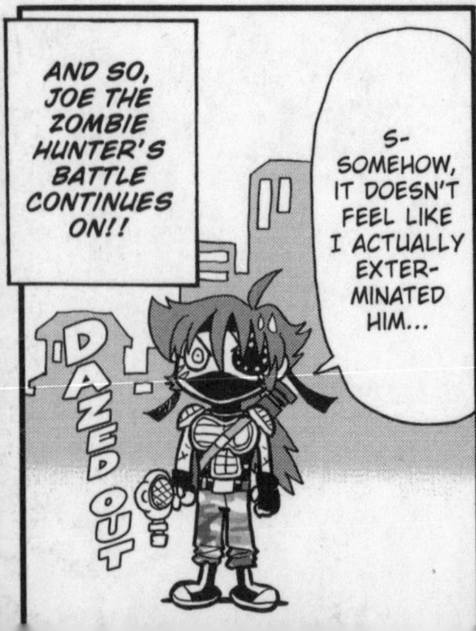
S-SOMEHOW, IT DOESN'T FEEL LIKE I ACTUALLY EXTERMINATED HIM...
AND SO, JOE THE ZOMBIE HUNTER'S BATTLE CONTINUES ON!!
DAZED OUT

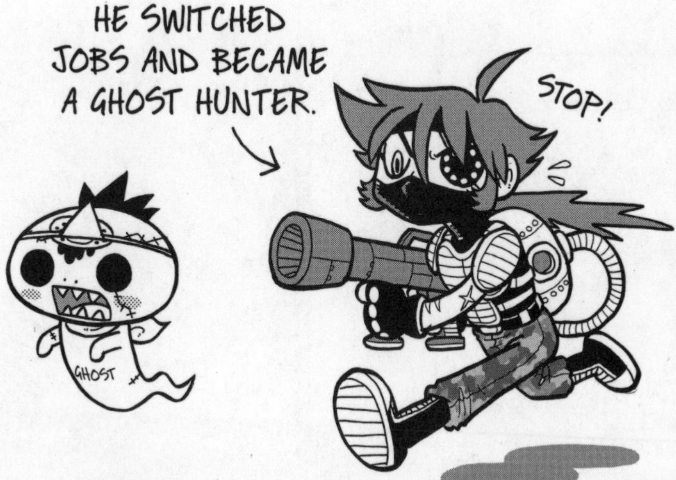
HE SWITCHED JOBS AND BECAME A GHOST HUNTER.
STOP!
GHOST

THE FARTZ JUZT WON'T ZTOP!

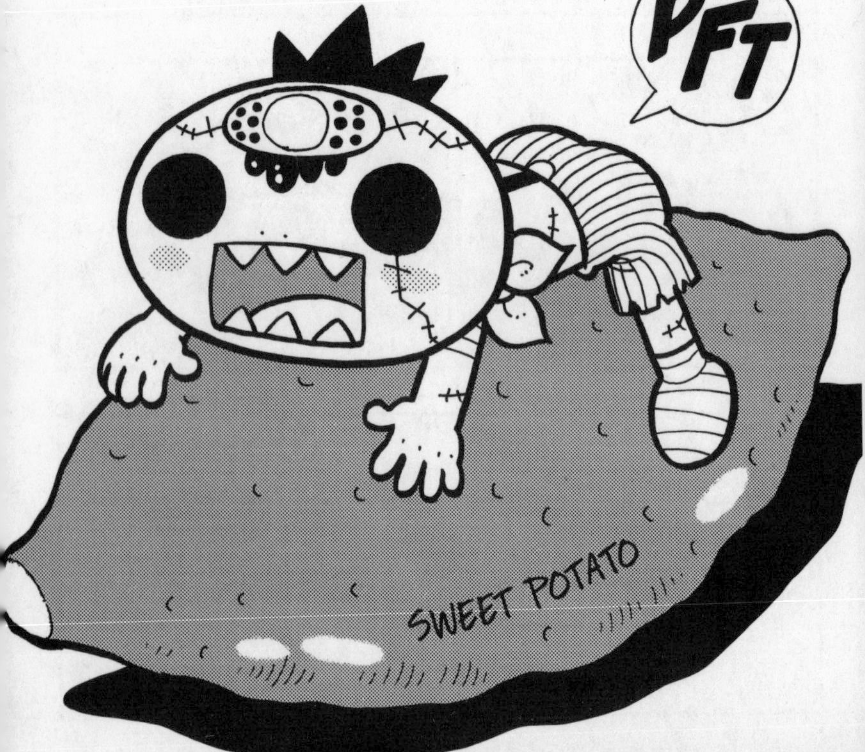
PFT
SWEET POTATO

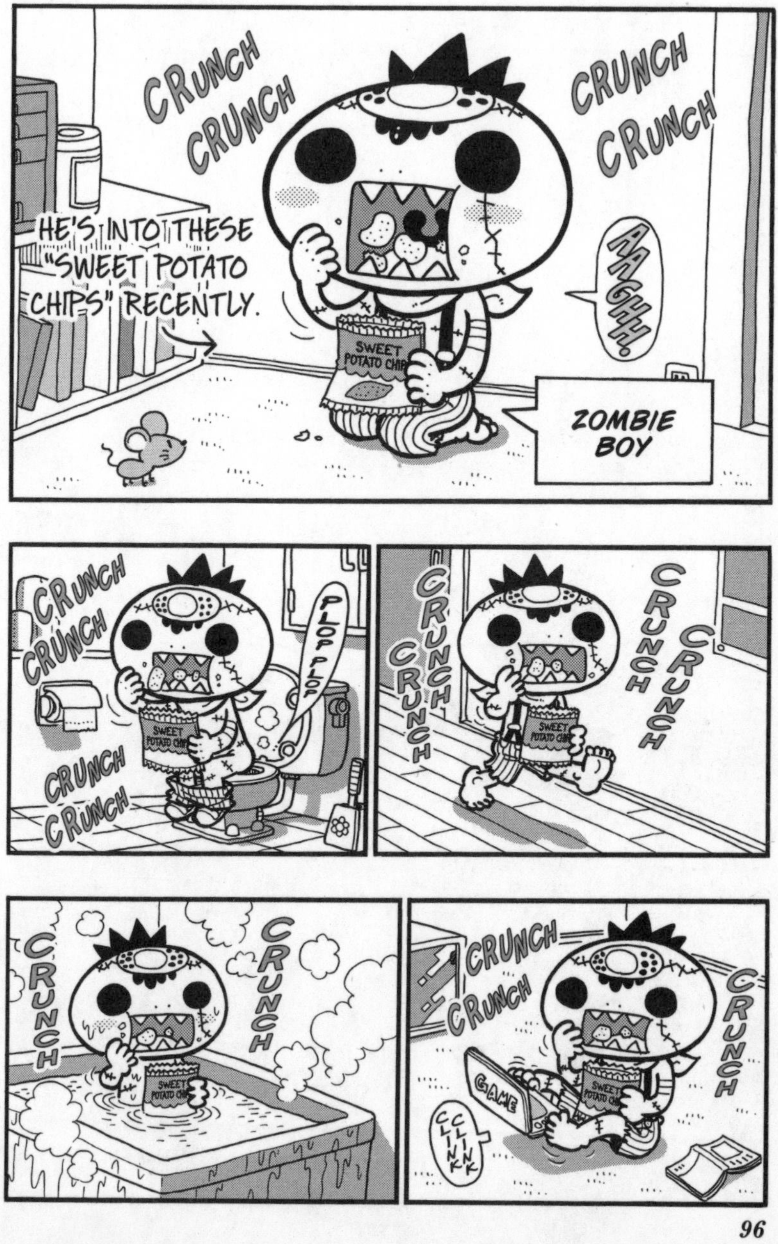
CRUNCH CRUNCH
CRUNCH CRUNCH
AAGHH!
ZOMBIE BOY
HE'S INTO THESE "SWEET POTATO CHIPS" RECENTLY.
SWEET POTATO CHIPS
CRUNCH CRUNCH
CRUNCH CRUNCH
SWEET POTATO CHIPS
PLOP PLOP
CRUNCH CRUNCH
SWEET POTATO CHIPS
CRUNCH CRUNCH
CRUNCH
CRUNCH CRUNCH
GAME
SWEET POTATO CHIPS
CLINK CLINK
CRUNCH
CRUNCH
SWEET POTATO CHIPS

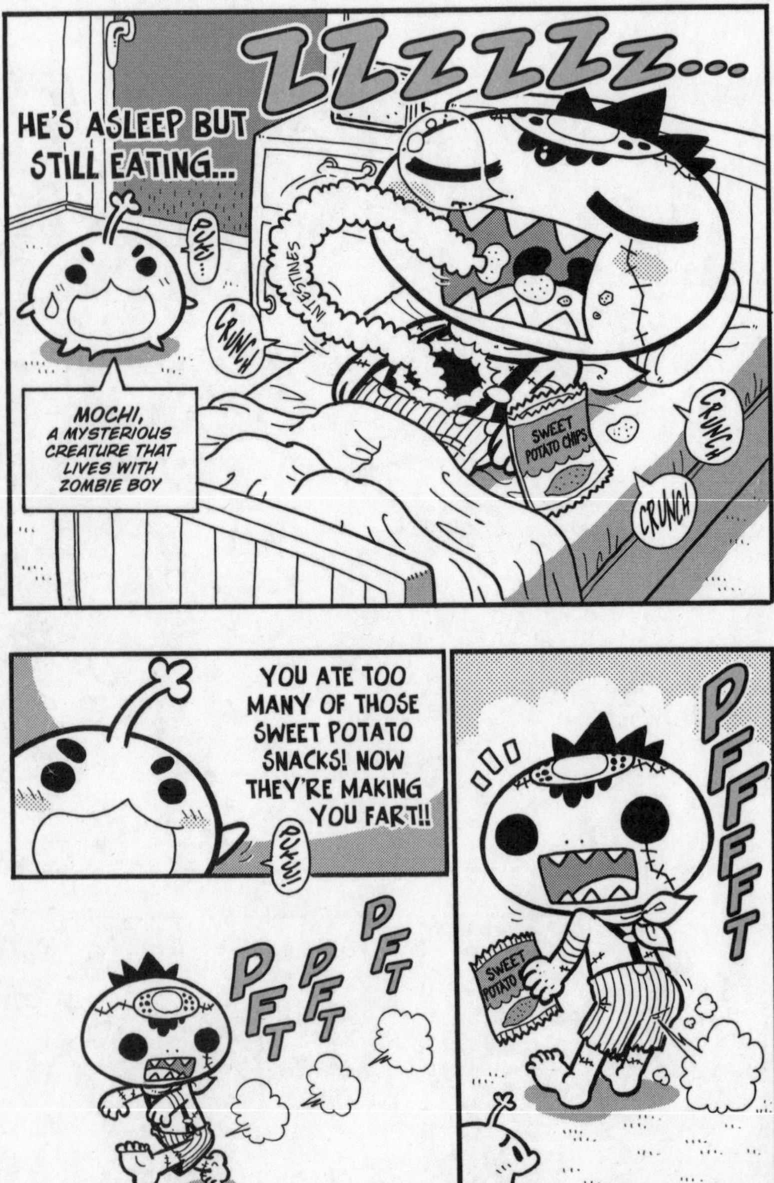

ZZZZZZz...
HE'S ASLEEP BUT STILL EATING...
PUKI...
CRUNCH
CRUNCH
SWEET POTATO CHIPS
INTESTINES
CRUNCH
MOCHI, A MYSTERIOUS CREATURE THAT LIVES WITH ZOMBIE BOY
PFFFFFT
SWEET POTATO
YOU ATE TOO MANY OF THOSE SWEET POTATO SNACKS! NOW THEY'RE MAKING YOU FART!!
PUKI!
PFT
PFT
PFT

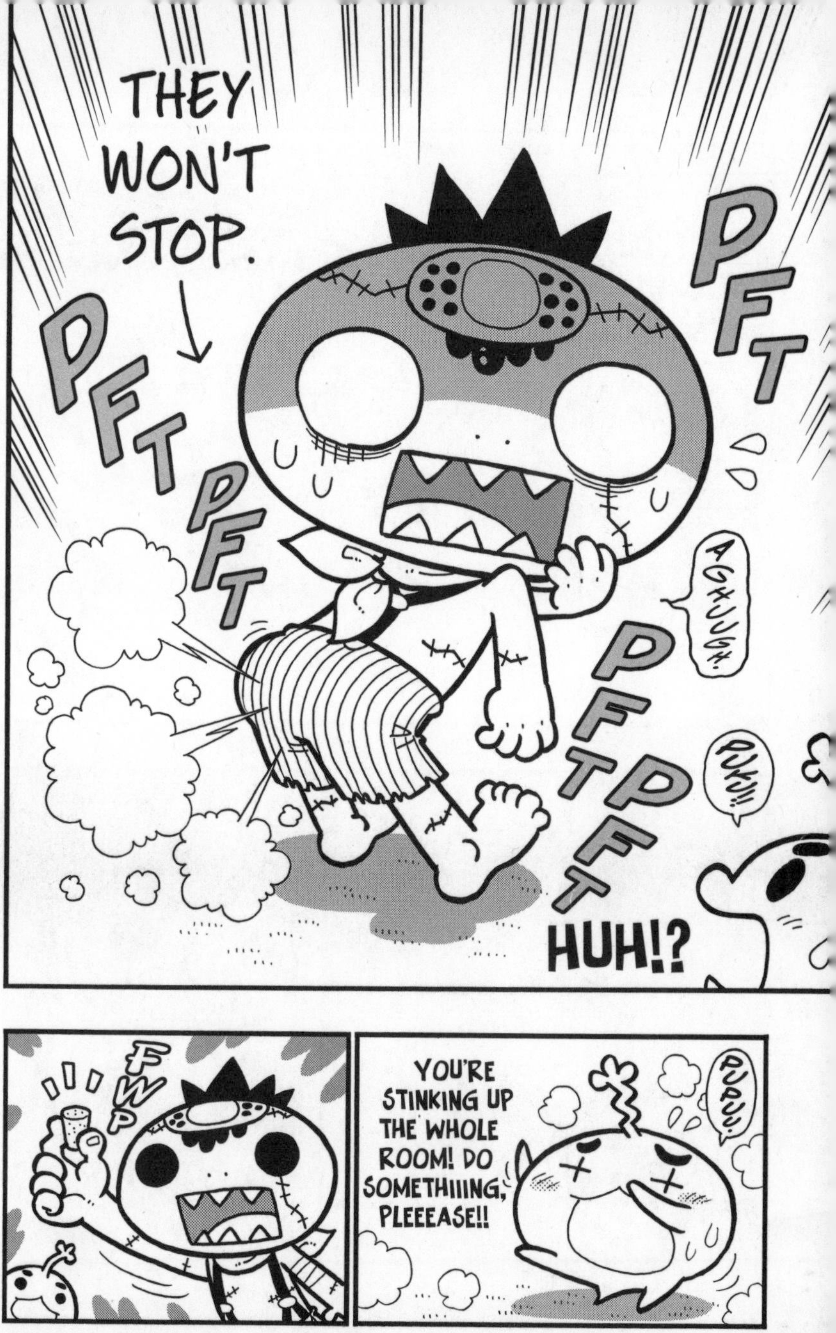
PFFT
THEY WON'T STOP.
PFFT
PFFT
AGHUUGH.
PFFT
PFFT
PUKU!!
HUH!?
PUPUU.
YOU'RE STINKING UP THE WHOLE ROOM! DO SOMETHIIING, PLEEEASE!!
FWP

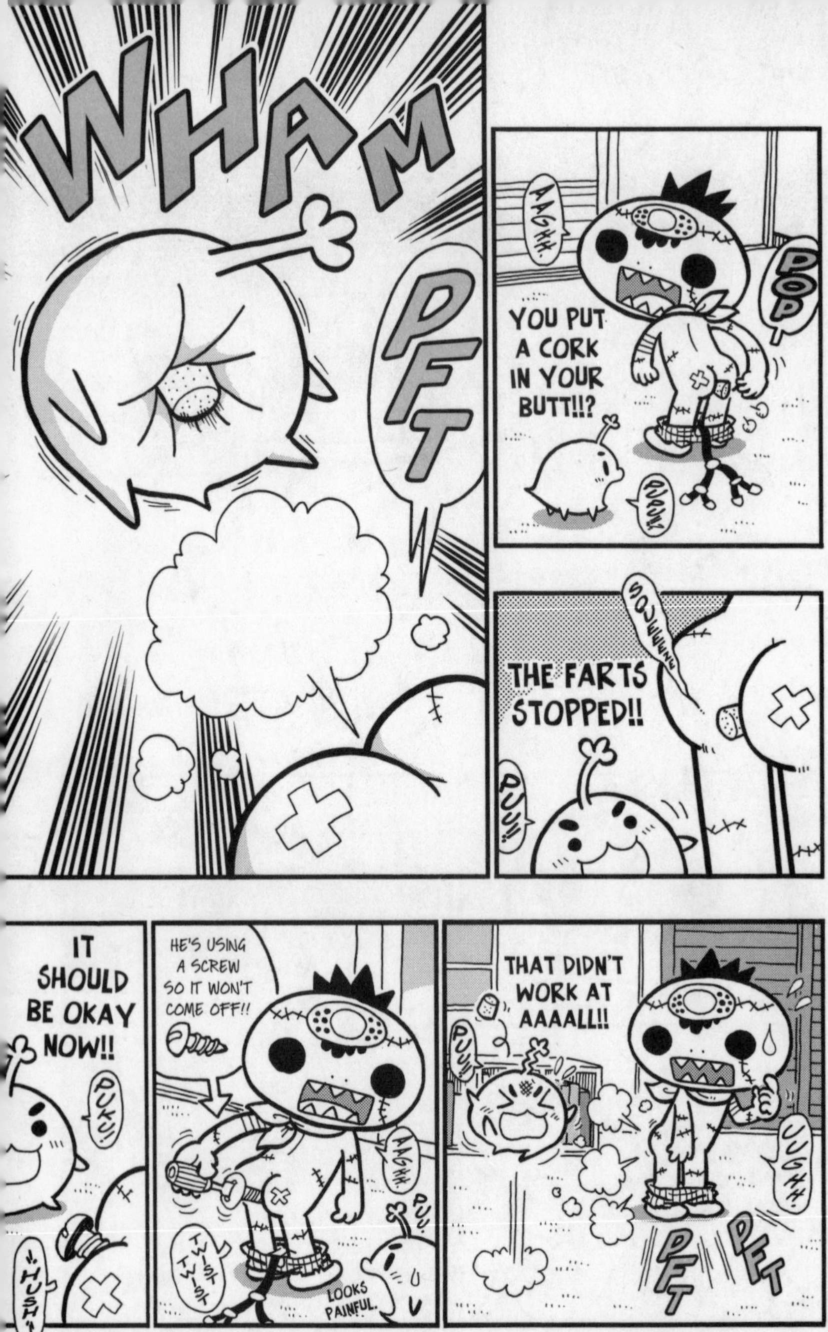
AAGHH.
POP
YOU PUT A CORK IN YOUR BUTT!!?
QUACK!?
SQUEEEEE
THE FARTS STOPPED!!
PUU!!
WHAM
PFT
THAT DIDN'T WORK AT AAAALL!!
PUU
UGHH.
PFT
PFT
HE'S USING A SCREW SO IT WON'T COME OFF!!
AAGHH.
PUU
TWIST TWIST
LOOKS PAINFUL.
IT SHOULD BE OKAY NOW!!
PUKU!
HUSH

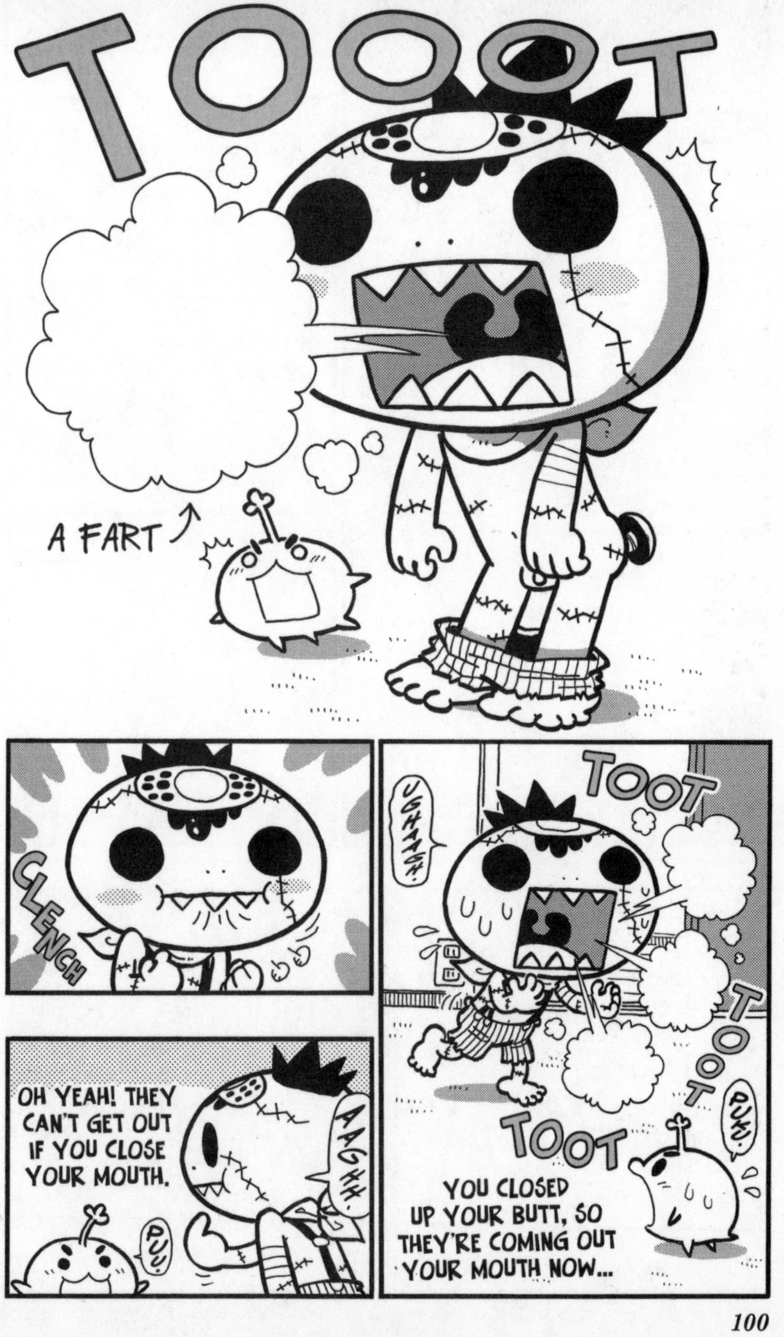
TOOOT
A FART
UGHAAAGH!
TOOT
TOOT
TOOT
PUU...
YOU CLOSED UP YOUR BUTT, SO THEY'RE COMING OUT YOUR MOUTH NOW...
CLENCH
AAGHH!
OH YEAH! THEY CAN'T GET OUT IF YOU CLOSE YOUR MOUTH.
PUU.

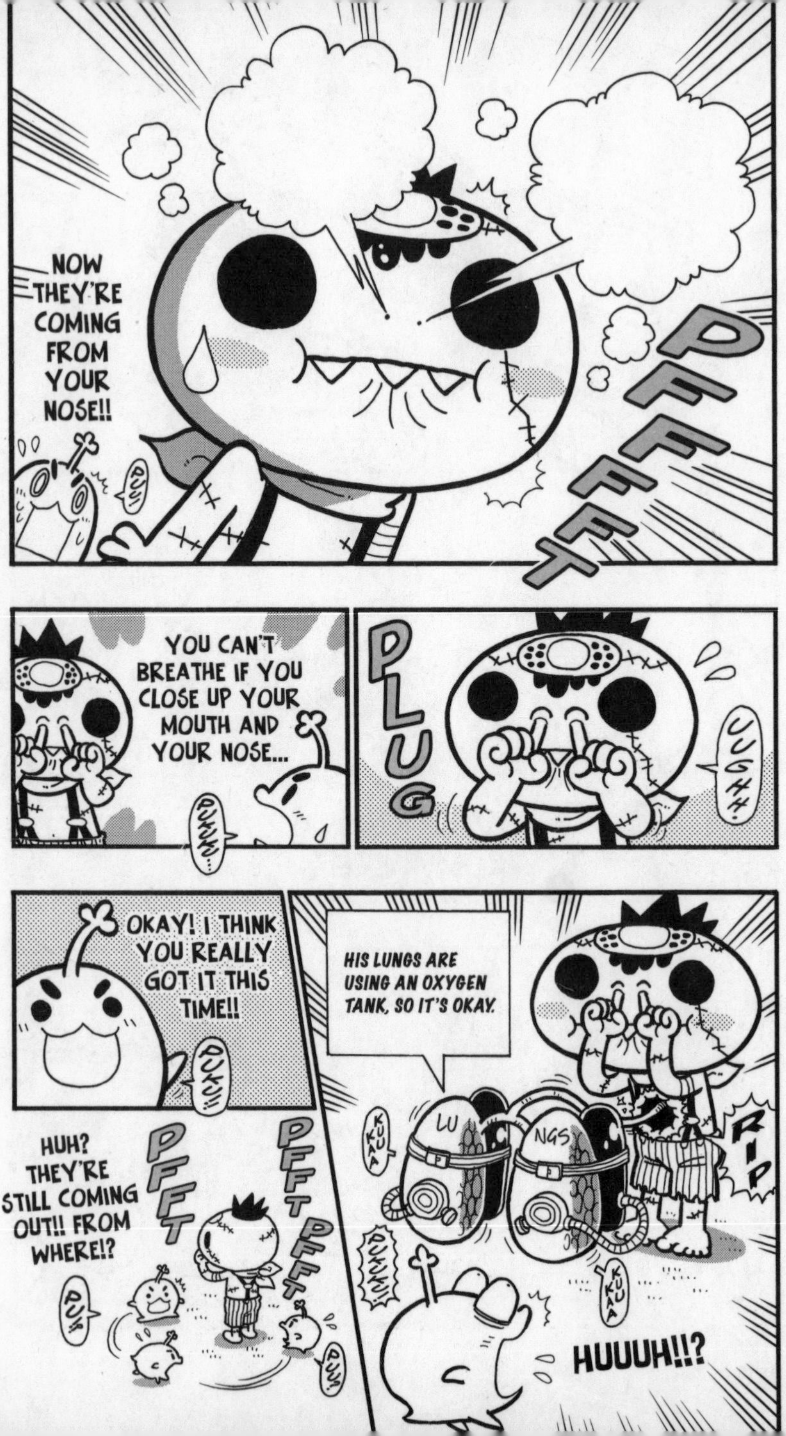
NOW THEY'RE COMING FROM YOUR NOSE!!
PFFFFT
PLUG
UGHH...
YOU CAN'T BREATHE IF YOU CLOSE UP YOUR MOUTH AND YOUR NOSE...
HIS LUNGS ARE USING AN OXYGEN TANK, SO IT'S OKAY.
RIP
KUUA
LU
NGS
KUUA
HUUUH!!?
OKAY! I THINK YOU REALLY GOT IT THIS TIME!!
HUH? THEY'RE STILL COMING OUT!! FROM WHERE!?
PFFT
PFFT
PFFT

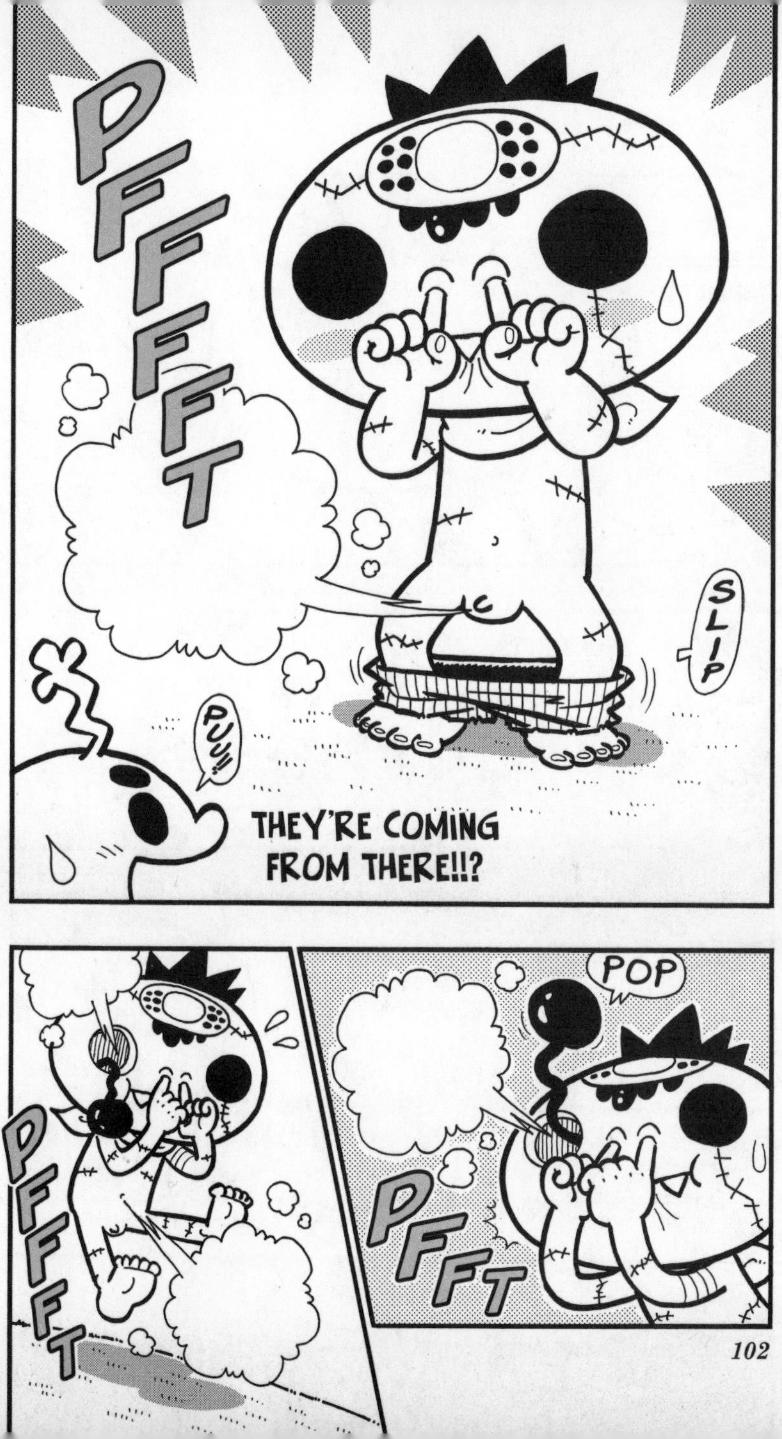
PFFFFT
SLIP
PUU!!
THEY'RE COMING FROM THERE!!?
POP
PFFT
PFFFFT

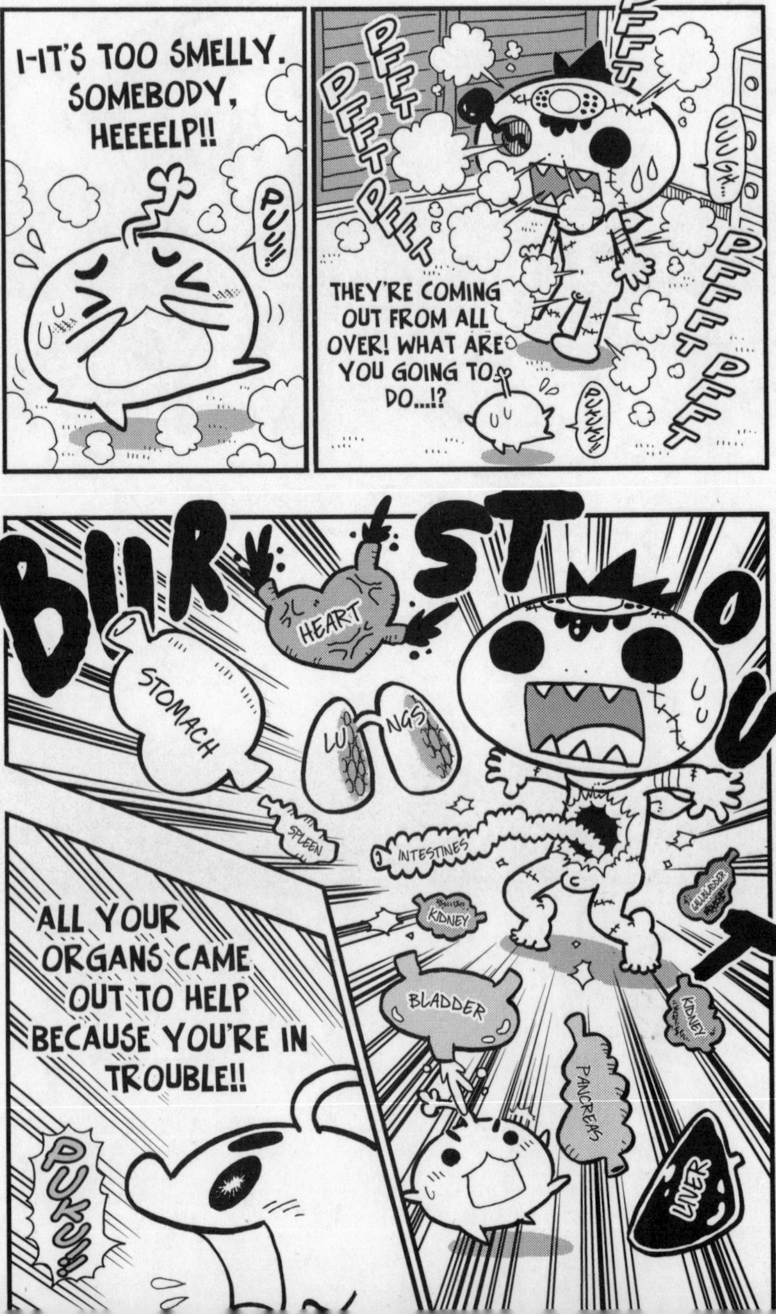
PFFT
UUUGH...
PFFT
PFFFT PFFFFT
PFFFFT PFFFT
THEY'RE COMING OUT FROM ALL OVER! WHAT ARE YOU GOING TO DO...!?
PUKUKU!!
I-IT'S TOO SMELLY. SOMEBODY, HEEEELP!!
PUUU!!
BURST OUT
HEART
STOMACH
LUNGS
SPLEEN
INTESTINES
GALLBLADDER
KIDNEY
BLADDER
KIDNEY
PANCREAS
LIVER
ALL YOUR ORGANS CAME OUT TO HELP BECAUSE YOU'RE IN TROUBLE!!
PUKU!!

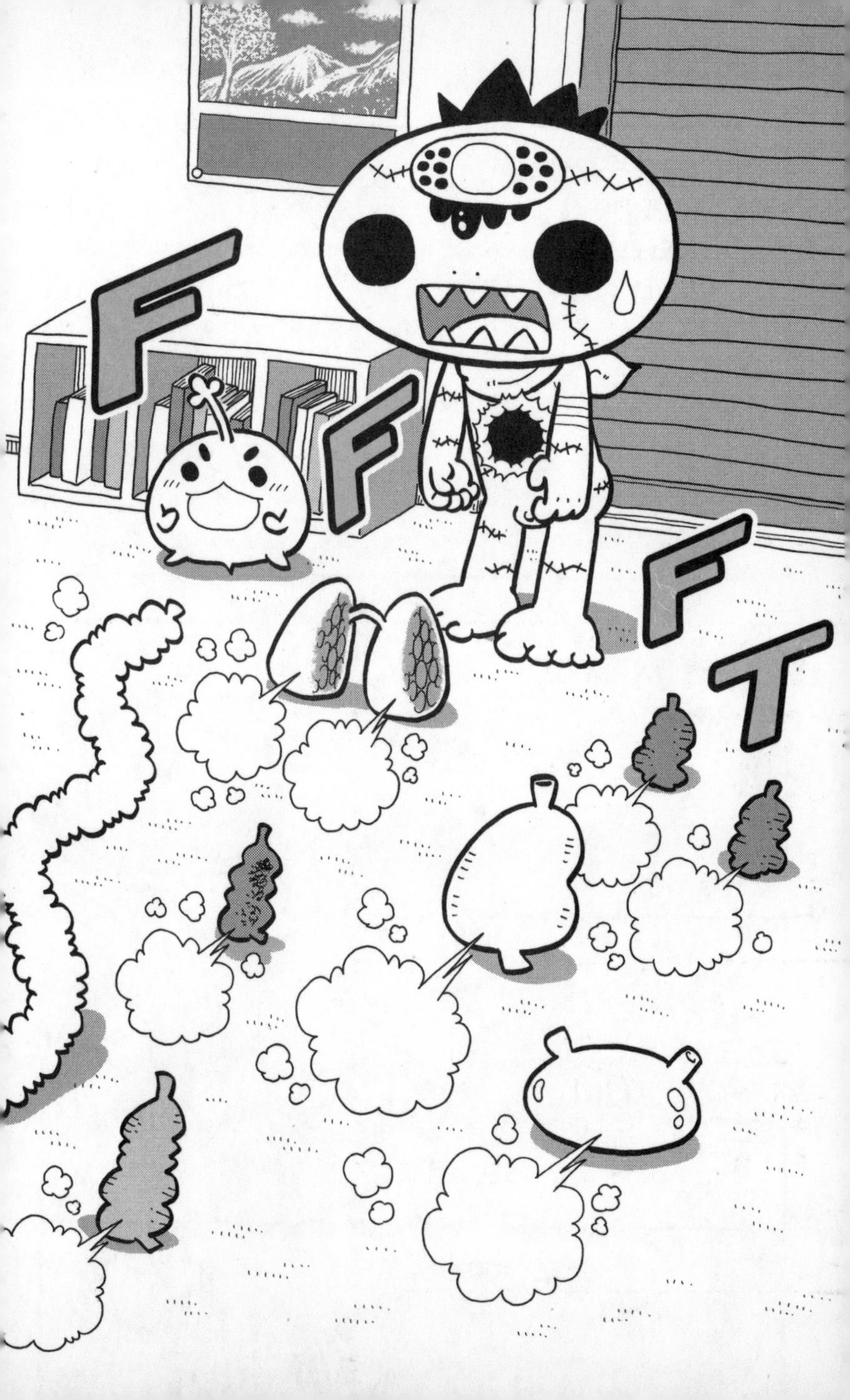
FFFT

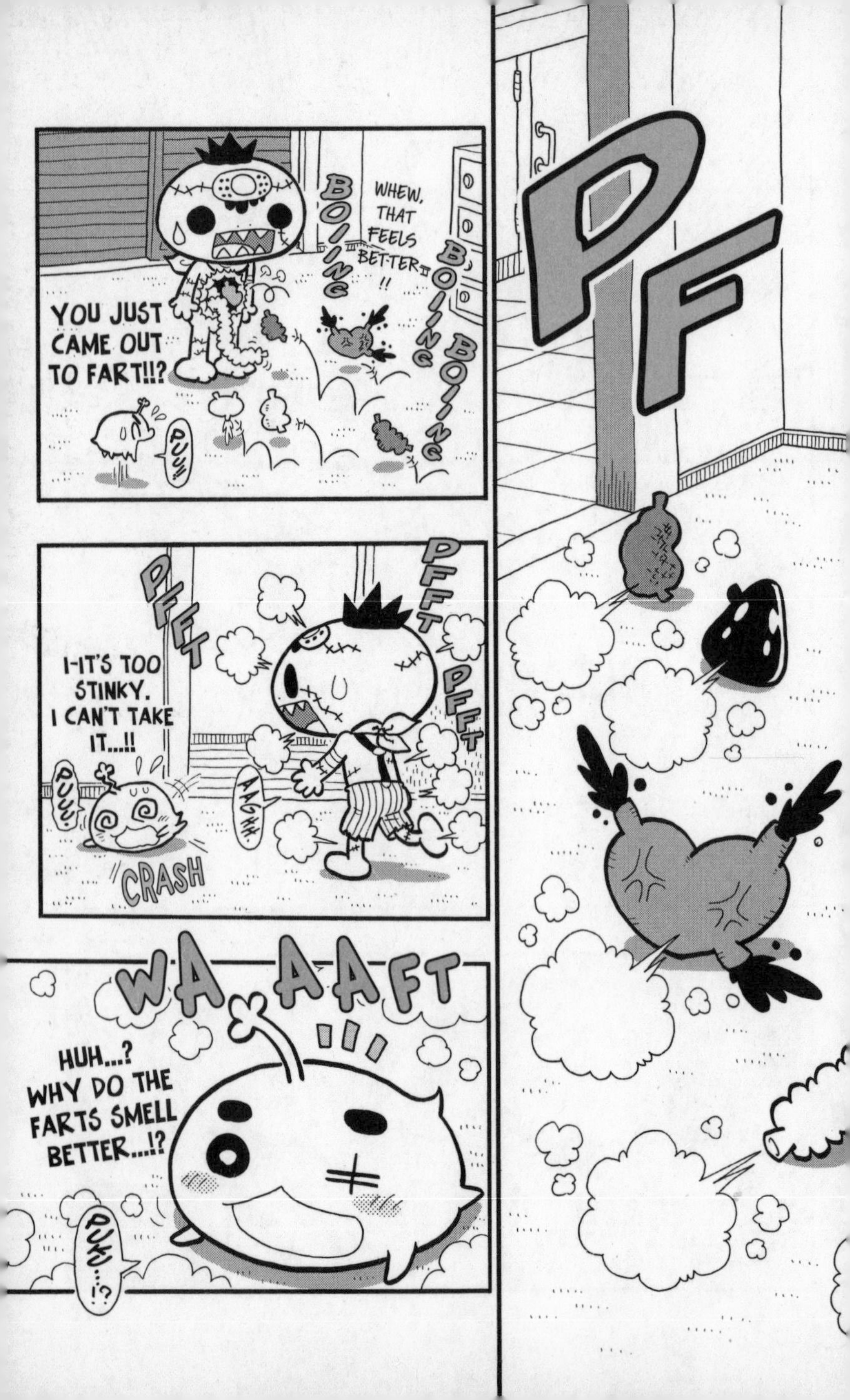
PF
BOING BOING
WHEW, THAT FEELS BETTER!!
BOING
YOU JUST CAME OUT TO FART!!?
PUU!!
PFFT
PFFT
PFFT
I-IT'S TOO STINKY. I CAN'T TAKE IT...!!
AAGHH
PUU...
CRASH
WAAAFT
HUH...? WHY DO THE FARTS SMELL BETTER...!?
PUU...!?

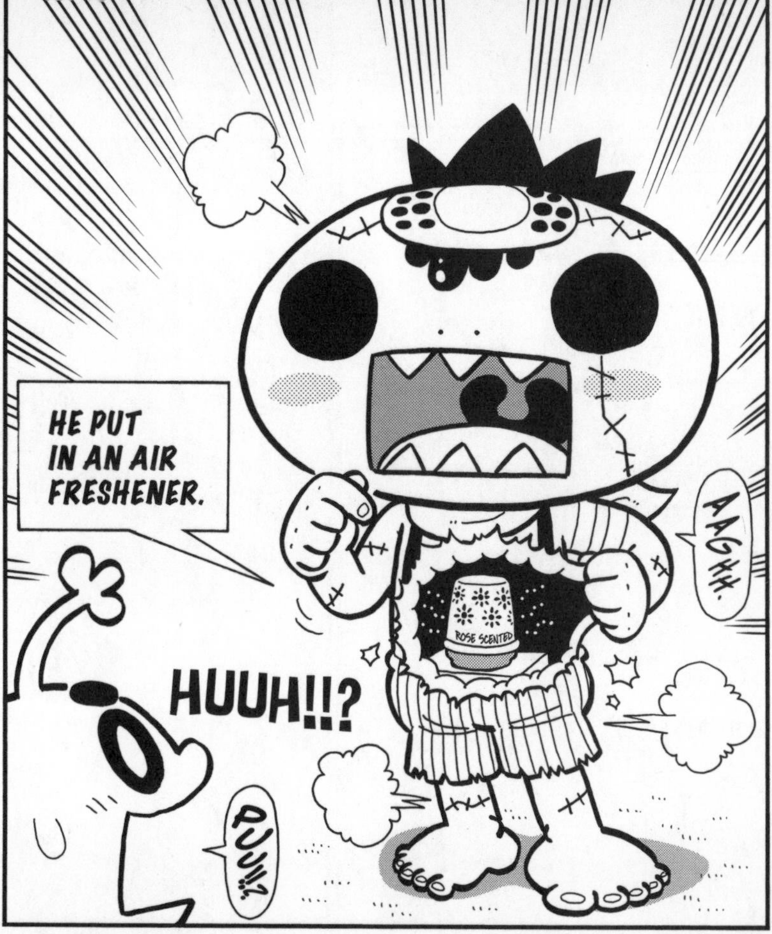
AAGHH.
HE PUT IN AN AIR FRESHENER.
ROSE SCENTED
HUUH!!?
PUU!!?

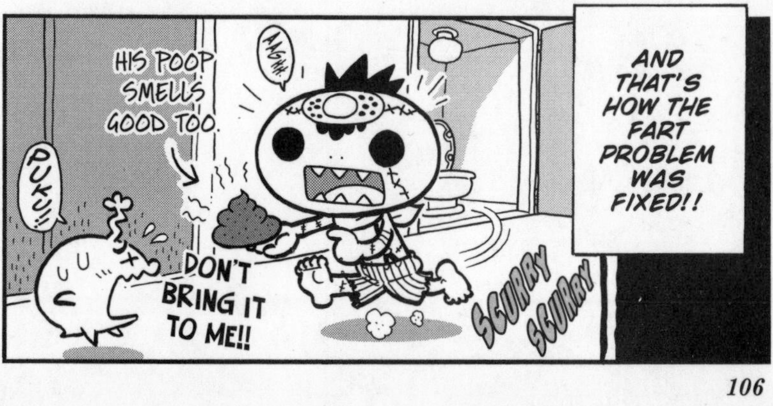
AND THAT'S HOW THE FART PROBLEM WAS FIXED!!
SCURRY SCURRY
AAGHH
HIS POOP SMELLS GOOD TOO.
PUKU!!
DON'T BRING IT TO ME!!

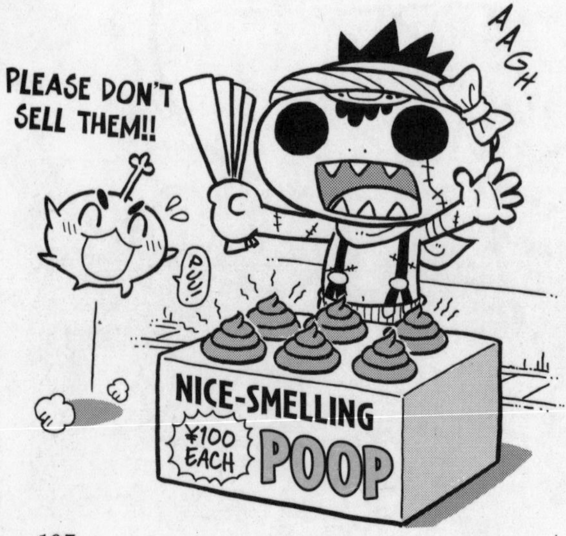
AAGH.
PLEASE DON'T SELL THEM!!
PUU!
NICE-SMELLING
¥100 EACH
POOP

LET'Z GO ON A ZUMMER GRAVEYARD ADVENTURE!

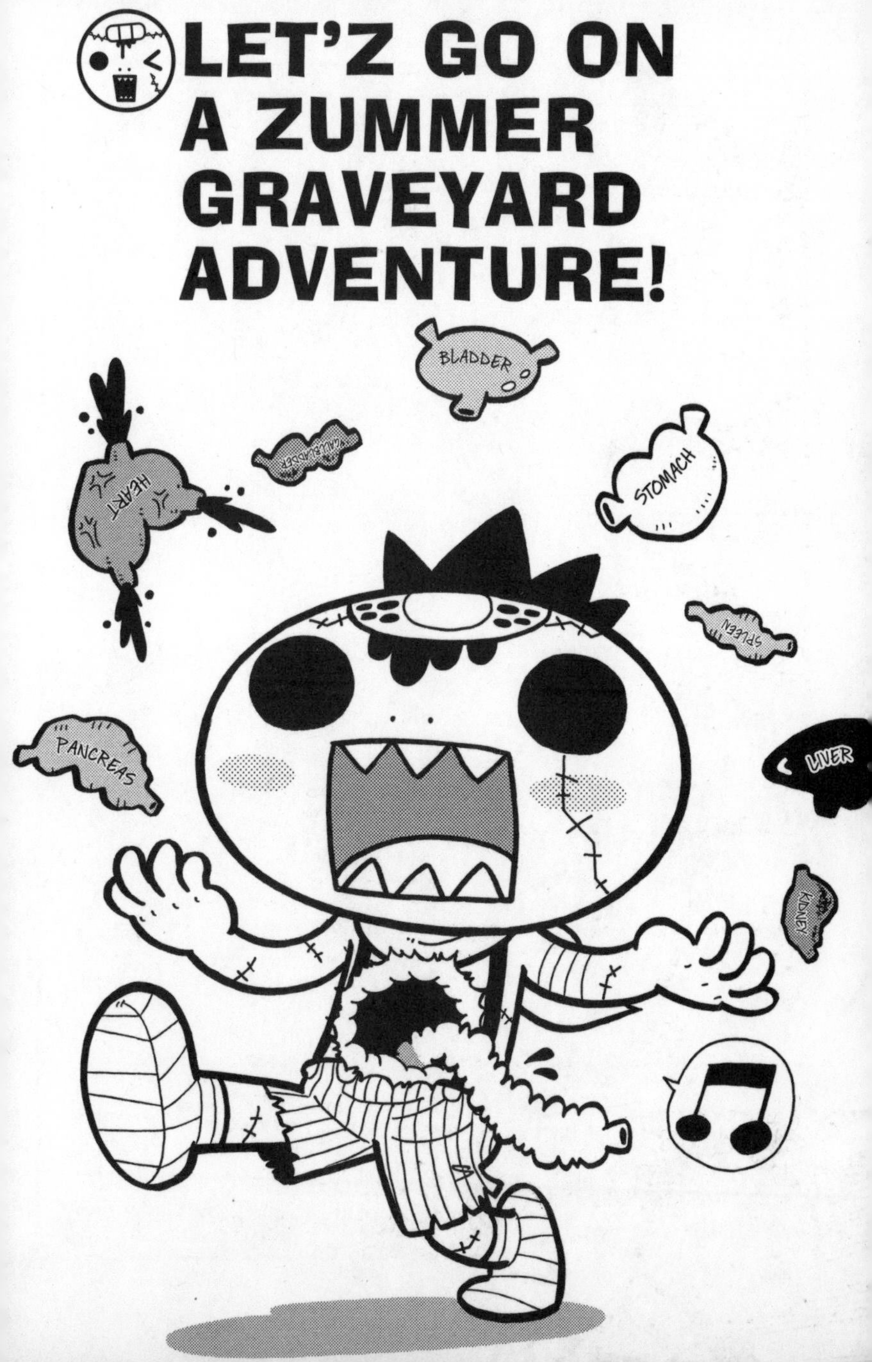
BLADDER
GALLBLADDER
HEART
STOMACH
SPLEEN
PANCREAS
LIVER
KIDNEY

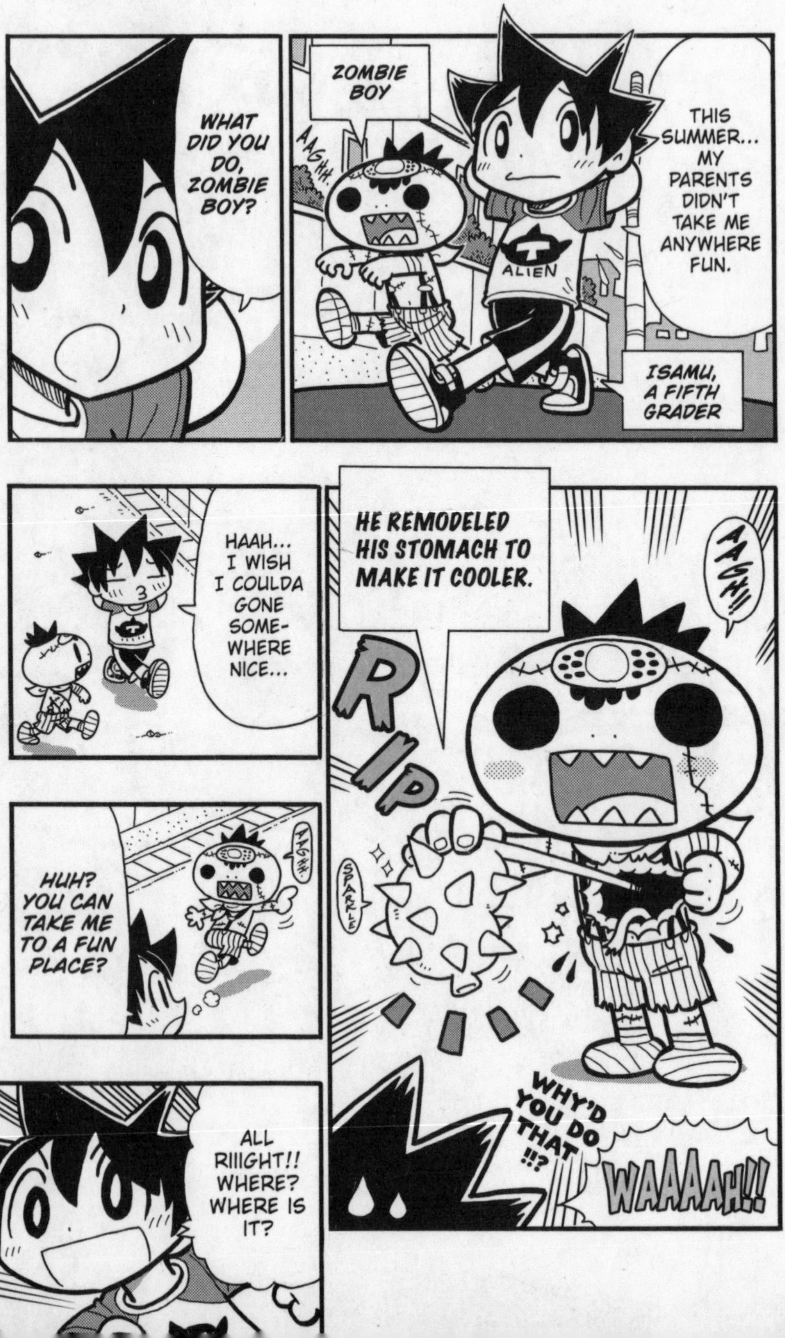
ZOMBIE BOY
AAGHH.
THIS SUMMER... MY PARENTS DIDN'T TAKE ME ANYWHERE FUN.
ISAMU, A FIFTH GRADER
WHAT DID YOU DO, ZOMBIE BOY?
HE REMODELED HIS STOMACH TO MAKE IT COOLER.
AAGH!!
RIP
SPARKLE
WHY'D YOU DO THAT!!?
WAAAAH!!
HAAH... I WISH I COULDA GONE SOME-WHERE NICE...
AAGHH.
HUH? YOU CAN TAKE ME TO A FUN PLACE?
ALL RIIIGHT!! WHERE? WHERE IS IT?

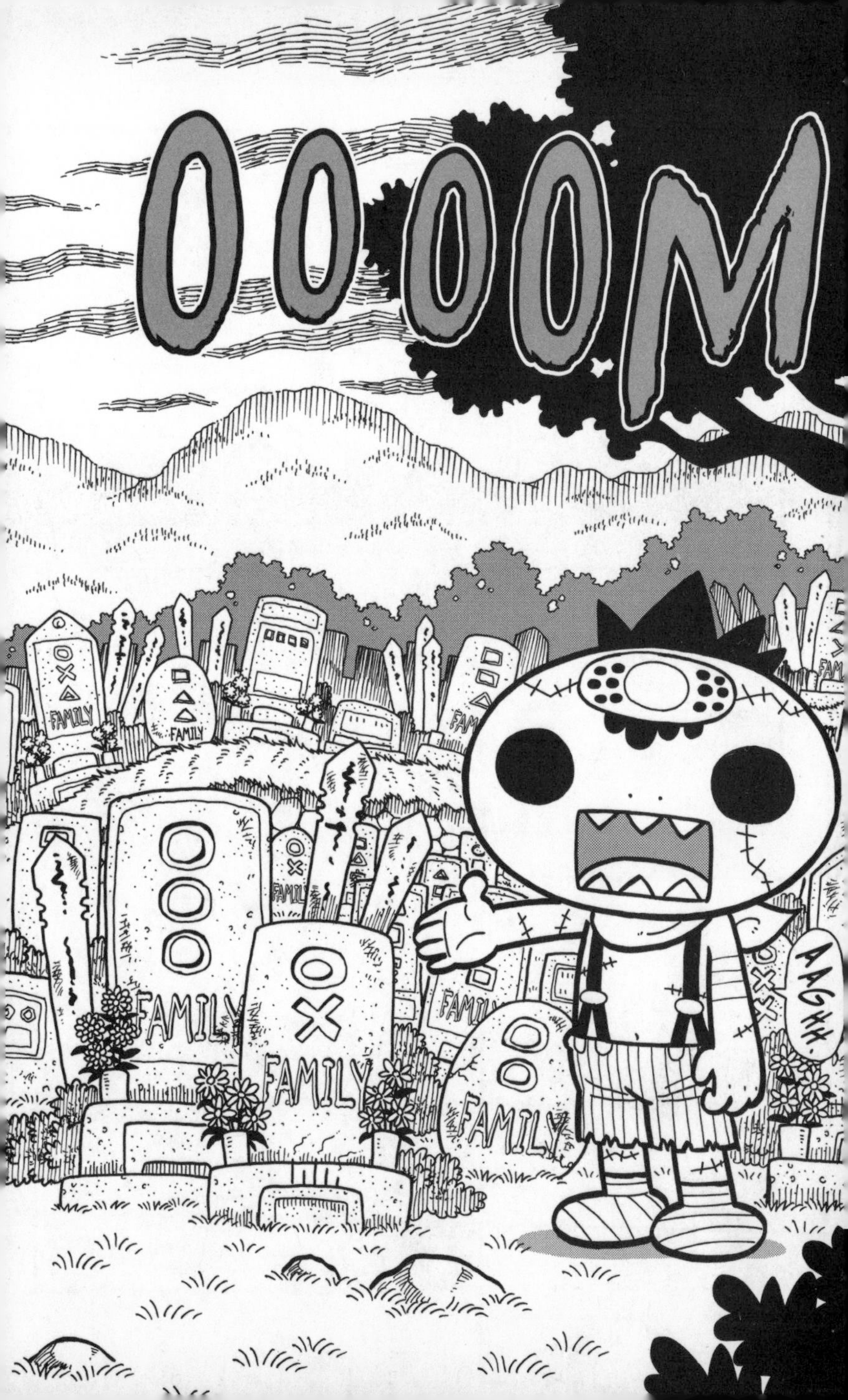
OOOOM
AAGHH.
FAMILY

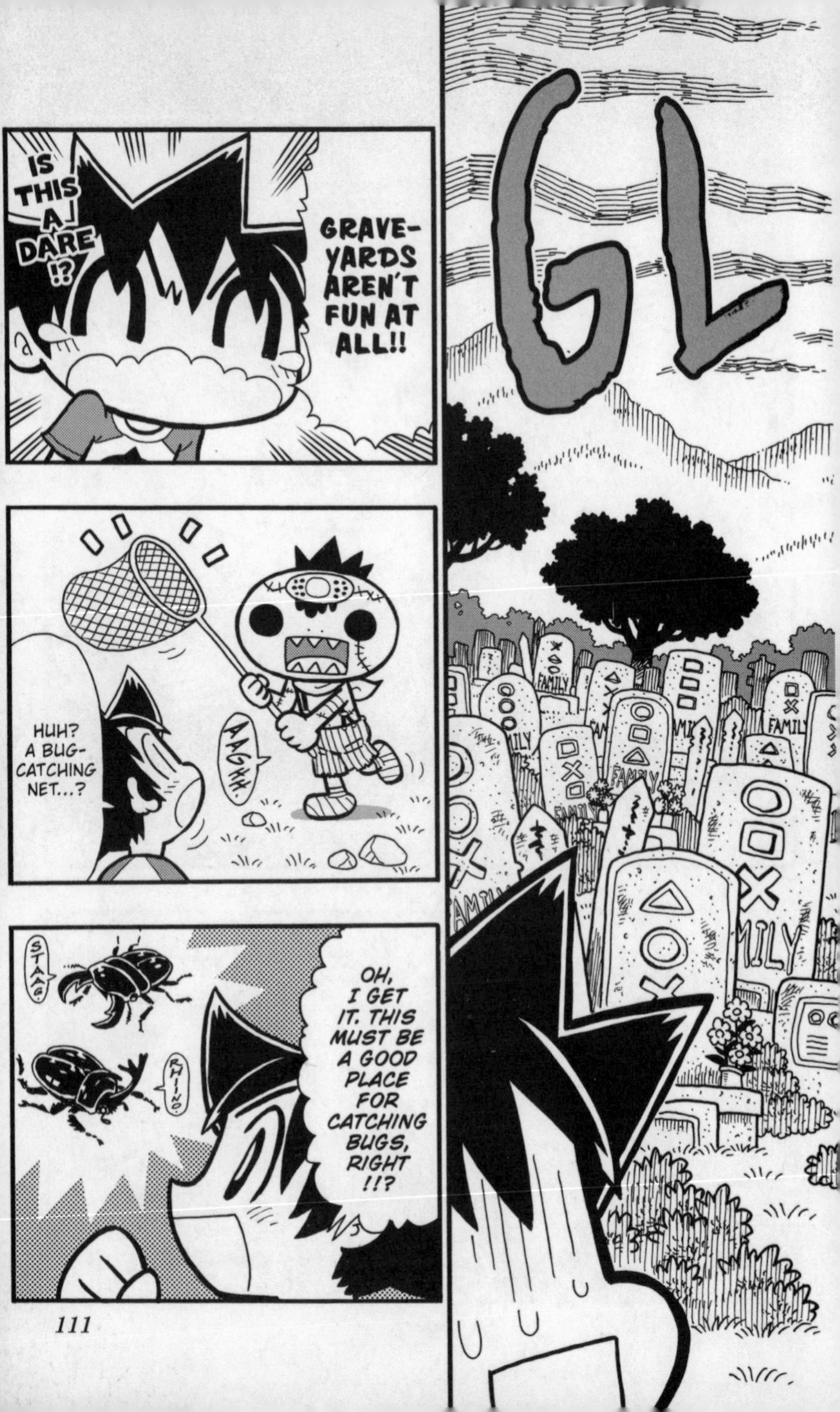
GL
GRAVE-YARDS AREN'T FUN AT ALL!!
IS THIS A DARE!?
AAGHH.
HUH? A BUG-CATCHING NET...?
OH, I GET IT. THIS MUST BE A GOOD PLACE FOR CATCHING BUGS, RIGHT!!?
STAAG.
RHINO.

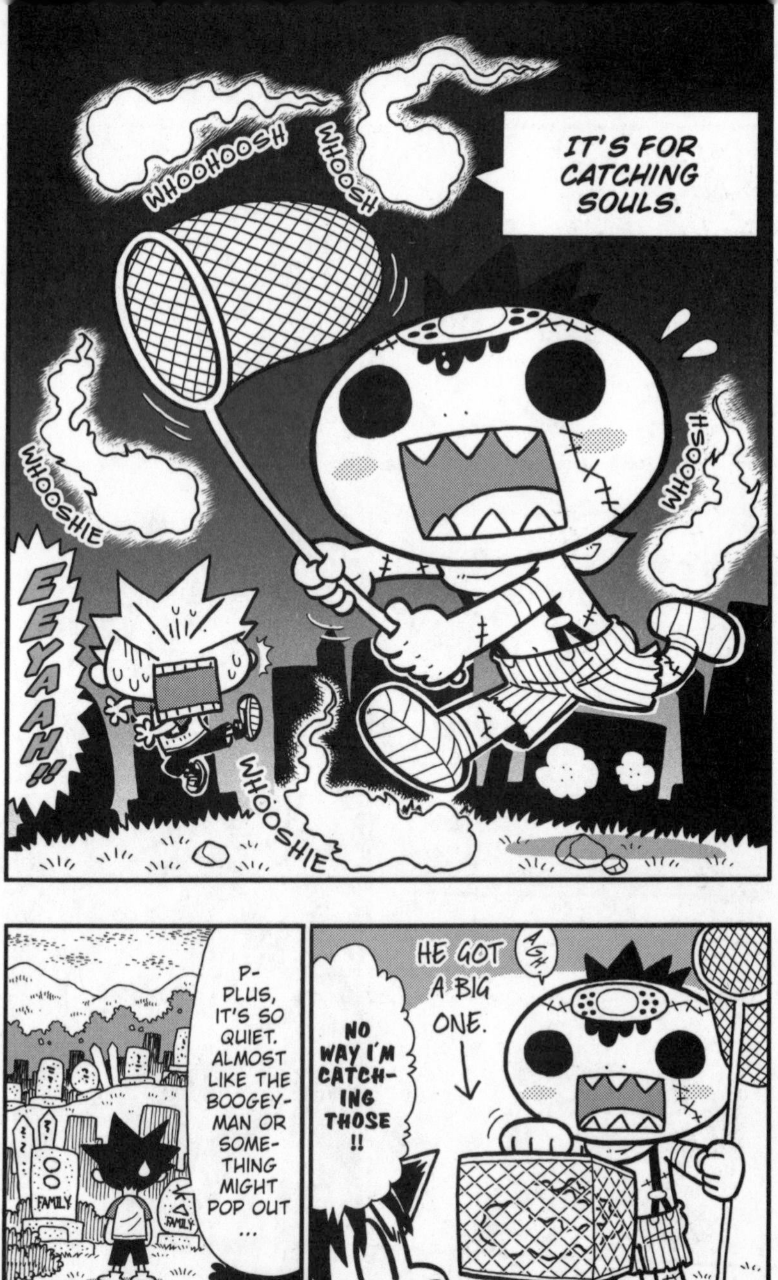
IT'S FOR CATCHING SOULS.
WHOOSH
WHOOHOOSH
WHOOSH
WHOOSHIE
EEYAAAH!!
WHOOSHIE
HE GOT A BIG ONE.
AGH
NO WAY I'M CATCHING THOSE!!
P-PLUS, IT'S SO QUIET. ALMOST LIKE THE BOOGEYMAN OR SOMETHING MIGHT POP OUT...
FAMILY
FAMILY

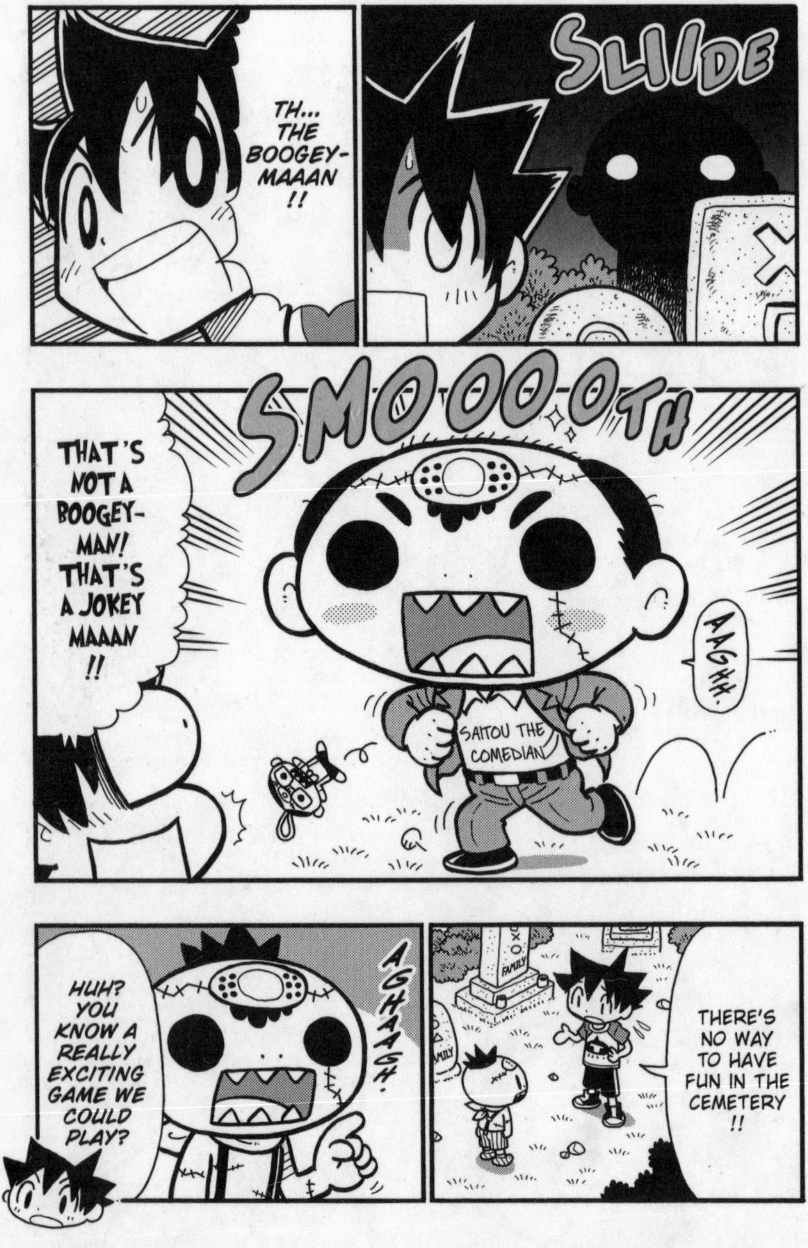
SLIIDE
TH... THE BOOGEY-MAAAN !!
SMOOOOTH
AAGHH.
SAITOU THE COMEDIAN
THAT'S NOT A BOOGEY-MAN! THAT'S A JOKEY MAAAN !!
THERE'S NO WAY TO HAVE FUN IN THE CEMETERY !!
AGHAAAGH.
HUH? YOU KNOW A REALLY EXCITING GAME WE COULD PLAY?

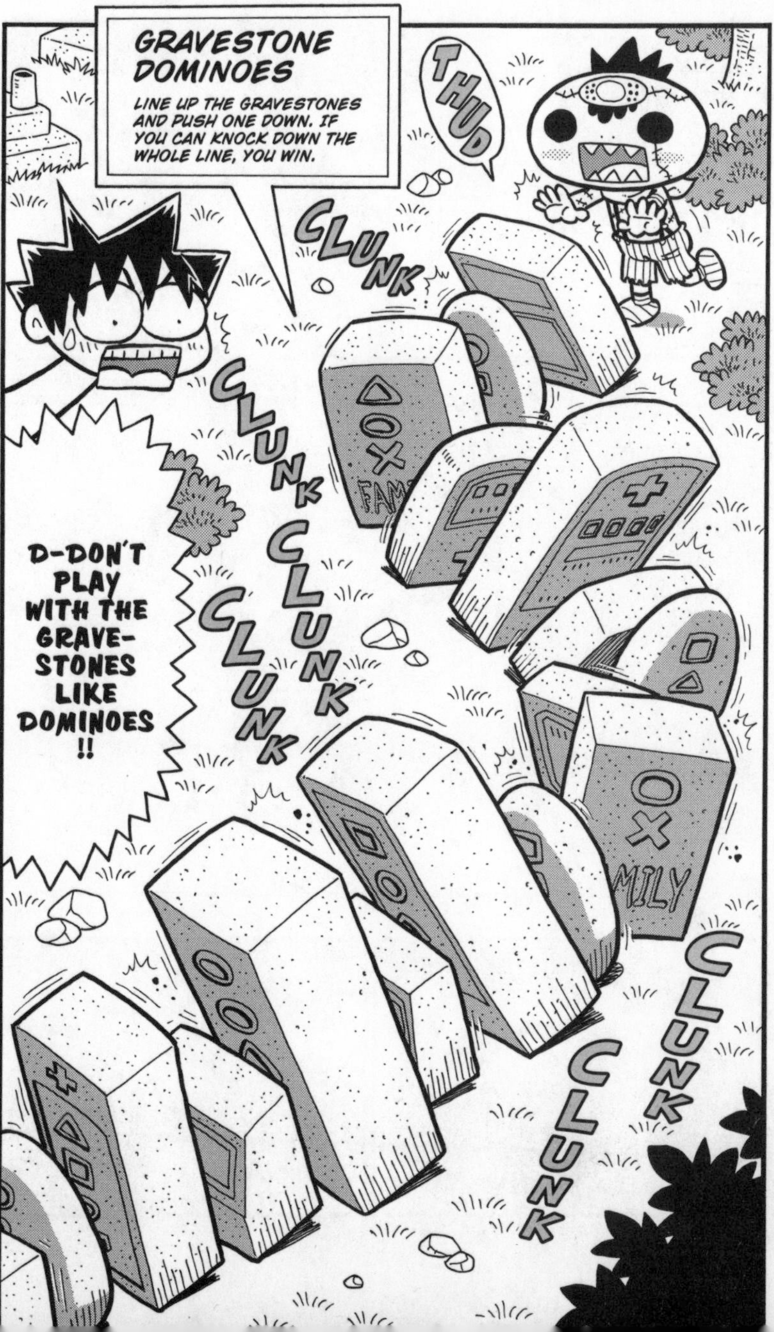
THUD
GRAVESTONE DOMINOES
LINE UP THE GRAVESTONES AND PUSH ONE DOWN. IF YOU CAN KNOCK DOWN THE WHOLE LINE, YOU WIN.
CLUNK
CLUNK
CLUNK
CLUNK
D-DON'T PLAY WITH THE GRAVE-STONES LIKE DOMINOES!!
CLUNK
CLUNK

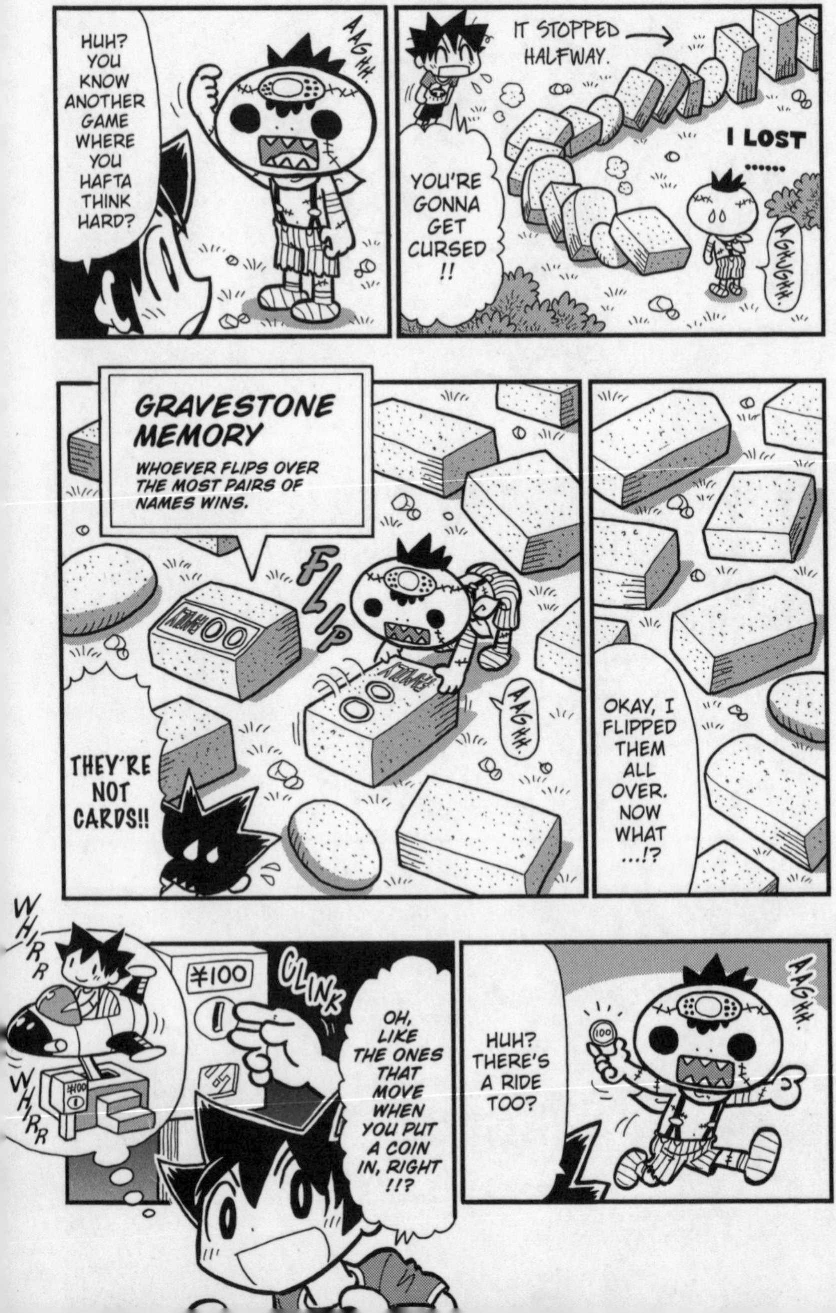
IT STOPPED HALFWAY.
YOU'RE GONNA GET CURSED!!
I LOST ......
AGUGHH.
AAGHH.
HUH? YOU KNOW ANOTHER GAME WHERE YOU HAFTA THINK HARD?
OKAY, I FLIPPED THEM ALL OVER. NOW WHAT ...!?
GRAVESTONE MEMORY
WHOEVER FLIPS OVER THE MOST PAIRS OF NAMES WINS.
FLIP
AAGHH.
THEY'RE NOT CARDS!!
AAGHH.
HUH? THERE'S A RIDE TOO?
¥100
CLINK
OH, LIKE THE ONES THAT MOVE WHEN YOU PUT A COIN IN, RIGHT!!?
WHIRR
WHIRR

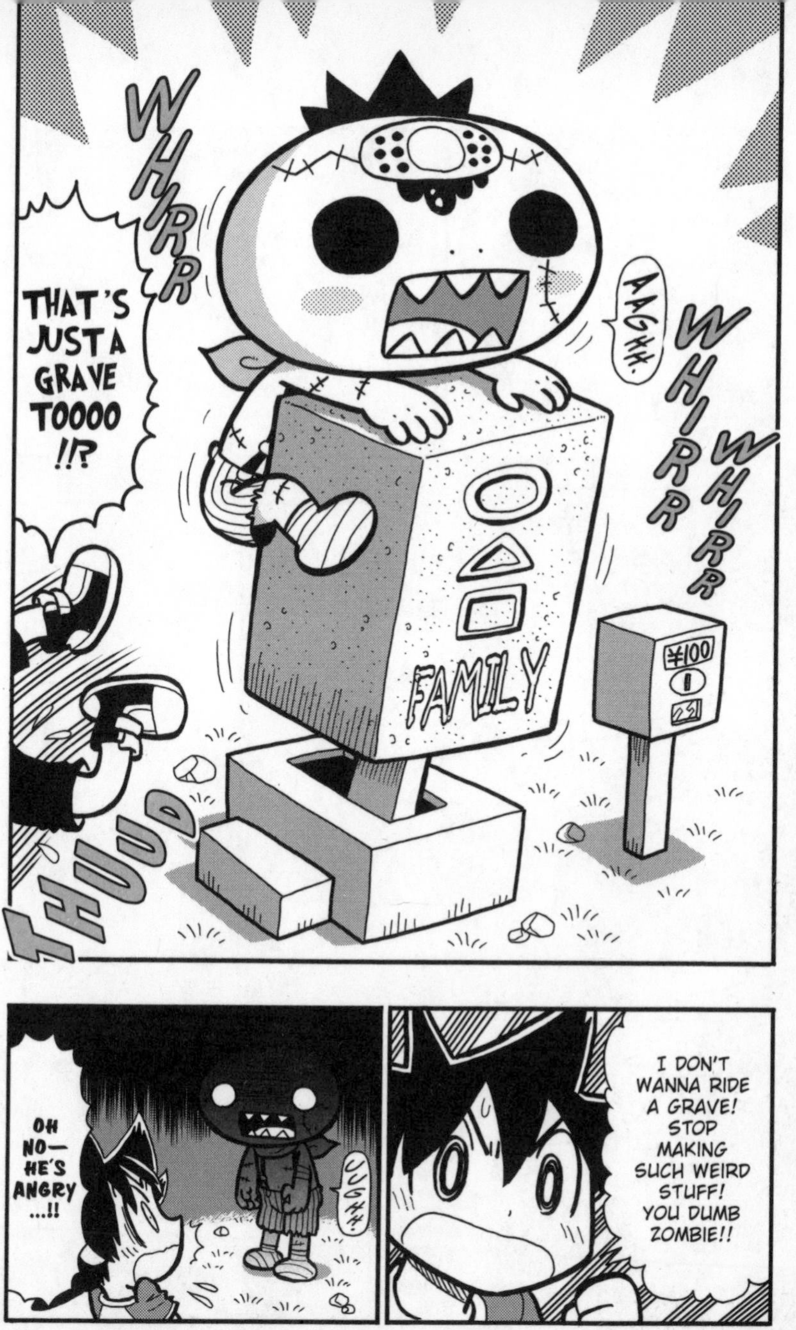
WHIRR
AAGHH.
WHIRR
WHIRR
FAMILY
¥100
WHIRR
THAT'S JUST A GRAVE TOOOO!!?
THUUD
I DON'T WANNA RIDE A GRAVE! STOP MAKING SUCH WEIRD STUFF! YOU DUMB ZOMBIE!!
UGHH.
OH NO—HE'S ANGRY ...!!

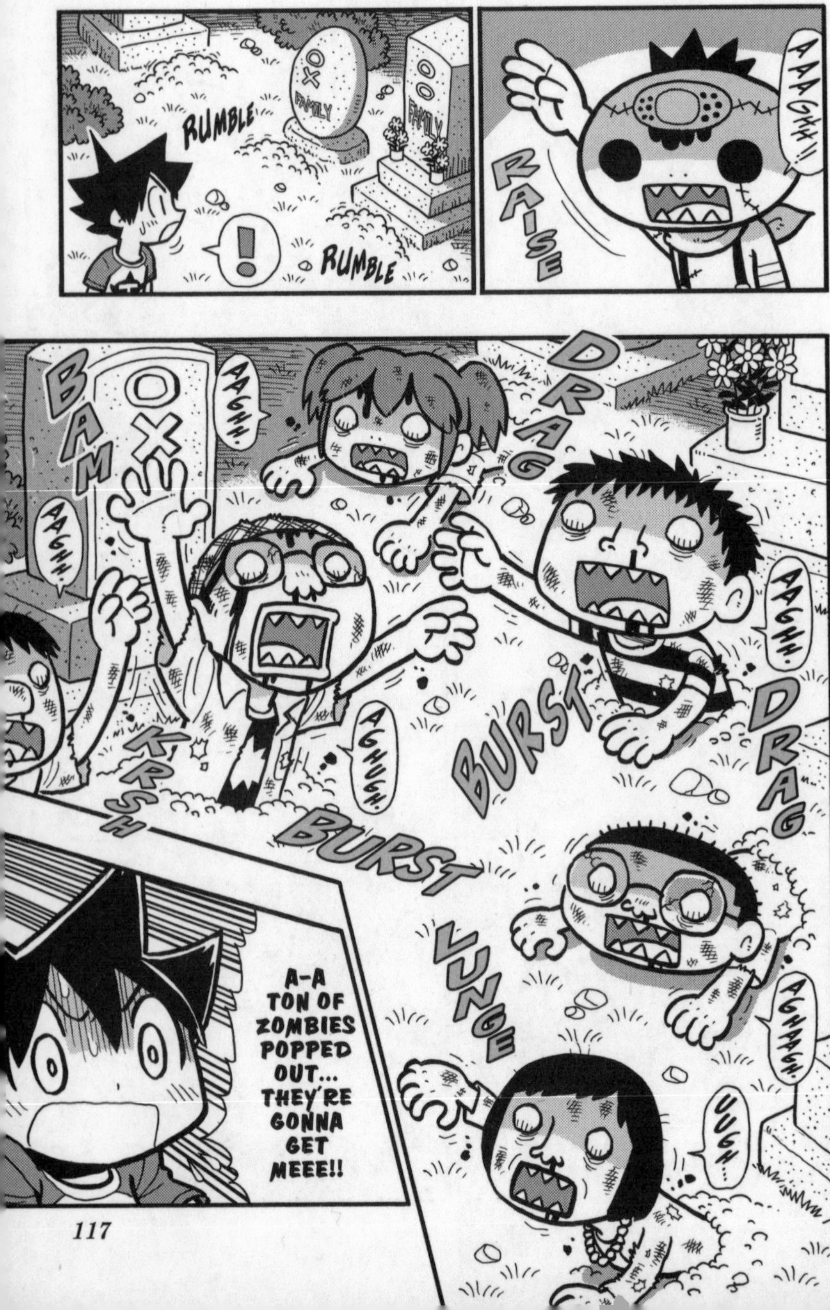
AAAGHH!!
RAISE
RUMBLE
!
RUMBLE
DRAG
AAGHH.
DRAG
BURST
AAGHH.
BAM
AAGHH.
AGHUGH.
KRSH
BURST
AGHAAGH.
VUNGE
UUGH...
A-A TON OF ZOMBIES POPPED OUT... THEY'RE GONNA GET MEEE!!

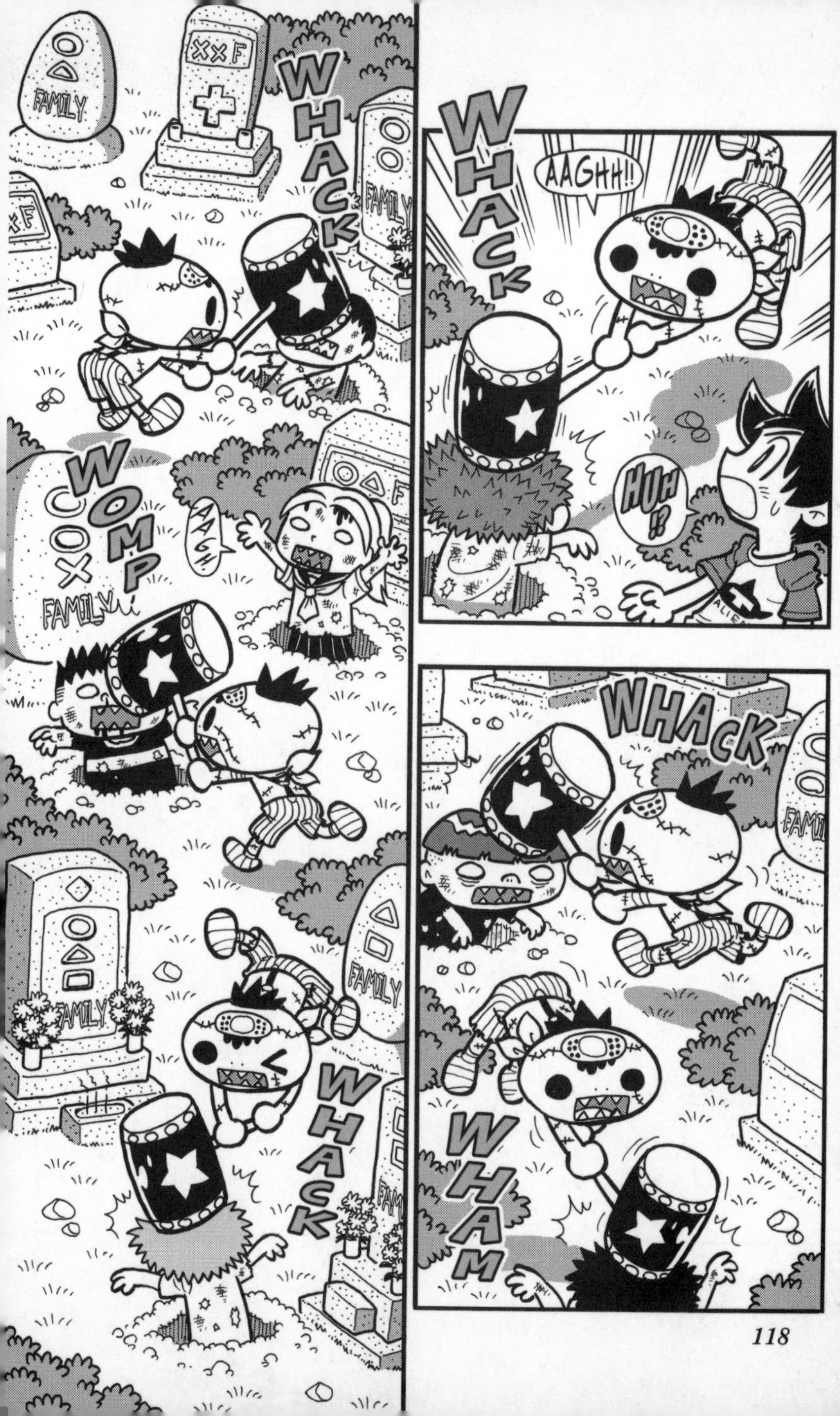
WHACK
AAGHH!!
HUH !?
WHACK
WHAM
WHACK
AAGH
WOMP
WHACK

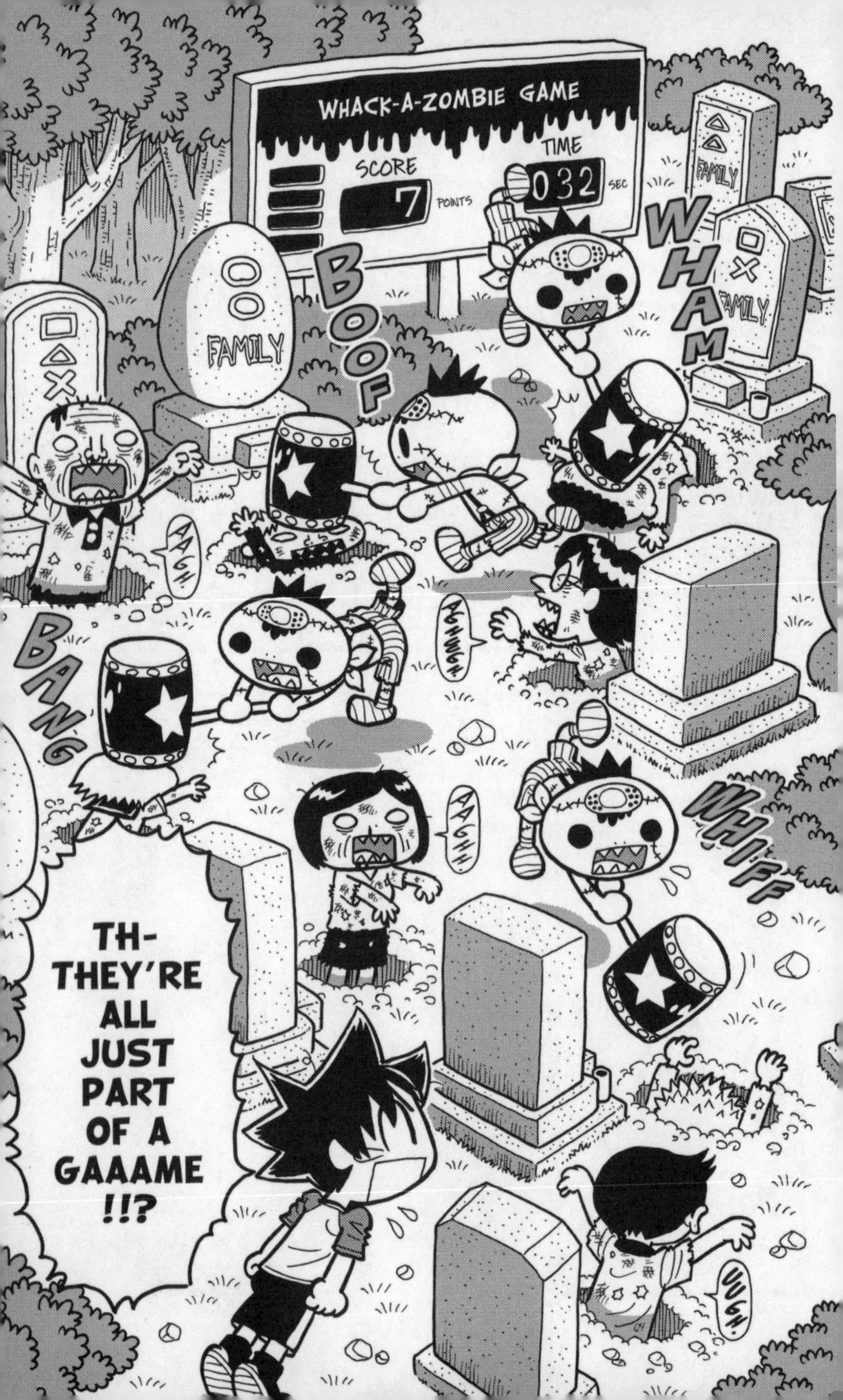
WHACK-A-ZOMBIE GAME
SCORE
7 POINTS
TIME
032 SEC
FAMILY
FAMILY
FAMILY
FAMILY
WHAM
BOOF
AAGH.
AGHHGH.
BANG
WHIFF
AAGHH.
TH-THEY'RE ALL JUST PART OF A GAAAME !!?
UUGH.

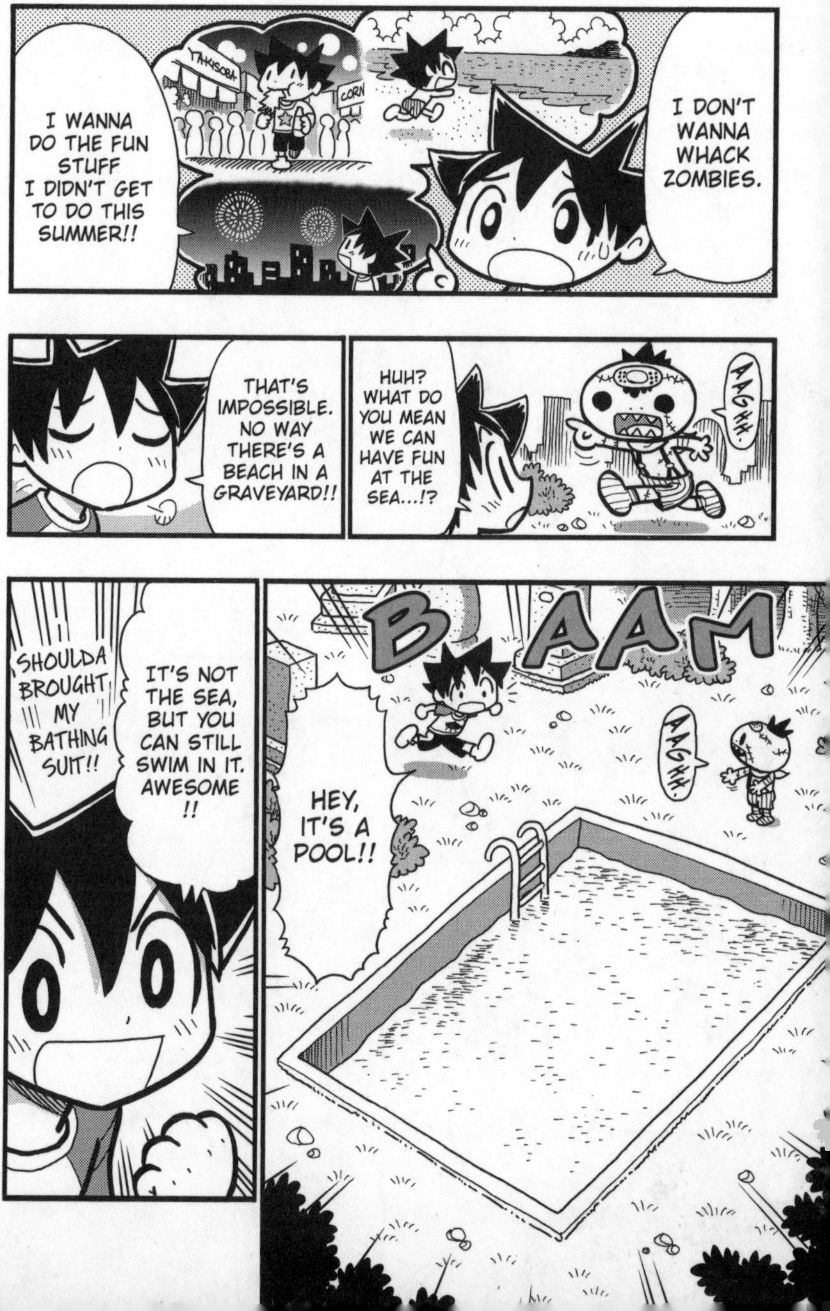
I DON'T WANNA WHACK ZOMBIES.
YAKISOBA
CORN
I WANNA DO THE FUN STUFF I DIDN'T GET TO DO THIS SUMMER!!
AAGHH.
HUH? WHAT DO YOU MEAN WE CAN HAVE FUN AT THE SEA...!?
THAT'S IMPOSSIBLE. NO WAY THERE'S A BEACH IN A GRAVEYARD!!
BAAM
AAGHH.
HEY, IT'S A POOL!!
IT'S NOT THE SEA, BUT YOU CAN STILL SWIM IN IT. AWESOME!!
SHOULDA BROUGHT MY BATHING SUIT!!

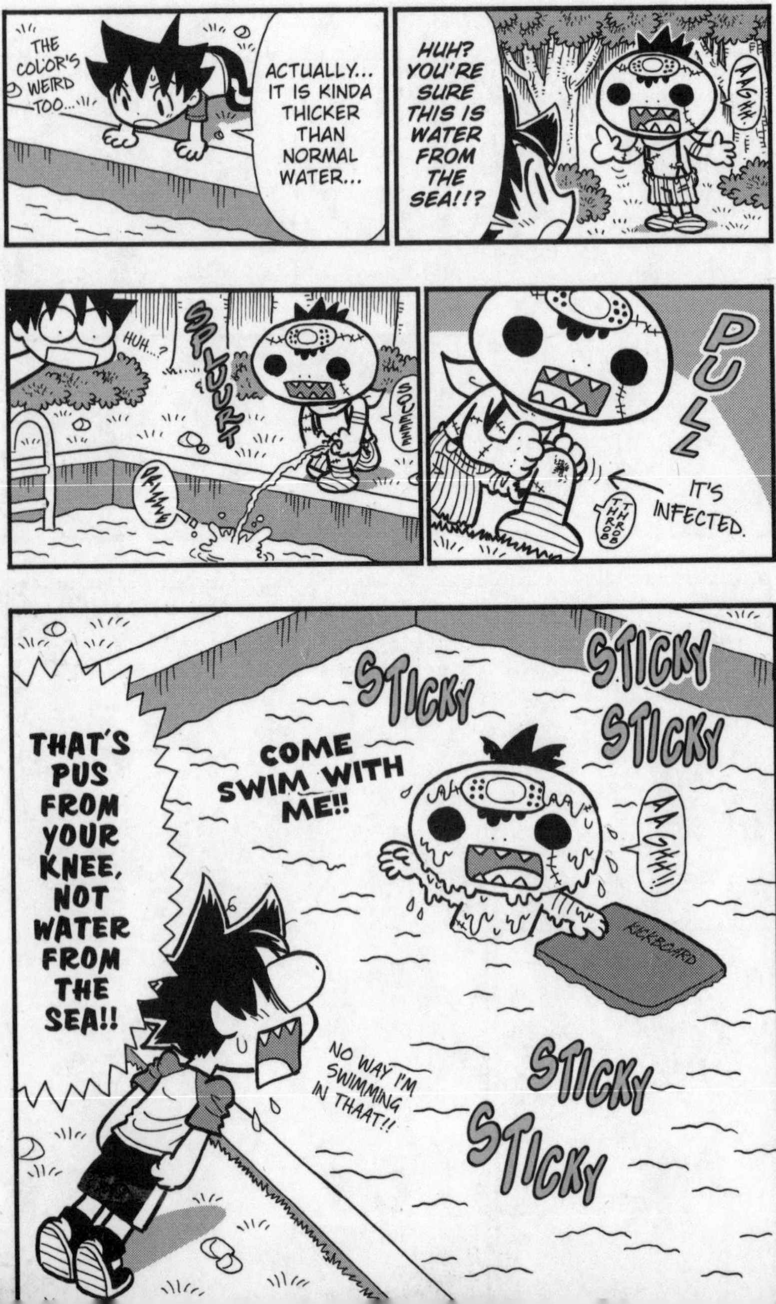
HUH? YOU'RE SURE THIS IS WATER FROM THE SEA!!?
AAGHH.
ACTUALLY... IT IS KINDA THICKER THAN NORMAL WATER...
THE COLOR'S WEIRD TOO...
PULL
IT'S INFECTED.
THROB THROB
SQUEEZE
SPLURT
HUH...?
STICKY
STICKY
STICKY
AAGHH!!
COME SWIM WITH ME!!
KICKBOARD
THAT'S PUS FROM YOUR KNEE, NOT WATER FROM THE SEA!!
NO WAY I'M SWIMMING IN THAAT!!
STICKY
STICKY

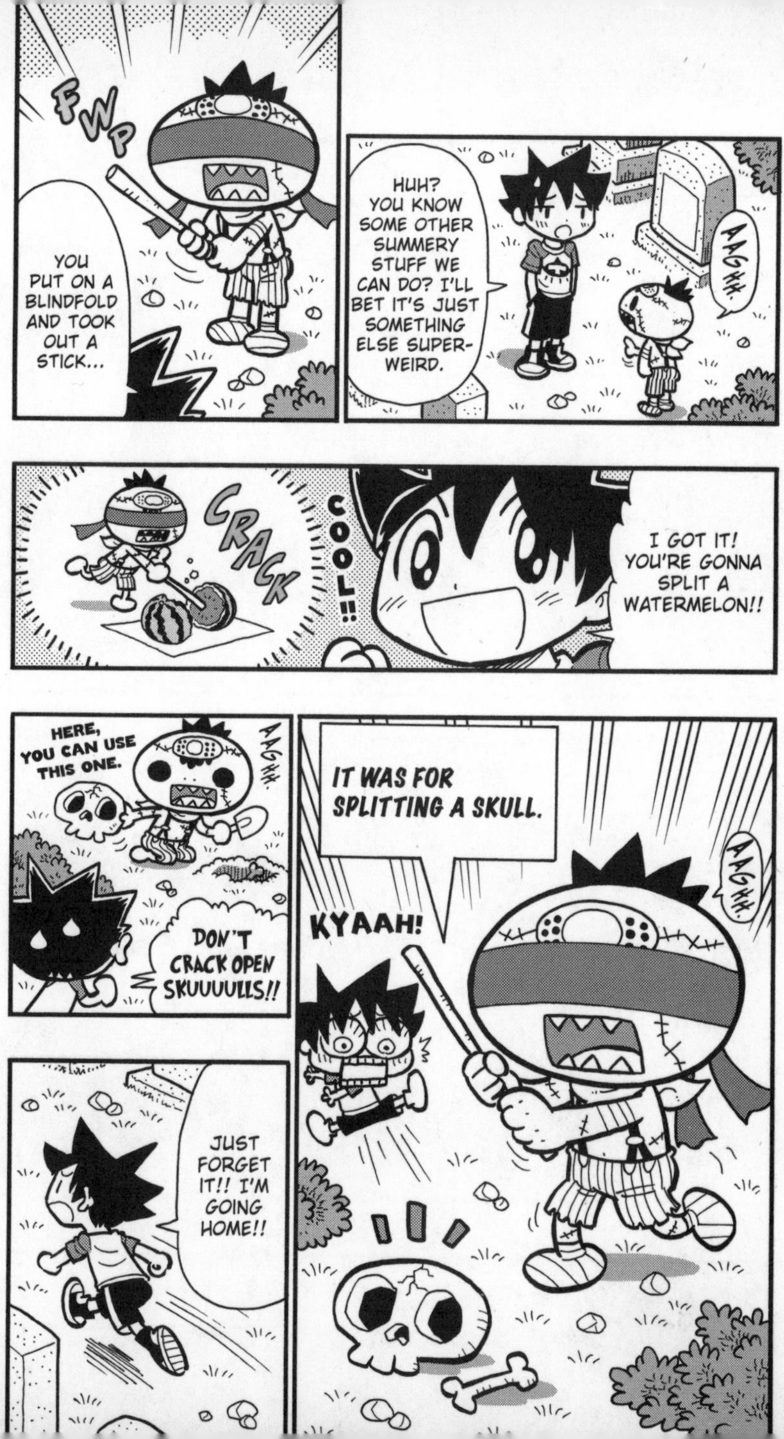
HUH? YOU KNOW SOME OTHER SUMMERY STUFF WE CAN DO? I'LL BET IT'S JUST SOMETHING ELSE SUPER-WEIRD.
AAGHH.
FWP
YOU PUT ON A BLINDFOLD AND TOOK OUT A STICK...
I GOT IT! YOU'RE GONNA SPLIT A WATERMELON!!
COOL!!
CRACK
IT WAS FOR SPLITTING A SKULL.
AAGHH.
KYAAH!
AAGHH.
HERE, YOU CAN USE THIS ONE.
DON'T CRACK OPEN SKUUUULLS!!
JUST FORGET IT!! I'M GOING HOME!!

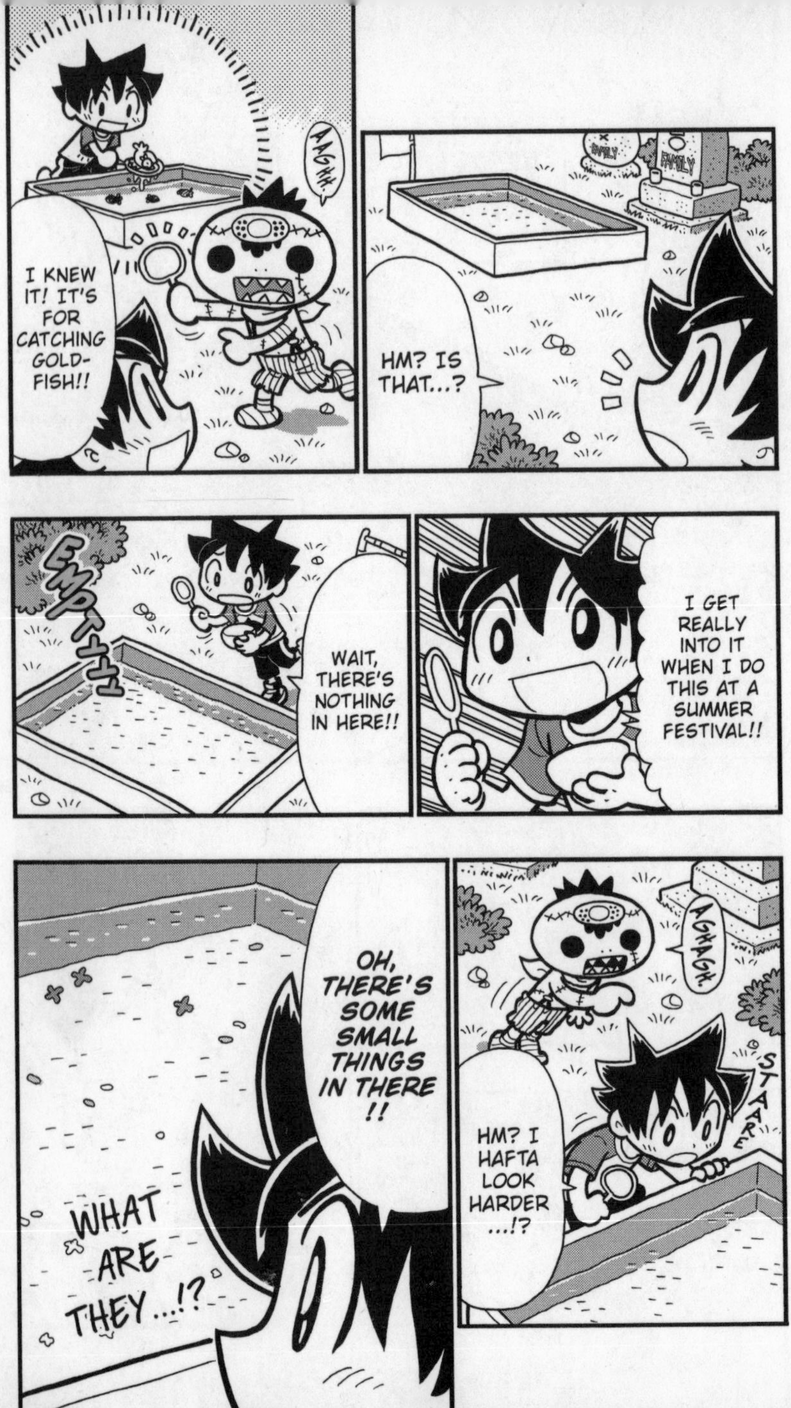
HM? IS THAT...?
AAGHH
I KNEW IT! IT'S FOR CATCHING GOLD-FISH!!
I GET REALLY INTO IT WHEN I DO THIS AT A SUMMER FESTIVAL!!
EMPTYYY
WAIT, THERE'S NOTHING IN HERE!!
AGHAGH
STAARE
HM? I HAFTA LOOK HARDER ...!?
OH, THERE'S SOME SMALL THINGS IN THERE !!
WHAT ARE THEY...!?

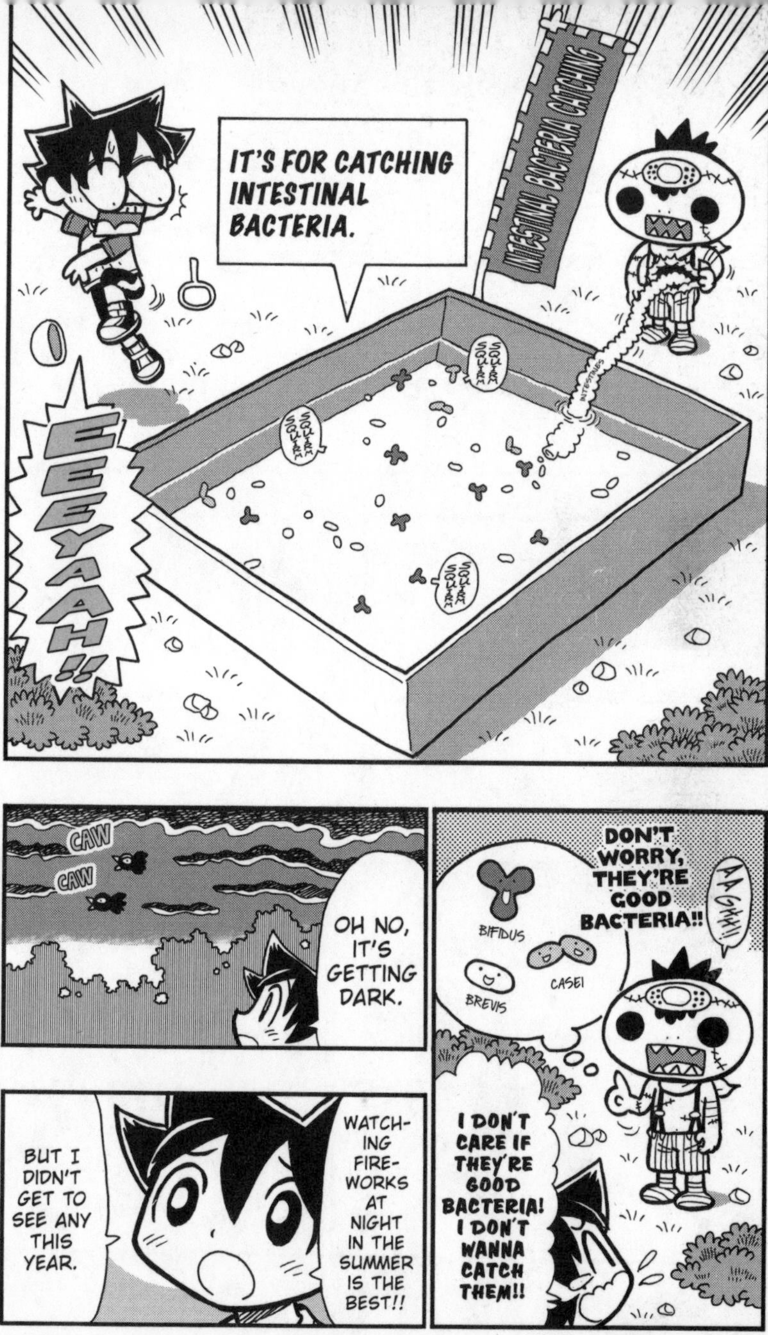
INTESTINAL BACTERIA CATCHING
IT'S FOR CATCHING INTESTINAL BACTERIA.
SQUIRM SQUIRM
INTESTINES
SQUIRM SQUIRM
SQUIRM SQUIRM
EEEEYAAAH!!
DON'T WORRY, THEY'RE GOOD BACTERIA!!
BIFIDUS
CASEI
BREVIS
AAGH!!
I DON'T CARE IF THEY'RE GOOD BACTERIA! I DON'T WANNA CATCH THEM!!
CAW
CAW
OH NO, IT'S GETTING DARK.
WATCHING FIREWORKS AT NIGHT IN THE SUMMER IS THE BEST!!
BUT I DIDN'T GET TO SEE ANY THIS YEAR.

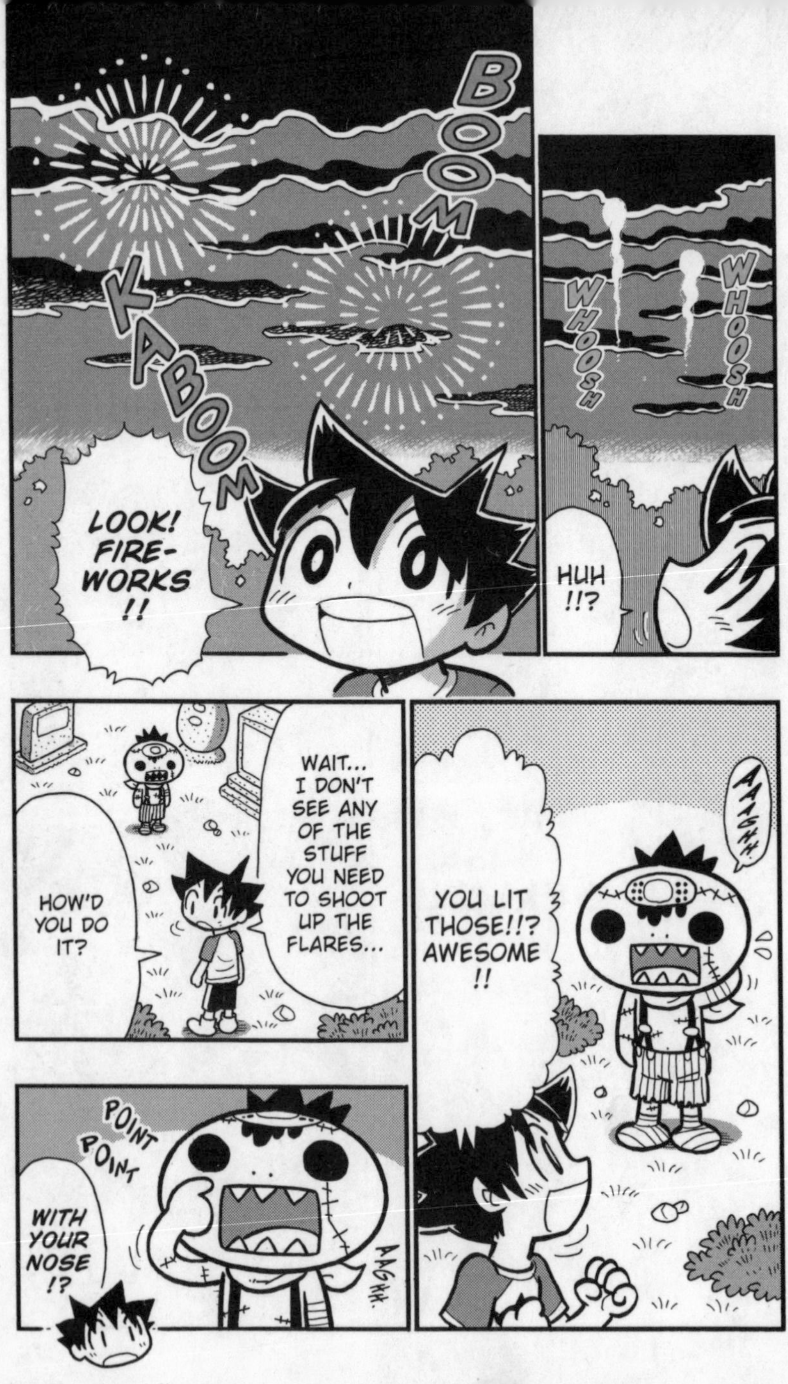
WHOOSH
WHOOSH
HUH !!?
BOOM
KABOOM
LOOK! FIRE-WORKS !!
AAAGHH
YOU LIT THOSE!!? AWESOME !!
WAIT... I DON'T SEE ANY OF THE STUFF YOU NEED TO SHOOT UP THE FLARES...
HOW'D YOU DO IT?
POINT
POINT
AAGHH.
WITH YOUR NOSE !?

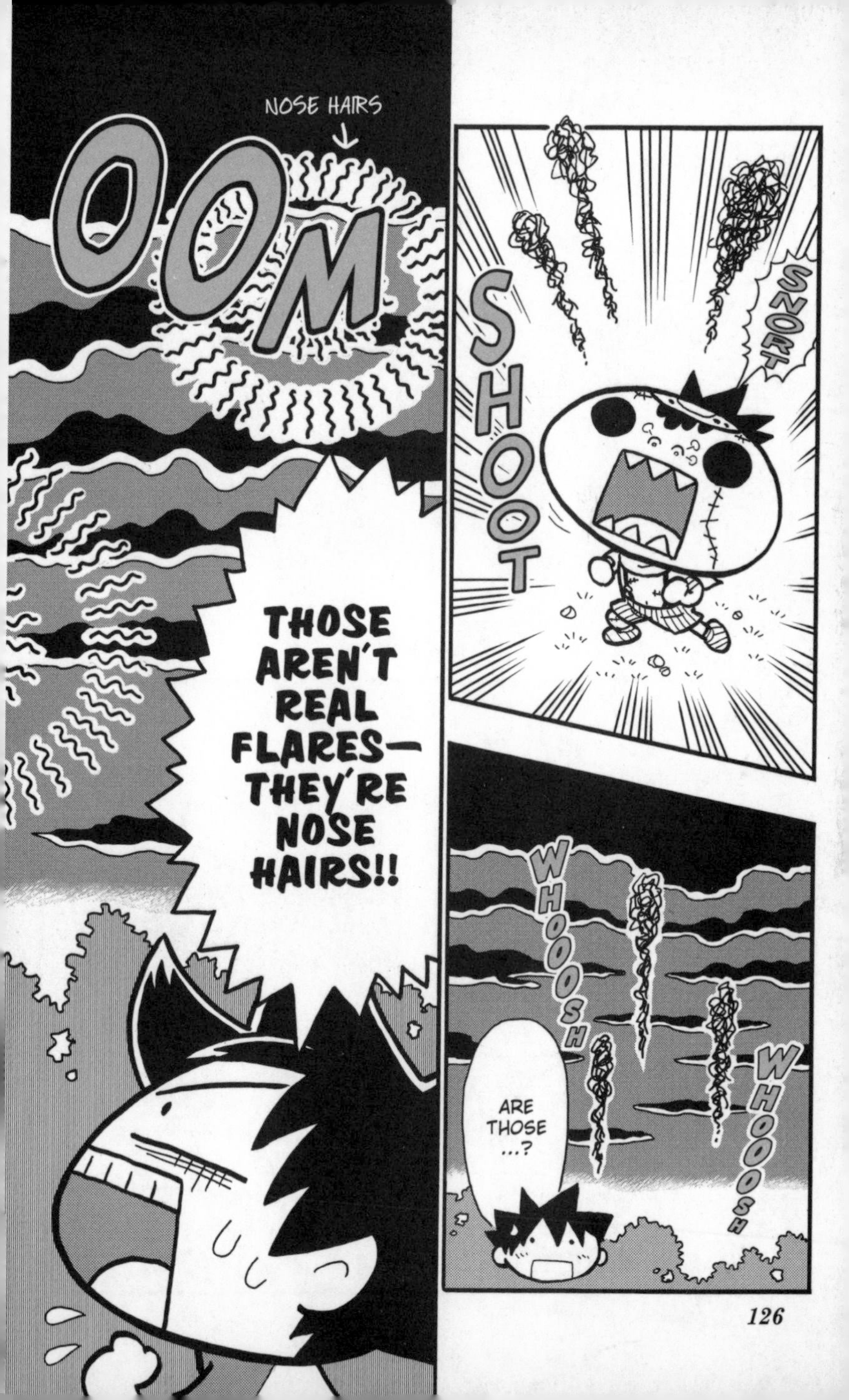
SNORT
SHOOT
WHOOOOSH
WHOOOOSH
ARE THOSE ...?
NOSE HAIRS
OOM
THOSE AREN'T REAL FLARES—THEY'RE NOSE HAIRS!!

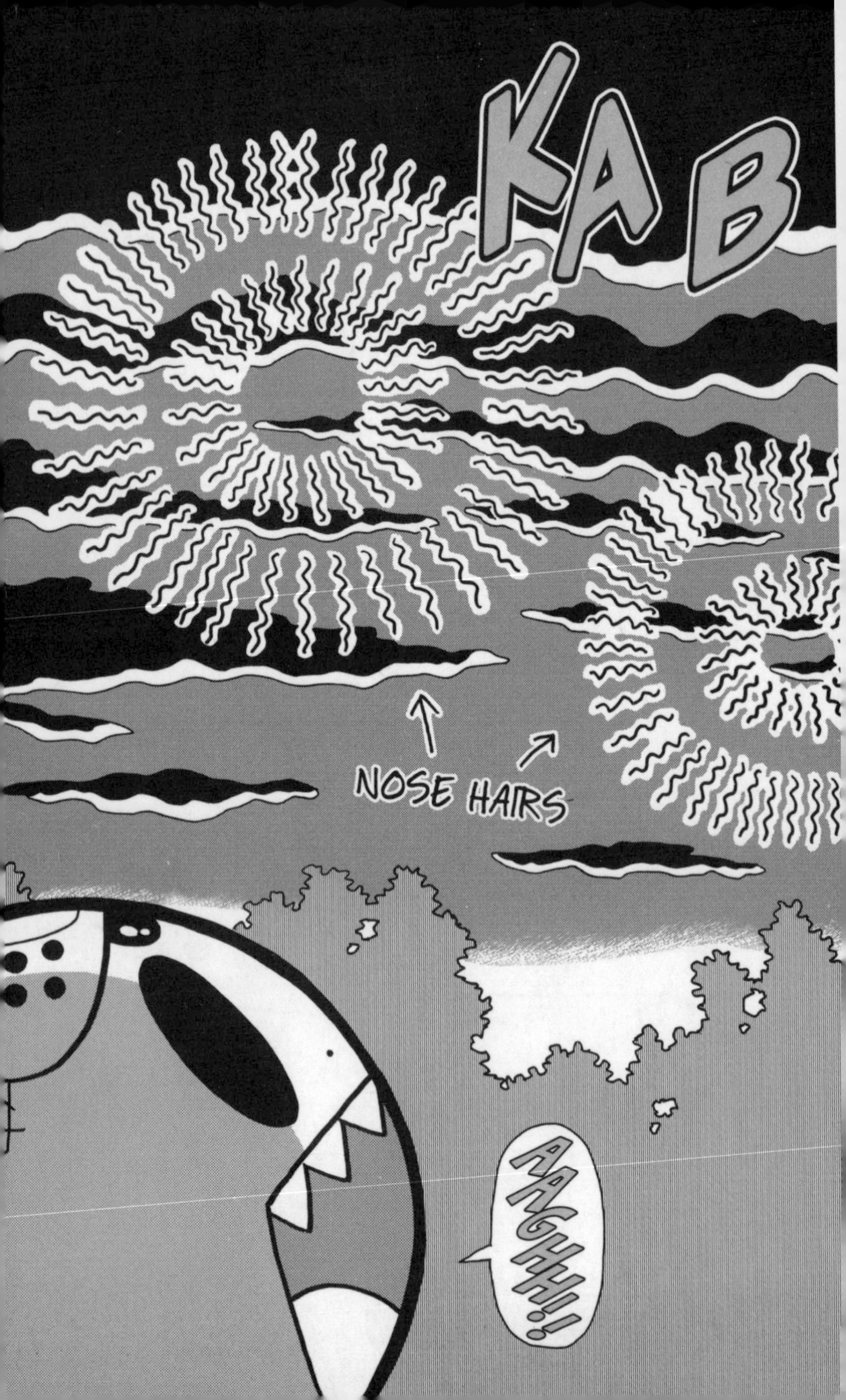
KAB
NOSE HAIRS
AAGHH!!

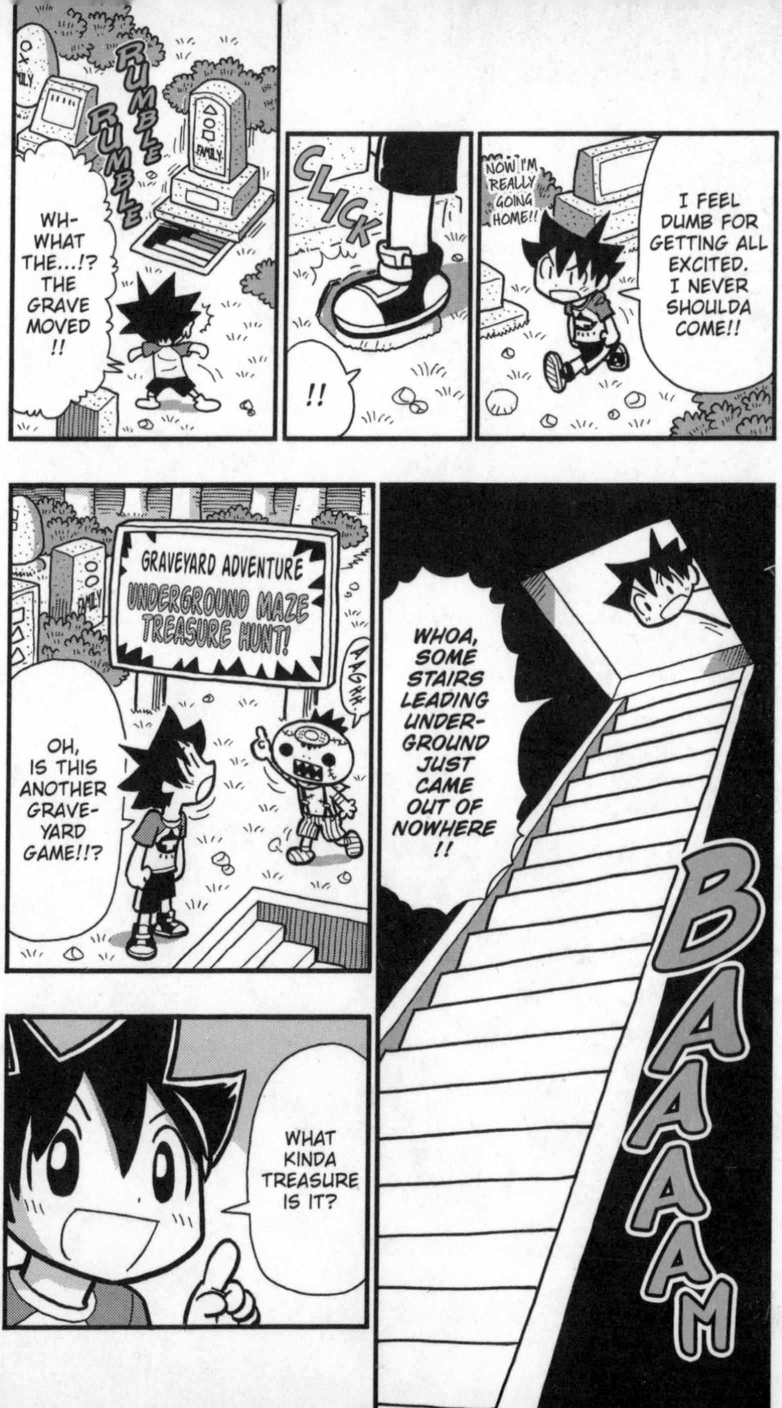

I FEEL DUMB FOR GETTING ALL EXCITED. I NEVER SHOULDA COME!!
NOW I'M REALLY GOING HOME!!
FAMILY
CLICK
!!
RUMBLE
RUMBLE
FAMILY
FAMILY
WH-WHAT THE...!? THE GRAVE MOVED!!
WHOA, SOME STAIRS LEADING UNDERGROUND JUST CAME OUT OF NOWHERE!!
BAAAAAM
GRAVEYARD ADVENTURE
UNDERGROUND MAZE TREASURE HUNT!
AAGHH
FAMILY
OH, IS THIS ANOTHER GRAVEYARD GAME!!?
WHAT KINDA TREASURE IS IT?

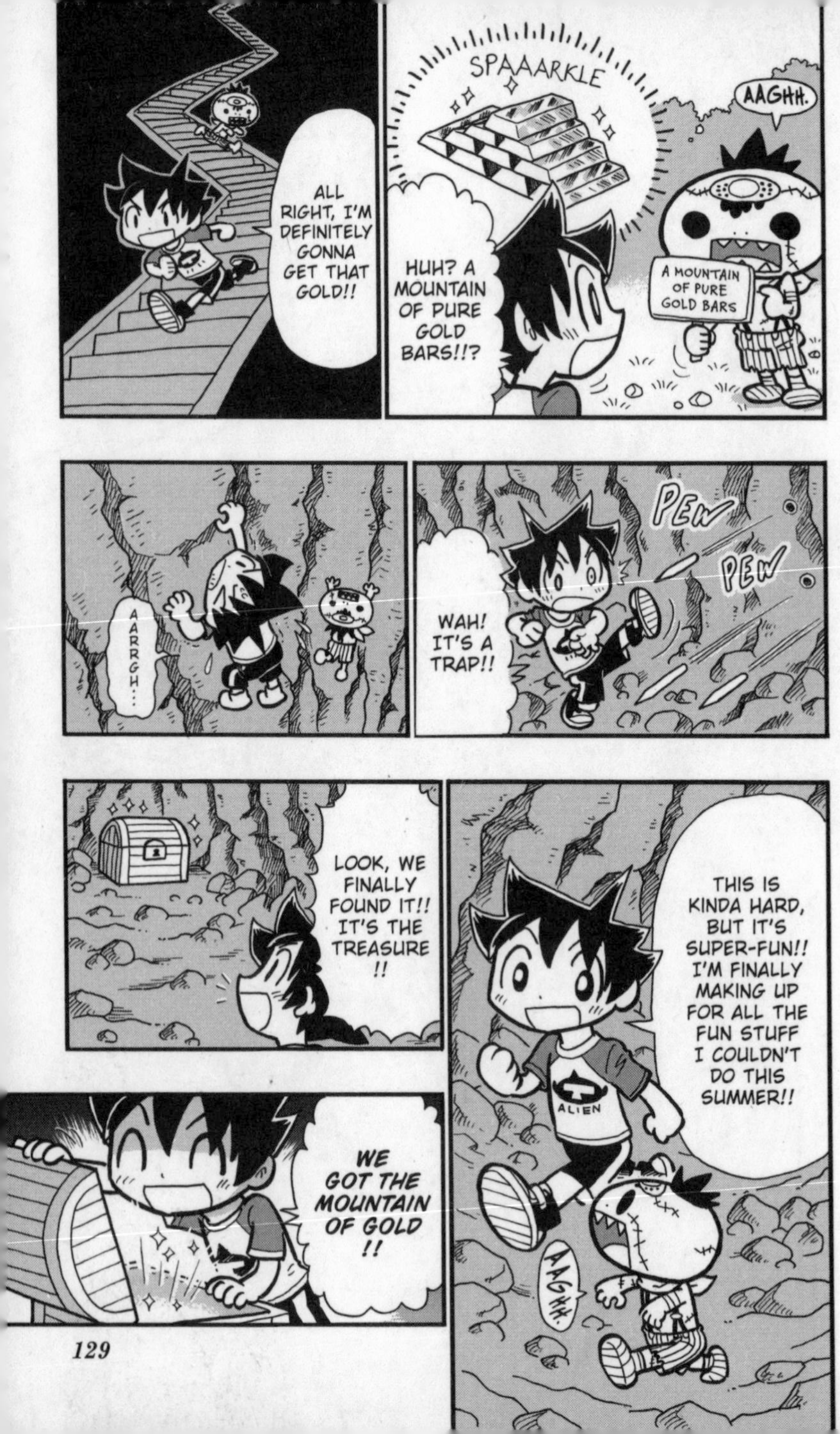

AAGHH.
SPAAARKLE
A MOUNTAIN OF PURE GOLD BARS
HUH? A MOUNTAIN OF PURE GOLD BARS!!?
ALL RIGHT, I'M DEFINITELY GONNA GET THAT GOLD!!
PEW
PEW
WAH! IT'S A TRAP!!
AARRGH...
THIS IS KINDA HARD, BUT IT'S SUPER-FUN!! I'M FINALLY MAKING UP FOR ALL THE FUN STUFF I COULDN'T DO THIS SUMMER!!
ALIEN
AAGHH.
LOOK, WE FINALLY FOUND IT!! IT'S THE TREASURE!!
WE GOT THE MOUNTAIN OF GOLD!!

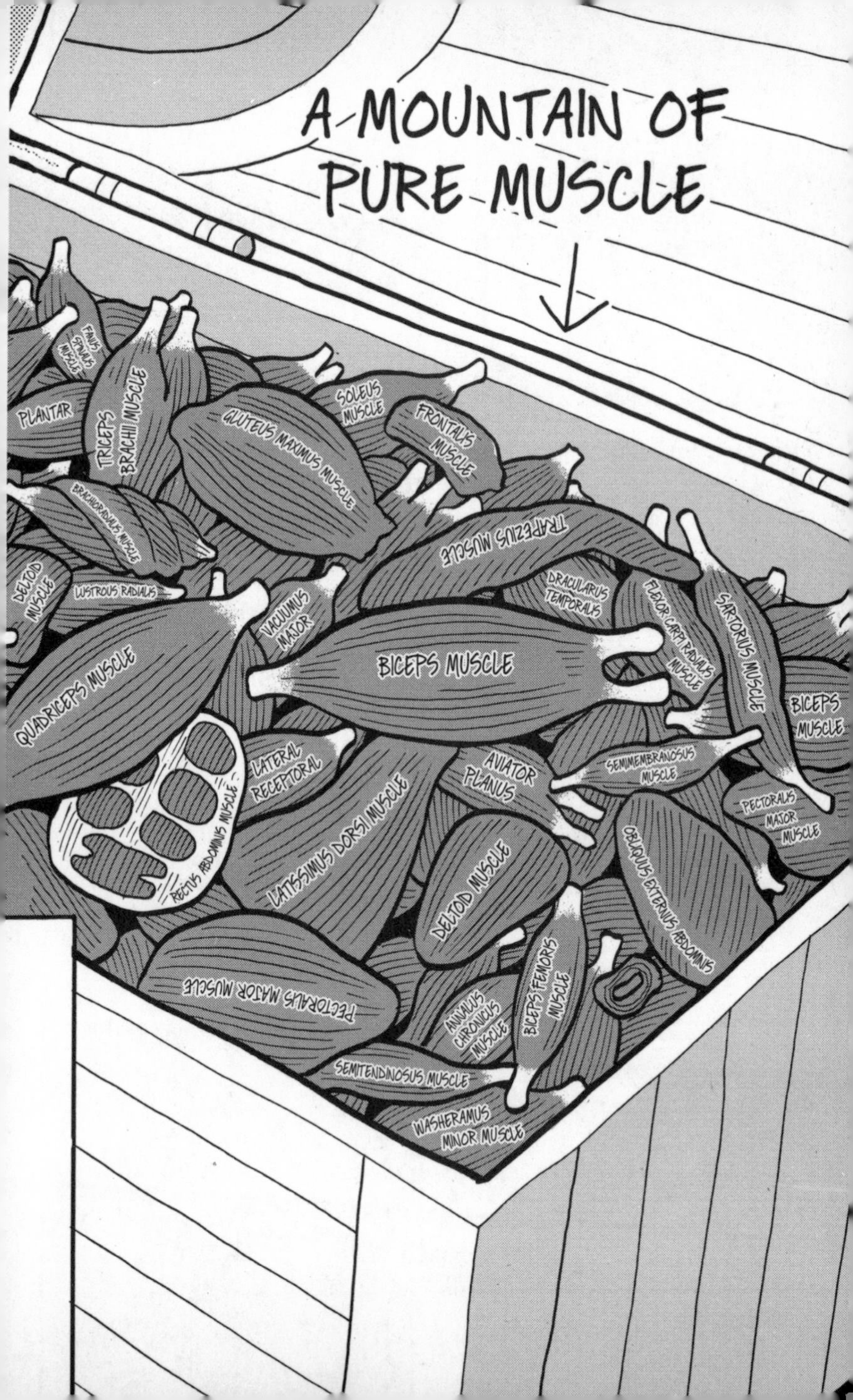
A MOUNTAIN OF PURE MUSCLE
FRONTALIS MUSCLE
SOLEUS MUSCLE
GLUTEUS MAXIMUS MUSCLE
TRICEPS BRACHII MUSCLE
FANUS SPINAUS MUSCLE
PLANTAR
TRAPEZIUS MUSCLE
BRACHIORADIALIS MUSCLE
SARTORIUS MUSCLE
FLEXOR CARPI RADIALIS MUSCLE
DRACULARUS TEMPORALIS
LUSTROUS RADIALIS
DELTOID MUSCLE
BICEPS MUSCLE
BICEPS MUSCLE
VACUUMUS MAJOR
QUADRICEPS MUSCLE
SEMIMEMBRANOSUS MUSCLE
AVIATOR PLANUS
LATERAL RECEPTORAL
PECTORALIS MAJOR MUSCLE
OBLIQUUS EXTERNUS ABDOMINIS
DELTOID MUSCLE
LATISSIMUS DORSI MUSCLE
RECTUS ABDOMINIS MUSCLE
BICEPS FEMORIS MUSCLE
ANNALUS CHRONICUS MUSCLE
PECTORALIS MAJOR MUSCLE
SEMITENDINOSUS MUSCLE
WASHERAMUS MINOR MUSCLE

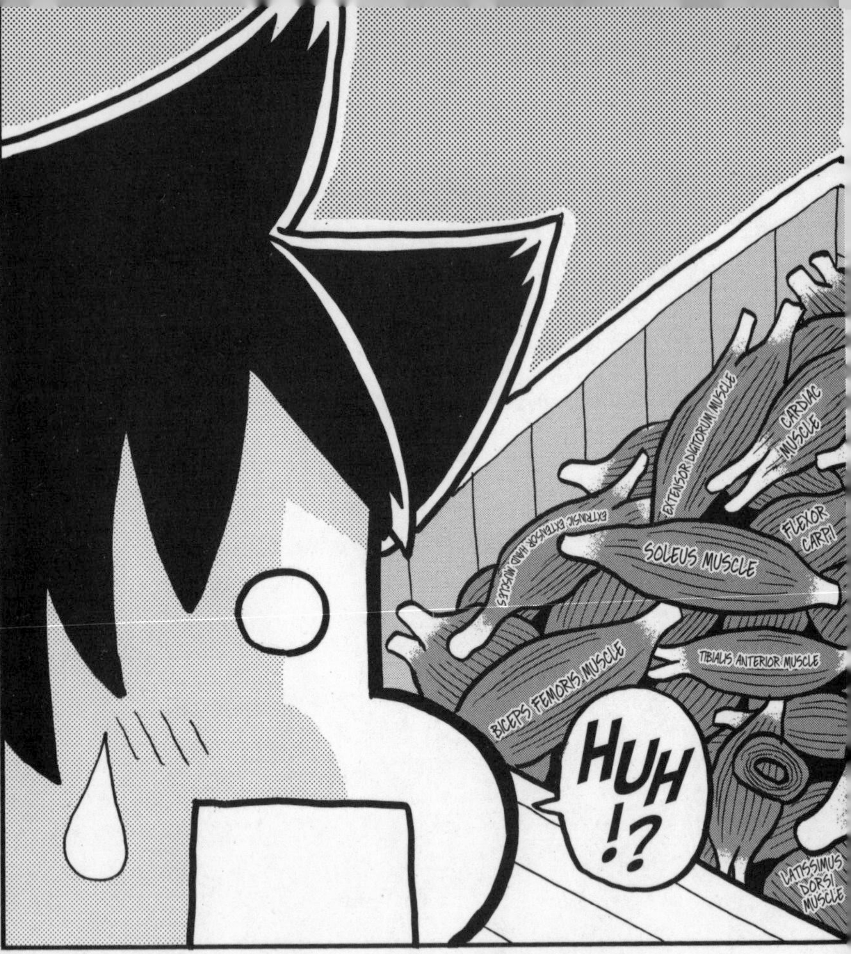
CARDIAC MUSCLE
EXTENSOR DIGITORUM MUSCLE
FLEXOR CARPI
SOLEUS MUSCLE
EXTRINSIC EXTENSOR HAND MUSCLES
TIBIALIS ANTERIOR MUSCLE
BICEPS FEMORIS MUSCLE
HUH!?
LATISSIMUS DORSI MUSCLE

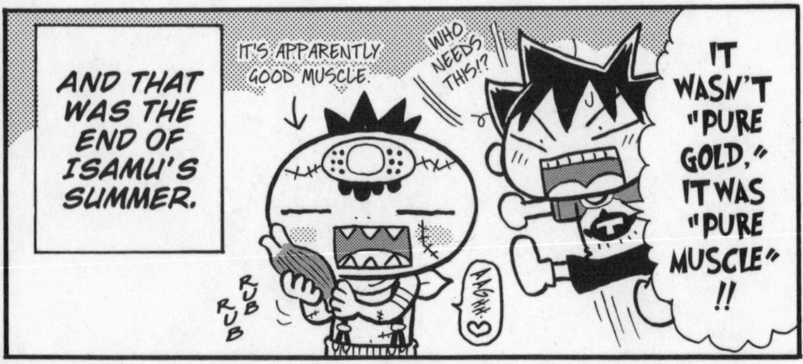
IT WASN'T "PURE GOLD," IT WAS "PURE MUSCLE"!!
WHO NEEDS THIS!?
IT'S APPARENTLY GOOD MUSCLE.
RUB RUB
AND THAT WAS THE END OF ISAMU'S SUMMER.

A MUSCLE
KEY CHAIN

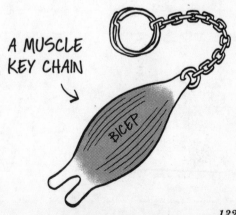

BICEP

LEZZONZ IN ATTACKING HUMANZ!

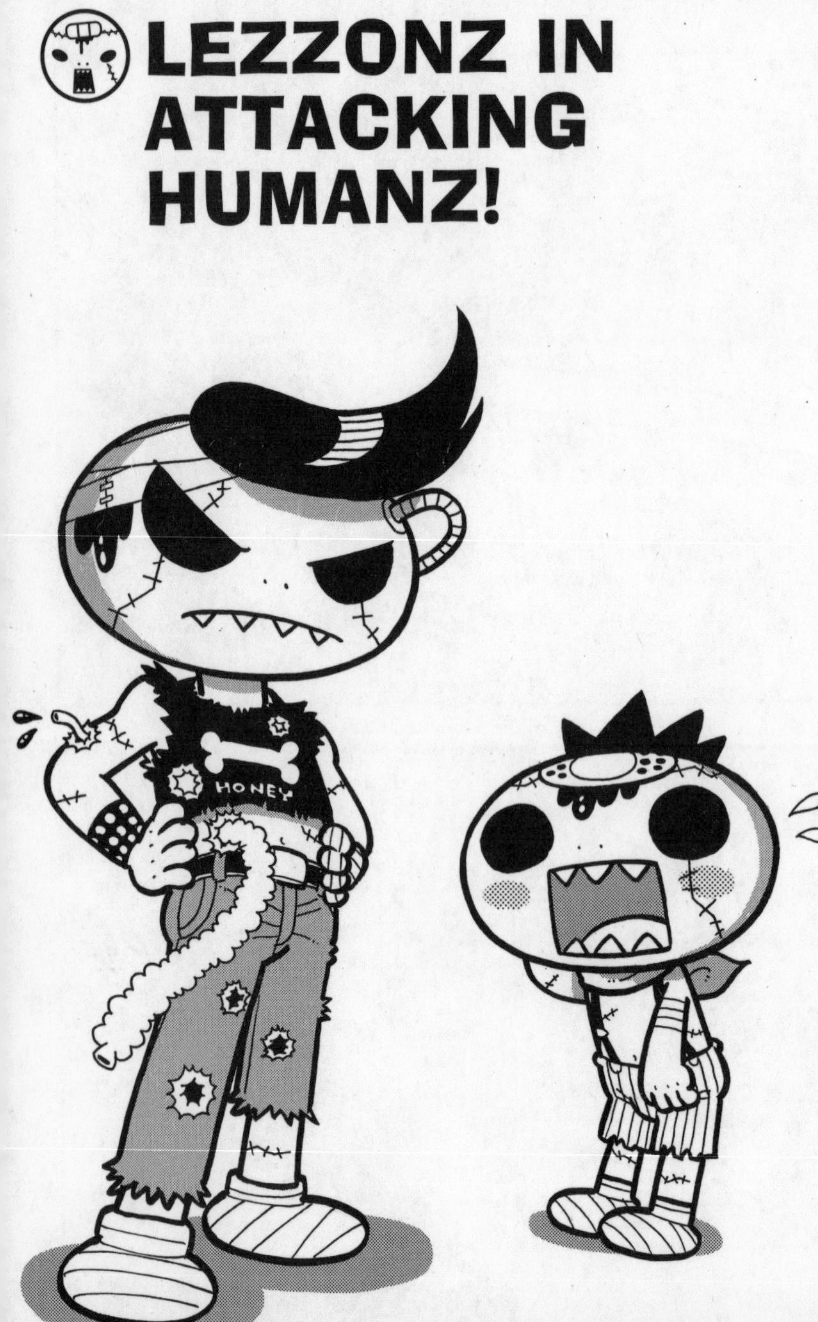
HONEY

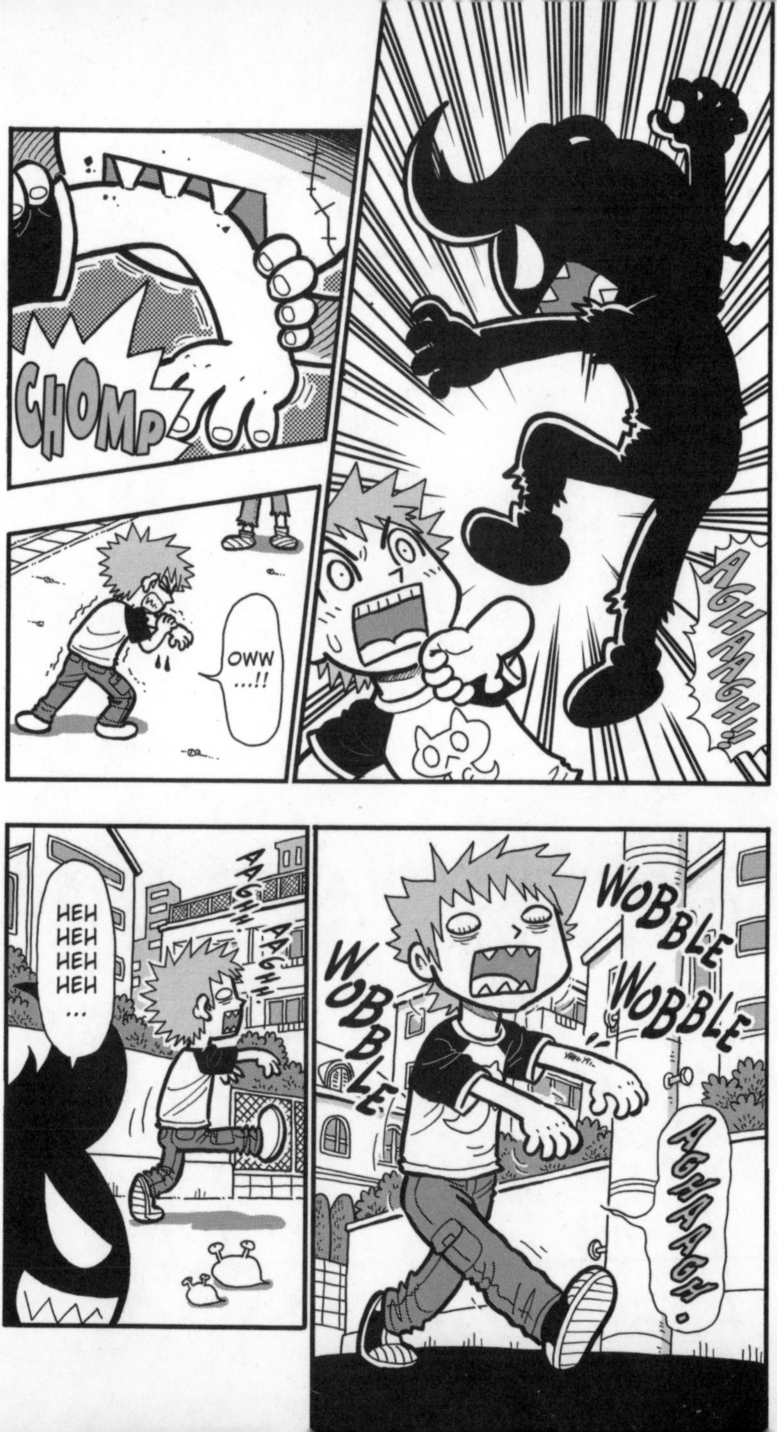
AGHAAGH!!
CHOMP
OWW ...!!
WOBBLE
WOBBLE
WOBBLE
AGHAAGH.
AAGHH AAGHH
HEH HEH HEH HEH ...

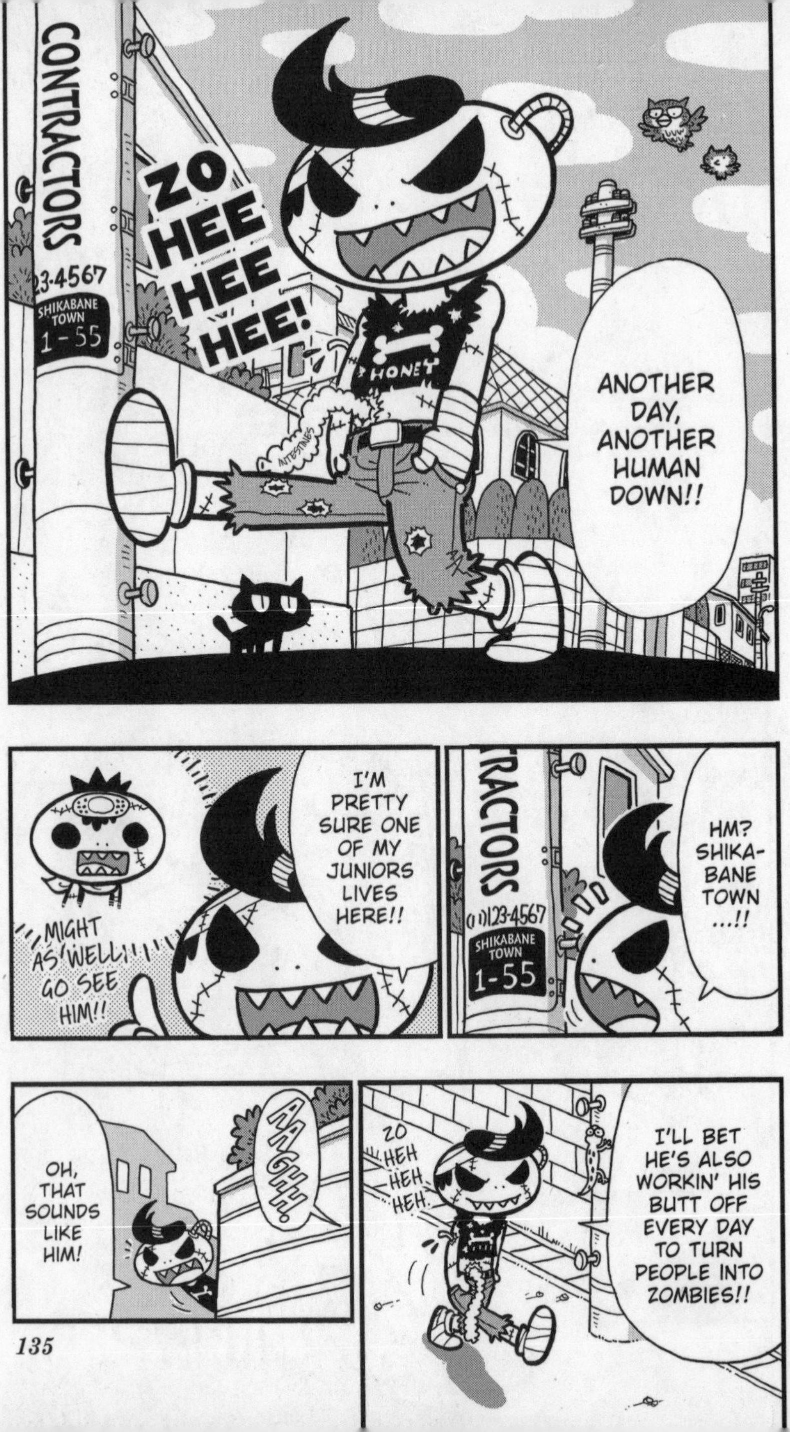
ANOTHER DAY, ANOTHER HUMAN DOWN!!
ZO HEE HEE HEE!
CONTRACTORS
23-4567
SHIKABANE TOWN 1-55
INTESTINES
HM? SHIKA-BANE TOWN ...!!
TRACTORS
SHIKABANE TOWN 1-55
I'M PRETTY SURE ONE OF MY JUNIORS LIVES HERE!!
MIGHT AS WELL GO SEE HIM!!
I'LL BET HE'S ALSO WORKIN' HIS BUTT OFF EVERY DAY TO TURN PEOPLE INTO ZOMBIES!!
ZO HEH HEH HEH
AAGHH!
OH, THAT SOUNDS LIKE HIM!

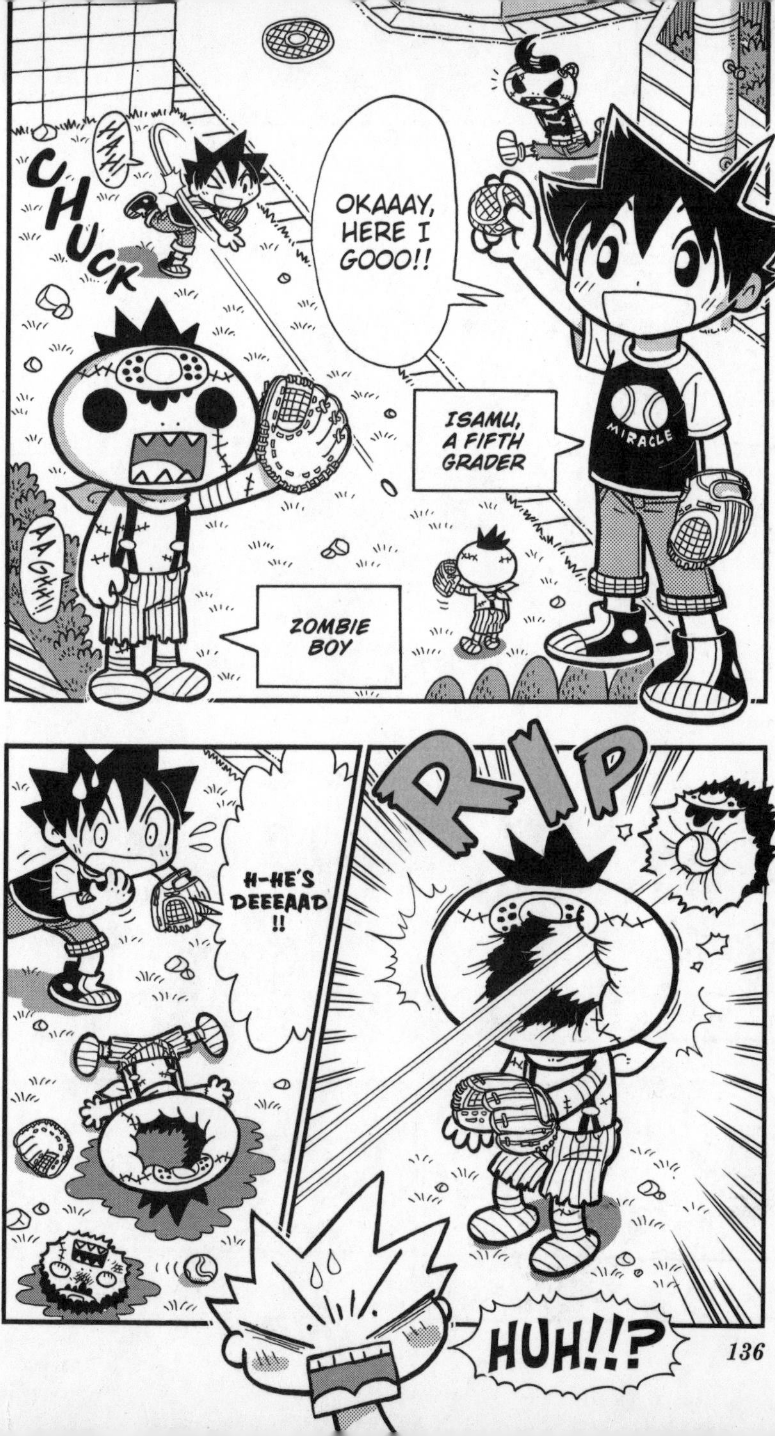
OKAAAY, HERE I GOOO!!
ISAMU, A FIFTH GRADER
HAH!
CHUCK
ZOMBIE BOY
AAGHH!!
RIP
HUH!!?
H-HE'S DEEEAAD !!

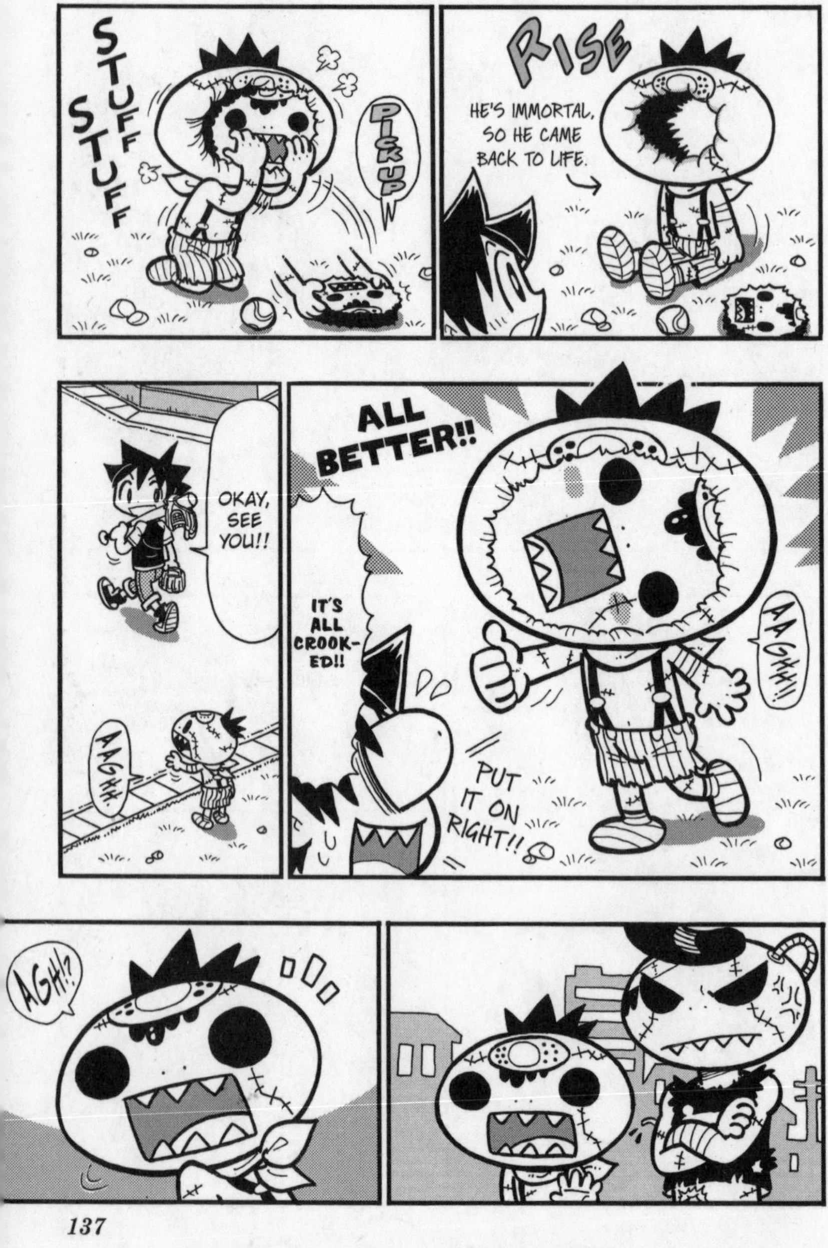
RISE
HE'S IMMORTAL, SO HE CAME BACK TO LIFE.
STUFF STUFF
PICK UP
ALL BETTER!!
AAGHH!!
IT'S ALL CROOK-ED!!
PUT IT ON RIGHT!!
OKAY, SEE YOU!!
AAGHH
AGH!?

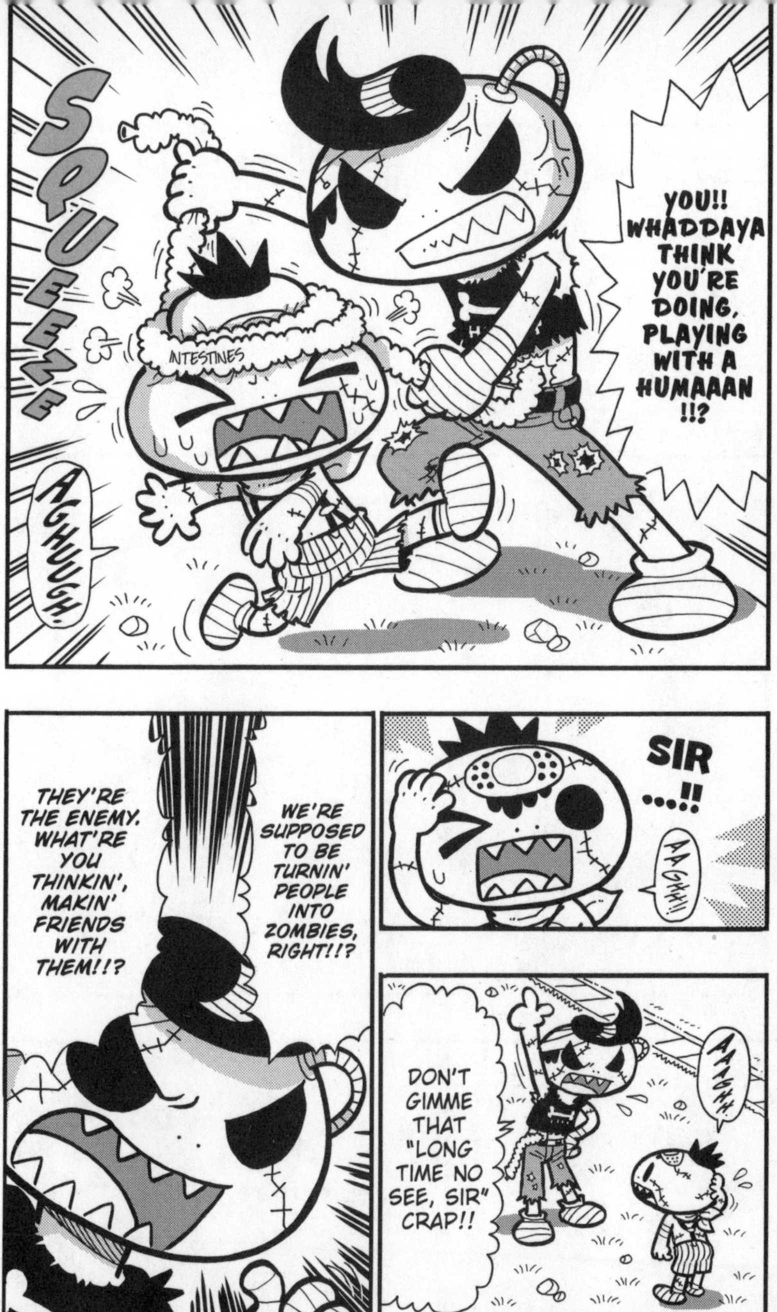
YOU!! WHADDAYA THINK YOU'RE DOING, PLAYING WITH A HUMAAAN!!?
SQUEEEZE
INTESTINES
AGHUUGH.
SIR...!!
AAGHH!!
AAAGHH.
DON'T GIMME THAT "LONG TIME NO SEE, SIR" CRAP!!
WE'RE SUPPOSED TO BE TURNIN' PEOPLE INTO ZOMBIES, RIGHT!!?
THEY'RE THE ENEMY. WHAT'RE YOU THINKIN', MAKIN' FRIENDS WITH THEM!!?

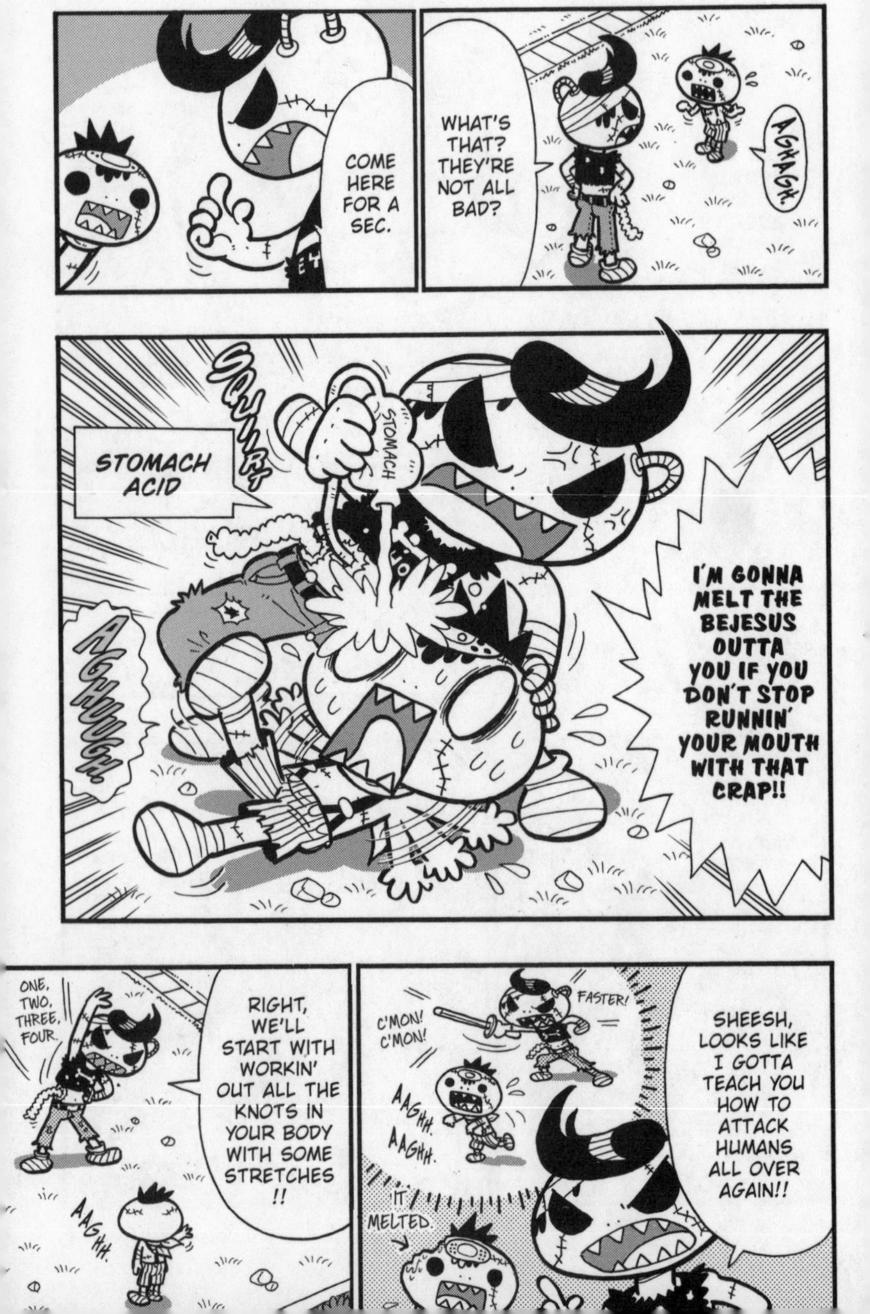
AGHAGH.
WHAT'S THAT? THEY'RE NOT ALL BAD?
COME HERE FOR A SEC.
I'M GONNA MELT THE BEJESUS OUTTA YOU IF YOU DON'T STOP RUNNIN' YOUR MOUTH WITH THAT CRAP!!
STOMACH
SQUIRT
STOMACH ACID
AGHUUGH
SHEESH, LOOKS LIKE I GOTTA TEACH YOU HOW TO ATTACK HUMANS ALL OVER AGAIN!!
FASTER!
C'MON! C'MON!
AAGHH. AAGHH.
IT MELTED.
RIGHT, WE'LL START WITH WORKIN' OUT ALL THE KNOTS IN YOUR BODY WITH SOME STRETCHES!!
ONE, TWO, THREE, FOUR.
AAGHH.

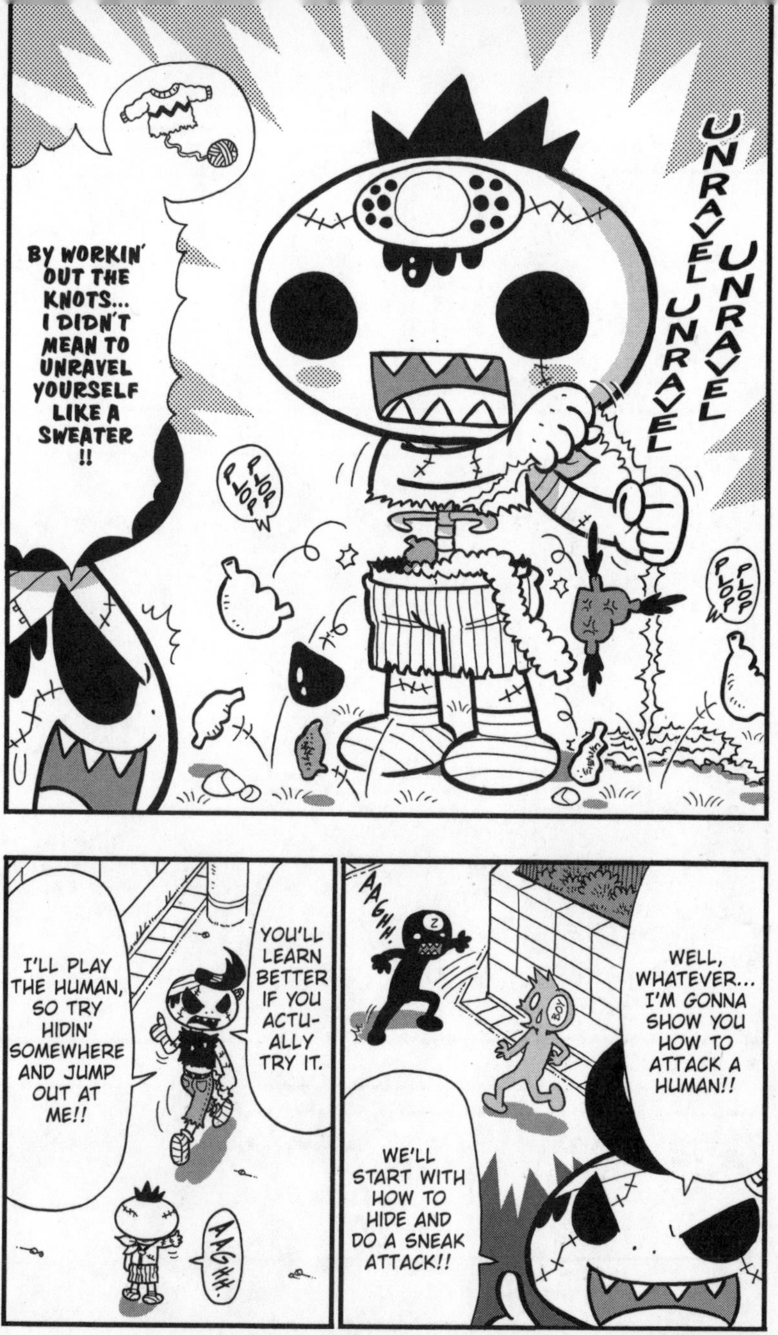
UNRAVEL UNRAVEL
UNRAVEL UNRAVEL
BY WORKIN' OUT THE KNOTS... I DIDN'T MEAN TO UNRAVEL YOURSELF LIKE A SWEATER!!
PLOP PLOP
PLOP PLOP
WELL, WHATEVER... I'M GONNA SHOW YOU HOW TO ATTACK A HUMAN!!
AAGHH!
BOY
WE'LL START WITH HOW TO HIDE AND DO A SNEAK ATTACK!!
YOU'LL LEARN BETTER IF YOU ACTU-ALLY TRY IT.
I'LL PLAY THE HUMAN, SO TRY HIDIN' SOMEWHERE AND JUMP OUT AT ME!!
AAGHH.

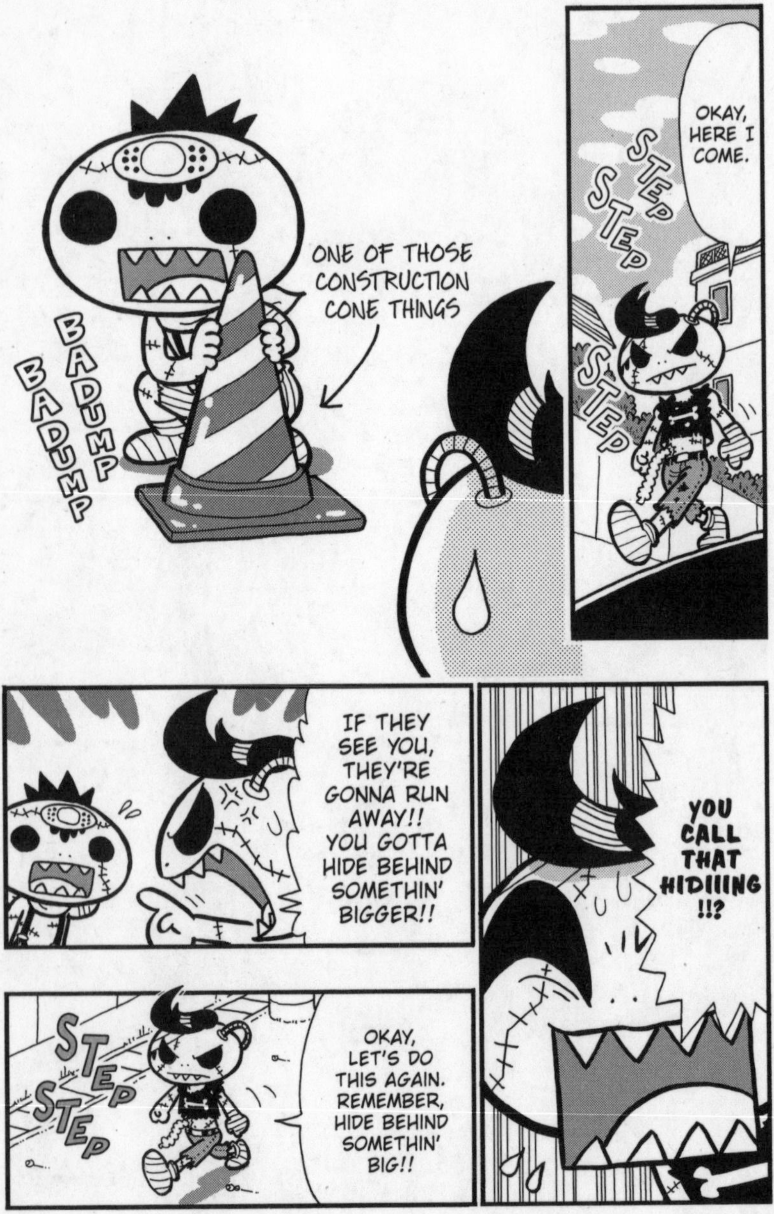
OKAY, HERE I COME.
STEP STEP
STEP STEP
BADUMP BADUMP
ONE OF THOSE CONSTRUCTION CONE THINGS
YOU CALL THAT HIDIIING!!?
IF THEY SEE YOU, THEY'RE GONNA RUN AWAY!! YOU GOTTA HIDE BEHIND SOMETHIN' BIGGER!!
OKAY, LET'S DO THIS AGAIN. REMEMBER, HIDE BEHIND SOMETHIN' BIG!!
STEP STEP

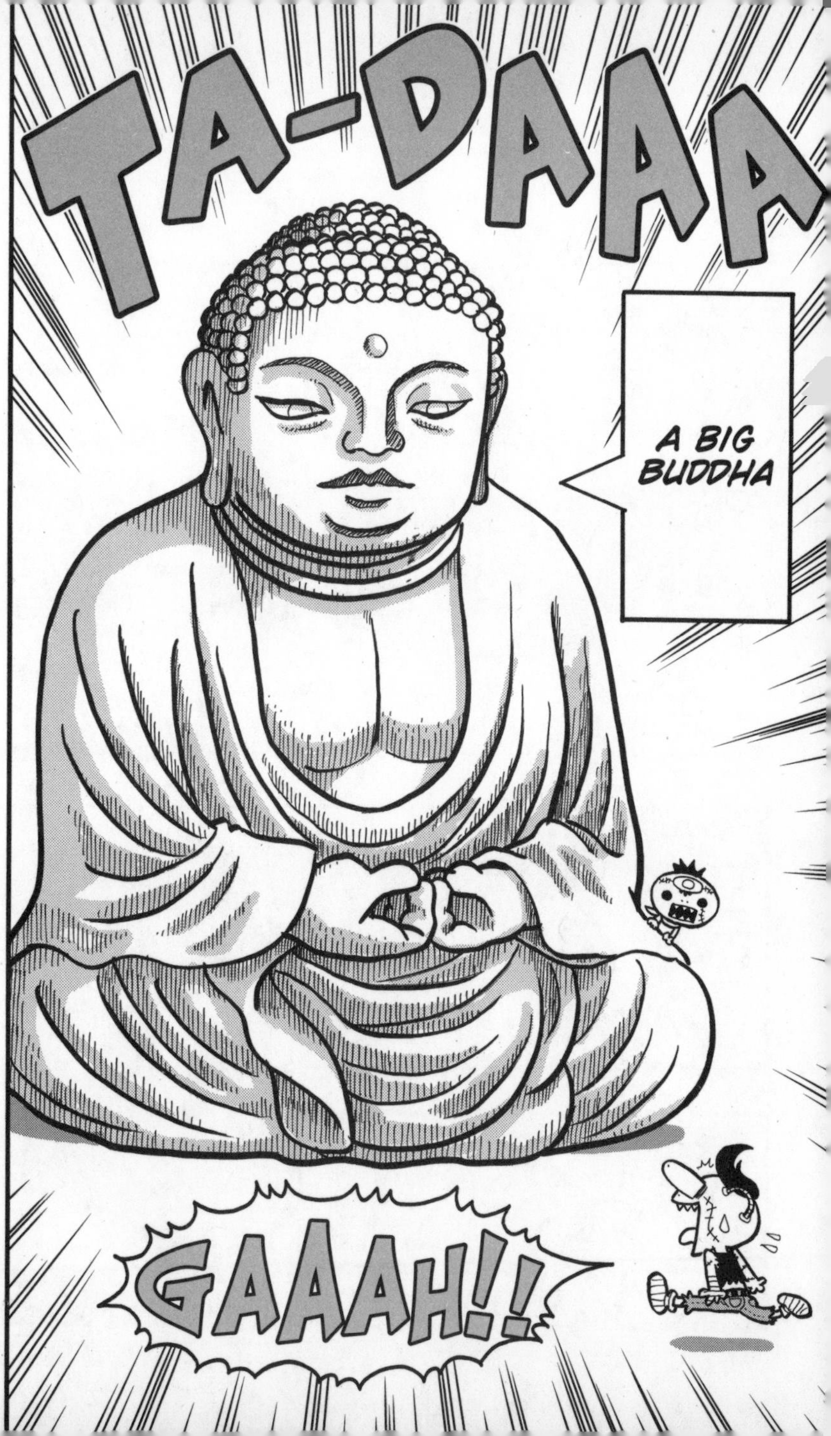
TA-DAAA
A BIG BUDDHA
GAAAH!!

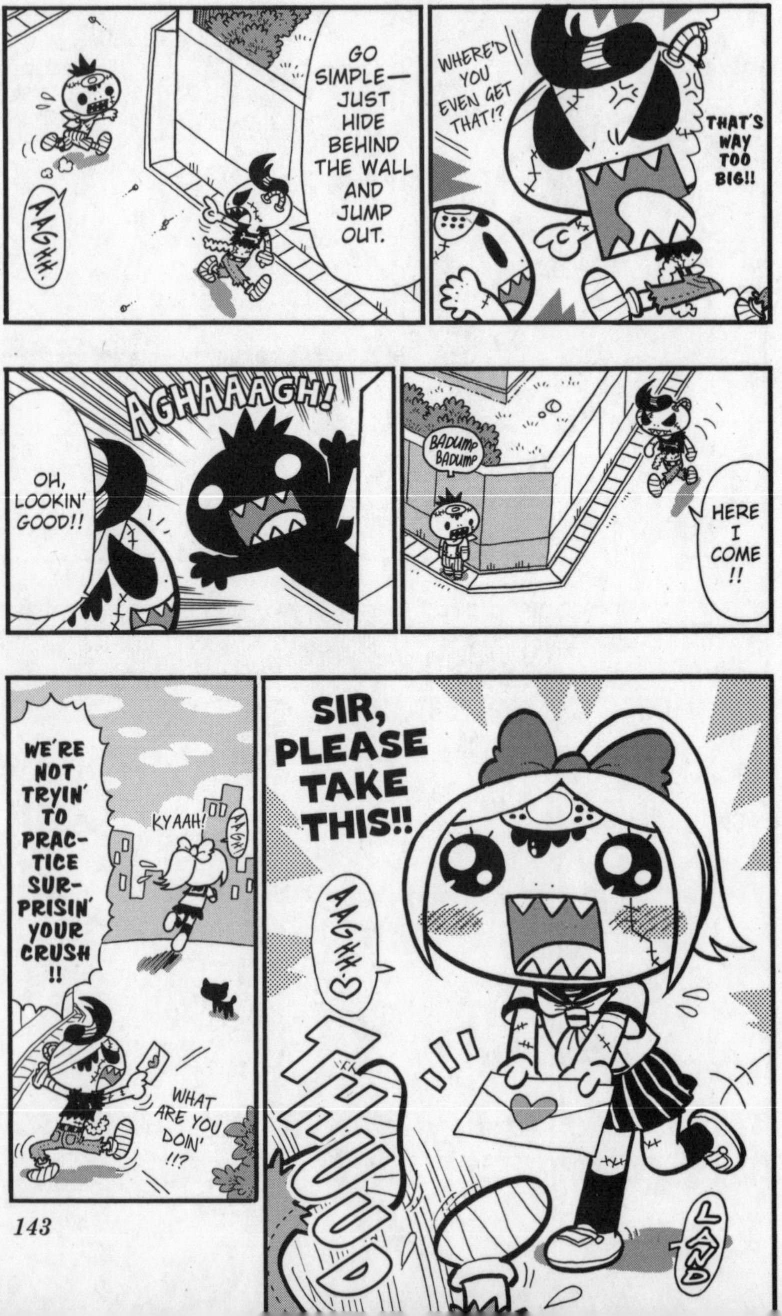
WHERE'D YOU EVEN GET THAT!?
THAT'S WAY TOO BIG!!
GO SIMPLE—JUST HIDE BEHIND THE WALL AND JUMP OUT.
AAGHH.
BADUMP BADUMP
HERE I COME!!
AGHAAAGH!
OH, LOOKIN' GOOD!!
SIR, PLEASE TAKE THIS!!
AAGHH.♡
THUUD
LAND
WE'RE NOT TRYIN' TO PRACTICE SURPRISIN' YOUR CRUSH!!
KYAAH!
AAGH!
WHAT ARE YOU DOIN'!!?

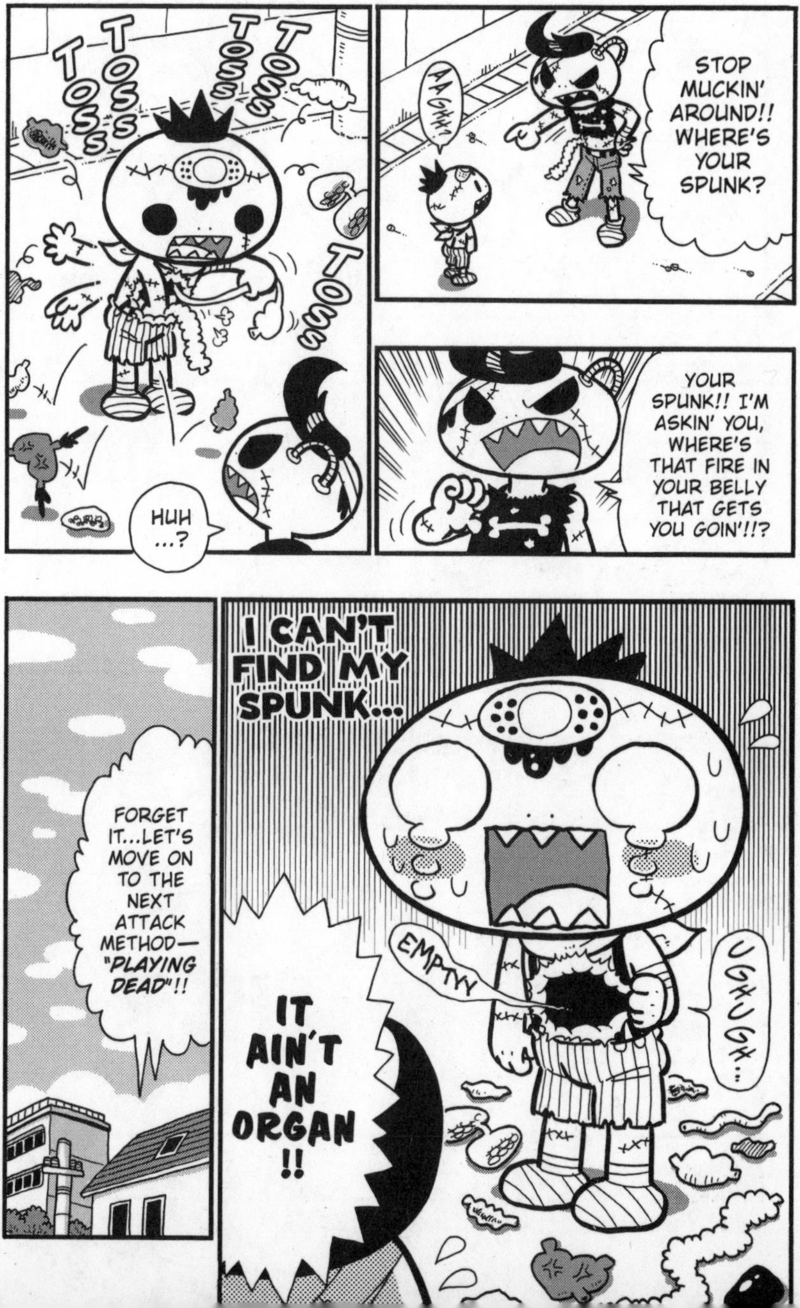
AAGHH?
STOP MUCKIN' AROUND!! WHERE'S YOUR SPUNK?
YOUR SPUNK!! I'M ASKIN' YOU, WHERE'S THAT FIRE IN YOUR BELLY THAT GETS YOU GOIN'!!?
TOSS
TOSS
TOSS
TOSS
TOSS
HUH ...?
I CAN'T FIND MY SPUNK...
UGH UGH...
EMPTYY
IT AIN'T AN ORGAN!!
FORGET IT...LET'S MOVE ON TO THE NEXT ATTACK METHOD—"PLAYING DEAD"!!

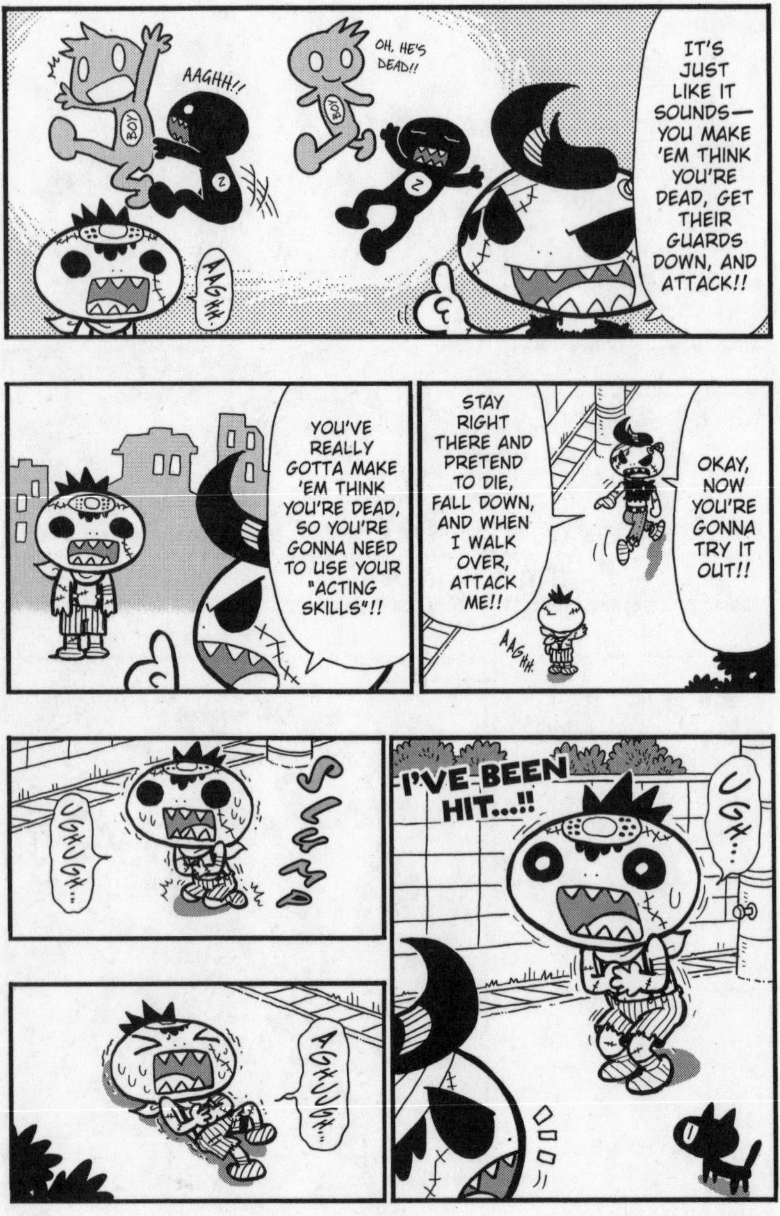
IT'S JUST LIKE IT SOUNDS—YOU MAKE 'EM THINK YOU'RE DEAD, GET THEIR GUARDS DOWN, AND ATTACK!!
OH, HE'S DEAD!!
AAGHH!!
AAGHH.
OKAY, NOW YOU'RE GONNA TRY IT OUT!!
STAY RIGHT THERE AND PRETEND TO DIE, FALL DOWN, AND WHEN I WALK OVER, ATTACK ME!!
AAGHH.
YOU'VE REALLY GOTTA MAKE 'EM THINK YOU'RE DEAD, SO YOU'RE GONNA NEED TO USE YOUR "ACTING SKILLS"!!
UGH...
I'VE BEEN HIT...!!
SLUMP
UGHUGH...
AGHUGH...

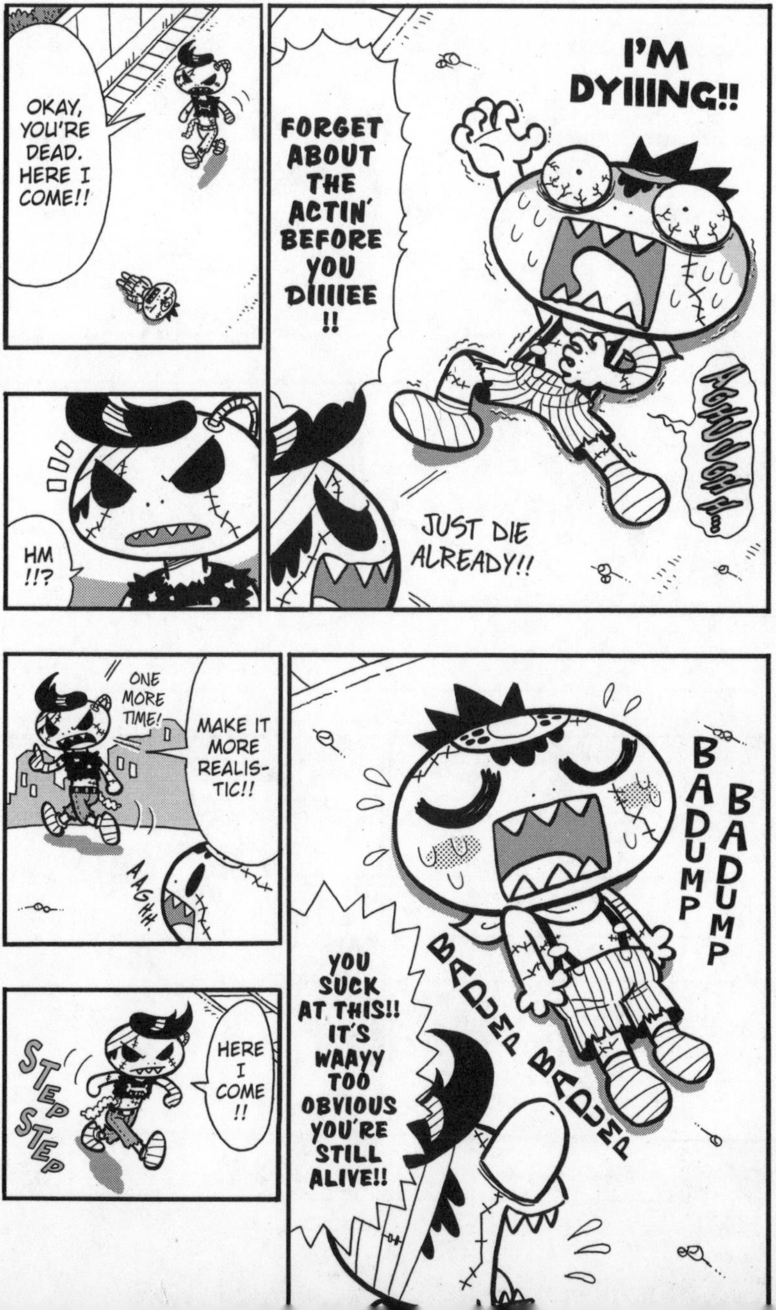

I'M DYIIING!!
AGHUUGHH...
FORGET ABOUT THE ACTIN' BEFORE YOU DIIIIEE!!
JUST DIE ALREADY!!
OKAY, YOU'RE DEAD. HERE I COME!!
HM!!?
BADUMP BADUMP
BADUMP BADUMP
YOU SUCK AT THIS!! IT'S WAAYY TOO OBVIOUS YOU'RE STILL ALIVE!!
MAKE IT MORE REALISTIC!!
ONE MORE TIME!
AAGHH
HERE I COME!!
STEP STEP

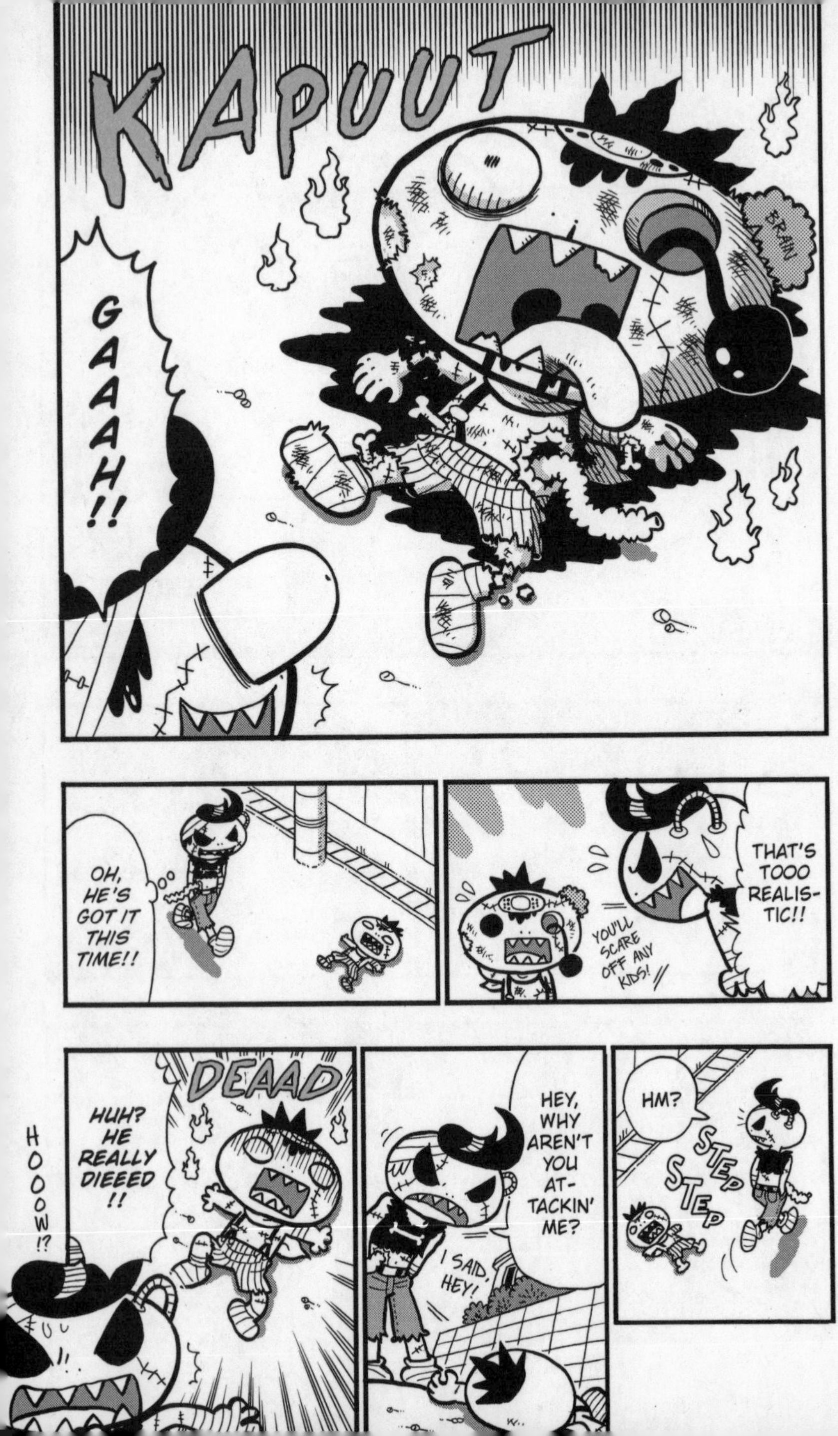
KAPUUT
BRAIN
GAAAAH!!
THAT'S TOOO REALISTIC!!
YOU'LL SCARE OFF ANY KIDS!
OH, HE'S GOT IT THIS TIME!!
HM?
STEP STEP
HEY, WHY AREN'T YOU AT-TACKIN' ME?
I SAID, HEY!
DEAAD
HUH? HE REALLY DIEEED!!
HOOOOW!?

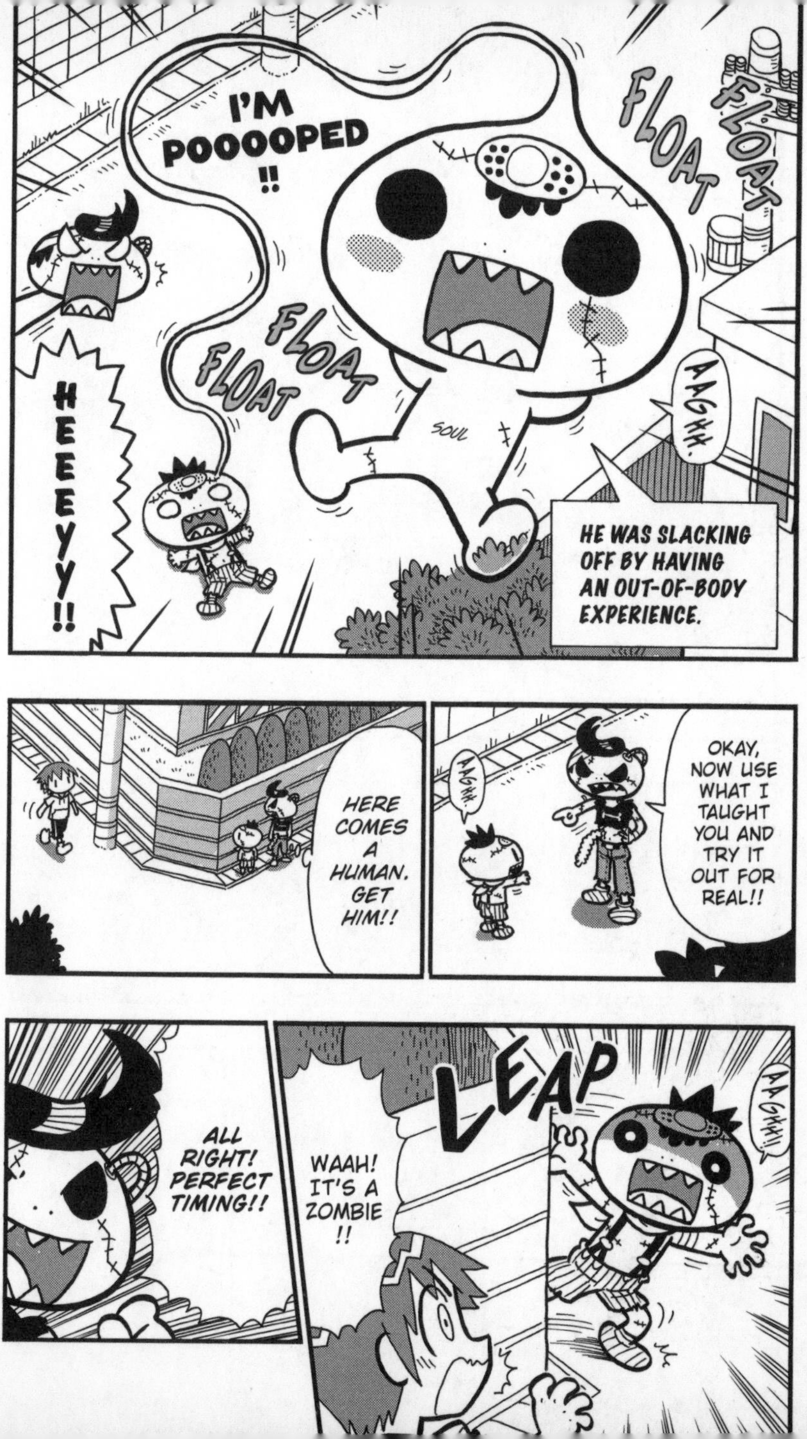
FLOAT
FLOAT
I'M POOOOPED!!
AAGHH.
FLOAT
FLOAT
SOUL
HE WAS SLACKING OFF BY HAVING AN OUT-OF-BODY EXPERIENCE.
HEEEEYY!!
OKAY, NOW USE WHAT I TAUGHT YOU AND TRY IT OUT FOR REAL!!
AAGHH.
HERE COMES A HUMAN. GET HIM!!
AAGHH!!
LEAP
WAAH! IT'S A ZOMBIE!!
ALL RIGHT! PERFECT TIMING!!

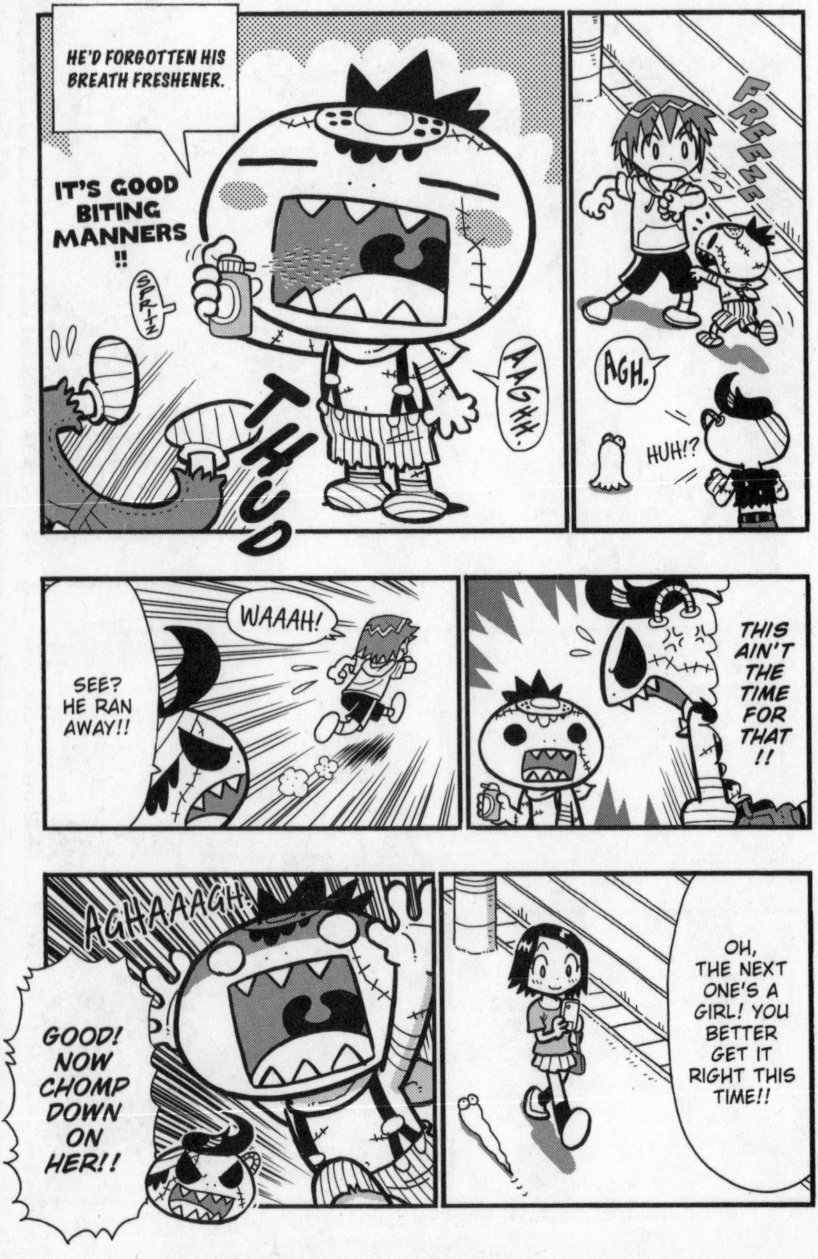
FREEZE
AGH.
HUH!?
HE'D FORGOTTEN HIS BREATH FRESHENER.
IT'S GOOD BITING MANNERS!!
SPRITZ
AAGHH.
THUD
THIS AIN'T THE TIME FOR THAT!!
WAAAH!
SEE? HE RAN AWAY!!
OH, THE NEXT ONE'S A GIRL! YOU BETTER GET IT RIGHT THIS TIME!!
AGHAAAAGH
GOOD! NOW CHOMP DOWN ON HER!!

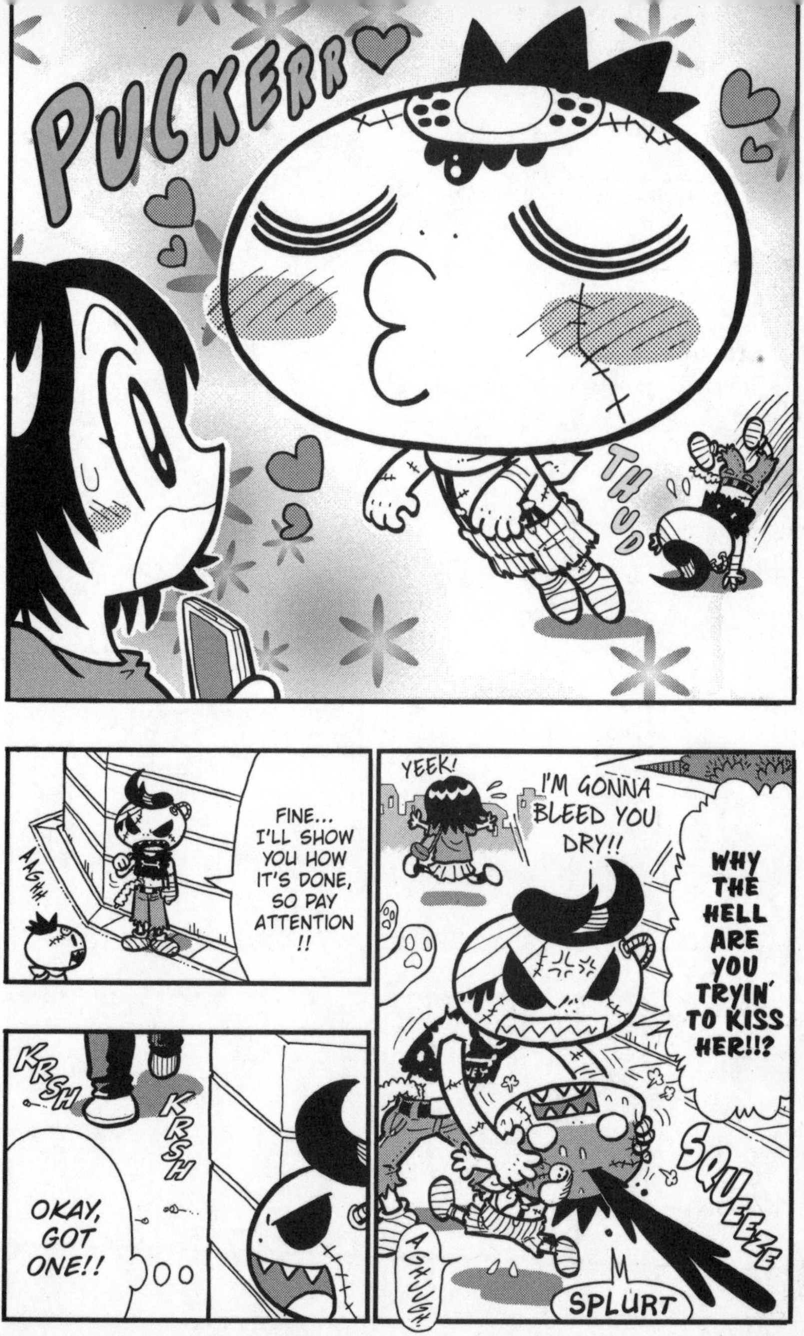
PUCKERR
THUD
YEEK!
I'M GONNA BLEED YOU DRY!!
WHY THE HELL ARE YOU TRYIN' TO KISS HER!!?
SQUEEZE
SPLURT
AGXUUGH.
FINE... I'LL SHOW YOU HOW IT'S DONE, SO PAY ATTENTION!!
AAGHH.
KRSH
KRSH
OKAY, GOT ONE!!

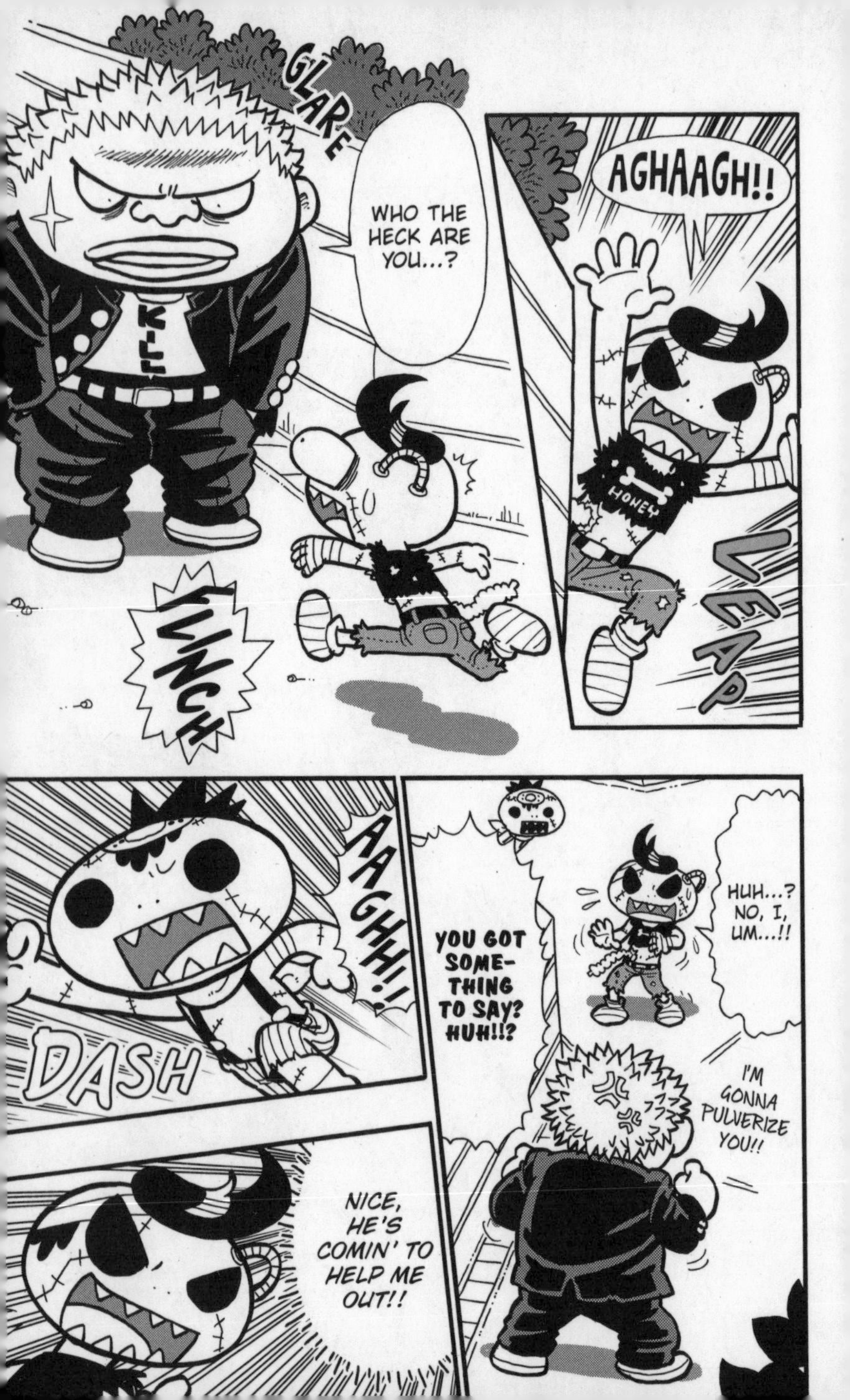
AGHAAGH!!
HONEY
LEAP
GLARE
WHO THE HECK ARE YOU...?
KILL
FLINCH
HUH...? NO, I, UM...!!
YOU GOT SOME-THING TO SAY? HUH!!?
I'M GONNA PULVERIZE YOU!!
AAGHH!!
DASH
NICE, HE'S COMIN' TO HELP ME OUT!!

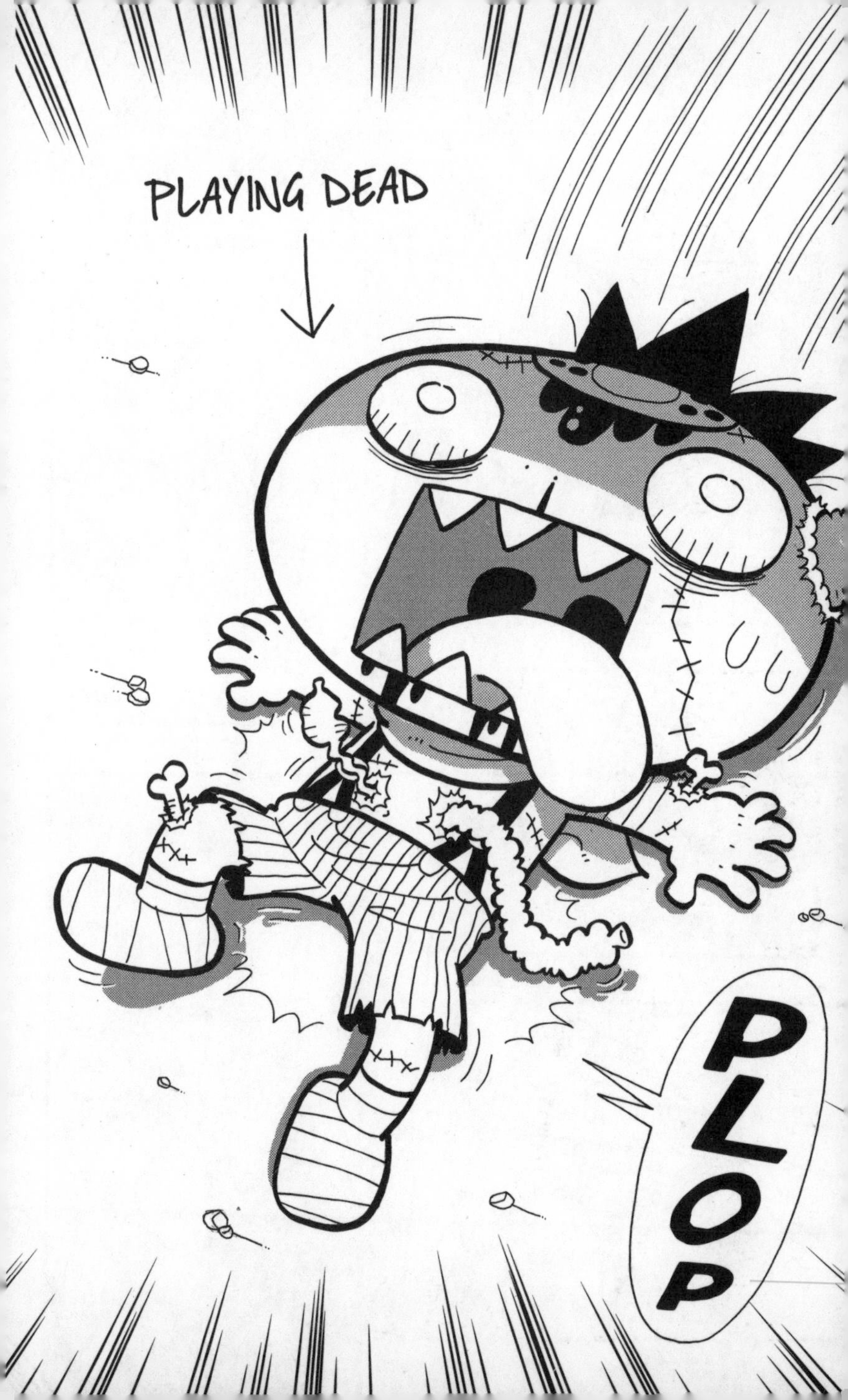
PLAYING DEAD
PLOP

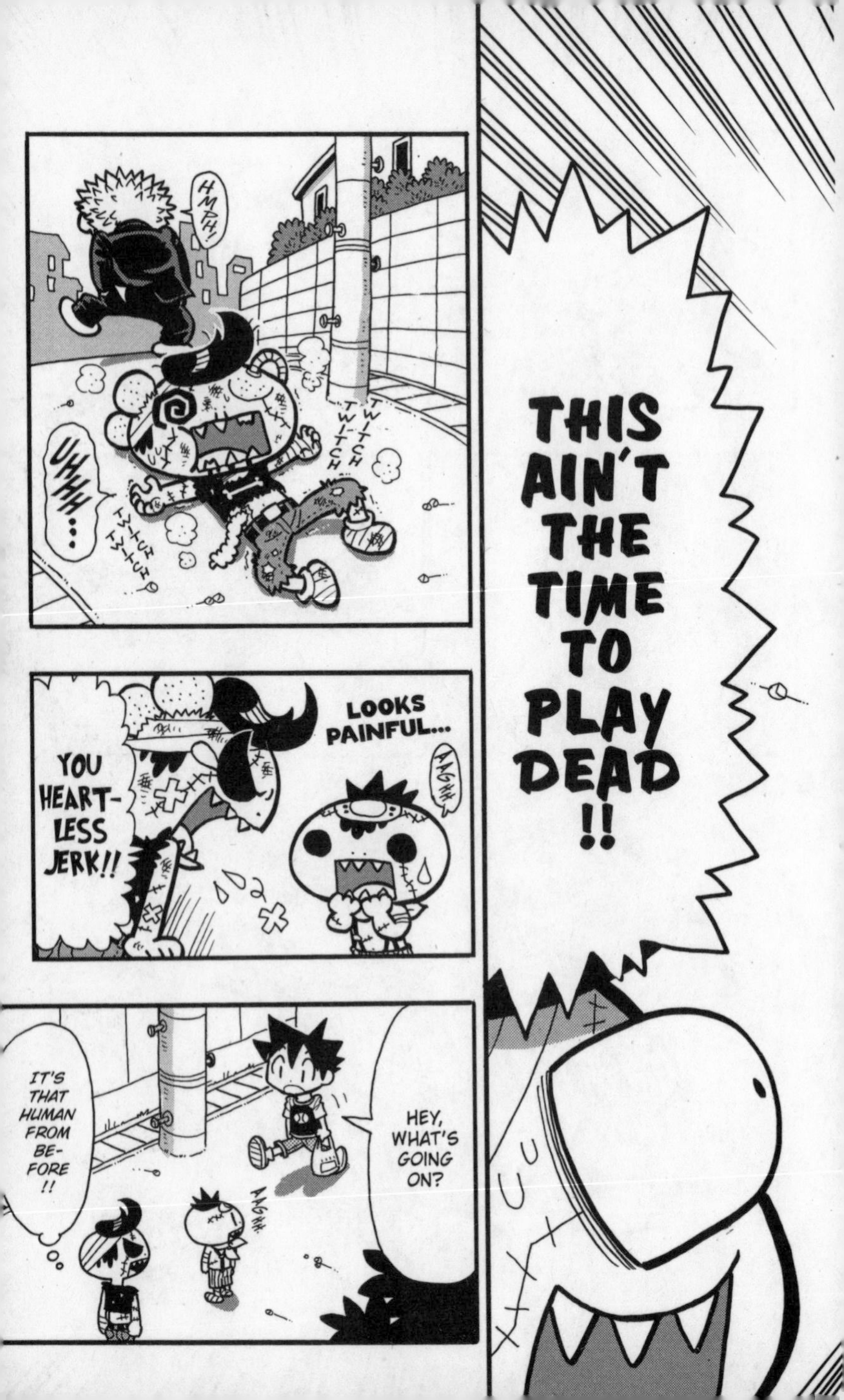
THIS AIN'T THE TIME TO PLAY DEAD!!
HMPH!
TWITCH TWITCH...
UHHH...
TWITCH TWITCH
LOOKS PAINFUL...
AAGHH
YOU HEART-LESS JERK!!
HEY, WHAT'S GOING ON?
AAGHH
IT'S THAT HUMAN FROM BE-FORE!!

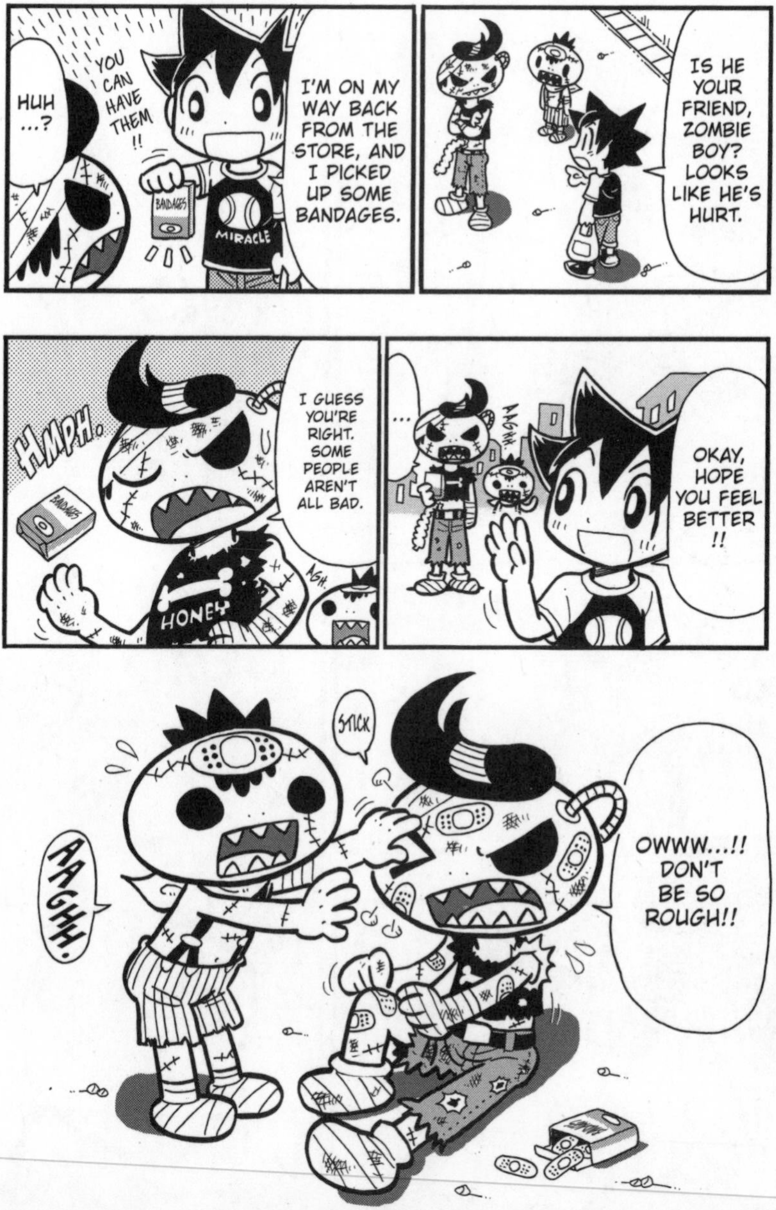
IS HE YOUR FRIEND, ZOMBIE BOY? LOOKS LIKE HE'S HURT.
I'M ON MY WAY BACK FROM THE STORE, AND I PICKED UP SOME BANDAGES.
YOU CAN HAVE THEM!!
HUH ...?
BANDAGES
MIRACLE
OKAY, HOPE YOU FEEL BETTER!!
AAGHH.
...
I GUESS YOU'RE RIGHT. SOME PEOPLE AREN'T ALL BAD.
HMPH.
AGH.
BANDAGES
HONEY
OWWW...!! DON'T BE SO ROUGH!!
STICK
AAGHH.

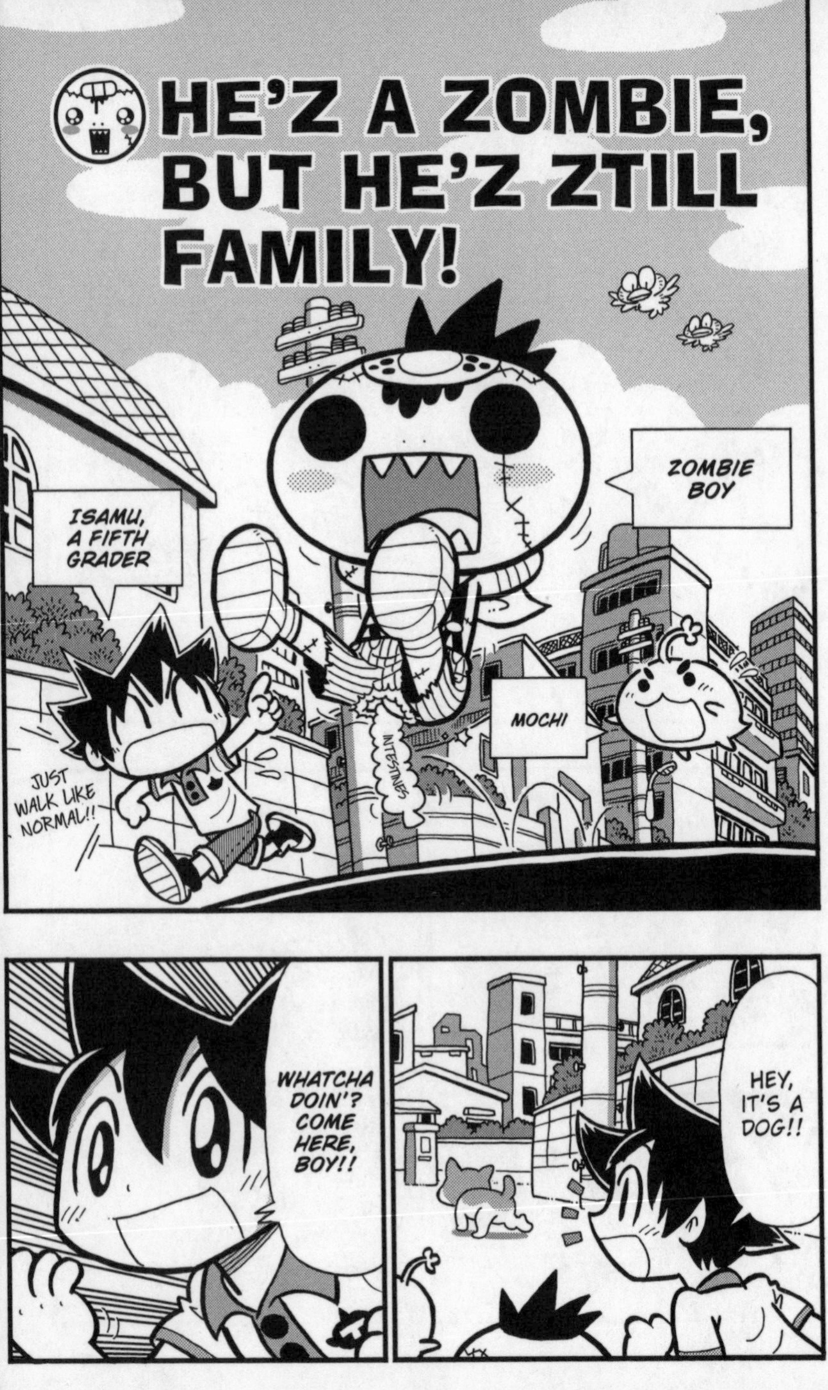
HE'Z A ZOMBIE, BUT HE'Z ZTILL FAMILY!
ZOMBIE BOY
ISAMU, A FIFTH GRADER
MOCHI
INTESTINES
JUST WALK LIKE NORMAL!!
HEY, IT'S A DOG!!
WHATCHA DOIN'? COME HERE, BOY!!

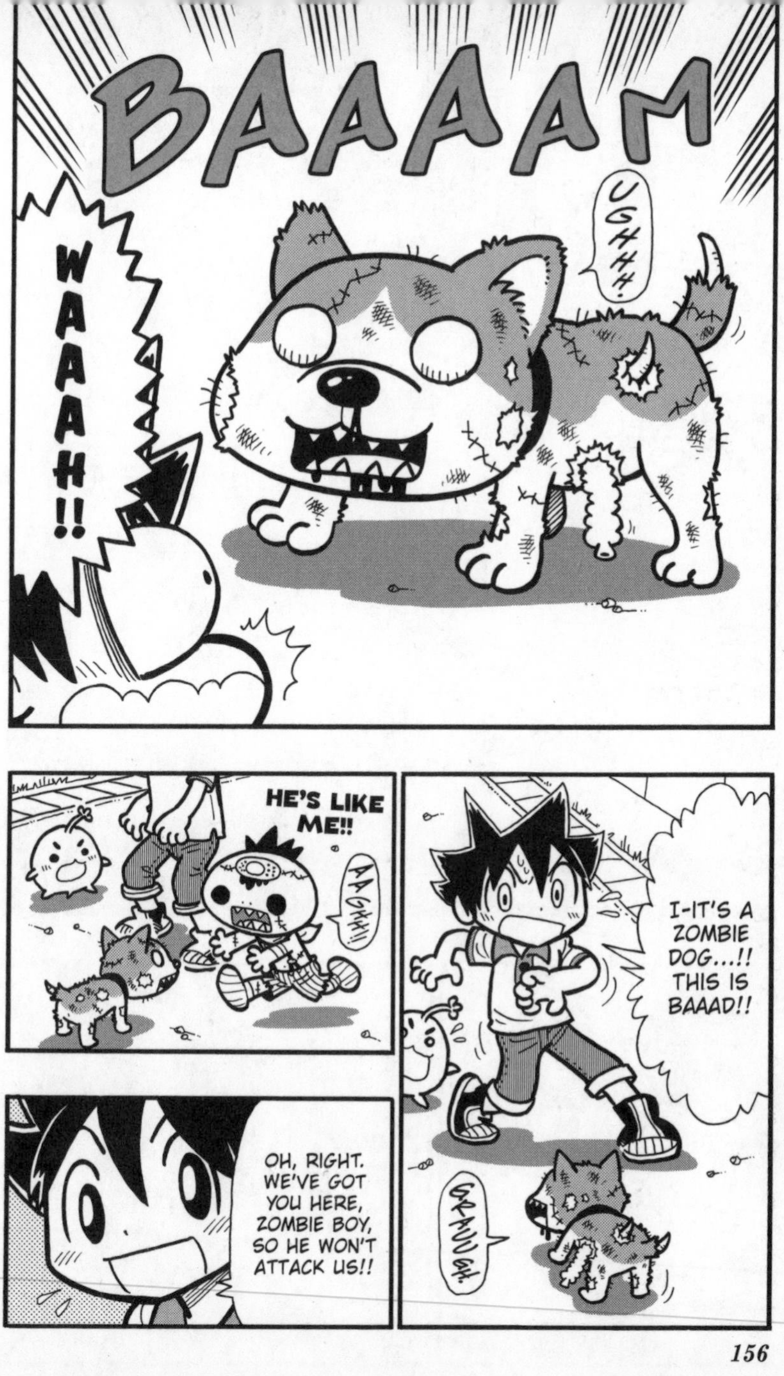
BAAAAM
UGHHH.
WAAAAH!!
I-IT'S A ZOMBIE DOG...!! THIS IS BAAAD!!
GRAUUGH.
HE'S LIKE ME!!
AAGHH!!
OH, RIGHT. WE'VE GOT YOU HERE, ZOMBIE BOY, SO HE WON'T ATTACK US!!

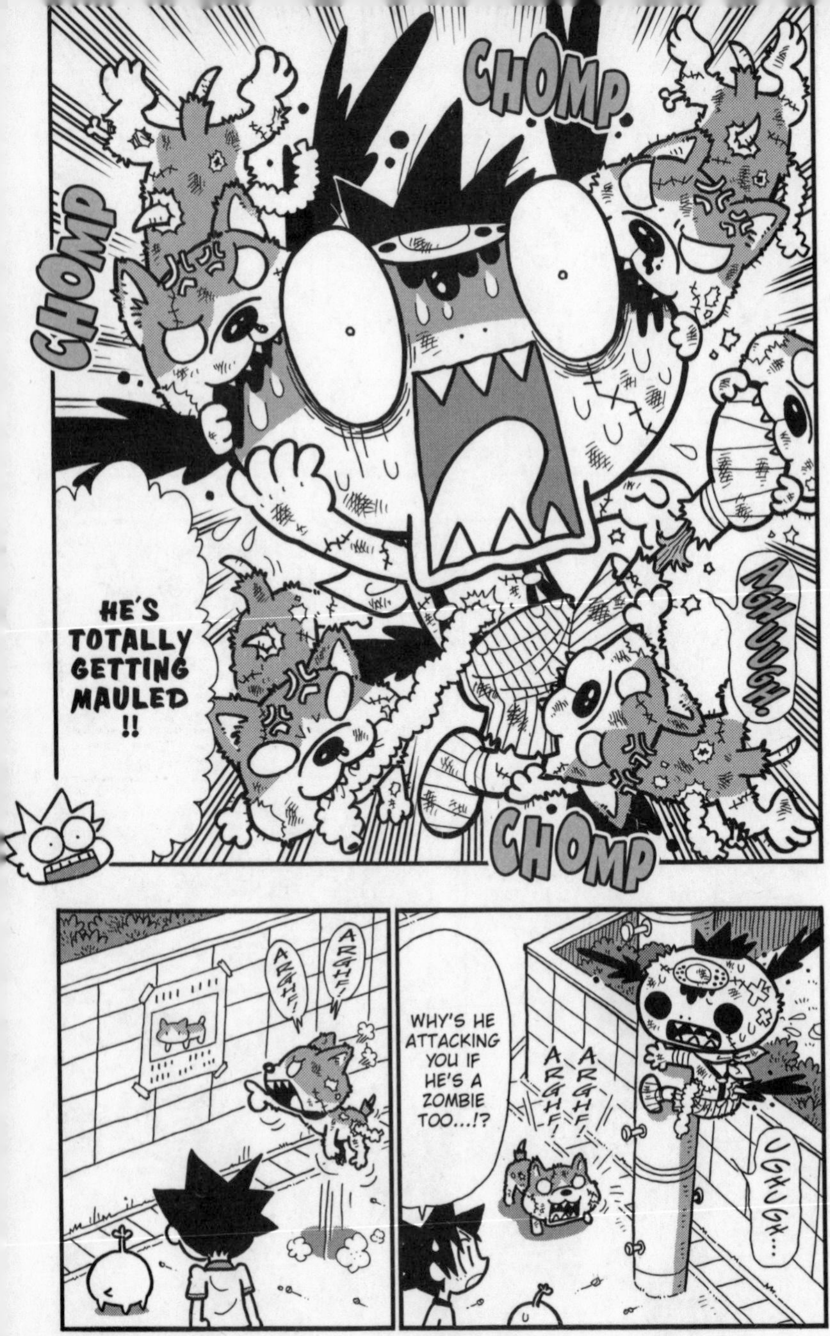
CHOMP
AGHUUGH!
CHOMP
CHOMP
HE'S TOTALLY GETTING MAULED!!
UGHUGH...
ARGHF!
ARGHF!
WHY'S HE ATTACKING YOU IF HE'S A ZOMBIE TOO...!?
ARGHF!
ARGHF!

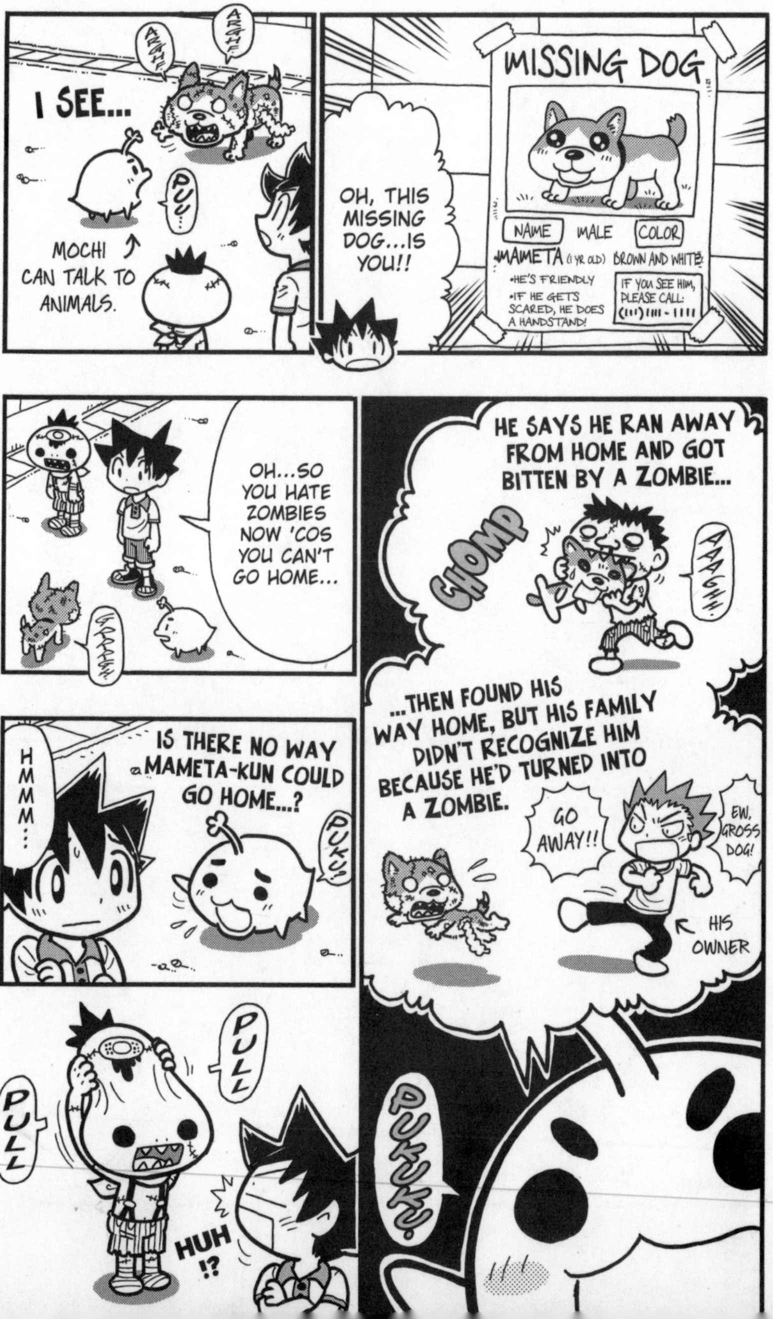
MISSING DOG
NAME
MALE
COLOR
MAMETA (1 YR OLD)
BROWN AND WHITE
•HE'S FRIENDLY
•IF HE GETS SCARED, HE DOES A HANDSTAND!
IF YOU SEE HIM, PLEASE CALL:
OH, THIS MISSING DOG...IS YOU!!
ARGHF
ARGHF
I SEE...
PUU...
MOCHI CAN TALK TO ANIMALS.
HE SAYS HE RAN AWAY FROM HOME AND GOT BITTEN BY A ZOMBIE...
AAAGHH
CHOMP
...THEN FOUND HIS WAY HOME, BUT HIS FAMILY DIDN'T RECOGNIZE HIM BECAUSE HE'D TURNED INTO A ZOMBIE.
EW, GROSS DOG!
GO AWAY!!
HIS OWNER
PUKUKU.
OH...SO YOU HATE ZOMBIES NOW 'COS YOU CAN'T GO HOME...
PUKU?!
IS THERE NO WAY MAMETA-KUN COULD GO HOME...?
HMMM...
PULL
PULL
HUH!?

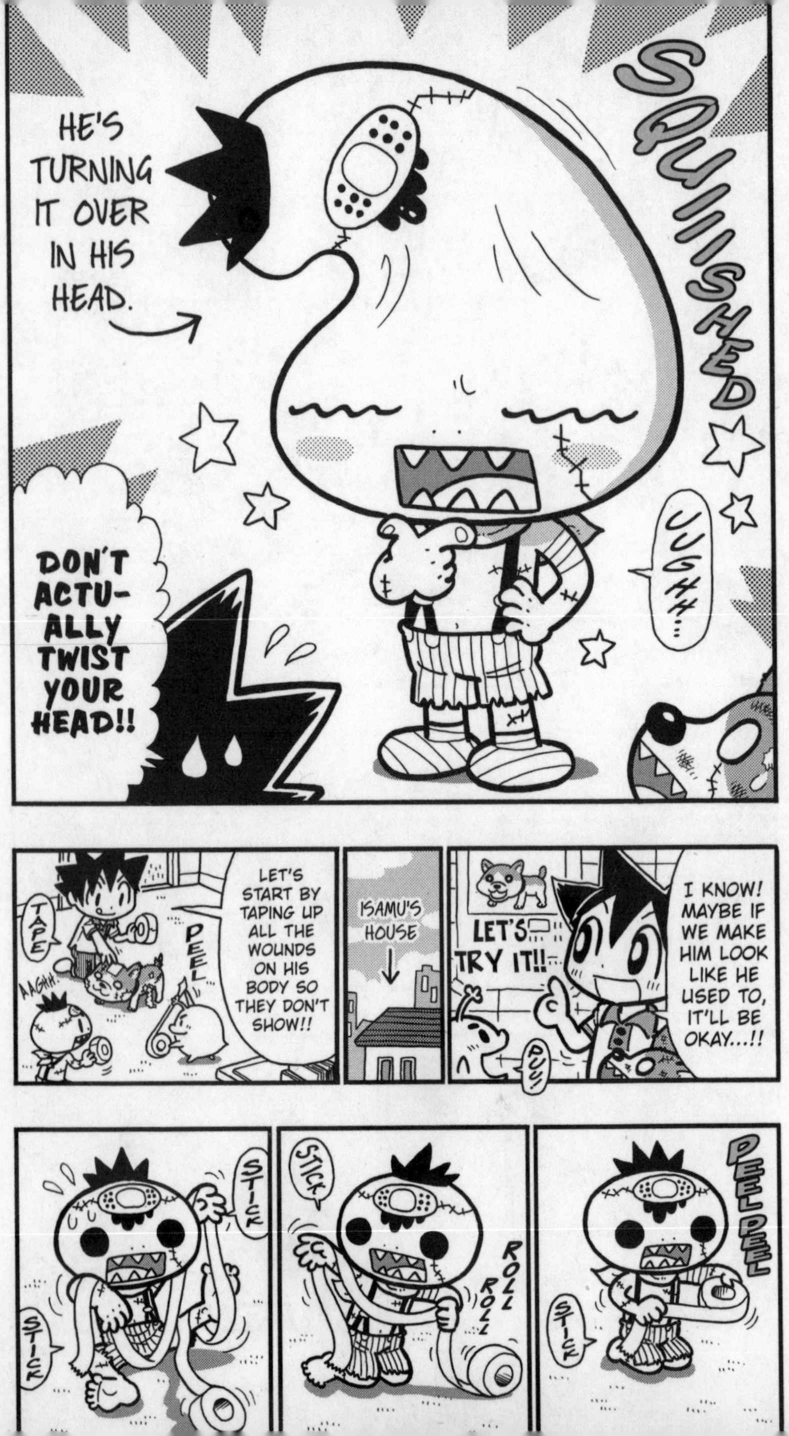
SQUIIIISHED
UGHHH...
HE'S TURNING IT OVER IN HIS HEAD.
DON'T ACTU-ALLY TWIST YOUR HEAD!!
I KNOW! MAYBE IF WE MAKE HIM LOOK LIKE HE USED TO, IT'LL BE OKAY...!!
LET'S TRY IT!!
PUU!
ISAMU'S HOUSE
LET'S START BY TAPING UP ALL THE WOUNDS ON HIS BODY SO THEY DON'T SHOW!!
PEEL
TAPE
AAGHH
PEEL PEEL
STICK
STICK
ROLL ROLL
STICK
STICK

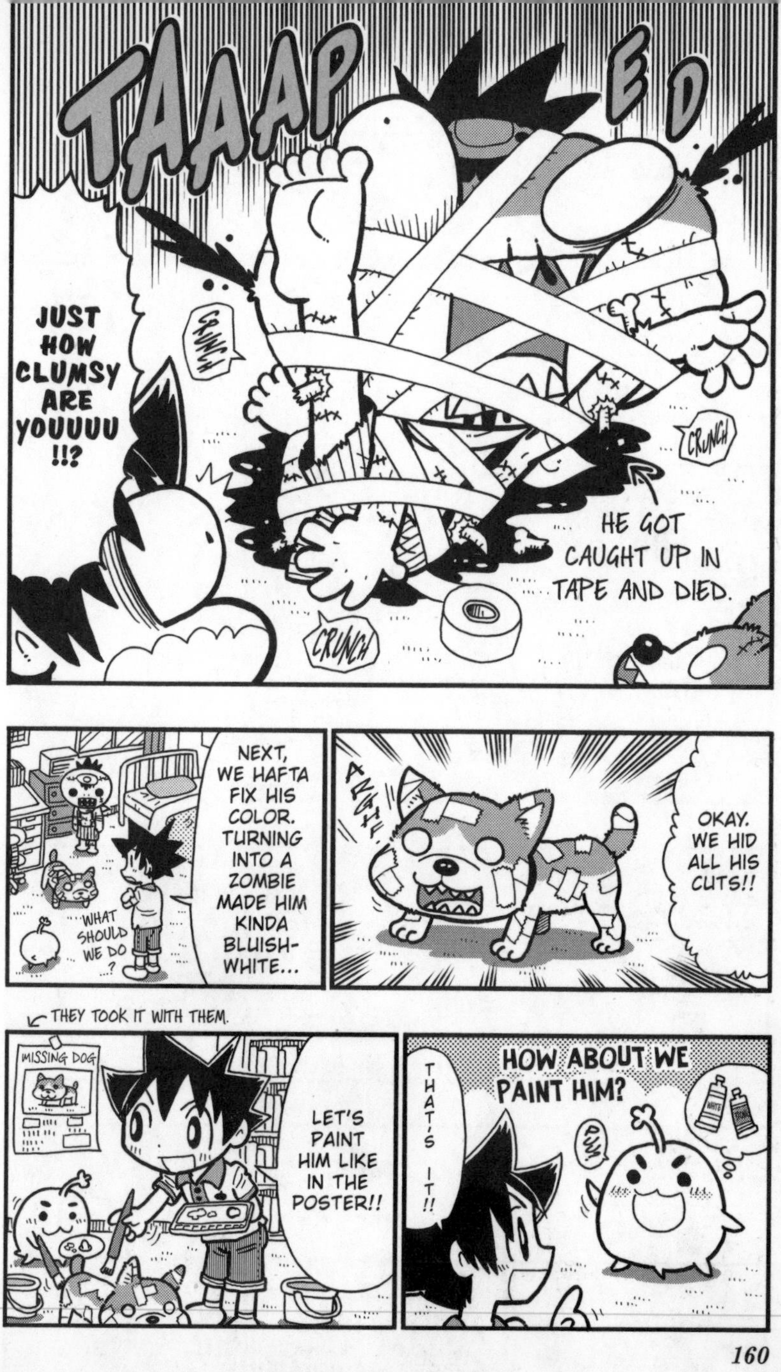
TAAAPED
CRUNCH
HE GOT CAUGHT UP IN TAPE AND DIED.
JUST HOW CLUMSY ARE YOUUUU!!?
CRUNCH
CRUNCH
OKAY. WE HID ALL HIS CUTS!!
NEXT, WE HAFTA FIX HIS COLOR. TURNING INTO A ZOMBIE MADE HIM KINDA BLUISH-WHITE...
WHAT SHOULD WE DO...?
THEY TOOK IT WITH THEM.
HOW ABOUT WE PAINT HIM?
WHITE
THAT'S IT!!
LET'S PAINT HIM LIKE IN THE POSTER!!
MISSING DOG

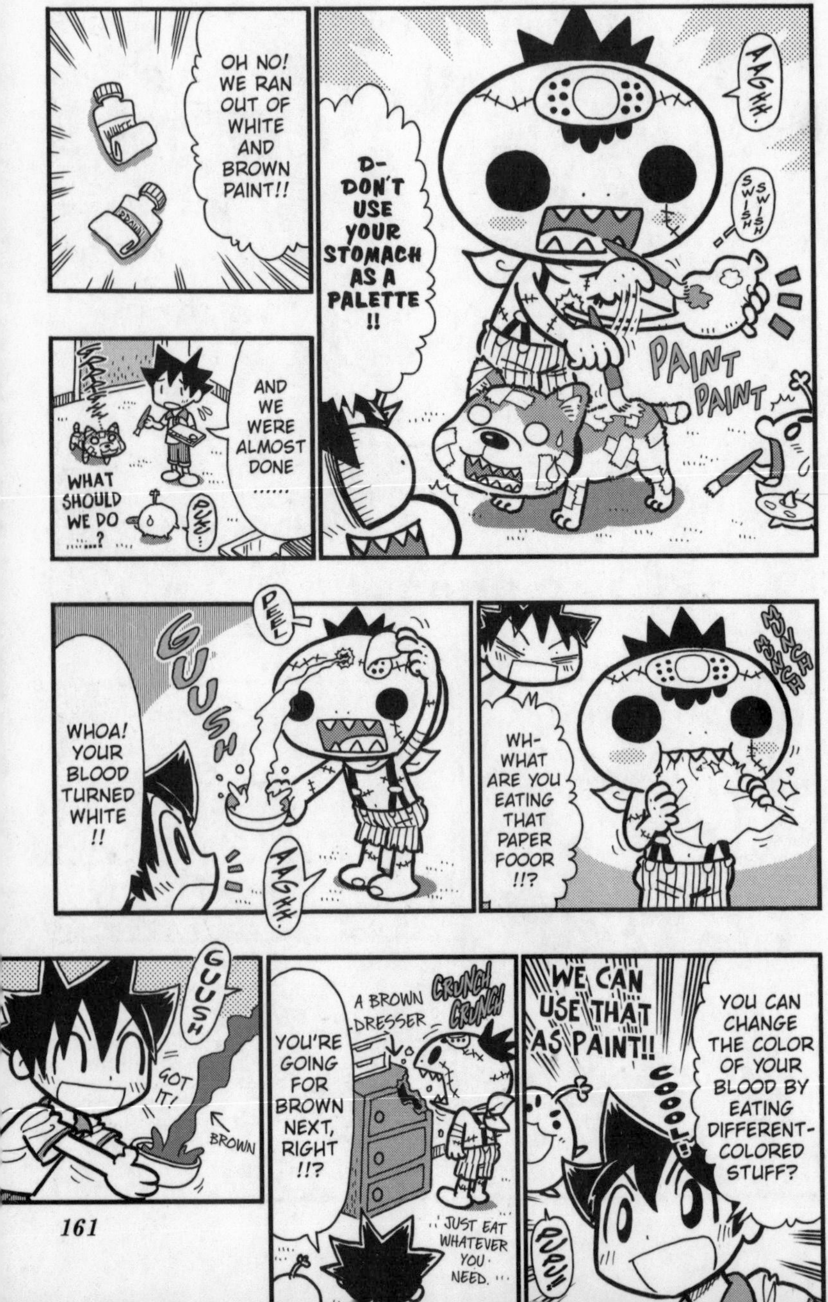
AAGHH.
SWISH SWISH
D-DON'T USE YOUR STOMACH AS A PALETTE!!
PAINT PAINT
OH NO! WE RAN OUT OF WHITE AND BROWN PAINT!!
WHITE
AND WE WERE ALMOST DONE......
WHAT SHOULD WE DO......?
PUKI...
MUNCH MUNCH
WH-WHAT ARE YOU EATING THAT PAPER FOOOR!!?
PEEL
GUUSH
WHOA! YOUR BLOOD TURNED WHITE!!
AAGHH.
WE CAN USE THAT AS PAINT!!
YOU CAN CHANGE THE COLOR OF YOUR BLOOD BY EATING DIFFERENT-COLORED STUFF?
COOOOL!!
PUPU!
A BROWN DRESSER
CRUNCH CRUNCH
YOU'RE GOING FOR BROWN NEXT, RIGHT!!?
JUST EAT WHATEVER YOU NEED.
GUUSH
GOT IT!
BROWN

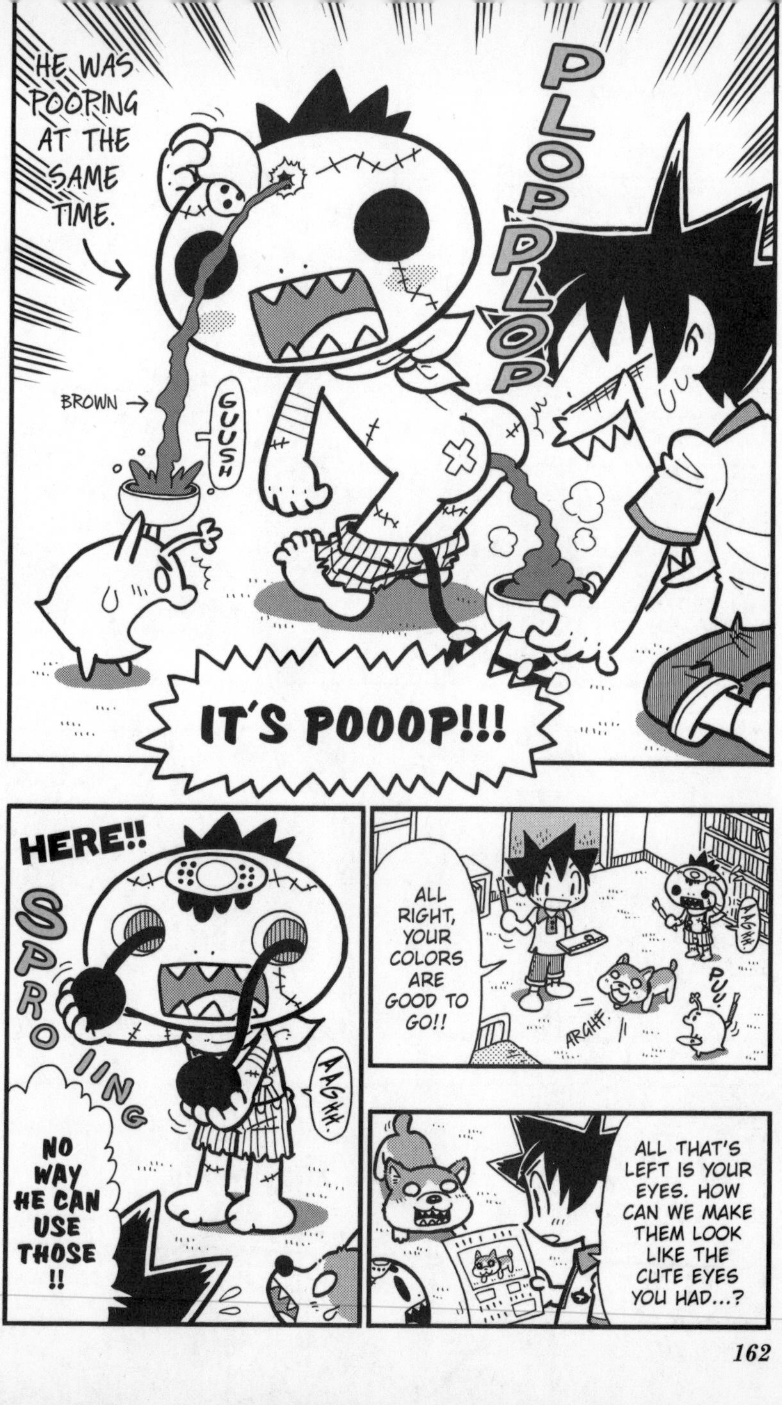
PLOP PLOP
HE WAS POOPING AT THE SAME TIME.
GUUSH
BROWN
IT'S POOOP!!!
AAGHH
PUU!
ALL RIGHT, YOUR COLORS ARE GOOD TO GO!!
ARGHF
ALL THAT'S LEFT IS YOUR EYES. HOW CAN WE MAKE THEM LOOK LIKE THE CUTE EYES YOU HAD...?
HERE!!
AAGHH
SPROIING
NO WAY HE CAN USE THOSE!!

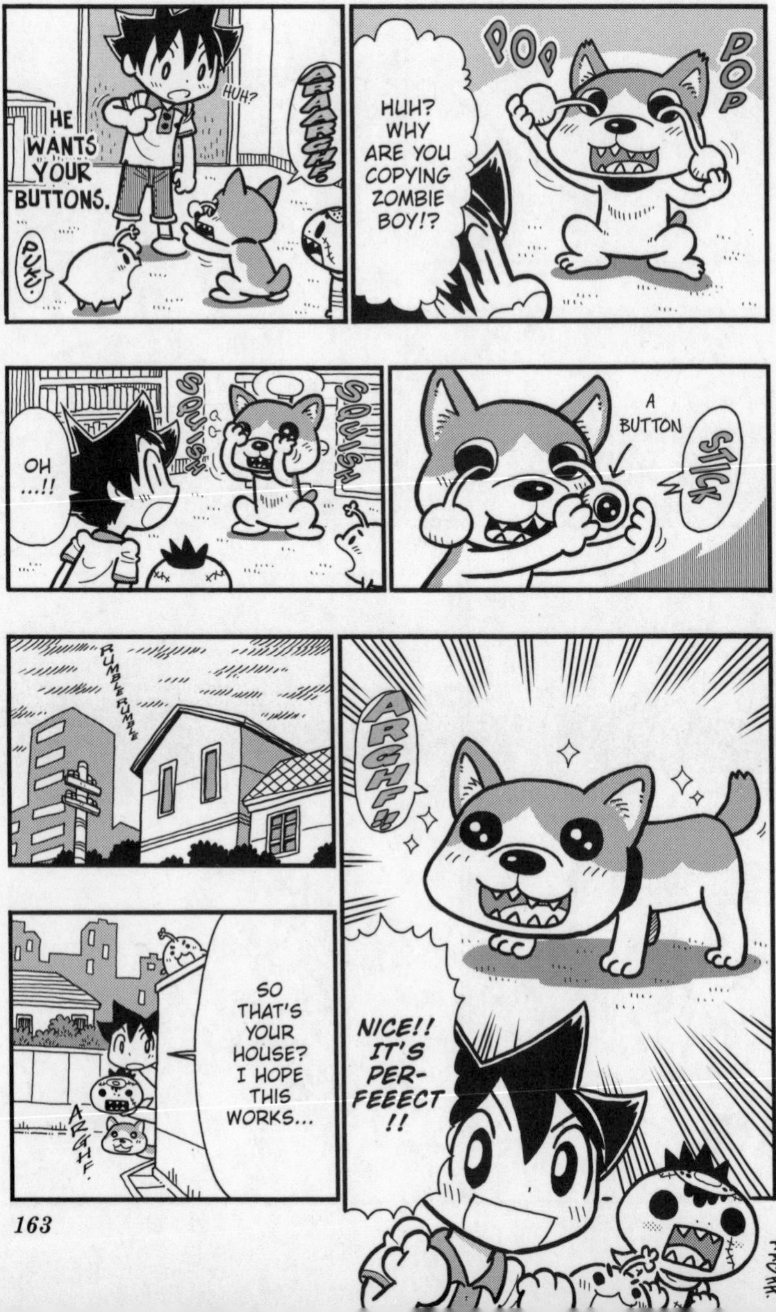
POP
POP
HUH? WHY ARE YOU COPYING ZOMBIE BOY!?
ARAARGHF
HUH?
HE WANTS YOUR BUTTONS.
PUKU.
A BUTTON
STICK
SQUISH
SQUISH
OH ...!!
ARGHF!!
NICE!! IT'S PER-FEEECT!!
AAGHH.
RUMBLE RUMBLE
SO THAT'S YOUR HOUSE? I HOPE THIS WORKS...
ARGHF.

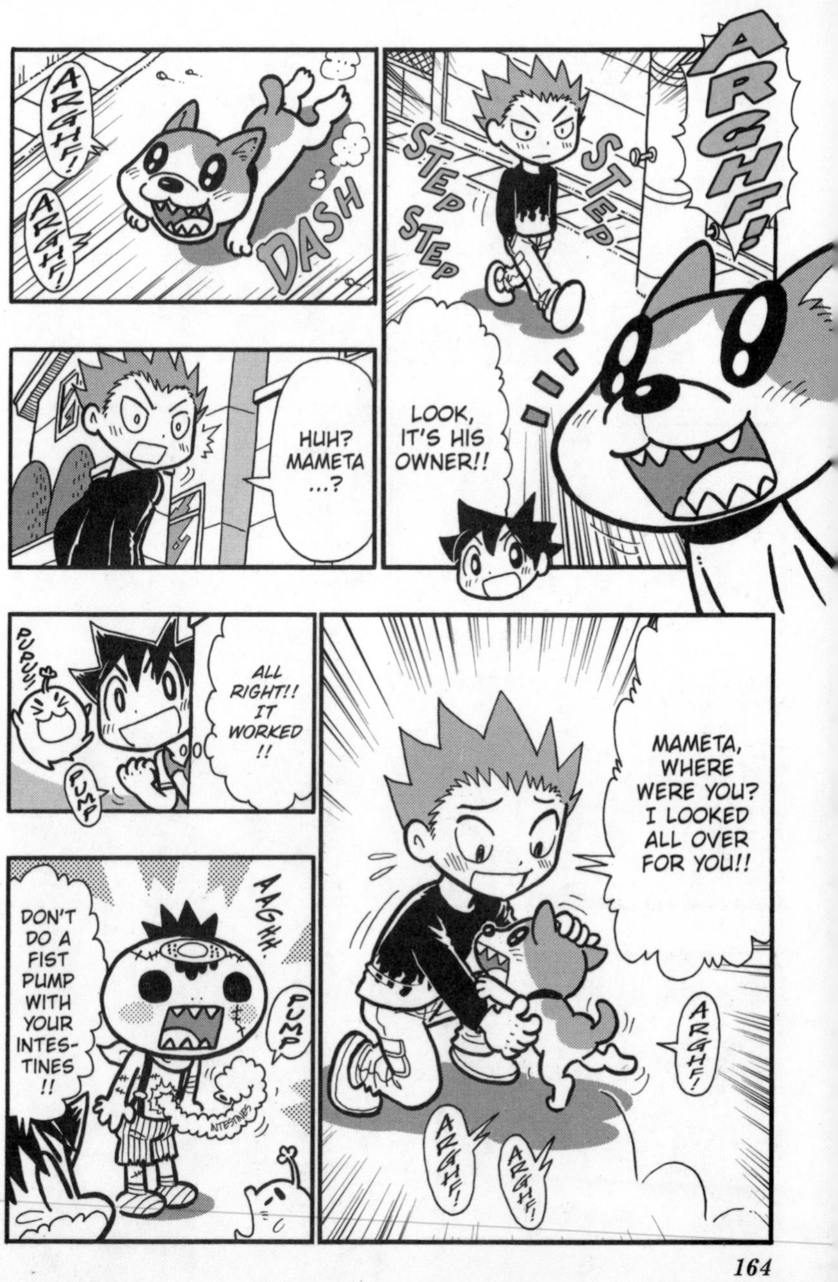
ARGHF!
STEP STEP
STEP STEP
LOOK, IT'S HIS OWNER!!
ARGHF!
ARGHF!
DASH
HUH? MAMETA ...?
MAMETA, WHERE WERE YOU? I LOOKED ALL OVER FOR YOU!!
ARGHF!
ARGHF!
ARGHF!
ALL RIGHT!! IT WORKED!!
PUPUU!!
PUMP
DON'T DO A FIST PUMP WITH YOUR INTES-TINES!!
AAGHH.
PUMP
INTESTINES

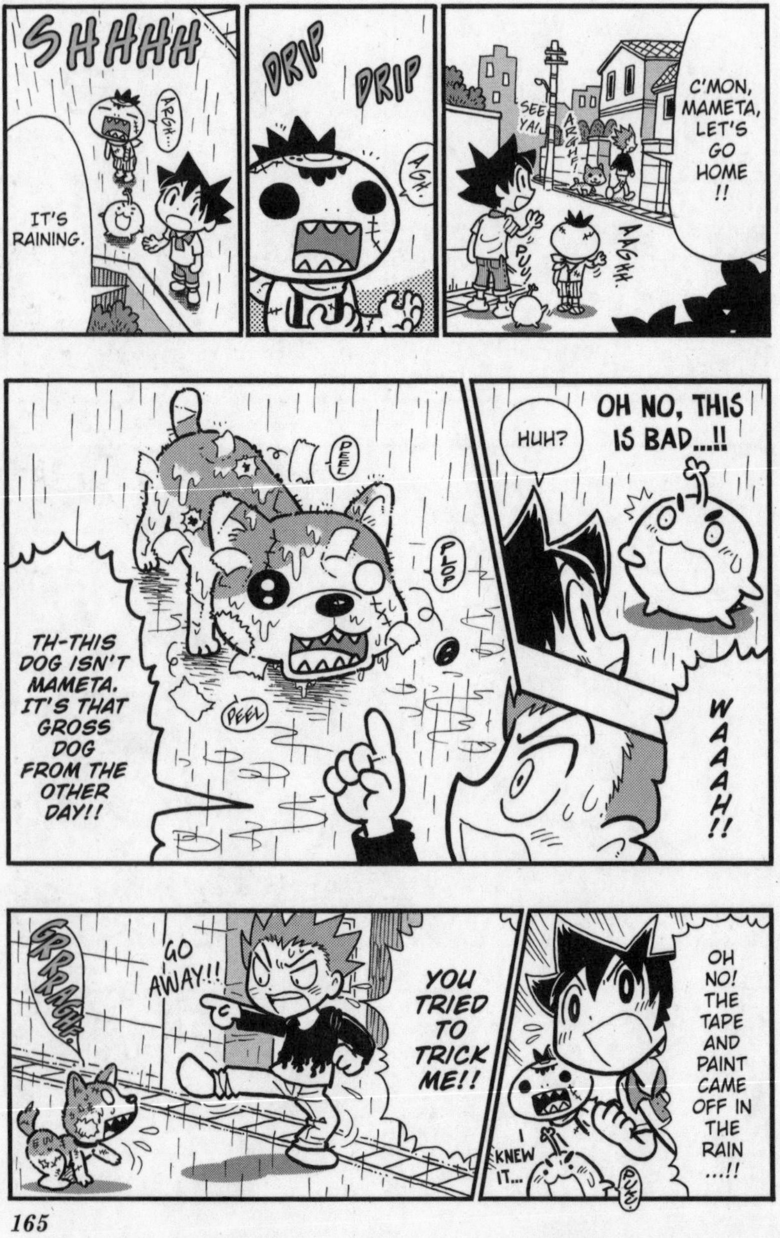
C'MON, MAMETA, LET'S GO HOME!!
SEE YA!
AAGHH
DRIP
DRIP
AGH
SHHHH
ARGH...
IT'S RAINING.
OH NO, THIS IS BAD...!!
HUH?
WAAAAH!!
PEEL
PLOP
PEEL
TH-THIS DOG ISN'T MAMETA. IT'S THAT GROSS DOG FROM THE OTHER DAY!!
OH NO! THE TAPE AND PAINT CAME OFF IN THE RAIN...!!
I KNEW IT...
YOU TRIED TO TRICK ME!!
GO AWAY!!

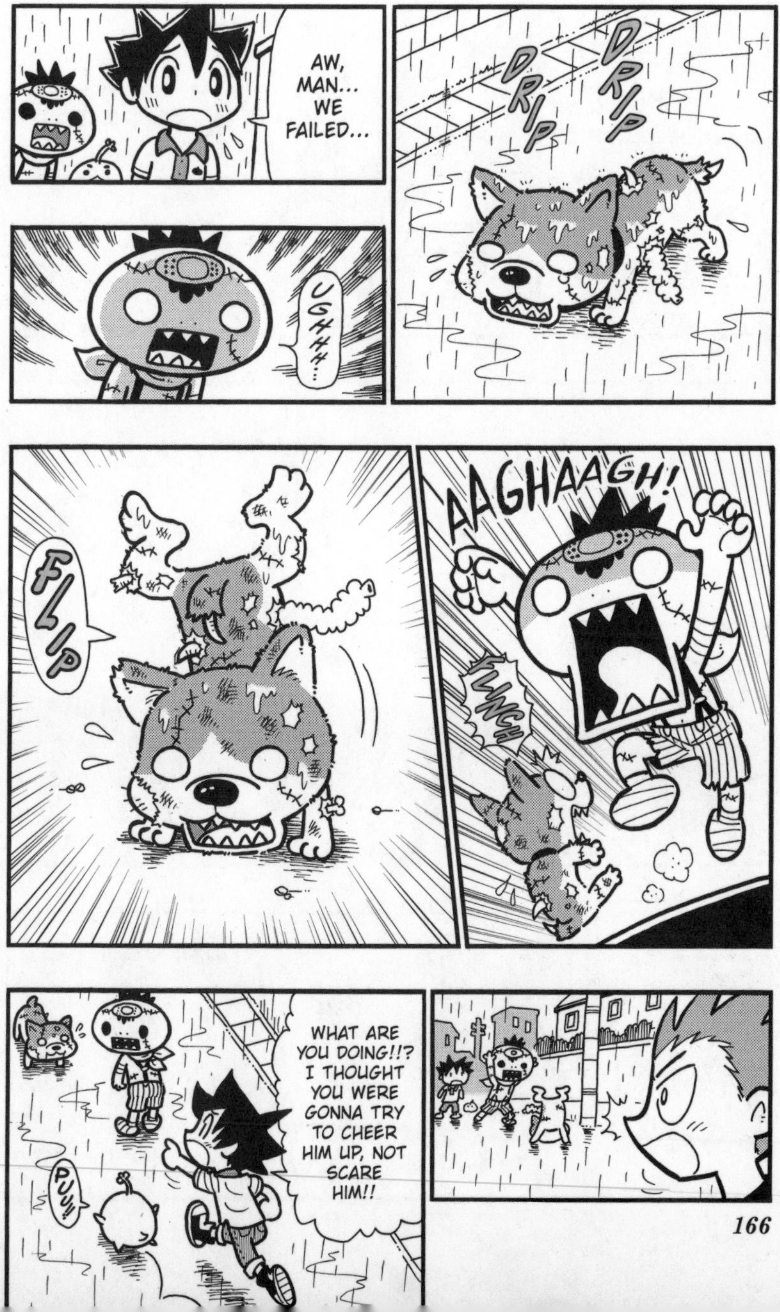
DRIP DRIP
AW, MAN... WE FAILED...
UGHHH...
AAGHAAGH!
FLINCH
FLIP
WHAT ARE YOU DOING!!? I THOUGHT YOU WERE GONNA TRY TO CHEER HIM UP, NOT SCARE HIM!!
PUU!!

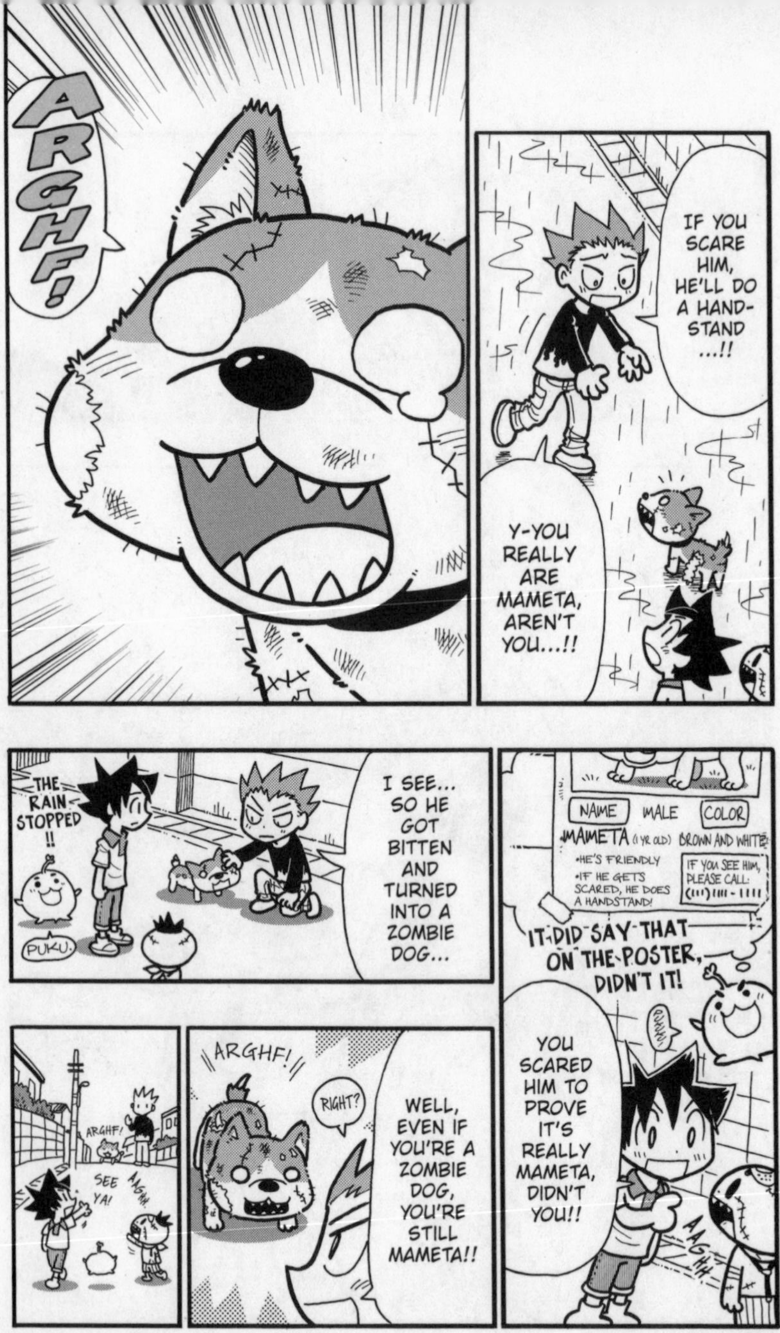
IF YOU SCARE HIM, HE'LL DO A HAND-STAND ...!!
Y-YOU REALLY ARE MAMETA, AREN'T YOU...!!
ARGHF!
NAME
MALE
COLOR
MAMETA (1 YR OLD)
BROWN AND WHITE
•HE'S FRIENDLY
•IF HE GETS SCARED, HE DOES A HANDSTAND!
IF YOU SEE HIM, PLEASE CALL:
IT DID SAY THAT ON THE POSTER, DIDN'T IT!
YOU SCARED HIM TO PROVE IT'S REALLY MAMETA, DIDN'T YOU!!
AAGHH
I SEE... SO HE GOT BITTEN AND TURNED INTO A ZOMBIE DOG...
THE RAIN STOPPED !!
PUKU
WELL, EVEN IF YOU'RE A ZOMBIE DOG, YOU'RE STILL MAMETA!!
RIGHT?
ARGHF!
ARGHF!
AAGHH
SEE YA!

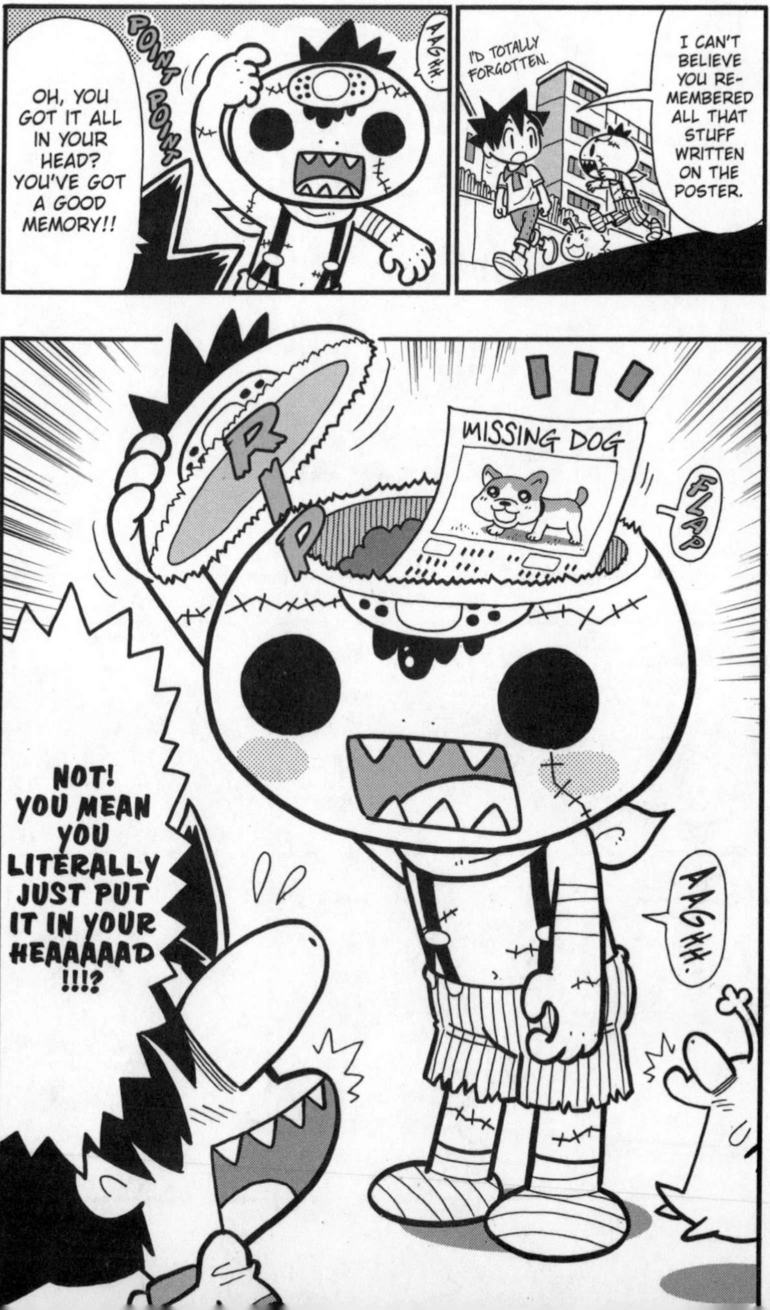

I CAN'T BELIEVE YOU RE-MEMBERED ALL THAT STUFF WRITTEN ON THE POSTER.
I'D TOTALLY FORGOTTEN.
AAGHH.
POINT POINT
OH, YOU GOT IT ALL IN YOUR HEAD? YOU'VE GOT A GOOD MEMORY!!
FLAP
MISSING DOG
RIP
AAGHH.
NOT! YOU MEAN YOU LITERALLY JUST PUT IT IN YOUR HEAAAAAD!!!?

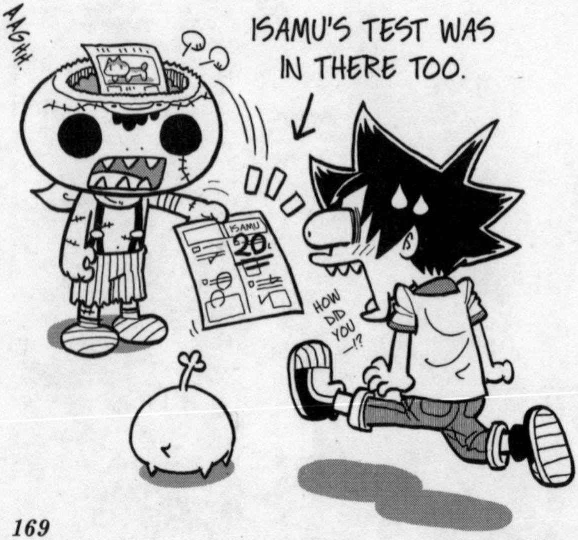
ISAMU'S TEST WAS IN THERE TOO.
HOW DID YOU—!?
ISAMU
20
AAGHH.

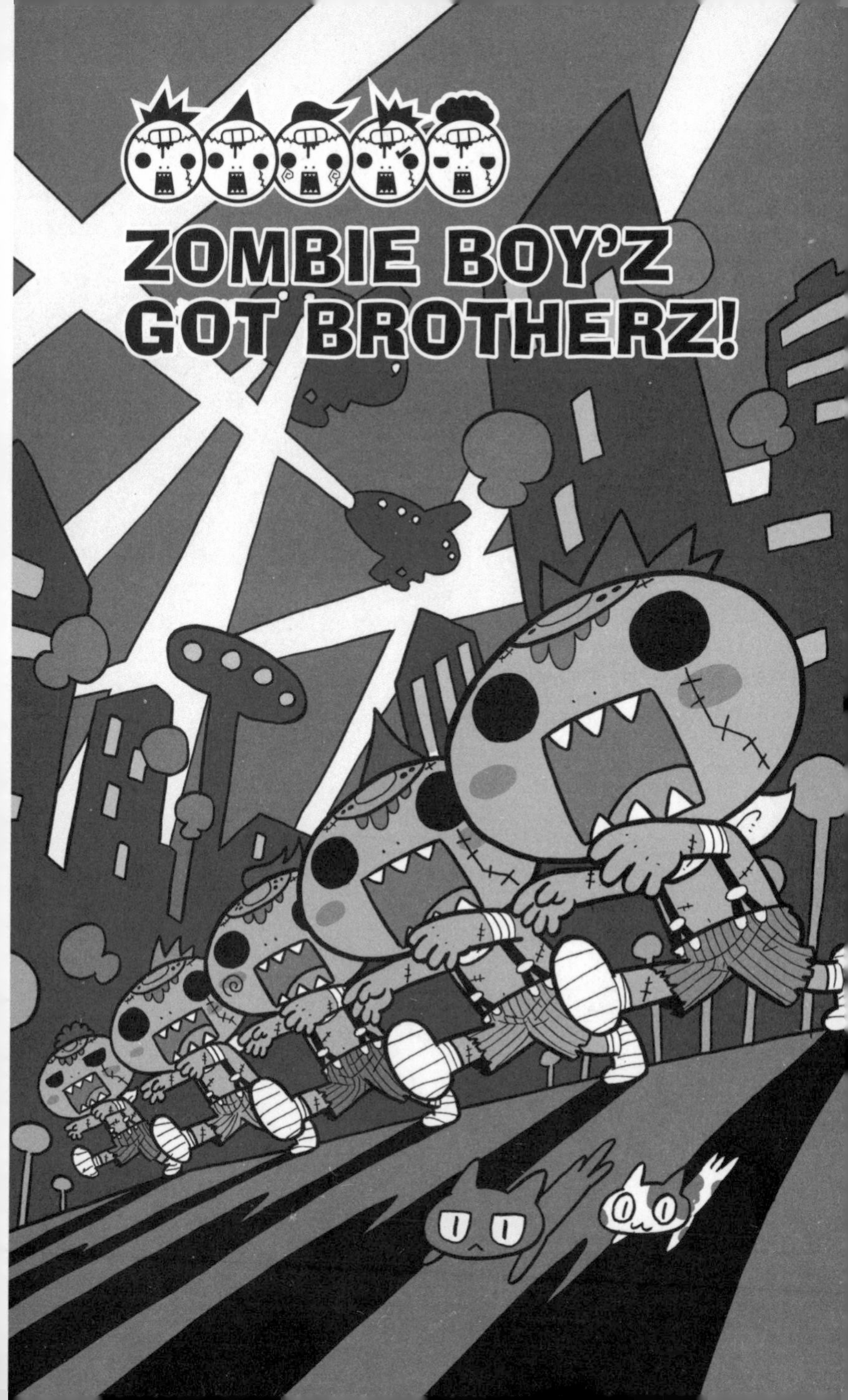
ZOMBIE BOY'Z
GOT BROTHERZ!

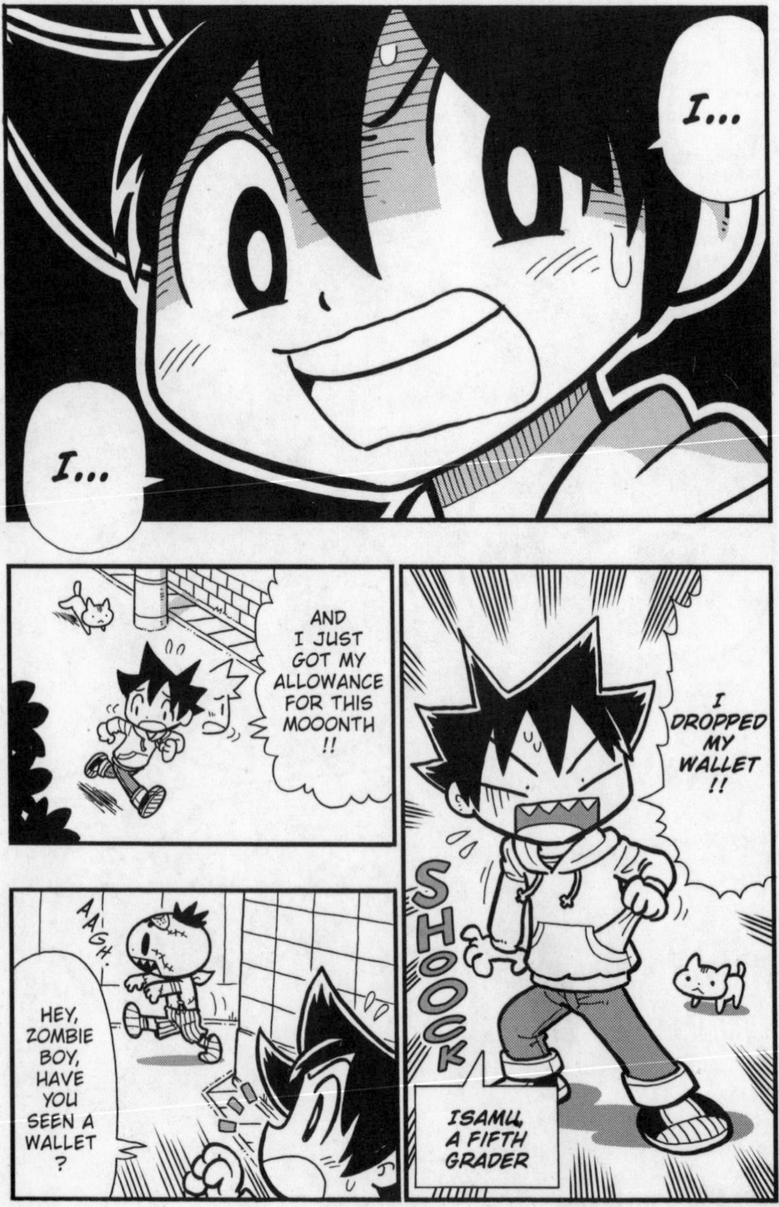
I...
I...
I DROPPED MY WALLET !!
SHOOCK
ISAMU, A FIFTH GRADER
AND I JUST GOT MY ALLOWANCE FOR THIS MOOOONTH !!
AAGH.
HEY, ZOMBIE BOY, HAVE YOU SEEN A WALLET ?

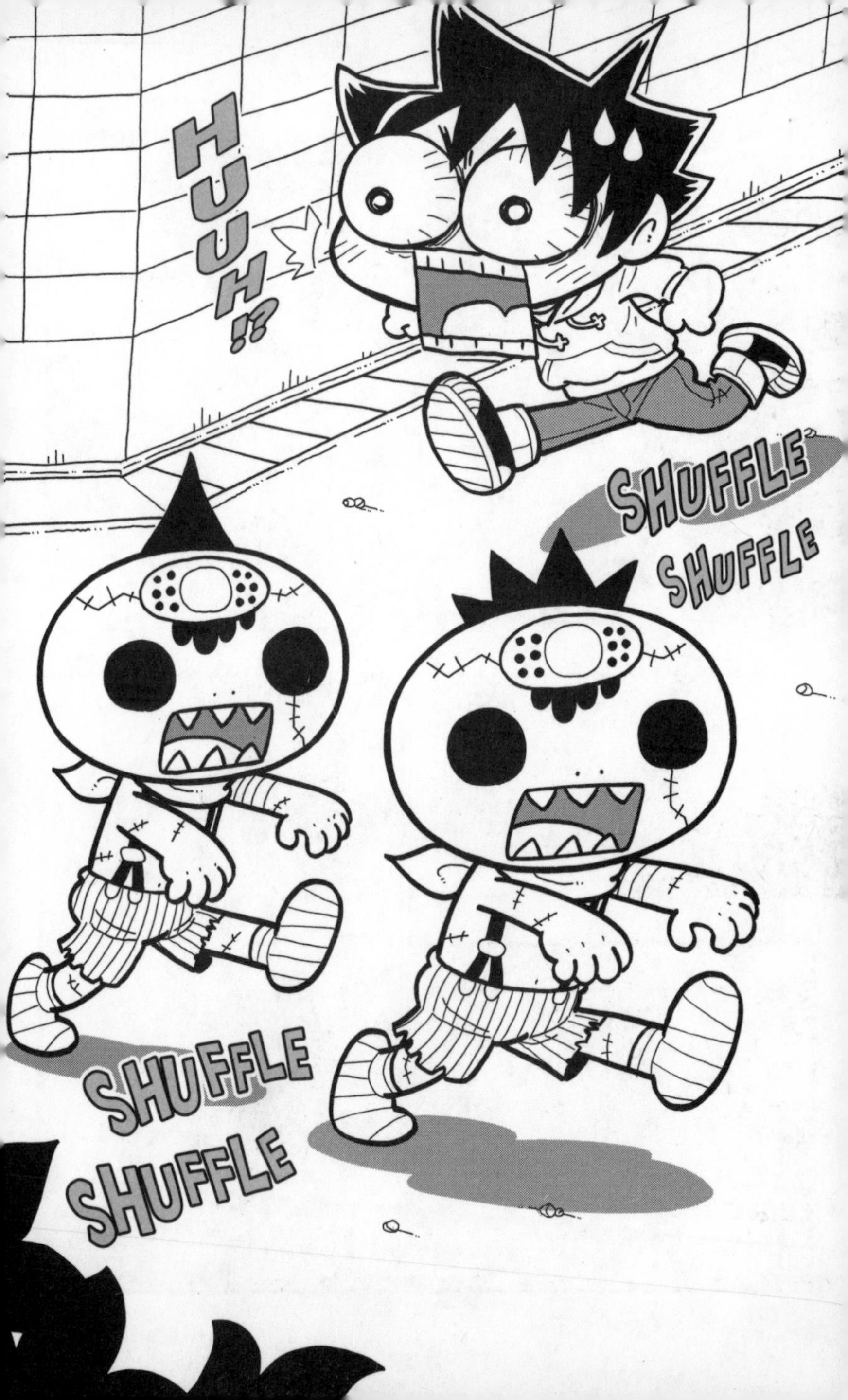
HUUUH!?
SHUFFLE
SHUFFLE
SHUFFLE
SHUFFLE

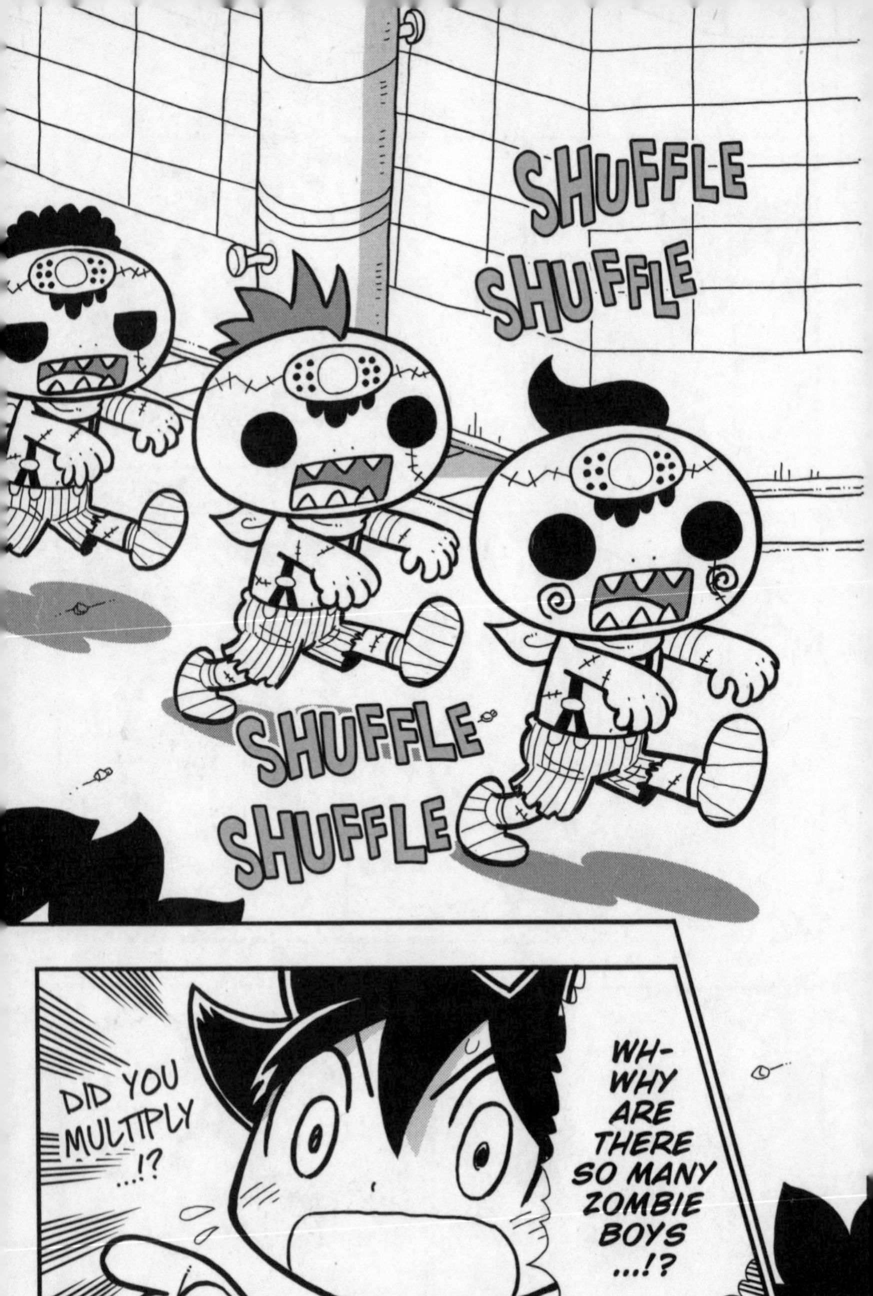
SHUFFLE
SHUFFLE
SHUFFLE
SHUFFLE
WH- WHY ARE THERE SO MANY ZOMBIE BOYS ...!?
DID YOU MULTIPLY ...!?

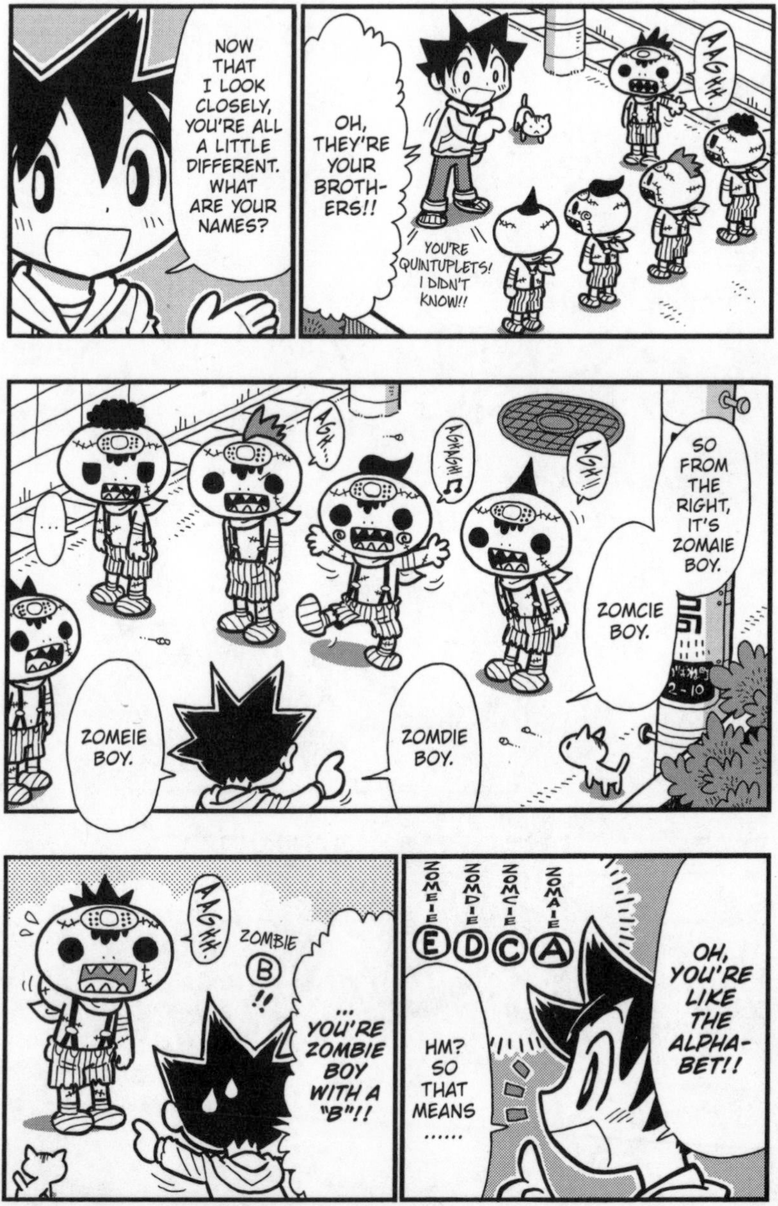
AAGHH.
OH, THEY'RE YOUR BROTH-ERS!!
YOU'RE QUINTUPLETS! I DIDN'T KNOW!!
NOW THAT I LOOK CLOSELY, YOU'RE ALL A LITTLE DIFFERENT. WHAT ARE YOUR NAMES?
SO FROM THE RIGHT, IT'S ZOMAIE BOY.
AGH!!
AGHAGH!♫
AGH...
...
ZOMCIE BOY.
ZOMDIE BOY.
ZOMEIE BOY.
ZOMAIE A
ZOMCIE C
ZOMDIE D
ZOMEIE E
OH, YOU'RE LIKE THE ALPHA-BET!!
HM? SO THAT MEANS ......
AAGHH.
ZOMBIE B !!
... YOU'RE ZOMBIE BOY WITH A "B"!!

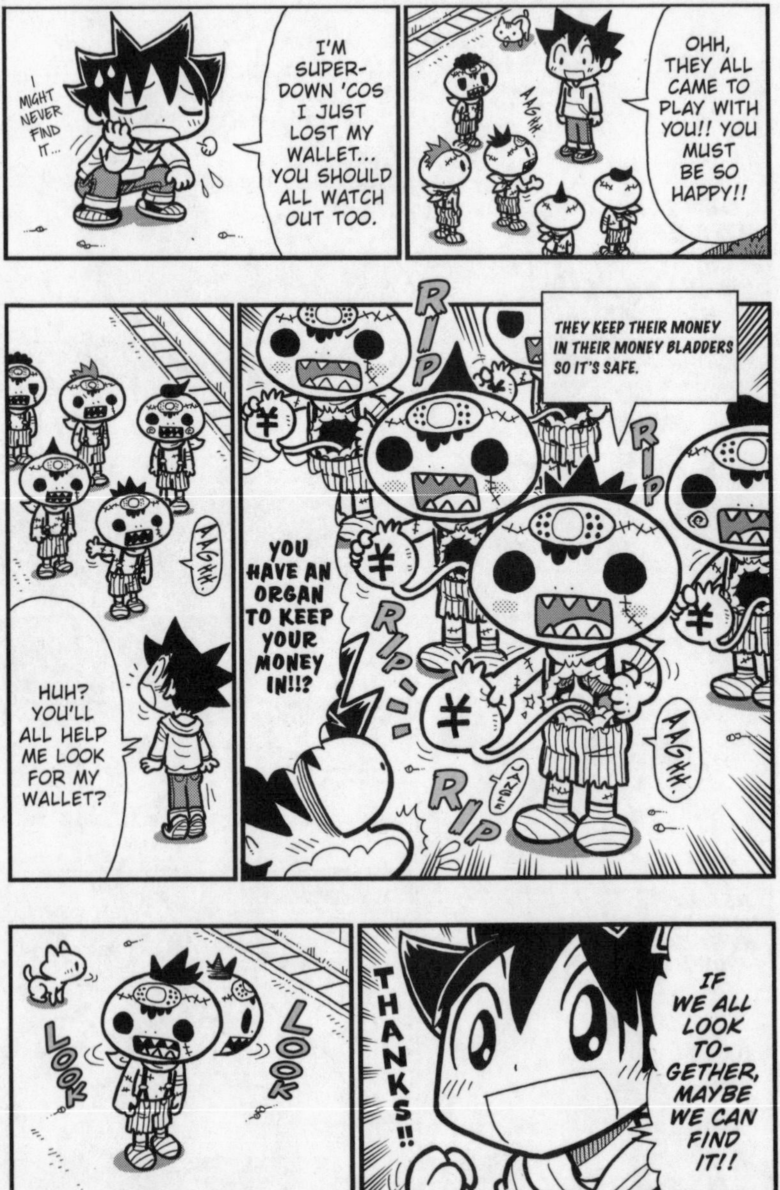

OHH, THEY ALL CAME TO PLAY WITH YOU!! YOU MUST BE SO HAPPY!!
AAGHH.
I'M SUPER-DOWN 'COS I JUST LOST MY WALLET... YOU SHOULD ALL WATCH OUT TOO.
I MIGHT NEVER FIND IT...
THEY KEEP THEIR MONEY IN THEIR MONEY BLADDERS SO IT'S SAFE.
RIP
RIP
AAGHH.
YOU HAVE AN ORGAN TO KEEP YOUR MONEY IN!!?
RIP
RIP
RIP
AAGHH.
HUH? YOU'LL ALL HELP ME LOOK FOR MY WALLET?
IF WE ALL LOOK TO-GETHER, MAYBE WE CAN FIND IT!!
THANKS!!
LOOK
LOOK

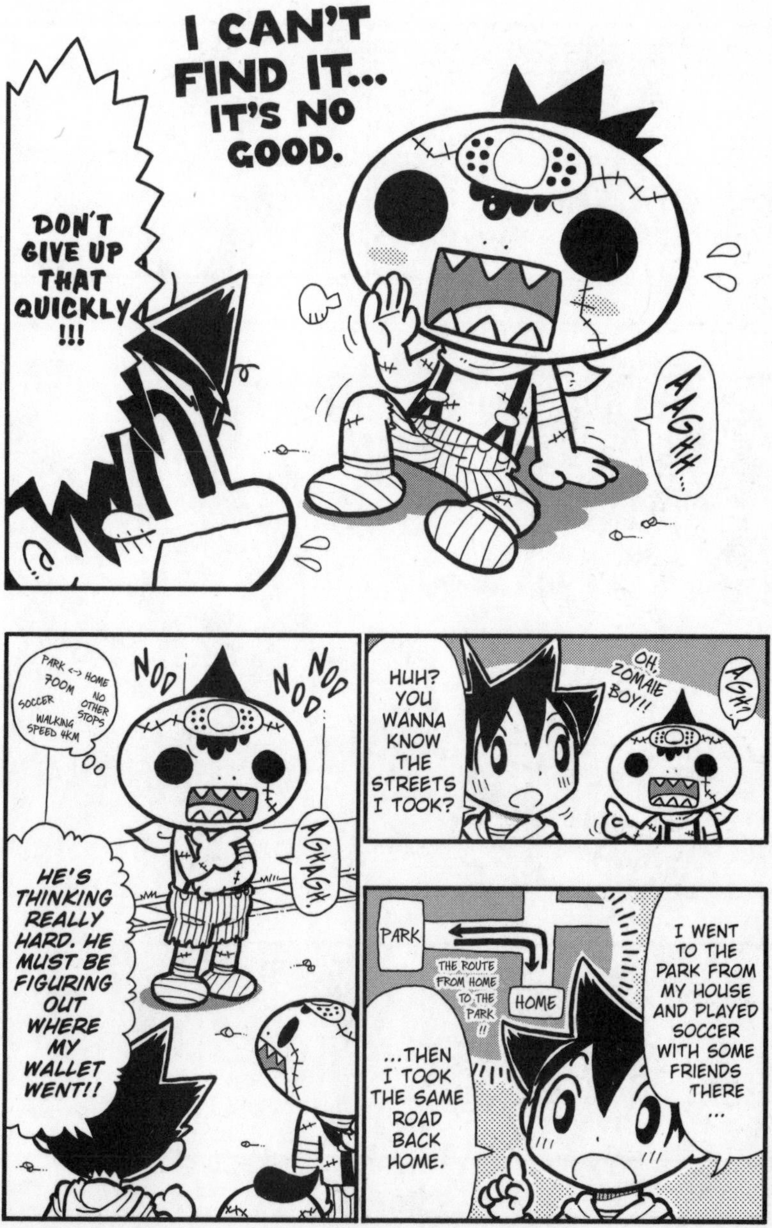
I CAN'T FIND IT... IT'S NO GOOD.
AAGHH...
DON'T GIVE UP THAT QUICKLY!!!
OH, ZOMBIE BOY!!
AGH!!
HUH? YOU WANNA KNOW THE STREETS I TOOK?
I WENT TO THE PARK FROM MY HOUSE AND PLAYED SOCCER WITH SOME FRIENDS THERE...
PARK
HOME
THE ROUTE FROM HOME TO THE PARK!!
...THEN I TOOK THE SAME ROAD BACK HOME.
NOD NOD NOD
PARK <-> HOME 700M NO OTHER STOPS SOCCER WALKING SPEED 4KM
AGHAGH.
HE'S THINKING REALLY HARD. HE MUST BE FIGURING OUT WHERE MY WALLET WENT!!

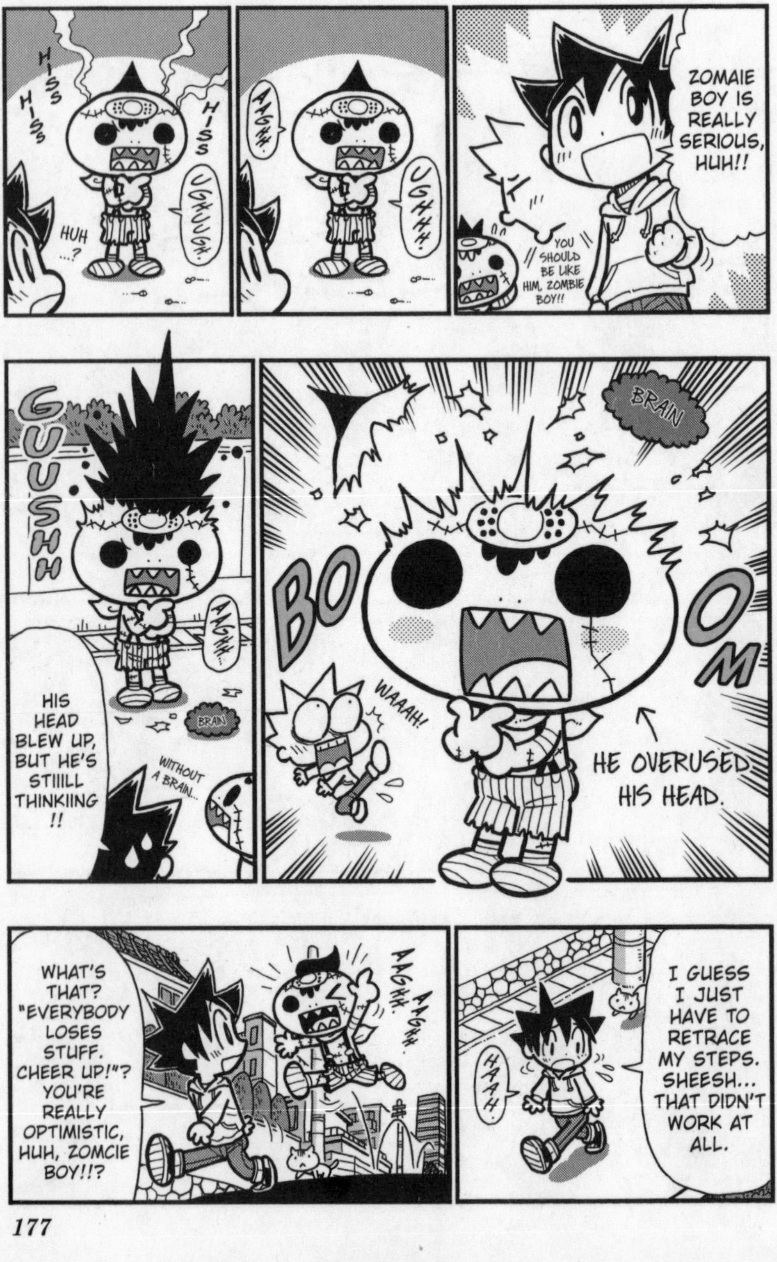
ZOMAIE BOY IS REALLY SERIOUS, HUH!!
YOU SHOULD BE LIKE HIM, ZOMBIE BOY!!
AAGHH.
UGHHH.
HISS
HISS
HISS
UGHUUGH.
HUH ...?
BRAIN
BOOM
WAAAH!
HE OVERUSED HIS HEAD.
GUUSHH
AAGHH...
BRAIN
HIS HEAD BLEW UP, BUT HE'S STIIILL THINKIING!!
WITHOUT A BRAIN...
I GUESS I JUST HAVE TO RETRACE MY STEPS. SHEESH... THAT DIDN'T WORK AT ALL.
HAAAH.
AAGHH.
AAGHH.
WHAT'S THAT? "EVERYBODY LOSES STUFF. CHEER UP!"? YOU'RE REALLY OPTIMISTIC, HUH, ZOMCIE BOY!!?

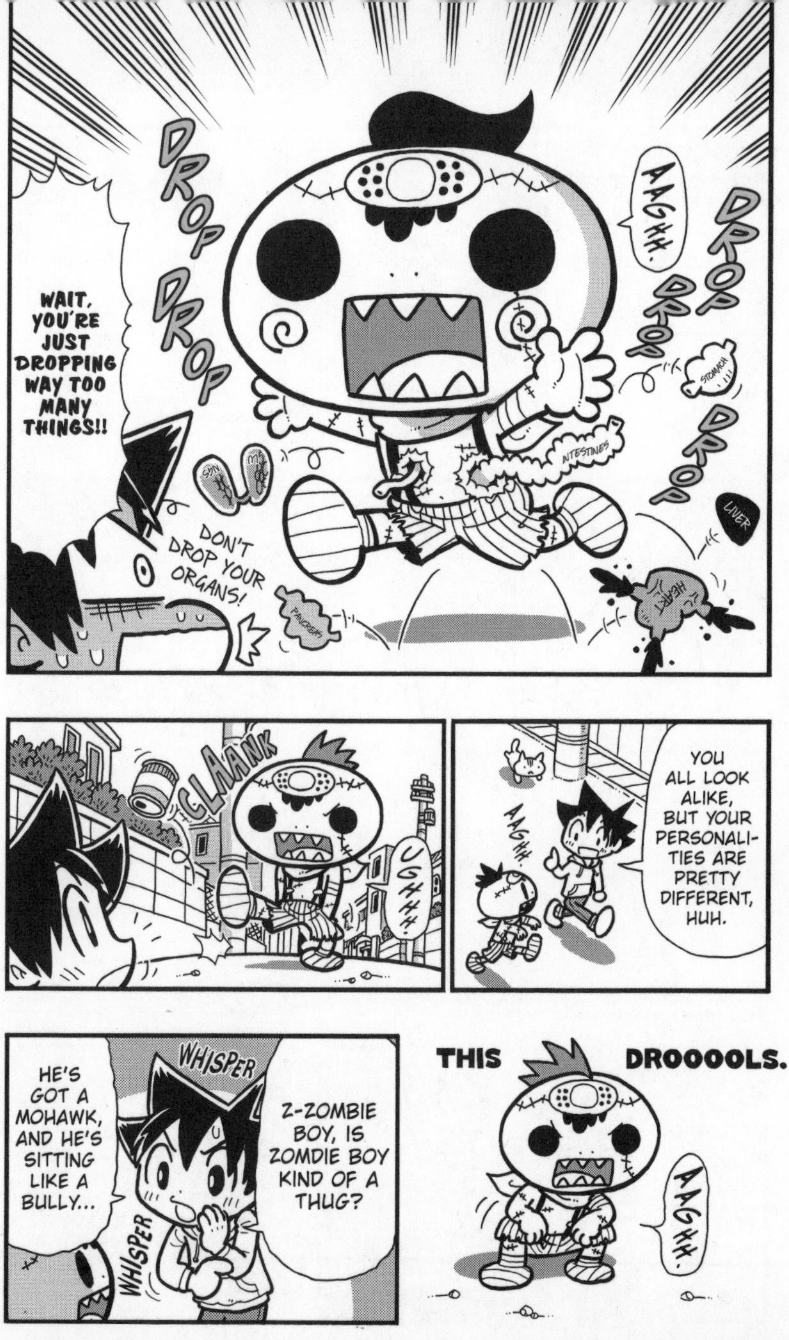
AAGHH.
DROP DROP
DROP DROP
STOMACH
INTESTINES
LIVER
HEART
PANCREAS
DROP DROP
DON'T DROP YOUR ORGANS!
WAIT, YOU'RE JUST DROPPING WAY TOO MANY THINGS!!
YOU ALL LOOK ALIKE, BUT YOUR PERSONALITIES ARE PRETTY DIFFERENT, HUH.
AAGHH.
CLAAANK
UGHHH.
THIS
DROOOOLS.
AAGHH.
WHISPER
Z-ZOMBIE BOY, IS ZOMDIE BOY KIND OF A THUG?
HE'S GOT A MOHAWK, AND HE'S SITTING LIKE A BULLY...
WHISPER

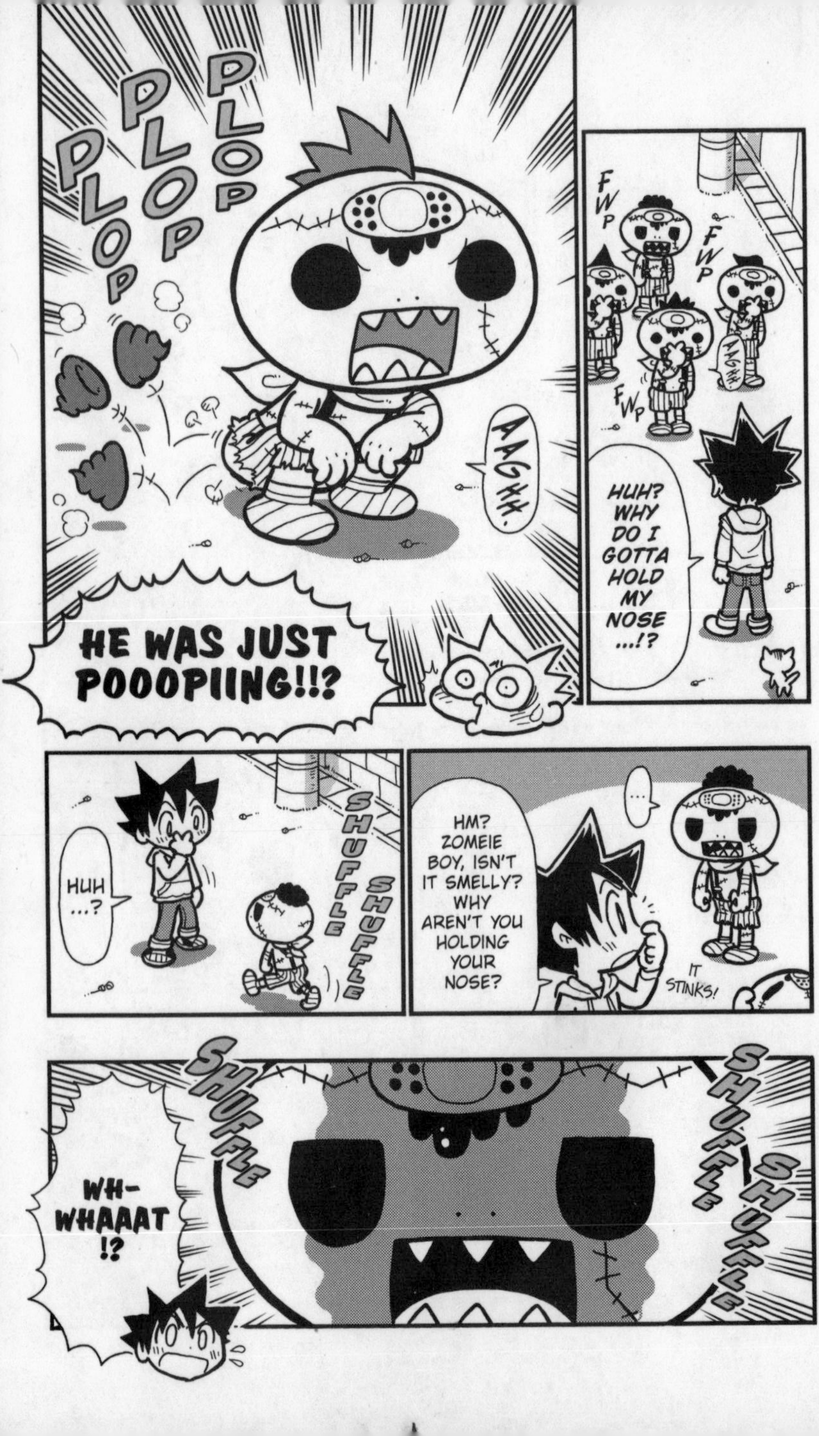
FWP
FWP
AAGHH.
FWP
HUH? WHY DO I GOTTA HOLD MY NOSE ...!?
PLOP PLOP PLOP
AAGHH.
HE WAS JUST POOOPIING!!?
...
HM? ZOMEIE BOY, ISN'T IT SMELLY? WHY AREN'T YOU HOLDING YOUR NOSE?
IT STINKS!
SHUFFLE SHUFFLE
HUH ...?
SHUFFLE-SHUFFLE
SHUFFLE
WH-WHAAAT!?

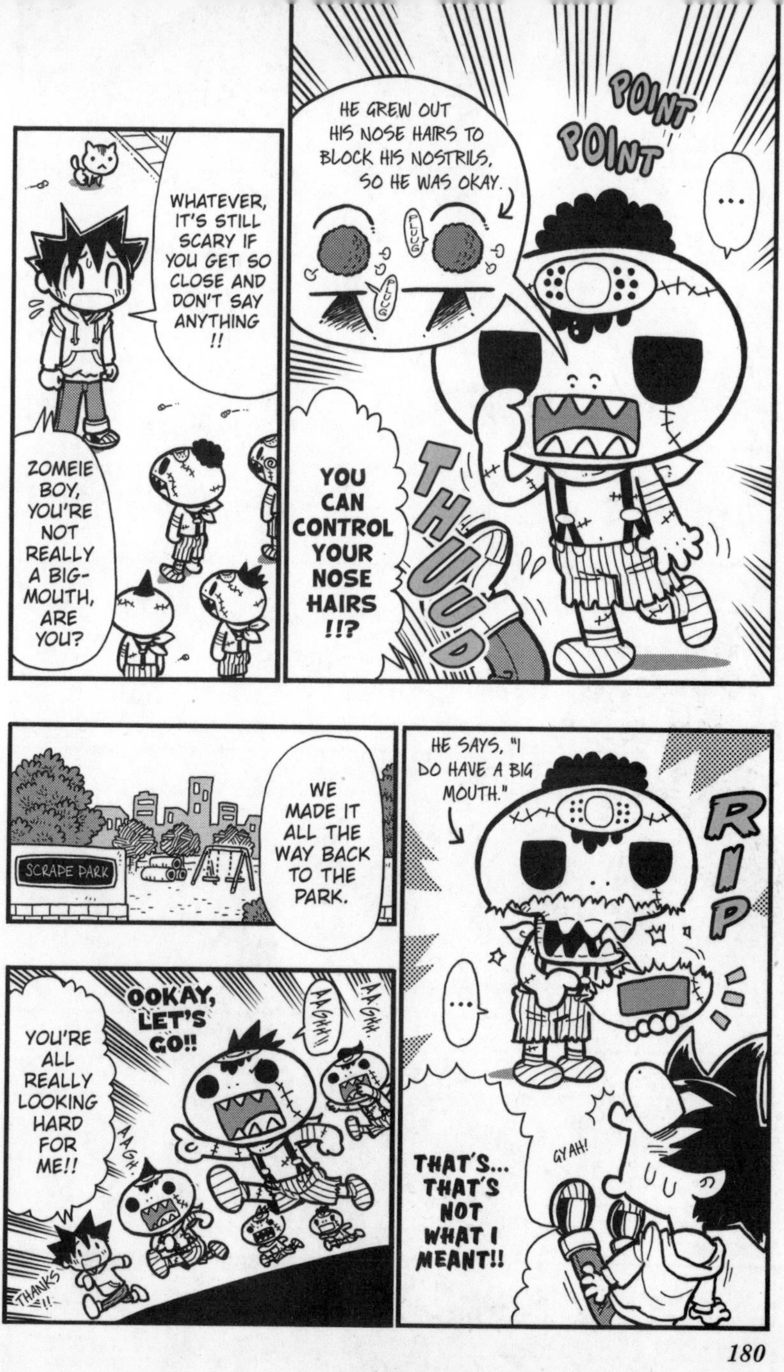
POINT
POINT
...
HE GREW OUT HIS NOSE HAIRS TO BLOCK HIS NOSTRILS, SO HE WAS OKAY.
PLUUG
PLUUG
YOU CAN CONTROL YOUR NOSE HAIRS !!?
THUUD
WHATEVER, IT'S STILL SCARY IF YOU GET SO CLOSE AND DON'T SAY ANYTHING !!
ZOMEIE BOY, YOU'RE NOT REALLY A BIG-MOUTH, ARE YOU?
HE SAYS, "I DO HAVE A BIG MOUTH."
RIP
...
GYAH!
THAT'S... THAT'S NOT WHAT I MEANT!!
SCRAPE PARK
WE MADE IT ALL THE WAY BACK TO THE PARK.
AAGHH!!
AAGHH.
OOKAY, LET'S GO!!
YOU'RE ALL REALLY LOOKING HARD FOR ME!!
AAGH.
THANKS!!

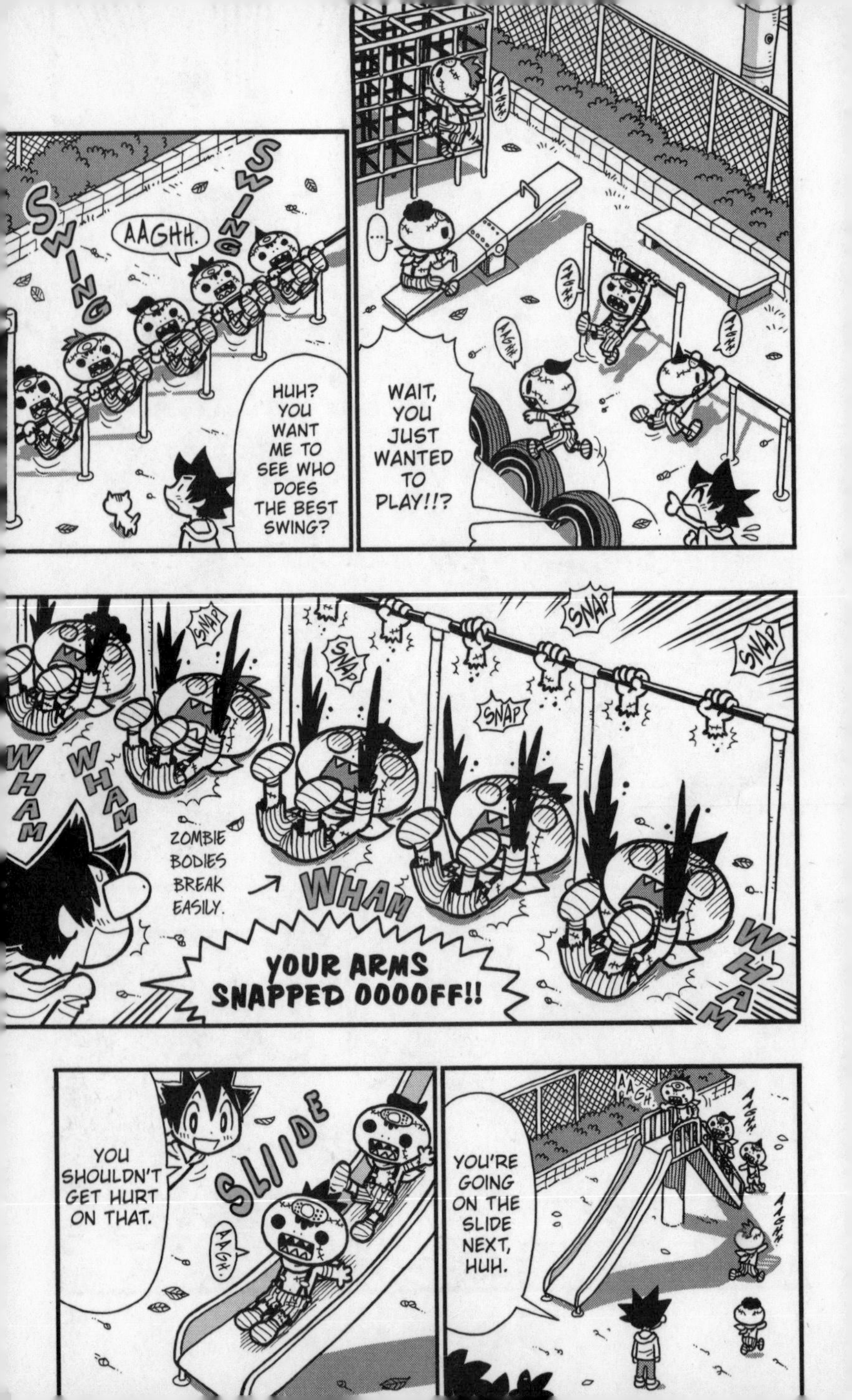
AAGH
...
AAGH
AAGH
AAGH
WAIT, YOU JUST WANTED TO PLAY!!?
SWING
SWING
AAGHH.
HUH? YOU WANT ME TO SEE WHO DOES THE BEST SWING?
SNAP
SNAP
SNAP
SNAP
SNAP
WHAM
WHAM
WHAM
WHAM
ZOMBIE BODIES BREAK EASILY.
YOUR ARMS SNAPPED OOOOFF!!
AAGH.
AAGHH
AAGHH
YOU'RE GOING ON THE SLIDE NEXT, HUH.
SLIDE
AAGH.
YOU SHOULDN'T GET HURT ON THAT.

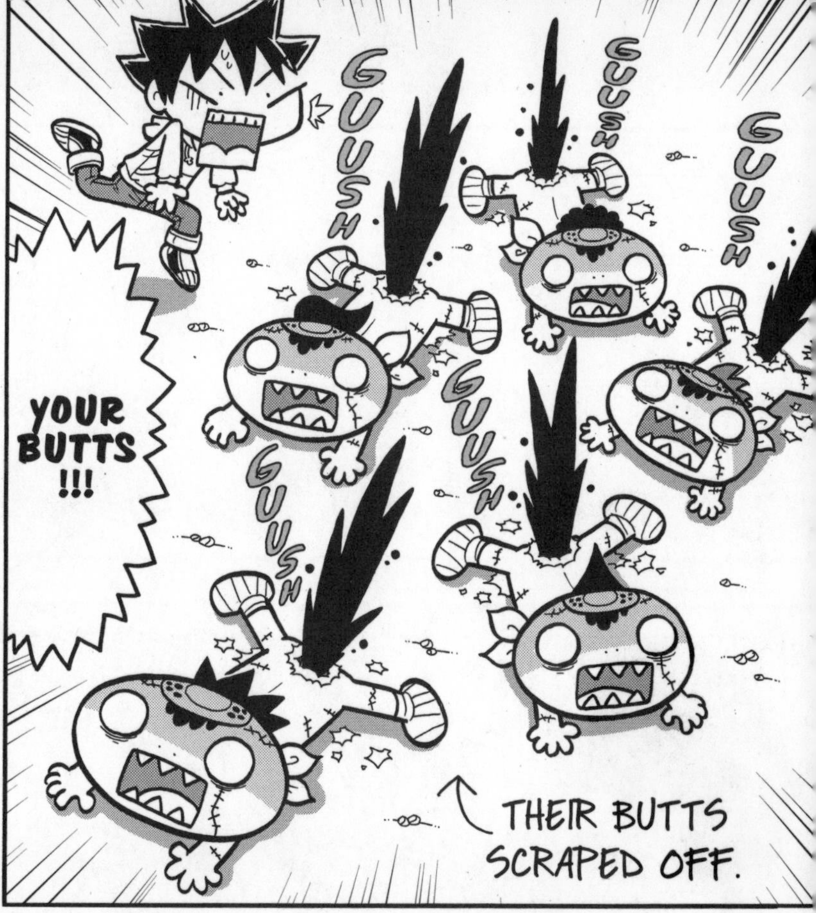
GUUSH
GUUSH
GUUSH
GUUSH
GUUSH
GUUSH
YOUR BUTTS!!!
THEIR BUTTS SCRAPED OFF.

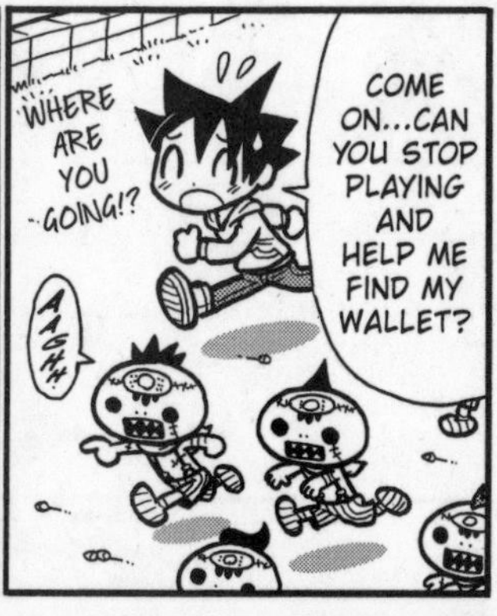
COME ON...CAN YOU STOP PLAYING AND HELP ME FIND MY WALLET?
WHERE ARE YOU GOING!?
AAGHH

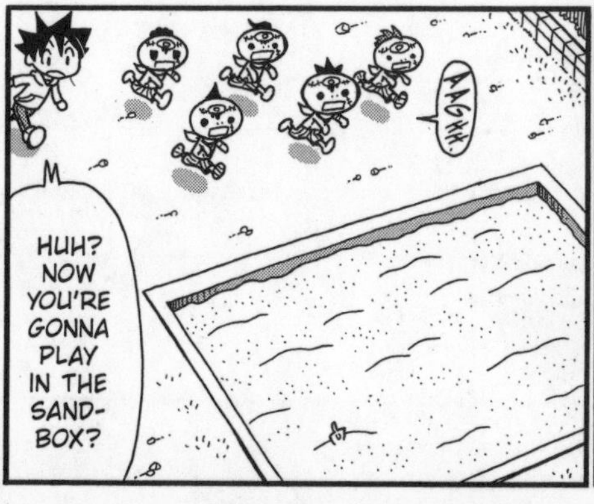
AAGHH
HUH? NOW YOU'RE GONNA PLAY IN THE SAND-BOX?

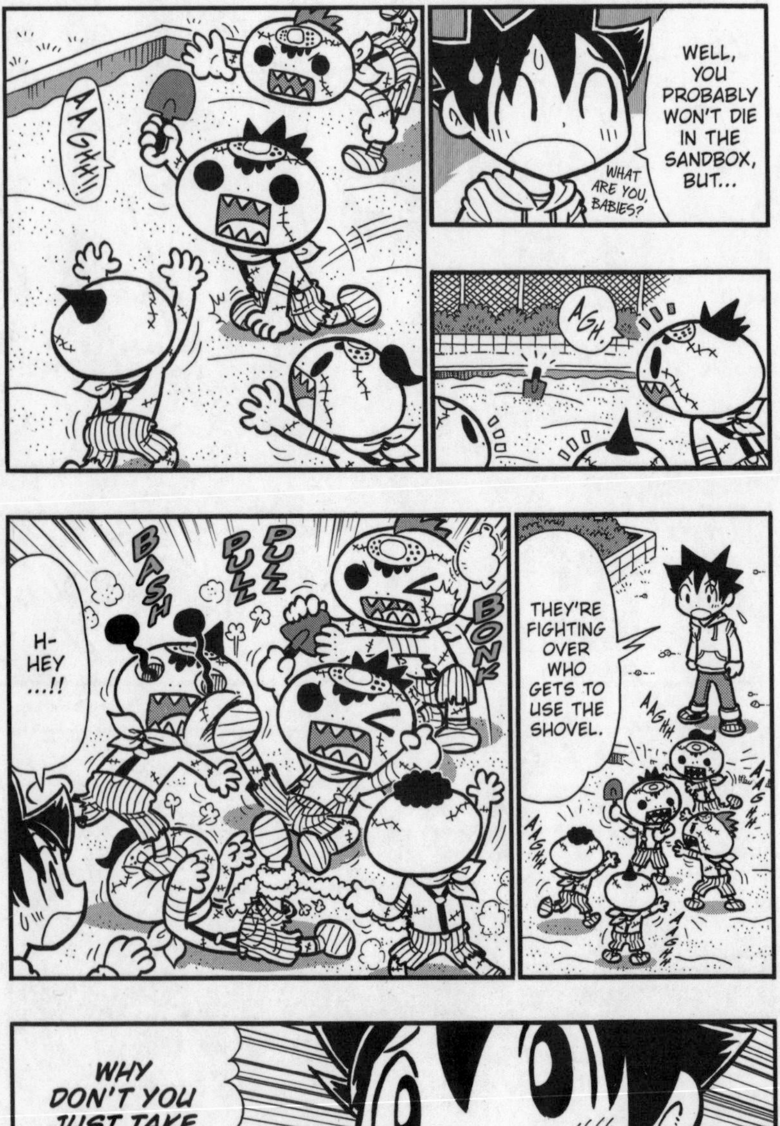
WELL, YOU PROBABLY WON'T DIE IN THE SANDBOX, BUT...
WHAT ARE YOU, BABIES?
AGH.
AAGHHH!!
THEY'RE FIGHTING OVER WHO GETS TO USE THE SHOVEL.
AAGHHH
AAGHHH
AAGHHH
AAGHHH
BASH
PULL PULL
BONK
H-HEY ...!!
WHY DON'T YOU JUST TAKE TURNS!!?

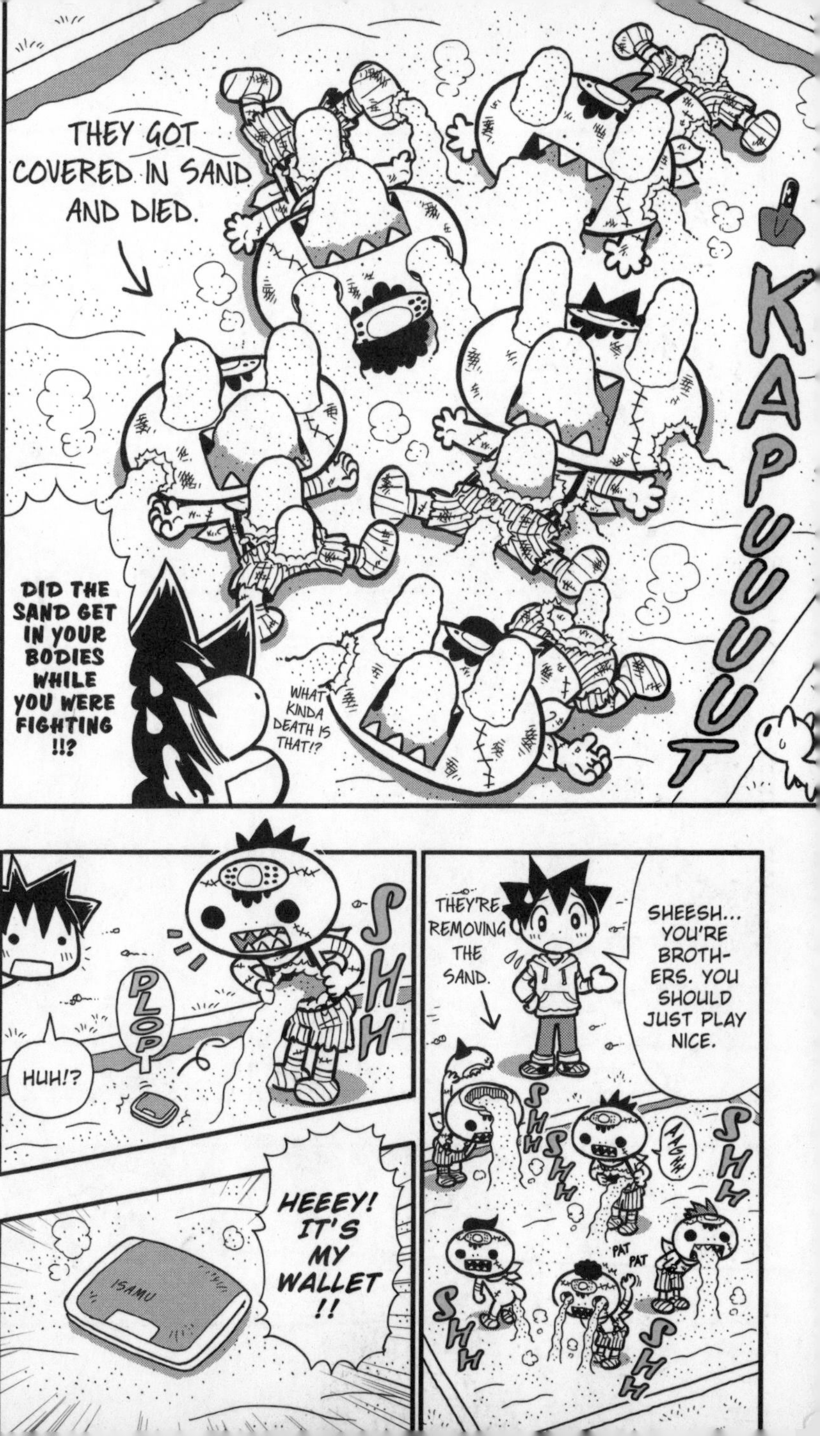
KAPUUUUUT
THEY GOT COVERED IN SAND AND DIED.
WHAT KINDA DEATH IS THAT!?
DID THE SAND GET IN YOUR BODIES WHILE YOU WERE FIGHTING!!?
SHEESH... YOU'RE BROTH-ERS. YOU SHOULD JUST PLAY NICE.
THEY'RE REMOVING THE SAND.
SHH
AAGH
SHH
SHH
PAT PAT
SHH
SHH
SHH
PLOP
HUH!?
HEEEY! IT'S MY WALLET!!
ISAMU

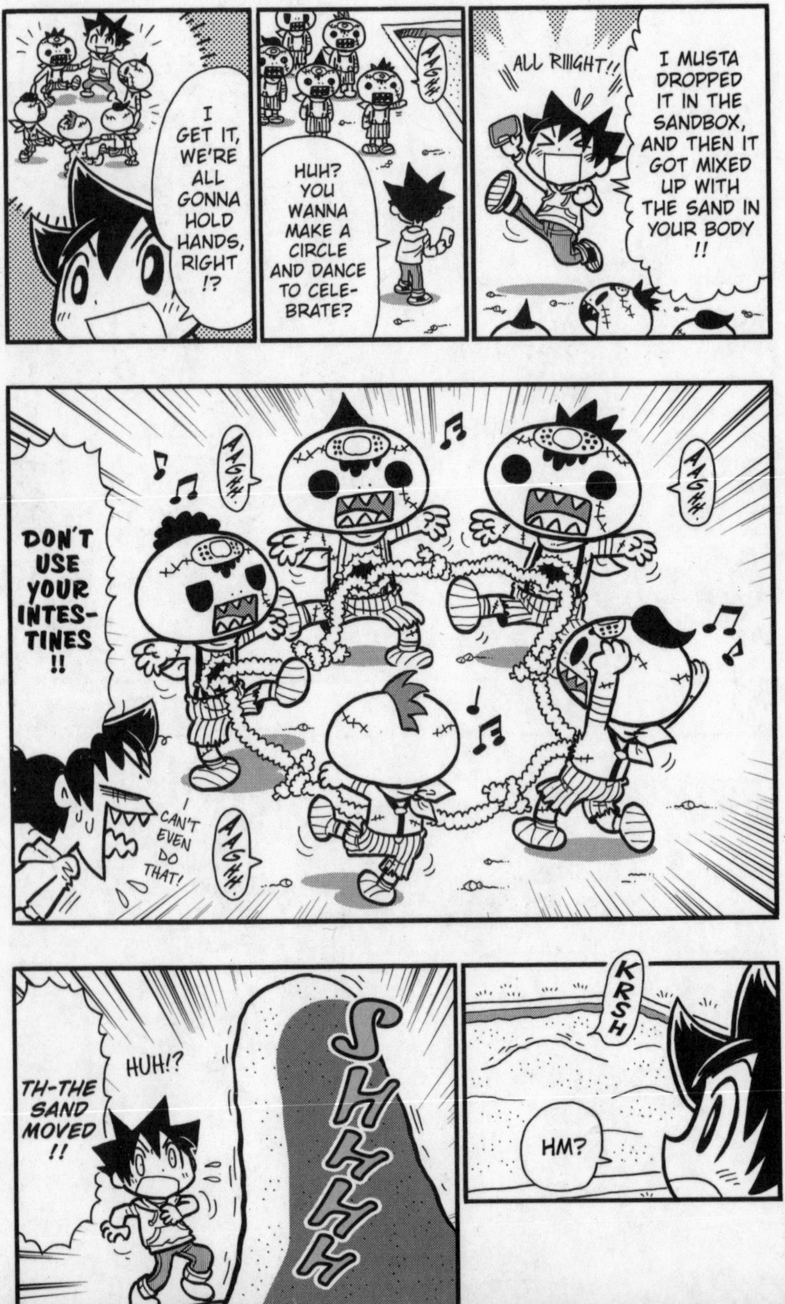

I MUSTA DROPPED IT IN THE SANDBOX, AND THEN IT GOT MIXED UP WITH THE SAND IN YOUR BODY!!
ALL RIIIGHT!!
AAGHH
HUH? YOU WANNA MAKE A CIRCLE AND DANCE TO CELEBRATE?
I GET IT, WE'RE ALL GONNA HOLD HANDS, RIGHT!?
AAGHH
AAGHH
DON'T USE YOUR INTESTINES!!
I CAN'T EVEN DO THAT!
AAGHH
KRSH
HM?
SHHHHH
HUH!?
TH-THE SAND MOVED!!

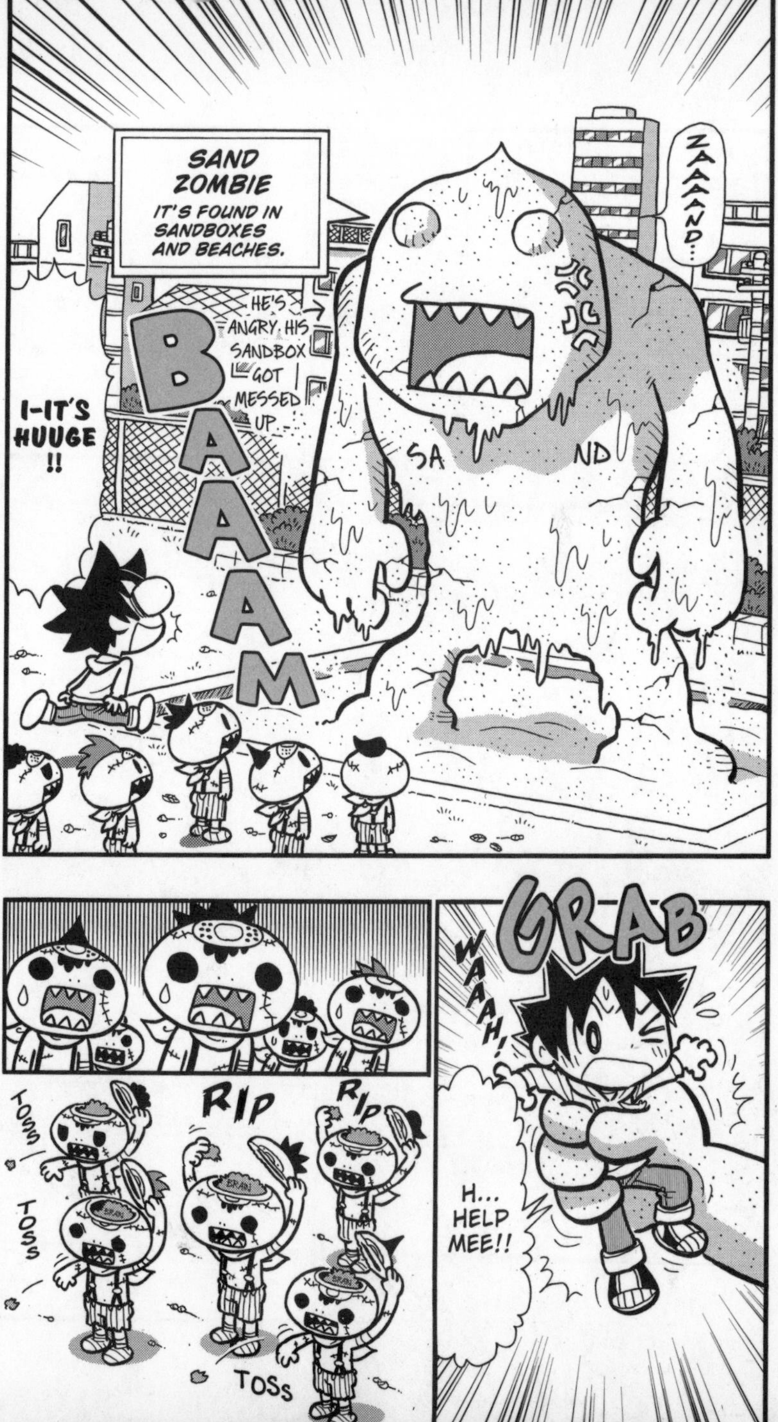
ZAAAAAND...
SAND ZOMBIE
IT'S FOUND IN SANDBOXES AND BEACHES.
HE'S ANGRY HIS SANDBOX GOT MESSED UP
BAAAM
SA
ND
I-IT'S HUUGE!!
GRAB
WAAAH!
H... HELP MEE!!
RIP
RIP
TOSS
TOSS
TOSS

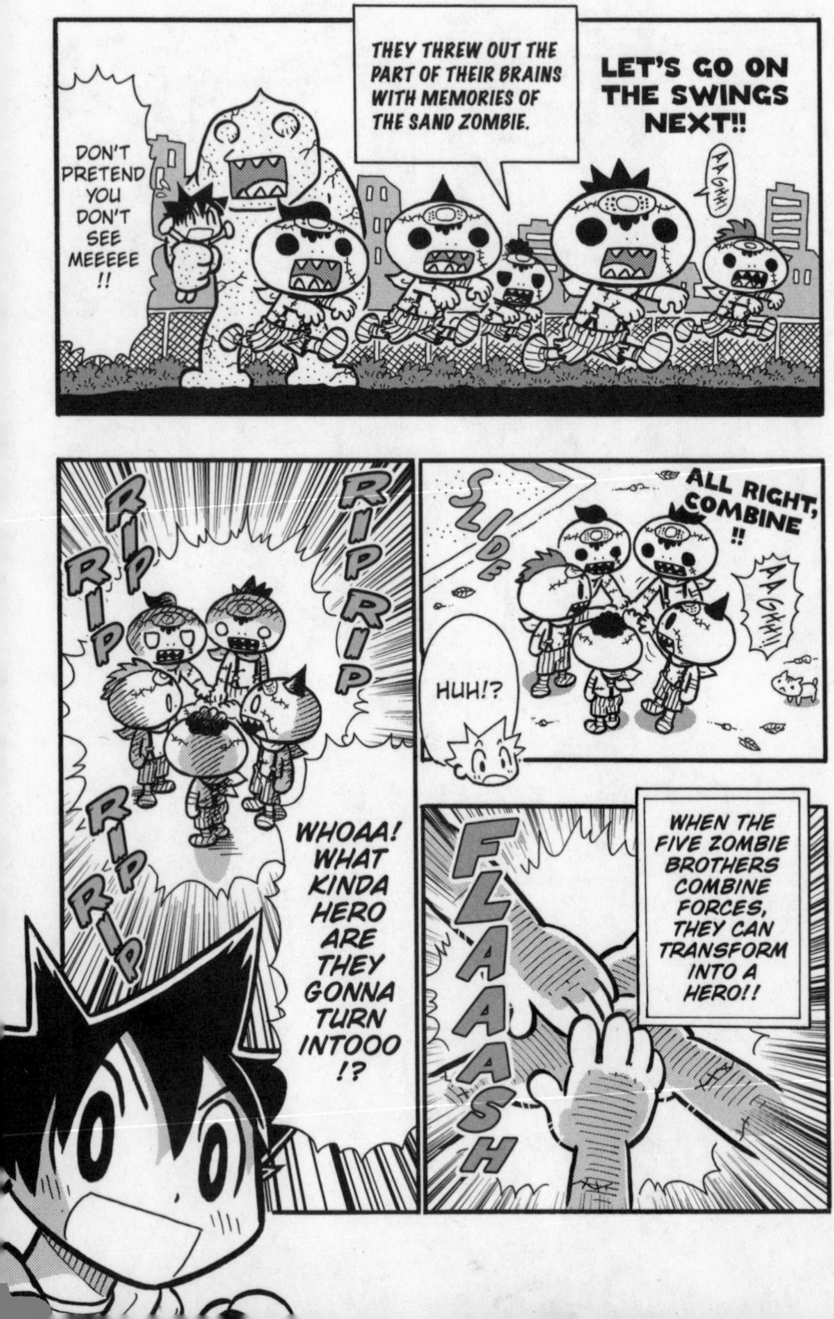
LET'S GO ON THE SWINGS NEXT!!
THEY THREW OUT THE PART OF THEIR BRAINS WITH MEMORIES OF THE SAND ZOMBIE.
AAGHH!
DON'T PRETEND YOU DON'T SEE MEEEEE!!
ALL RIGHT, COMBINE!!
AAGHH!!
SLIDE
HUH!?
WHEN THE FIVE ZOMBIE BROTHERS COMBINE FORCES, THEY CAN TRANSFORM INTO A HERO!!
FLAAAASH
RIP RIP
RIP RIP
WHOAA! WHAT KINDA HERO ARE THEY GONNA TURN INTOOO!?
RIP RIP

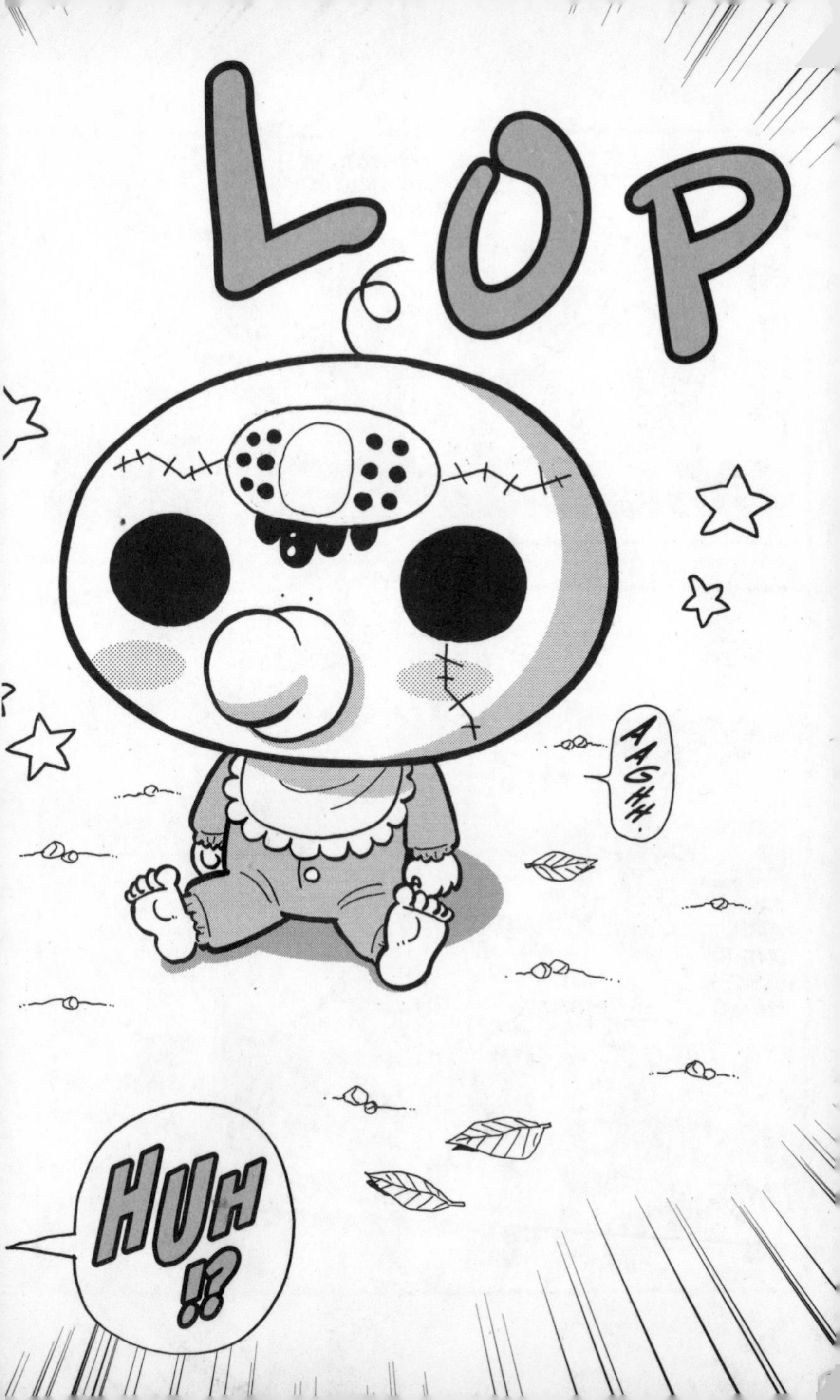
LOP
AAGHH.
HUH !?

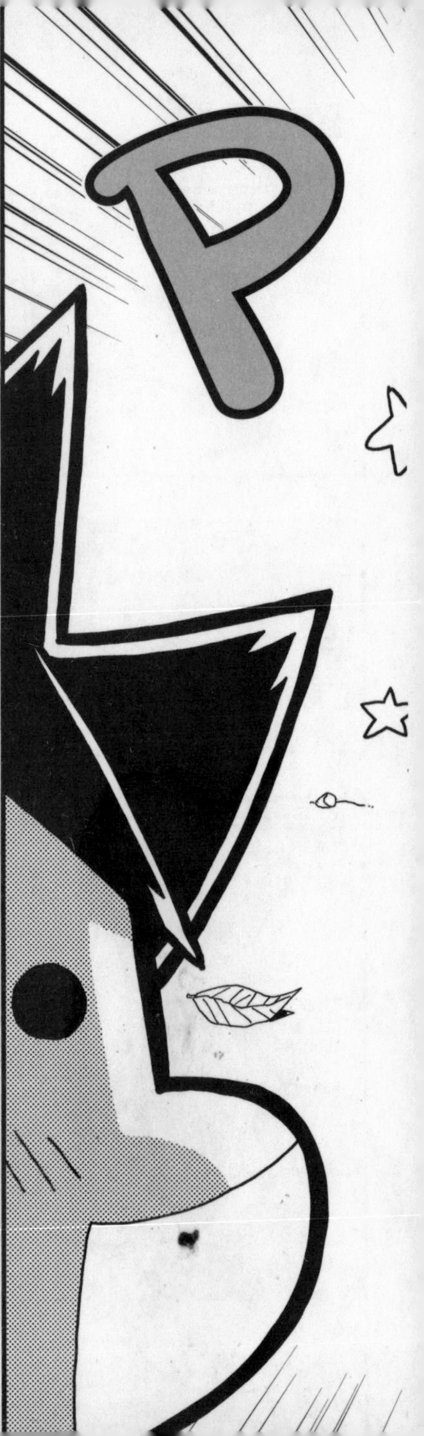
P
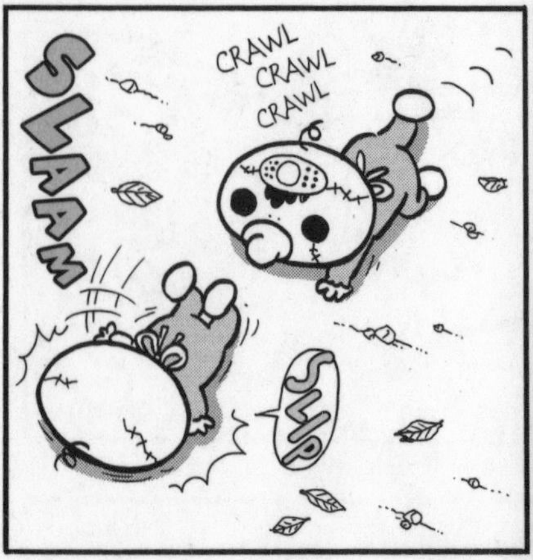
CRAWL CRAWL CRAWL
SLAM
SLIP
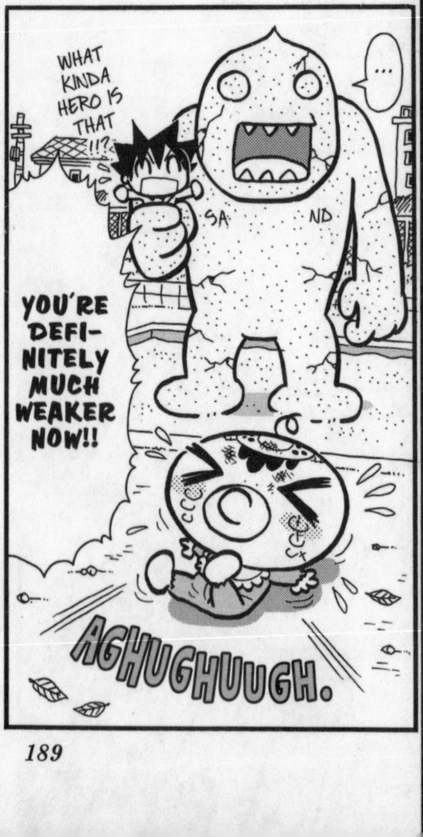
...
WHAT KINDA HERO IS THAT!!?
SA ND
YOU'RE DEFI-NITELY MUCH WEAKER NOW!!
AGHUGHUUGH.

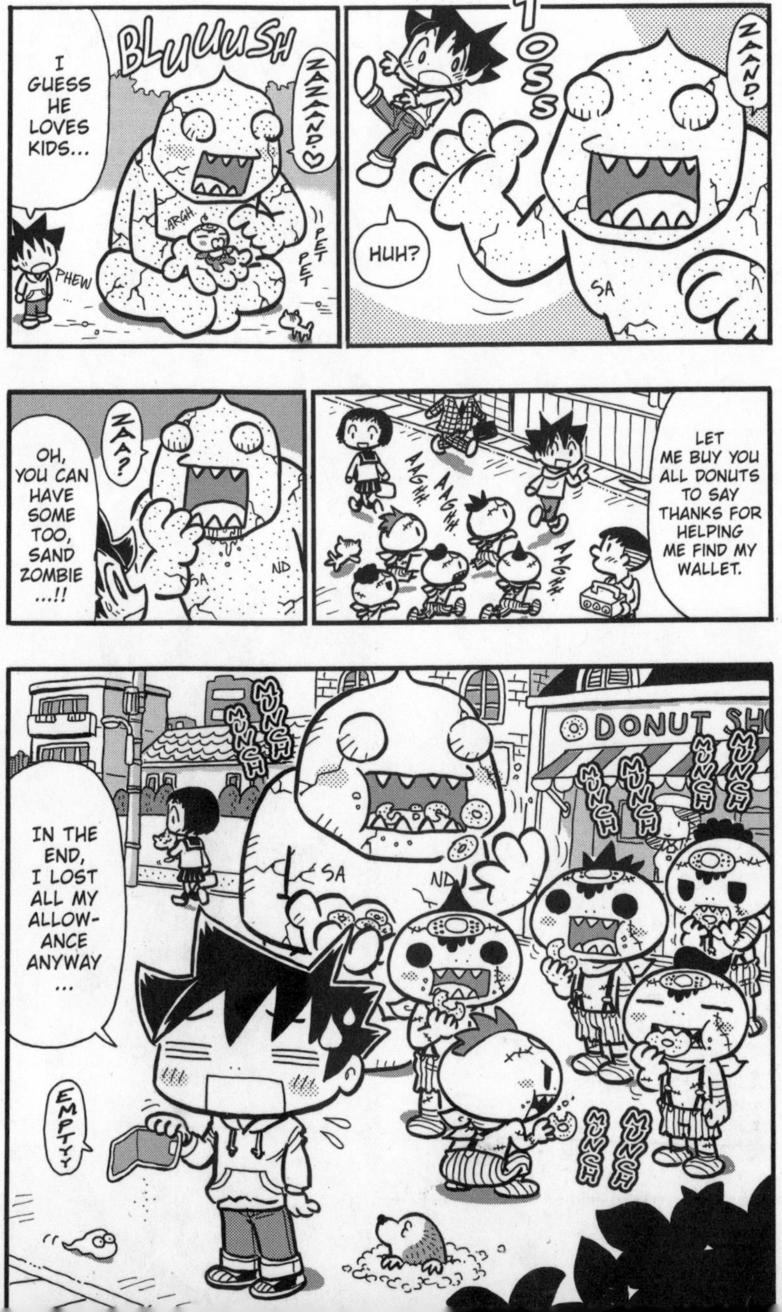
ZAAAND.
TOSS
HUH?
SA
ZAZAAND.♡
BLUUUSH
I GUESS HE LOVES KIDS...
ARGH.
PET PET
PHEW...
LET ME BUY YOU ALL DONUTS TO SAY THANKS FOR HELPING ME FIND MY WALLET.
AAGHH
AAGHH
AAGHH
ZAA?
OH, YOU CAN HAVE SOME TOO, SAND ZOMBIE...!!
SA
ND
DONUT SH
MUNCH
MUNCH
MUNCH
MUNCH
MUNCH
MUNCH
SA
ND
IN THE END, I LOST ALL MY ALLOW-ANCE ANYWAY...
EMPTYY
MUNCH
MUNCH

ZO ZO ZOMBIE

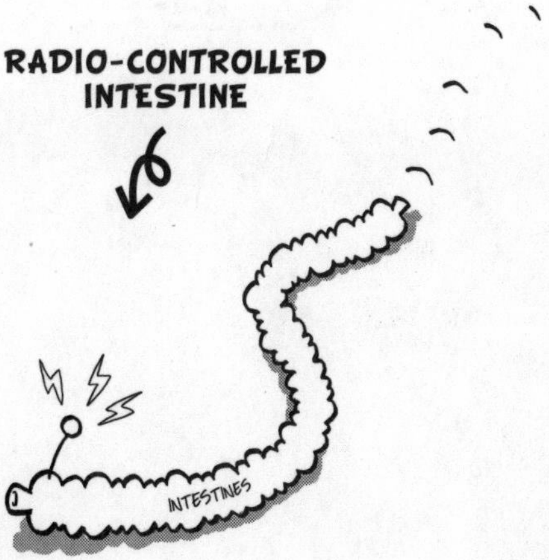
RADIO-CONTROLLED
INTESTINE
INTESTINES

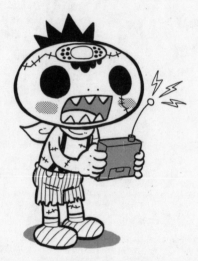

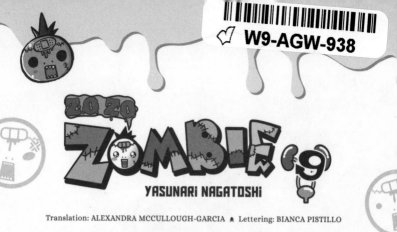

ZOZOZO ZOMBIE 9

YASUNARI NAGATOSHI

Translation: ALEXANDRA MCCULLOUGH-GARCIA ♣ Lettering: BIANCA PISTILLO

This book is a work of fiction. Names, characters, places, and incidents are the product of the author's imagination or are used fictitiously. Any resemblance to actual events, locales, or persons, living or dead, is coincidental.

ZOZOZO ZOMBIE-KUN Vol. 9
by Yasunari NAGATOSHI
© 2013 Yasunari NAGATOSHI
All rights reserved.
Original Japanese edition published by SHOGAKUKAN.
English translation rights in the United States of America, Canada, the United Kingdom, Ireland, Australia and New Zealand arranged with SHOGAKUKAN through Tuttle-Mori Agency, Inc.

English translation © 2020 by Yen Press, LLC

JY
150 West 30th Street, 19th Floor
New York, NY 10001

Visit us at jyforkids.com ♣ facebook.com/jyforkids
twitter.com/jyforkids ♣ jyforkids.tumblr.com ♣ instagram.com/jyforkids

First JY Edition: October 2020

JY is an imprint of Yen Press, LLC.
The JY name and logo are trademarks of Yen Press, LLC.

The publisher is not responsible for websites (or their content) that are not owned by the publisher.

Library of Congress Control Number: 2018948323

ISBNs: 978-1-9753-5349-0 (paperback)
978-1-9753-8638-2 (ebook)

10 9 8 7 6 5 4 3 2 1

WOR

Printed in the United States of America

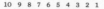